Praise for *As Above, So Below* and Rudy Rucker

"A delightful book, one that carries us through the sixteenth-century picture-plane at extraordinary angles, illuminating Bruegel, his art and his world, with warmth and candor."
—William Gibson, author of *Pattern Recognition*

"As intricate . . . as one of its subject's own vivid depictions of sixteenth-century life in the Spanish-dominated Low Countries, Rucker's fictionalized life of Bruegel draws its readers into a teeming world of politics, art, love, sin, and loss. . . . He skillfully interlaces his account of Bruegel's various artistic and literary influences with insights into the genesis of some of his most renowned works. This is clearly a labor of love and . . . it grapples handily with Bruegel's genius—his ability to wittily and gracefully re-create all human activity, from the sublime to the scatological."
—*Publishers Weekly*

"A lively and well-narrated tale that will appeal to Bruegel fans and may awaken newcomers to an interest in his work."
—*Kirkus Reviews*

"Rudy Rucker is an oddity and a treasure. . . . In these days of neat little marketing categories, few writers attempt to cover so much ground."
—*Wired*

"Rucker is an artist well worth discovering, reading, and keeping up with. . . . [His novels] sparkle with deadpan wit and a natural storyteller's flair."
—*The Washington Post*

BOOKS BY RUDY RUCKER

NOVELS
AS ABOVE, SO BELOW: A NOVEL OF PETER BRUEGEL (FROM TOR)
SPACELAND (FROM TOR)
REALWARE
FREEWARE
THE HACKER AND THE ANTS
THE HOLLOW EARTH
WETWARE
THE SECRET OF LIFE
MASTER OF SPACE AND TIME
THE SEX SPHERE
SOFTWARE
WHITE LIGHT
SPACETIME DONUTS

NONFICTION
SAUCER WISDOM (FROM TOR)
ALL THE VISIONS
MIND TOOLS
THE FOURTH DIMENSION
INFINITY AND THE MIND
GEOMETRY, RELATIVITY AND THE FOURTH DIMENSION

COLLECTIONS
GNARL!
SEEK!
TRANSREAL!
THE FIFTY-SEVENTH FRANZ KAFKA

AS ABOVE, SO BELOW

▓▪▓▪▓▪▓▪▓▪▓▪▓▪▓▪▓▪▓▪▓▪▓

A NOVEL OF
PETER BRUEGEL

RUDY
RUCKER

 A TOM DOHERTY ASSOCIATES BOOK
NEW YORK

AS ABOVE, SO BELOW: A NOVEL OF PETER BRUEGEL

Interior art by Peter Bruegel

Book design by Mark Abrams

A Forge Book
Published by Tom Doherty Associates, LLC
175 Fifth Avenue
New York, NY 10010

www.tor.com

Forge® is a registered trademark of Tom Doherty Associates, LLC.

ISBN 0-765-30403-1 (hc)
ISBN 0-765-30404-X (pbk)

First Hardcover Edition: November 2002
First Paperback Edition: November 2003

Printed in the United States of America

0 9 8 7 6 5 4 3 2 1

FOR *SYLVIA*

CONTENTS

AS ABOVE, SO BELOW

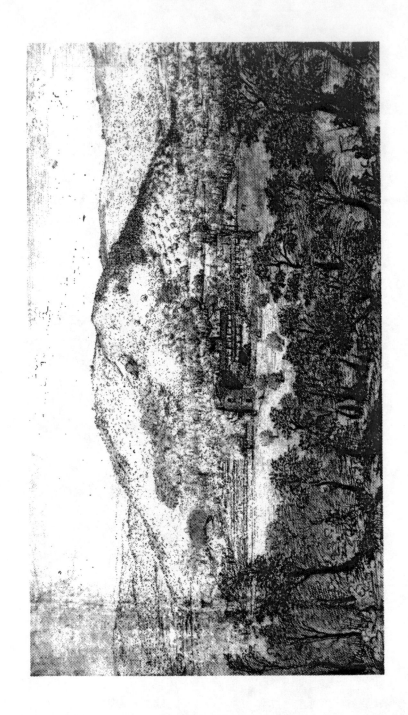

ONE

MOUNTAIN LANDSCAPE
THE FRENCH-ITALIAN ALPS, MAY 1552

Peter Bruegel was looking at his first mountain, a steep, rounded foothill at the edge of the Alps. He and his friend Martin de Vos had never seen anything like it.

"The land swoops right up into the air," said Bruegel. He was a tall young man with a high brow, a big nose, and alert clear gray eyes. "Just like it's supposed to."

"Like a great ocean wave," said de Vos. He leaned on his long staff, peering out from under the low brim of his hat. He had a snub nose and a cheerful smile. "It was worth coming all this way from Antwerp."

"Do you notice how the mountain's flank tilts up towards us?" continued Bruegel. "It's like we're looking down at it from the sky. With everything spread out next to each other. All there for us to see." He stepped off the stony road into the green grass and held out his arms as if to embrace the landscape before him.

It was a rain–kissed afternoon in May. Puffy little clouds were scattered across the watery blue sky, some hanging so close to the ground that Bruegel could almost touch them. A small river ran beside the road, lit just now by a patch of sun. Slanting gray streaks of rain caressed the green mountain. Bruegel felt as if his heart were blooming.

"I have to draw this," he told de Vos. He shrugged the strap of his satchel from his shoulder, peeled off his skirted jerkin, and sat down cross–legged upon it. He found ink and pen and a bottle of water in his satchel, and pulled a sheet of paper out of a special flap in his jerkin's lining. All the while he was staring at the mountain. "It's quite unlike what we've seen in paintings back in the Low Lands, Martin. Different than what we've been taught. It's less contorted, more like a living thing. It's saying hello to me."

De Vos smiled and sat down to watch his friend begin making tiny brown ink marks on his paper. Rather than drawing a scene with long continuous outlines, Bruegel preferred to nibble away at the edges of things with an accumulation of dots and strokes. The progress was steady and surprisingly rapid.

Some other travelers passed by, distracting de Vos. This was a busy road, with any number of merchants moving their goods back and forth between Italy and Northern Europe. Beyond the little mountain before them was one of the few passes where a wagon could get through the Alps.

"I'll meet you at that monastery by the mountain's base," said de Vos, looking off down the road. "See it? I'll warrant we can find food and lodging there."

"Be sure and tell them that we're guild artists," said Bruegel. "Maybe we can make something for them instead of paying cash."

"They might want to own the drawing that you're doing right now," suggested de Vos. "It's off to a nice start, I'd say."

"The monks won't want a plain nature sketch," said Bruegel. "If I were to offer them this drawing, I'd need to add something Scriptural."

"Joseph and Mary on the way to Egypt," suggested de Vos. "The hermit St. Anthony. The repentant Mary Magdalene taking a piss."

"I'd like that," said Bruegel, smiling. He was known among his friends for his fondness of sketching people in their private moments. "But the monks are surely beyond such low concerns. I imagine they're educated men. Humanists, perhaps. I could add some Classical figures for them. Mercury and Psyche in the sky. Or Daedalus and Icarus."

"Well, in any case be sure to draw their monastery!" said de Vos. "But leave the figures for when you've found your patron."

"Good idea, Martin," said Bruegel. "Meanwhile, less of you and more of my pen and this mountain. They're talking to me."

"All I hear is the bells of the monks' cows," said de Vos, rising to his feet. "Fat cattle mean good cheese. Bread and cheese and ale and some dark-green mouse-ear lettuce. It's the season for radishes too! There's quite a few buildings over there beyond the monastery. It looks like a regular village. Maybe I'll find a young widow with a hungry eye." De Vos had little more experience with women than Bruegel, but he liked to talk big.

He stepped down to the river and splashed some water on his face. He scrambled back to the road, gave Bruegel a cheery wave, and walked off whistling. Bruegel continued to draw, sinking into a kind of conversation with the mountain.

Whenever Bruegel concentrated on objects they seemed to talk to him. The quill pen told him how stiff it was and how it loved to be dipped in ink. Its squeaks were as the faint honks of a goose. The sepia ink spoke of the squid and cuttlefish sacks it came from, of water and writhing tentacles. The paper stretched itself out like a dog in the sun; it sighed with satisfaction at being scratched.

Most of all, though, it was the mountain that spoke to Bruegel.

"I'm alive too," the great mound said. "I move slower than you, but yes, I roll and turn within my sweet green skin. See the cleft at my top? Like the tip of your prick. I leak a stream from there and it's of a marvelous purity, refined by my mineral body. Be sure to sketch in the rim of my stream's gully, Peter. I used to be much taller than the younger mountains beyond me, so make me the highest thing in your picture. I'm old and wise, but on this summer day I feel young. The trees on my flanks are feathered with leaves that shelter all manner of birds, beasts, and men. I'm glad that you're drawing me. Yes, I have a dent halfway up, so shade it dark like that, good, and right before the ridge I'm a bit flat, so the bumps you make for trees should be closer together there. Fine. Leave the paper blank where the sun's very bright upon me, that's perfect. And now fill in that tangle of trees that march up my gorge—I'm lovely in there, Peter, you should walk up onto me and see."

After an hour of this, the pleasant mountain had been well depicted. Now Bruegel drew the monastery as well. It had a tidy Gothic chapel, a stone refectory, and a long two-storied wooden residence house with a red tile roof. Just like the mountain, the building spoke to Bruegel as he sketched it, talking about right angles and perspective, about monkishness, and about the joy of having windows. And then the sketch was done.

Bruegel sighed and stretched, got to his feet, and looked down at his new drawing, its corners weighted down by little stones. The sun was low in the sky behind him, glazing the world with shades of gold. How lucky he was to be an artist, a guild member in good standing. If all went well—and surely it would!—he'd come into his own before much longer. He'd have his own studio, a string of wealthy patrons, apprentices to make up his paints, and a fine house in the center of Brussels. All this assuming—and here lay Bruegel's great worry—assuming there was a market for the things he saw, and for his way of seeing them.

Seeing, seeing, seeing—very nearly the sum of what he did. So often he was the onlooker, off to the side of the street fairs and artists' gatherings in Antwerp, alone with his eyes and the pictures in his head. Peter the Watcher—more than one woman had called him that, and not as a compliment. Someday he'd have his studio, and his patrons, and his house; he'd have a wife and a family and he'd be a watcher no more.

Even as he reviewed these overfamiliar thoughts, Bruegel was examining his drawing, feeling each bit with his eyes, looking for any weakness or excess. Now and then he stooped to make a hook or a dash with the nib of his pen. Soon he was done. The picture was outside him now, born into the world, leaving a hole he could only fill with the next picture to come.

He put away his ink, pen, and paper and walked down the road, observing, as always, the way that a landscape sprang into a new kind of life when he moved through it. Bruegel savored the suave way in which the world's perspectives rotated: the nearby trees turned as if on spindles; the fields and orchards constellated themselves into new alignments; and the most distant landmarks seemed to sail along with him, keeping pace with his passage. The world danced a stately jig about you, if only you watched.

The little road arced away from a bog by the river and passed through a wet field crisscrossed with streams. The peach-colored clouds were reflected in the scattered patches of green water—exquisite. The road swung back to a ford in the river beside a couple of farmhouses. Behind Bruegel were Nice, Provence, and the setting sun, ahead of him lay the Alps, the Po Valley, Lombardy, Parma, Florence, and Rome. Some cattle stood in the river drinking water, with a peasant boy watching over them.

Bruegel had his own memories of tending cattle for Graaf de Hoorne, the nobleman who owned the estates where he'd been raised. Long, peaceful days those had been, off on his own with some bread and cheese, keeping the cows from the crops, leading them to good pastures, herding them home at night, with no company save a dog or, on the best days, the merry Anja. Sometimes, to make Anja laugh, he'd drawn faces with a muddy stick upon a cow's great, round side. Naughty Anja, more and less than a sister—where was she now? He'd never seen her once since they'd sent him away from the village. Out to seek his fortune. And here he was at the Alps, seeking ever farther afield.

Bruegel tipped his hat to the boy and picked his way across the water. A line of cypresses grew along the uphill road to the monastery. The trees' tops blended into one long worm, and the bare trunks twisted down like legs. Viewed as one great chimerical being, the line of trees was a caterpillar. Bruegel walked up the slope; he was happy to be finally starting up the slope of an Alp. According to de Vos, this was the route that Hannibal took up through the Alps in ancient times. Bruegel tried to visualize the Moorish troops and their elephants.

There had been an elephant in Antwerp last year, the property of a financier. But Bruegel had been off working as an artist's assistant in Mechelen right then, and before he could get back to Antwerp to perhaps sketch the elephant, the hot-blooded beast had died of the damp winter cold. The financier's partners had eaten the monster in a banquet that was a nine-days' wonder. Bruegel had only managed to see the tusks and a bit of the skin; perhaps he'd finally see a whole elephant in Rome.

At the top of the rise he found three low covered wagons standing in the monastery courtyard. It seemed that the monks ran an inn with the sign of a White Stag. Looking past the monastery, Bruegel saw that the village was larger than he expected, with perhaps as many as a hundred houses. It must have been a local holiday, for everyone was outdoors, noisy as Carnival. They were rushing about in ragtag groups, chatting and whooping, ever more of them streaming into the village for some unseen event higher up the peaceful mountain.

"Peter!" It was Martin de Vos, sitting out on a stone bench in front of the inn. He was holding a large white radish and a pot of beer. He looked uncharacteristically gloomy. "I've got beds for us in the common sleeping room. The Brothers have declared a firm lack of interest in our art, but I've haggled them to a very reasonable cash fee for our stay. Beer, supper, and morning porridge included." This sounded like good news, but de Vos was upset about something.

Bruegel sat down at his side, took a bite of the radish and a gulp of the beer. "Here it is," he said, getting out his drawing. "What's set the villagers a-buzz?"

"An 'Act of Faith,'" said de Vos with a great sigh. "It seems there was an old couple who lived next to the monastery's estate." He pointed. "In that stone hut right over there where the village begins. See how the door's been kicked in? The Brothers arrested the couple last week—they were named Joseph and Marie, of all things. They were deemed a sorcerer and a witch by the prior of the monastery, a Father Lorenzo. The ecclesiastics staged a quick trial, and today the villagers buried Marie alive and hung Joseph by the neck. The Golgotha is somewhere up in that woodsy valley upon your hill. The peasants have been straggling down for the last hour. Quite a festival they've made of it." De Vos took Bruegel's drawing and pointed to a spot on it. "I think the gibbet will be just about there. We'll have a look on our way to the pass tomorrow. Joseph the alchemist will still be dangling. Perhaps you can sketch him."

Bruegel experienced the quick phantasm of an imaginary smell as distinctly as if his foot had just skidded through a patch of human waste. The thought of hanged men always brought to mind this one particular stench. It came from three years ago, when he'd still been the apprentice of Master Coecke. They'd been in Brussels making a great faux-marble arch of wood and canvas to celebrate a state visit by the Habsburg Emperor Charles V and his foppish son Philip. To add to the pomp of the reception, an exemplary heretic had been hung upon a gibbet to one side of the arch, a stocky weaver who'd made so bold as to own a printed copy of the Bible. Windy spring weather was in play, and the man's corpse was continually dripping a sharp-stinking brown fluid, the drawn-out evacuation of his watery bowels. The body was so close to the arch that, over the course of any given day, the fitful breezes would noticeably besmirch the vibrating cloth of the Emperor's hollow mock monument. Charles V's arrival kept being delayed, so Bruegel had to repaint the same panel four separate times, surrounded by the astounding smell of the hanged man.

"What folly," said Bruegel, reflexively rubbing his long, straight nose. "An alchemist?"

"An indifferent one. He used up too much of the prior's gold, it seems. And his wife was said to have made a potion to help a woman drive off an unwanted quickening of her womb. But I fear the central issue was quite mundane: a long-running dispute over grazing rights. Joseph and Marie's bit of land has joined the Church's holdings now. Prompt pontifical justice, just like back in the Low Lands. Can you remind me why we're going to Rome, Peter? To the rotten lair of the foul maggots who inflict the Inquisition upon us?"

"Shut your crack," snapped Bruegel, giving a quick look around. "Do you want to get stretched as well?" He got to his feet and tucked his picture back into his jerkin. "I'm going inside."

"Bring me another beer," said de Vos, tipping up his mug.

"Get your own, fool. If you're to hang, I barely know you." For the moment, any fondness he had for de Vos was gone. Bruegel felt tired, hungry, and beset by folly on every side. Without any further look at his companion, he headed into the inn.

It was a surprisingly airy room, with a high ceiling and tall windows in the walls. The windows glowed with orange and purple from the setting sun. Their casements were open and an evening breeze wafted in. A tonsured brown-robed monk tended a great wooden vat of beer. In here, all was order and peace. Bruegel took a deep, shaky breath, calming himself. He approached the vat.

"You are the other artist from Antwerp," said the monk in Latin. He was a portly man with sharp eyes. Bruegel knew a little of the international language, and he answered "*Sane*" for "Yes."

The monk topped off a mug whose foam had been settling, and handed it to Bruegel. "Your companion's already paid for your food and lodging. Sit down anywhere you like, and one of the novices will bring you some bread, cheese, and radishes."

Bruegel walked towards a long table with some men who were talking a Low German dialect which was close enough to Flemish for Bruegel to understand. Seating himself, he recognized one of the men. It was the young merchant Hans Franckert, a fat, powerful fellow with a wide, slitlike mouth. Though Franckert was originally from Nuremberg, he'd moved to Antwerp and become a citizen several years ago.

Franckert was a convivial man known for carousing with artists. He was often seen, for instance, at the gatherings of the Violet Chamber of Rhetoric. The so-called Chambers of Rhetoric were street-theater groups—they performed plays and skits at festivals, using their own scripts, costumes, and backdrops. As a matter of pride, nearly every crafts guild had an associated Chamber of Rhetoric—no less so the St. Luke's Guild for artists. The Violet Chamber's meetings were fecund with wordplay and creative ferment—small wonder that Franckert enjoyed them. The more calculating of the artists viewed the meetings as a good place to scout for patrons—or for friendly women. Though Bruegel would have liked to be one of these fishers of men—or of women—he inevitably ended up at the fringes of the Chamber's gatherings—watching. Though Franckert was only five years older than him, he'd never actually spoken to Franckert before. Somewhat to Bruegel's surprise, the merchant knew him.

"Peter Bruegel!" exclaimed Franckert, raising his beer. "You were the apprentice of Master Coecke, were you not? He was a mighty artist; may he rest in peace."

"I'm an apprentice no longer," said Bruegel. "I've been a Master of the St. Luke's Guild for over a year."

"Congratulations," said Franckert. "Meet my bookkeeper, Klaua, and my teamsters, Max and Moritz. We're on our way to Antwerp! My new hometown. Max here is a native of the Low Lands as well, the good Max Wagemaeker, my guide in all things Flemish. We've got two wagons filled with colors, spices, and Venetian silks. Whither are you bound, Peter?"

"I'm out to fill my eyes with the Alps and the treasures of Italy. I sketched my first mountain today."

"Show me," said Franckert. So Bruegel took his drawing out from inside his coat, holding it a careful few inches above the beery table. Franckert leaned forward, studying the image. "It's a mountain all right," he said presently. "Like looking out a window." He gave Bruegel a friendly clap on the shoulder. "Well done."

"I could sell it to you," said Bruegel. "I'm short of funds."

"The artist's fate," said Franckert. "I'm not averse to helping out a son of Antwerp. How much might you charge?"

"Could you pay a gold piece?"

"Not out of the question. I'm having a good trip." Franckert patted his heavy double-walled silk purse, which rested on the bench at his side, attached to his belt by a leather cord. The purse clinked fatly. "But let's enjoy each other's company a bit before pushing matters to a head."

"So what was your cargo to Venice?" asked Bruegel, stowing away his drawing. If conversation was what was wanted, he'd provide it. He'd learned from Master Coecke that some patrons were as interested in knowing the artist as they were in owning the art.

"German copper and quicksilver. We went down through Austria. I sold twelve big flasks of quicksilver to the Venetian mirror makers."

"I've never seen any large amount of quicksilver," said Bruegel, intrigued.

"The metal of Mercury," said Franckert. "It's wonderful stuff, as unexpected as amber or a lodestone. I keep a little sample of it with me." He fished in the folds of his leather coat and came up with a thick-walled, tightly corked bottle of heavy, shiny liquid. "Look," said Franckert, spilling a little puddle of the quicksilver onto the table. "Touch it, Peter."

Bruegel poked the puddle and it shuddered. The room was partly reflected in it. The great room's patterned ceiling, which Bruegel hadn't noticed before, was clearly visible, a tessellation of red squares and yellow octagons. The edges of the silver puddle dropped off steeply; the long lines of the windows were mirrored with abrupt bends. Now Franckert tapped the puddle hard, and it splattered into dozens of little balls, each of them a miniature round mirror.

"How wonderful!" exclaimed Bruegel. "And we can join them back together?"

"Just push them," said Franckert. "They melt together when they touch, unless there's dirt between them."

A tonsured boy appeared with a plate of food for Bruegel. Franckert used a scrap of paper to scoop up his puddle of quicksilver, pouring it back into its little bottle. He splashed a little water onto his hands and rubbed them on his shirt.

"Mercury harbors evil humors for the unwary," said Franckert. "Few of the men in the cinnabar mines live past thirty."

A few tiny balls of the mercury remained wedged down in the cracks of the table, peeping up at Bruegel like sly silver eyes.

Bruegel munched his bread and cheese, thinking first about the quicksilver, and then about the meal. The monks' bread was coarse and friendly on the tongue; the soft, shiny cheese was ripe and salty. Delicious.

It was pleasant to sit in the company of Franckert and his party. Their slurred, guttural speech, though not quite Flemish, was homey and comforting. For over a week now, de Vos had been Bruegel's only conversation partner, and the man's many peculiarities and character flaws had become galling.

Franckert was likable, with a manner less pompous than expected from a merchant. Back in Antwerp, Bruegel had regarded Franckert only from a distance, usually carousing and shouting with other, better-known artists. As Franckert's noisy jests and drolleries had never included Bruegel, he'd imagined that Franckert was a vain man who looked down on him. But now that fate had thrown them together, Franckert showed every sign of friendship and interest. Far from being a braggart, he was perfectly ready to share a laugh at his own expense. He seemed, if anything, more eager to impress Bruegel than Bruegel was to impress him.

Bruegel asked for some advice about the roads ahead, which got the teamsters talking not only about the highways but about the adventures they led to. The leather-faced Max told a ribald story about an amorous interlude in a Venetian stable, the tale embroidered with comments by the others. For Moritz's sake, Max was speaking in a low German that Bruegel found hard to follow, but his broad gestures and onomatopoeic grunts filled out the picture. The very haziness of the tale thus heard made it the more universal. Warmed by the beer, Bruegel found himself laughing easily and making his own remarks, fully part of the group.

The bookkeeper Klaua mentioned that they'd passed the gallows on their way down the mountain. The villagers had been gathered there in great numbers, making it hard to get one's wagons through. Franckert's company hadn't stopped to watch, lest some of their cargo be pilfered by the boisterous crowd.

As they ate and talked, Bruegel noticed de Vos repeatedly nipping into the eating hall for more beer to take outside—two mugs at a time. It was getting dark now, and a monk moved about lighting torches in the dining room and in the courtyard. Bruegel went outside to see what had become of his companion. De Vos was sitting on the same bench as before, drinking beer with a local woman who loudly used a few words of Flemish. Though it was hard to be sure in the torchlight, the woman was no longer in the flower of her first youth. She was plump rather than wrinkled; she had a fixed smile and a missing front tooth. Her name was Lisette.

"She wants me to spend the night in her cottage, Peter," said de Vos. "I can meet up with you in the morning." His earlier gloom had given way to cheerful abandon.

"Leave your purse and other valuables with me," muttered Bruegel in Flemish.

"Yes," hissed de Vos. "I'll do it as we piss together."

"This Lisette, this well-aged prickpocket, was she at the execution?" asked Bruegel as the two of them wetted the wall of the monastery.

"Indeed," said de Vos. "She said it put her blood all in a fever." He passed Bruegel his purse, his pocketknife, and the small brooch he wore on his cape. "She said the hanged man got a magnificent cock-stand, and that the buried woman screamed for nearly an hour. Yes, yes, Lisette wants me on top of her, as heavy as a fathom of earth."

"And you're done with raging at Rome, Martin?"

"We have but this one world to live in," said de Vos with his old cheerful grin. "It pleases God to test us." He persuaded the tapster monk to draw him two more mugs of beer, and then he and Lisette toddled off into the night.

Franckert appeared in the courtyard, checking up on his covered wagons. Their sides were made of lapped-together boards like a boat's hull, and they had big springs and huge spoked wheels. Hoops held the covers slightly domed up over the wagons, making room for extra storage. "Did I tell you I'm bringing painters' colors to Antwerp, Peter? They fill half this wagon. Look." Franckert loosened a corner of the covering canvas and prodded some bundles. "These packages hold a pigment called Indian yellow. Do you know it?"

"I've heard of it," said Bruegel. "But Master Coecke never used it. He preferred a yellow massicot made of roasted white lead." Bruegel peered closer, trying to make out the tint in the half-light of the flickering torch.

"The Indian yellow is remarkably rich and intense," said Franckert. "It's made from dried cow piss! A special kind of Calicut cow, fed only on mango leaves. And look here, see my blues? The most precious of the lot. I have both azurite and the true ultramarine, made of ground lapis lazuli, painstakingly separated from its gray matrix, twenty guilders per ounce."

"Peter Baltens got the chance to use some ultramarine for a chapel triptych I helped him on this past year," said Bruegel. "His contract with the sponsoring guild specified a full four ounces. We had a lot of sky."

Bruegel didn't mention that Baltens had hogged all of the color painting, limiting Bruegel to the monochrome underpainting of the landscapes on the front of the panels. At least Baltens had let Bruegel fully execute the gray-tone grisaille images on the backs of the triptych wings. Baltens had been able to make the rules, since it was he who'd obtained the commission from the guild steward. Bruegel still hadn't managed to obtain any commissions of his own, and sometimes it felt like he never would.

"You're lucky to be an artist," Franckert was saying. "If I hadn't inherited my father's business, I might have been one too. And, oh yes, it would have helped if I had the eye and the hand for drawing." Franckert laughed self-deprecatingly. He really was a very pleasant man.

"What other colors are in the wagon, Hans?"

"Since I knew I was heading for the artists of Antwerp, I brought along some vermilion made of Austrian quicksilver ore, so bright it pricks the eye. If that's too sharp, I've a rosier sort of red from the roots of the Venetian madder plant. I've laid in a full palette of Italian earth colors: burnt Sienna, raw umber, a mossy green, Verona brown, deep reds and ochers. The very soil bursts with tint in

sunny Italy. I've an exquisite green malachite as well, azurite's sister. Have you
finished many paintings since leaving your Master, Peter?"

"It's only been a year now," said Bruegel. "So there's been but the one triptych I just mentioned. The chapel piece for the Mechelen glove-makers' guild.
Figures in a mountain landscape. Only now it occurs to me that Baltens and I
had never seen a real mountain! We paint pictures of pictures; we repeat twice-
told tales."

"I'm sure the triptych was every bit as fine as any Flemish painter's, my good
Peter."

"I dream of a higher level of mastery," said Bruegel, responding to the
encouragement. "I'll paint what lives and breathes and thinks—not what you see
in dusty lesson-pictures. God's world, we creatures in it, and the world as mirrored in the phantasmagoria of our souls—that's my theme. Oh yes, Hans, someday I'll come into my own. In Mechelen, for instance, I made the backs of the
triptych panels a grisaille of grotesques."

"Such as?" inquired Franckert.

"The creatures before the Flood. I put in a great number of man-lobsters."
For emphasis, Bruegel made pinching motions with his fingers as he said the
Flemish word for lobster, that is, *kreeft*. Franckert laughed and clapped Bruegel
on the back.

Back inside, the monks had laid out pallets on the floor of the great room; the
dining room was the inn dormitory as well. Cheered by the evening's good
companionship, Bruegel slept soundly, his pack under his head.

In the morning, over their breakfast porridge, Franckert asked Bruegel to take
out his drawing and show it to him again. He was actually acute enough to comment upon the way Bruegel had used the pockmarks and bumps of little shrubs
to build up the long, shaggy curve of the mountain's edge. "It's like your hand
was just pecking away at it," said Franckert. "So much pecking deserves a grain
of corn! I'll buy it, my friend. But—hmm—I wonder if you could add some
human figures in it? Perhaps some travelers?"

"Actual travelers?" said Peter, getting out his pen. "No saints or kings? You're
a man to my liking, Hans. Real people for a real mountain." Working quickly, he
put a few men in the corner, and signed the picture.

They completed the exchange out in the courtyard. Bruegel had made his
first independent sale. His heart rose to the high blue heavens.

Franckert's party clattered off down the slope. A bare-legged little local girl
who'd been standing around watching them suddenly began to shout. "Pee-ter
Bruu-gel! Pee-ter Bruu-gel!"

"I'm your man," said Bruegel. "What is it?"

But the girl spoke a dialect which Bruegel couldn't understand.

"Do you come from Lisette?" asked Bruegel in halting French.

The little girl nodded vigorously and repeated the name Lisette. She seized hold of Bruegel's cape and pulled him forward. "Pee-ter Bruu-gel!"

"Wait," said Bruegel and ran back into the monastery to get his satchel. No point leaving it here to be pillaged. The noisy urchin led Bruegel through the village streets at a trot. The slowly stirring locals watched them going by. Some of them smirked knowingly. Finally on the uphill side of the village they came to a stop.

The sun was peeping over the high green ridge of the mountain and the sky was a luminous blue. It was peaceful in the heavens, but there was strife below, here at Lisette's little cottage. De Vos was lying on the ground nude, smeared with shit and feathers. A red-faced peasant stood over him with knife and a scythe. Lisette was in the cottage door, looking more sly than sorrowful. A few more feathers lay at her feet.

"Thank God you here," she said in broken Flemish. "My man want cut off you friend's sausage!"

"Help me, Peter," groaned de Vos.

Bruegel looked at the agitated peasant. He was toothless, and his chin was a grizzled knob right up under his nose. He gestured menacingly with his knife and sickle, looking for all the world like a lobster.

"You've riled a *kreeft*," chortled Bruegel. With Franckert's coin in his pocket, the world was a merry jape. "Martin de Vos, beshitted and befeathered for his sins."

De Vos managed the ghost of a smile. "A red *kreeft*, yes. He emptied the night pot upon me and slashed the pillow. I suppose he wants money for Lisette. Give him some."

"We want to go on our way," Bruegel told the toothless peasant. He pointed up the mountain and then, seeing no reaction, he made a gesture of handing out coins. "I can pay you a little bit."

The *kreeft*-man's eyes glittered, and his chin worked back and forth. He made an encouraging gesture with his knife.

"Here," said Bruegel, holding out some of the small coins de Vos had entrusted to him yesterday. Lisette skipped over and counted them. She said something to her man, who seemed prepared to back off. But now the little messenger girl piped up with new information. She'd been there to witness Bruegel's sale to Franckert, alas.

"We want the gold coin," announced Lisette. "If you no give, then off come you friend's sausage." The *kreeft* leaned over de Vos, rubbing his knife along his sickle. The clashing metals made an unsettling, slithery sound.

"You stupid, clumsy pig," said Bruegel to de Vos, all his good humor gone. But there was nothing for it but to draw out his fine new coin. When the *kreeft* saw the gold, a streamer of saliva flopped down from one corner of his mouth.

These were very simple people. Lisette tucked the coin into her bosom, then brought out a basin of water for de Vos to clean himself a little. His clothes appeared next. And then they were on their way up the mountain, with Lisette calling a sweet "*Au revoir!*"

"Where did you get the gold piece?" asked de Vos presently.

"I sold my drawing of this mountain to Hans Franckert," snapped Bruegel, his humor still spoiled. "You're an idiot."

"Franckert? He was at the inn?"

"Yes," said Bruegel. "Didn't you see him? He had wagons of Venetian spices and colors for Antwerp. Too bad you didn't stay with us. Did you enjoy your night with the trull?"

"Nothing special," said de Vos with a rueful smile. "Push push, squirt squirt. We were drunk. And then this morning that man came crashing in. Yes, yes, he was very like a lobster. I'm sorry for the gold coin, Peter. You're a noble friend."

Bruegel didn't answer. They walked on in silence for a while. The morning sun was burning off the clouds; birds were singing all around them. Slowly Bruegel's anger faded away. "You're noble, too, Martin," he said, finally. "We're all noble. Even with the coin gone, I still have the memory of making the sale. Franckert was quite taken with my drawing. He wasn't the usual run of customer, expecting to see the same things over and over again. I sold my drawing and now I'm hiking up the very Alp I drew. What a fine day it's turning into."

"I'm still in a cloud of stink," said de Vos. "If we cross a stream, let's stop so I can have a proper wash."

They proceeded up the mountain, with the sun growing brighter. They heard the rushing of a stream, and another sound, the music of—a bagpipe? The path bucked up and turned a corner, bringing them into a level little spot in the side of the mountain. A stream flowed along the far side of the glen. In the middle of the flat spot was a big, slanted rock with a gallows mounted on it: two square-cut beams rising four times the height of a man, with a stoutly braced crosspiece on top. There were a dozen men and women in the glen, sweaty and dirt stained, dancing to the music of a bagpipe.

"They've taken down the alchemist," said de Vos. "Perhaps they're his friends or relatives?"

Dirt was mounded high upon a single fresh grave. Bricks scattered to one side attested to the weight the executioners had used to smother the old Marie. Seemingly the mourners had cut down the hanged Joseph and buried him with his wife. They'd erected a makeshift cross upon the grave, hallowing the earth where the unfortunate old couple lay.

The little company continued their piping and dancing. They smiled, in a solemn kind of way, but they didn't try to speak to Bruegel and de Vos. While de Vos bathed himself in the stream, Bruegel sat to one side, seeing.

Owing to the slope of the rock, the far leg of the gallows was longer than the near one. This had the odd effect that, if Bruegel imagined the rock to be flat, the farther leg seemed closer. This gave the gallows a twisted, illogical appearance, as if produced by a clumsy painter's mistake in perspective. Yes, the gallows seemed part of a Crooked World, an apparition that should dissolve in the light of day.

Bruegel opened his senses, feasting upon the details of the moment: the shapes of the thick round tree trunks, the leaves spotted with bright sunlight, the little river in the plain below, and here in this glen, the dancers and the grim instrument of execution. The sane daily world was so different from the Crooked World of the gallows.

How odd to think of the two fresh corpses beneath the disturbed earth and bricks, the two old people dead down there. Up here, the breeze and the sunlight and the music continued. Death was close and real; there was no cure for it but to live as deeply as one could, no answer but work and love.

Bruegel saw a quick darting movement at the top of the gallows: a magpie, black on top and white below. It let out a melodious trill, quickly answered by a second magpie perched on a stump below. A married pair, two wise old birds, hopping this way and that, singing and pecking, letting out little spurts of white shit with the twitches of their tails.

Now de Vos came back from his ablutions, clean and happy. He and Bruegel headed farther up the mountain. The music of the bagpipe followed them for quite some time.

※ ※ ※ ※ ※ ※ ※ ※ ※ ※ ※ ※ ※

TWO

THE TOWER OF BABEL
ROME, JULY 1553

Bruegel loved the colors of Rome. Though some buildings were bare stone, most were covered in stucco and painted a particular shade of red or yellow. The Roman red was a dusky rose and the yellow was a pale orange with the slightest hint of green. After repairing a patch of any wall, the Romans seemed to paint it with whichever of the two tints lay closest to hand, so everywhere there were pink shapes on yellow walls and yellow forms atop the pinks.

The sky was a hot, glowing blue never seen in the Low Lands, and, wonder of wonders, there were palm trees growing in some of the squares. Bruegel itched to get out his little pouch of watercolor pigments and try mixing up the hues brought out by the warm autumn sun.

But the first order of business was to try to find the studio of Giulio Clovio, a successful artist who'd been recommended to Bruegel by Mayken Verhulst. Mayken was the widow of the Master Coecke with whom Peter had apprenticed. She was an artist herself, and something more than a mentor to the young Peter.

Their parting was still clear in his mind, Mayken in the tall brick Brussels house Master Coecke had bought, with upper floors for his workshop's studios. Mayken's hair had been, as always, in a messy bun, and she'd had paint on her fingers. She'd been smiling at him, seeing him just as he was with her clever blue eyes, while her daughter, young Mayken, crawled around under the table imitating a lost pig she'd seen in the street earlier that day, and then attacking Bruegel's ankle as if to bite it. He'd drawn a picture for the merry little girl, and then he'd been on his way. Bruegel's highest dream was to have a house, studio, wife, and family like Master Coecke's. Yet he found himself unwilling to paint in the polished, Italianate style of the Master's that sold so well.

It took them all day to find Clovio's workshop, using their Latin to ask directions, mostly from the ubiquitous ecclesiastics, the fluent de Vos doing most of the talking. The Italians seemed a handsome race, well formed and with smooth warm-toned skin. Their rapid speech and lively gestures made Bruegel think of tropical birds. He and de Vos got lost over and over, not that it much mattered to either one of them, surrounded by this architecture, these people, and these sun-hot colors, the whole city a crowded canvas come to life. Bruegel's big nose was filled with smells of brick, dust, and stone, of saffron, cinnamon, and anise, of jasmine, magnolia, and gardenia, of modern corruption and ancient decay.

He found Clovio's studios on the top floor of a yellow building in an old part of town, across the Tiber from the Vatican, not far from the Colosseum. Sweating with the heat, Bruegel and de Vos climbed four flights of stairs and knocked on the door, a handsome piece of oak with a bronze Turk's head for a knocker. A grinning olive-skinned youth answered; he was an apprentice, with his hands stained from grinding paint. He introduced himself as Giampietrino and ushered them in through the cluttered apartments.

The first room was filled with paintings, drawings, banners, rugs, tapestries, and vases, all very smooth and polished in the high Italian style, very like the kinds of work prized by Bruegel's dead Master Coecke. In the next room were exotic items from the East: intricately tooled cushions, screens of gilded leather, Arabian tankards, Moorish weapons, bows, shields, and a spiky black suit of armor that reminded Bruegel of a cricket.

They passed a kitchen with rich smells that set Bruegel's empty stomach to growling. The lady of the house was in there, busy giving orders to a stout cook and a slender young woman with a graceful neck. This was Giulio Clovio's dwelling as well as his studio. It would have been nice to go into the kitchen, to taste the food and talk to the girl, but Giampietrino led on.

The next room was filled with dusty white copies of classic statues, one whole wall a glorious disorder of plaster casts of busts and friezes. Bruegel stopped to stare, enjoying both the art and the smell of unfamiliar spices that had followed him from the kitchen. The sculptures were arid, but not without interest. Many of the busts had names engraved on them; it was remarkable to see these ancient Romans' names and physiognomies preserved for the ages by the transforming power of art.

"Cows!" smiled de Vos, pointing to some garlanded cattle skulls depicted in an ancient frieze. The humble cow was part of classical Rome, and now Bruegel was part of Rome too, transported all the way here from the Low Lands. He noticed a particularly evil-looking fellow among the busts, the inscribed name Massimino meant, he reasoned, "Biggest Smallest." Bruegel himself, was he to be big or small?

"This way," urged Giampietrino, and now they entered a corner room to find Giulio Clovio, a vigorous older man with curly gray hair and a round, clean-shaven face. He was working on three miniature paintings at the same time, using the last light from the setting sun. Using an exceedingly fine brush, he repeatedly moved down the row of paintings: touch, touch, touch.

"I am Peter Bruegel, student of the late Master Coecke," said Bruegel in his slow, stiff schoolboy Latin. He'd been mentally preparing the words all afternoon. "And this is my friend Martin de Vos. We are artists of the St. Luke's Guild in Antwerp. We have come to visit Rome. Mayken Verhulst told us to visit you. Can you help us?"

"*Mayken mirabila,*" said Clovio, his Latin very vulgar and smooth. "The lamented Coecke often spoke of her to me. A vigorous wife and a paragon of talent. She paints miniatures, what could be nobler? Coecke showed me two of her works that he carried with him, a picture of a windmill and a portrait of the artist. Your Mayken has a kind face and a very human brush. The Master Coecke always smoothed his images too much for my taste. He was too Italian even for me. His works resemble porcelain."

"*Sane,*" agreed Bruegel, and then he tried to say more. "I learned from Mayken as well as from Coecke. I can paint miniatures too." He leaned over to peer at Clovio's work. The miniatures were on ovals of ivory, perhaps four inches high by three inches wide, painted with incredible detail and delicacy. They were identical portraits of an old man wearing an intricately chased silk cassock. The portraits had a very immediate and lively look, indeed, the triply depicted old man looked so stern and irritable that one almost imagined his lips would twitch to spit out some withering remark.

"Portraits sell the best," said Clovio. "Closely followed by nude goddesses and startled nymphs."

"Who is this you paint?" asked Bruegel, pointing at the miniatures.

"Our good Pope Julius the Third," said Clovio. "Cardinal Farnese ordered these as presents for his three mistresses."

"You know the Pope and the cardinals personally?" marveled de Vos in his smooth Latin. "Are they good or are they evil?"

"They're Romans." Clovio laughed and swept his hand through a complicated curve. "Crooked and devious. Rotten to the core."

"Aren't you Italian too?" asked Bruegel.

"I was born in Croatia," said Clovio. "One is very honest there, I'm sure. But by now I'm a Roman too. You can meet Cardinal Farnese for yourself later this week. And I'll tell you something, boys, he's the one to get you in to see the Sistine Chapel. Even in the Low Lands you've heard of Michelangelo, no?"

"The engraver Jerome Cock saw Michelangelo's ceiling on his trip to Rome," said de Vos in a hushed voice. "He said it blinded him, made him lay down his paintbrush forever."

"Non timeo," said Bruegel, meaning, "I'm not afraid." Bruegel's Master Coecke had often spoken of Michelangelo's Sistine Chapel frescoes, and Bruegel was bound and determined to see them himself. Why else travel all this way? A cow in Rome must surely see the sun.

"I'll ask Cardinal Farnese." Clovio put his hands on his hips, looking at his two young visitors with some amusement. "Two parasites in search of a host, eh? Leeches! Blood worms! Cow birds! Why do the Flemings come to Rome, but no Romans go to the Low Lands?"

Giampietrino, busy grinding paint at one side of the room, let out a guffaw at his master's badinage.

"We'll be no trouble," said de Vos. "We can sleep on cushions or on the floor, Master Clovio. We hardly eat at all. Perhaps we can do some work for you? Or trade you something?"

"It's my pleasure to aid young artists," tut-tutted Clovio, still looking them over. "Think nothing of it. But what would you trade me? What do you have?"

Bruegel took off his jerkin and reached down into the flat pouch of the lining. He pulled out his drawings and the two watercolors he'd managed to do, hoping for just an opportunity like this.

"I admire that one," said Clovio, immediately pointing to the best, a watercolor of Lyons.

"Please accept it," said Bruegel, flushing with pleasure. He handed over the painting with a low bow. It had been too long since he heard the praise of a Master.

"This is worth a good week's room and board for the two of them, don't you agree, Giampietrino?" said Clovio, holding the picture out at arm's length. "An artist can always learn something new, even an old dog like me. Look at our Bruegel's perspective. He paints like a bird high up in the air. He has the cosmic landscape style of the fine Flemish masters. And how about you, de Vos, what's your style?"

"I don't have any pictures with me," confessed de Vos who, grasshopperlike, had accumulated nothing during their travels. "But I can make something for you. I'm very handy with the human figure. I can limn a most plausible Christ."

"Maybe I can get you boys a commission," said Clovio. "De Vos could paint a Christ, and Bruegel could paint the background." He studied the view of Lyons some more, smiling at it. "I'd like to see Bruegel at work."

"A mountain lake?" suggested Bruegel. "I'm full up to here with Alps," he added, touching the base of his throat. "They filled my soul. An Alpine lake as a miniature, Master Clovio?"

"You would fit the Alps onto an ivory disk?" said Clovio with a laugh.

"I can't paint in miniature," interrupted de Vos. "We should make a nice big picture. It'll be worth more to your patrons."

"You're wrong there," said Clovio with a hint of annoyance. "The smaller the painting, the more refined is the art. Let's suppose your 'nice big picture' will be worth enough to lodge you gentlemen for two more weeks after the first," he continued. "And after three weeks—*basta!*"

A sweet voice called from the kitchen. Dinnertime! Bruegel and de Vos sat down with Clovio, Clovio's wife, Beatrice, the apprentice, Giampietrino, the young woman from the kitchen, and the cook, Sophia, a large ill-tempered woman whose few words sounded like shouted curses. Beatrice had a melodious voice, though Bruegel could only guess at what she was saying. He had the feeling she was strict; there was a forbidding vertical line between her eyes.

The young woman, whose name was Francesca, had to keep hopping up to get things from the kitchen. At first Bruegel thought she was a maid, but then he figured out that she was Giulio and Beatrice's unmarried daughter. She seemed a bit odd. With a sense of foreboding, he noticed that de Vos couldn't keep his eyes off her.

The food was interesting. First there was a great mound of slippery strings of dough called spaghetti, accompanied by some kind of meat in a thick brown sauce and a mass of wilted bitter vegetables resembling celery and spinach. Then there was a big bowl of sweet, creamy pudding and a slab of soft, blue-veined cheese. Clovio poured a generous amount of red wine during the meal and de Vos of course got stinking drunk.

At the end of the meal, de Vos slid his hand up under Francesca's skirt when she leaned across the table to carry the great pudding dish out to the kitchen. Francesca gave a yelp of surprise and dropped the dish onto the table, breaking the bowl into several big pieces. She picked up a shard with a great blob of nutmeg-scented pudding upon it and flipped the pudding into de Vos's face, where it stuck. And then Francesca started laughing uncontrollably. The cook shouted, the mother said something curt in Italian, and Clovio's face clouded with fury. A moment later Giampietrino was showing Bruegel and de Vos to a small guest room off the front room.

"You sleep now," said Giampietrino.

"I love Francesca," mumbled the sodden de Vos, clumsily scraping the thick custard from his face and licking it off his fingers. Several rooms away, Francesca's laughter was still going on. De Vos made as if to start back out the door to look for her.

"Don't bother her," cautioned Giampietrino with a stern wag of his finger and slipped out the door, closing it tight behind him. When de Vos started fumbling with the door handle, Bruegel grabbed him by the shoulders and flung him onto the bed.

"You. Stay. Here," Bruegel hissed at de Vos. He was sitting upon de Vos with his hands around his neck. De Vos was too drunk and too surprised to do much of anything. He looked up at Bruegel with such a bewildered expression that Bruegel almost felt sorry for him. But the memory of the lost gold coin had blossomed up fresh in his mind. "If you get up, I'll kill you!" added Bruegel, clenching his teeth and giving a sharp squeeze to the hapless de Vos's throat. Everything in the room seemed red, everything but de Vos's pale, trembling face, still sticky with custard. He was trying to say something, but Bruegel couldn't hear him.

And then Bruegel caught himself and let de Vos go. De Vos groped about the bed, found one of the pillows, pulled it over his head, and fell asleep.

In the morning Bruegel felt ashamed for getting so angry. He must have looked like an underworld demon, throttling his traveling companion. He woke de Vos and apologized to him, but de Vos professed not to remember the threat. So then Bruegel went over the events a bit, pointing out what a good situation they'd found here and imploring de Vos not to ruin things.

On stepping out into Clovio's apartment, they found their host slicing up a melon with a sizable knife. He was still in a choleric state over de Vos's insult to his daughter.

"I'm of a mind to put you two rustics out on the street," exclaimed Clovio as soon as he caught sight of them. "You misapprehend what it is to be an artist. I'm a family man, not a libertine. I paint here and I have a drink with my meals, but this isn't a brothel."

De Vos flushed and seemed on the point of making things worse. But Bruegel spoke before him. "Forgive my friend's conduct last night," said Bruegel. "He has but a weak head for wine. I can assure you that he's quite overcome with remorse." Bruegel paused to glare at de Vos, who for once kept silent. And then he continued. "I've so been looking forward to working with you, Master Clovio. Master Coecke often said that Giulio Clovio has no equal. Be patient with two young Flemish artists abroad. Let us learn from you."

The old artist nodded and set down his knife. And then de Vos made proper amends, beginning with Giulio Clovio and ending with Francesca, who was once again sitting quietly in the kitchen. Francesca gave no particular sign of knowing what de Vos was talking about; today she seemed quite dull and withdrawn. Bruegel had a vague memory of having heard her laughter continuing well into the night.

For the next few days they spent the mornings in Giulio Clovio's studio and the afternoons looking around Rome. In the evenings they'd dine all together and, for now, de Vos was staying fairly sober. Francesca's behavior was unpredictable; sometimes she looked at them as if they were nothing but statuary, other times she was all winks and smiles. Once she threw a fava bean at de Vos's head. But de Vos kept his distance; he'd switched his romantic aspirations to a young woman who sold flowers in a nearby market.

A steady stream of patrons and fellow artists came in and out of Clovio's studio, and on the very first day, one of the patrons showed an interest in commissioning a genuine Flemish landscape painting by the two young artists. He was a conservatively dressed merchant with an eye for a bargain. He used the Italian word for "Flemish," which was *Fiammingo*. The picture was to be called *Landscape with Christ Appearing to the Apostles at the Sea of Tiberias*. Though Bruegel would have liked to base his landscape upon his Alpine sketches and memories, the patron was very definite that he wanted a landscape "in the style of Patinir," that is, a landscape of fantastic, tortured rocks shaped like nothing found in nature.

How dull, thought Bruegel, why did I bother to hike through the Alps? Once again it's to be a painting of a painting. He confided some of his thoughts to Clovio and de Vos. But de Vos was no longer sympathetic—perhaps he remembered his choking after all—and the old painter shrugged off Bruegel's protests.

"You don't like the job, so what?" said Clovio. "You've got a customer. You sell the picture and then you paint another one. Maybe the next one is the way you like."

"I could waste my life that way," said Bruegel. "Waiting to begin."

"Don't give yourself airs, Peter," put in de Vos. "If you can't paint the landscape, I will."

"Don't you two spongers get wise," said Clovio, growing sterner. "You'll do this job for your rent, exactly as I say. Landscape by Bruegel, Christ and Apostles by de Vos." And that was that.

Clovio gave Bruegel a seasoned oak panel to paint his landscape on, which was something of a treat. And, just so that de Vos wasn't idle while waiting for his chance to add Jesus, Clovio put him to work shaping and polishing ivory disks for miniatures. The disks were cut from an actual pair of elephant tusks that lay on Clovio's studio floor. When the master wasn't around, Giampietrino liked to hoist one tusk beneath each arm and race around the room being an elephant.

Eager to impress Master Clovio with his skill as a Flemish artist, Bruegel worked at building his picture up by the Van Eyck "egg-oil method" which Master Coecke had taught him.

Van Eyck's innovation for Flemish painting had been to use both egg and oil. In general, one prepared paint by mixing powdered pigments with a liquid; the Van Eyck trick was to mix one batch of paints with egg yolk, and to mix a separate batch with oil. The virtue of the egg-based paint, also known as egg tempera, was that it dried as rapidly as watercolor; in addition, egg temperas were good for drawing an accurate line. Oil-based paint, on the other hand, had great transparency and luminosity, and was ideal for putting a colored glaze over a previously flat area. Oil paint also had the virtue that it was easy to blend different hues of the slow-drying oils together, creating effects that could only be achieved with egg tempera by laborious crosshatching. Since Van Eyck, it had become customary for a Flemish master to use both. You started by making a neutral-colored egg tempera underpainting, glazed the underpainting with oil colors, added additional details in egg, laid on more oil colors, and so on. Bruegel knew all about it—or so he thought.

Bruegel gessoed his panel, carefully outlined his landscape upon it, and used shades of ocher mixed with egg yolk to flesh the drawing out into a fully modeled monochrome underpainting, brightening the highlights with white lead. The egg-tempera work dried to a fine hardness each afternoon, and before long he began layering on colored glazes of dilute oil paints, modeling the fantastic contours of the imaginary rocks.

The danger with the mixed method was that one could easily lose control of the technique, particularly when working with new materials for the first time. Clovio's brushes, pigments, and oils were unlike the ones Bruegel was used to, and the eggs that Clovio's cook gave Bruegel were rather lacking in freshness. Things didn't go all that well. The painting was oily and smeared in spots, dry and dull colored in others. And it was taking up all of Bruegel's time. Here he'd come to Rome to expand his horizons, and he was pissing away the precious sunny days on a picture doomed by its very conception to be a failure. And making a remarkably poor job of it, at that.

Meanwhile de Vos was getting impatient to put his figures on, as he was tired of endlessly polishing Clovio's ivory blanks. He began nagging and rushing Bruegel, which made the picture go even worse. Noticing the tension, Clovio gave de Vos something else to do: he got him to start engraving designs onto the fancy bronze hinges that Clovio used on the little rosewood boxes that he put his finished miniatures in.

Nearly two weeks went by, and then Clovio's miniatures were done and Cardinal Farnese showed up at the studio with a retinue of three lesser ecclesiastics, all of them dressed in fine silks, the Cardinal of course in red. He was a corpulent man with a face like a roast leg of mutton—quite brown and shiny, with lips that were crisp dark ridges of fat. He talked volubly, endlessly, in Italian. He showed every evidence of satisfaction with Clovio's three miniatures of Julius III. Clovio nestled each of them into its velvet-lined, bronze-hinged rosewood case and accepted his pay. Still the Cardinal continued to talk.

Bruegel couldn't tell whether or not Clovio had remembered to mention the Sistine Chapel, so he spoke up in his halting Latin to ask the Cardinal if he and de Vos could see it. Cardinal Farnese replied that, as it happened, he himself was to celebrate a private afternoon requiem mass in the Sistine Chapel this very day; the mass was being said for the soul of a very dear friend of the Pope's. It would be no trouble at all for him to arrange admission for the foreign artists—"you little *Oltramontani*" as he addressed them, meaning "People from Beyond the Mountains"—provided that they could make a donation to his charity fund. The figure he named was surprisingly high.

"Too much," said de Vos in Flemish. "Forget it, Peter."

"Hush," snapped Bruegel. It was impossible that this opportunity might be snatched away. He looked imploringly at Clovio, but the older painter seemed unmoved. "I'll paint you a miniature," he told Clovio. "I'll paint it my way and you'll love it. Please pay for us." Clovio sighed, shook his head, and opened his freshly filled purse.

So Bruegel and de Vos attached themselves to the Cardinal's party, who were riding back to the Vatican in two elegant open carriages. Clovio himself declined to accompany them. "I've seen it," he said. "I prefer miniatures."

As for de Vos, even though he was paying nothing himself, he was angry about the deal, and, as now became more and more evident, he was deeply uneasy about seeing Michelangelo's work at all. De Vos seemed to be afraid that somehow the sight of these masterpieces would emasculate him as an artist. All the way to the Vatican, he was muttering angry Flemish sayings about the degeneracy of the Italian Church.

Their carriage rattled across the Tiber and pulled up before the partly finished St. Peter's Basilica, which was covered in scaffolding and surrounded by great piles of marble. In the little spare time that he'd had in Rome, Bruegel hadn't made it here yet. St. Peter's and the Vatican, the very center of the world. They'd been building the Basilica for almost fifty years now; indeed the sale of papal indulgences had begun as a way to raise money for this, the largest church in history.

Beggars crowded around them as they dismounted. One of the Cardinal's assistants cleared the way. He was a hard-looking young priest with a big jaw and a black cane. Bruegel had wondered why such a sturdy fellow needed a cane, but now he saw the cane spring into action; the priest slashed away at the beggars as if he were beating rugs—though without managing to land a solid blow. There was a jut to the priest's jaw and mocking agility to the beggars' motions that Bruegel would have loved to draw. What a waste it was to be spending his days painting fake rocks.

Beyond the beggars were crowds of peddlers hawking relics, medals, and long printed prayers that were said only to work if one read them exactly word for word. A group of nuns sat behind a long table filled with painted plaster statues of the Virgin, St. Christopher, St. Barbara, St. Hipolytus, and St. George, with each statue's face wearing the same blank simper. Their deadening uniformity put Bruegel in mind of the innumerable Italianate religious paintings he'd seen. Why did people want to see the same thing over and over and over?

A sleek priest offered him a fresh-printed indulgence, good for one hundred years off from the time that was owed to Purgatory as a residual "temporal debt" even after a sin was forgiven. A curtained confession booth was set up nearby, with a second priest prepared to calculate your current temporal debt. The booth resembled an outhouse. It was a melancholy sight to see such japery in full swing. And only last year Julius III had made proclamations about reforming the Church.

Past St. Peter's and before entering the buildings of the Vatican Palace proper, they paused by an elegantly tiled villa where the Cardinal had his private apartments. Using a great iron key, the Cardinal unlocked a gate and the little party entered the building's enclosed courtyard. A trio of voluptuous women appeared on the second floor balcony, calling lewdly down to the Cardinal. The Cardinal sent Clovio's three boxed paintings upstairs with an assistant, and then his three mistresses began blowing kisses down to him. Actually, it was more than kisses, they were gesturing to him with their tongues, yes, their full-lipped mouths were wide open and their fat tongues licked about. The plump trulls tried to outdo each other in their bawdy display of licentiousness: cooing, giggling, and showing off their breasts and legs. The Cardinal seemed tempted to lug his carcass up to join them, but he still had his requiem mass to do, so it was onward to the Sistine Chapel.

Seeing the three courtesans had thrown de Vos into a frenzy of outrage and lust. "It's said that the degenerate Emperor Nero had his gardens here," he said in a quiet, angry tone. "Things haven't changed a bit." His short nose had gone quite red. Seeing him this way made Bruegel regret being a fellow Low-Lander.

Inside the Vatican Palace, Cardinal Farnese disappeared down a corridor to put on his vestments. One of his assistants ushered Bruegel and de Vos past the guards and into the chapel. There were a few mourners near the altar and a few sightseers, but other than that, Bruegel and de Vos had the place to themselves. They sat down on a bench by one wall and looked things over. The walls and ceilings were covered with frescoes: Botticelli and Rosselli on the walls, Michelangelo's brilliantly colored panels on the ceiling, and behind the altar his immense new *Last Judgment.*

Bruegel stared upwards, all of his being concentrated into his eyes. It was quite some time until he thought to form any words. At first only scattered phrases came to mind. A window into Paradise. On Earth as it is in Heaven. God into Man. As above so below. His lips moved a bit, thinking out loud. And all the while Bruegel's gaze continued to caress the living shapes and masses of Michelangelo's men and women. Off in the distance of the chapel a sweet voice sang.

"What do you think, Peter?" asked de Vos in a low tone.

"As above so below," repeated Bruegel. "Paintings like sculptures. Wonderfully solid. I wish I had the man's grasp of anatomy."

"Lord, yes," said de Vos with something like a sob. "The proportions, the perspective, the shading, everything so dreadfully perfect."

They sat staring in silence a little longer. When de Vos spoke again, his voice had a truculent tone. "Nevertheless, I say Michelangelo's no better than you or me. His figures are masterful, but you know something? They're all the same. Look at the people in that *Last Judgment.* It's like a plate of mussels. Each one no different from the next. It's boring."

"I almost agree," said Bruegel, allowing himself a smile. "And look down at the bottom of the *Last Judgment*—for his Hell, Michelangelo puts Charon and the river Styx. Classicism. Clean, good, noble, sanitized, bloodless, without scent. Where are the flaming cities and the gibbering grotesques?"

"The man doesn't hold a candle to our Hieronymus Bosch," said de Vos. "Oh, look, here comes Cardinal Farnese to say the mass. What a porker. Wouldn't it be great to paint him as a pig? A pig in an alb saying mass. Say, if I ran back to his apartments now, I could catch his whores alone."

"Oh, that's enough," said Bruegel, once again regretting de Vos's presence. Yes, the man was a loyal companion, but he always went too far. "This is a church, Martin. We're here to look and think and pray."

De Vos wandered off and left Bruegel alone. At the other end of the chapel, the Cardinal and choir began the singsong of the prayers. Bruegel leaned back, again staring up at Michelangelo's great paintings. Despite the brave and impudent words he and de Vos had said, he was very much in awe of these masterpieces. For Michelangelo, the classical and Christian iconography were, after all, but trappings. His real interest was Man, the ideal human form in all its aspects. How might it be to paint like this, but to move beyond classicism and the

Bible—why not paint people as they truly were down here Below? Why not paint a peasant feast or the howling mob at a public execution?

Bruegel's thoughts turned to God and the Church—the Church in all her decadence. God had made and was even now making everything there was: Rome and the Popes, Michelangelo and his paintings, Bruegel and de Vos, the bench upon which Bruegel sat. The divine Light lived in each and every fiber of being. God was perfect; Man was flesh, doomed to die, to rot, to stink. All works of Man were imperfect, but the Light was within them all. Degenerate though the Church might be, God could heal it.

Bruegel had been carrying a knot of anger at the corruption he'd seen today, but as he thought of God, the knot let go. He felt as if a rusty wire were being unwrapped from around his heart. With his eyes half-closed, Bruegel had the sense that Jesus was standing right beside him, resting His hand upon his shoulder. Bruegel's heart filled with love, compassion, and a deep trust in God. There was, after all, only this one Church. The Cardinal's voice sang on, and if the Cardinal were but a greasy bagpipe, the sound was nonetheless the voice of God. God's Light had flowed through Michelangelo, and it could flow through Bruegel as well. With God all things were possible.

The singing had stopped; the mass was over. To Bruegel's eyes, everything looked warm and rich, filled as he was with the ecstasy of—had it been a vision? De Vos came hurrying up to him.

"The guards say we have to leave." Three formidable Italian men stood nearby.

With a last look up at Michelangelo, Bruegel exited the chapel into the palace corridors, his surroundings still lit by the numinous glow of his vision. And just now, for a wonder, de Vos wasn't saying anything to bring him back to earth.

As they exited the palace, Bruegel heard a Flemish accent, and recognized one of the other sightseers. It was his friend Abraham Ortelius from Antwerp, accompanied by a lean old Italian man.

Ortelius was an unprepossessing fellow with a thin nose in a serious face. He had blue eyes and wispy blond hair. Ortelius's father had died young, saddling the boy with early responsibilities. He looked older than Bruegel, even though he was the same age of twenty-six. Ortelius was a fellow member of the St. Luke's Guild of artists, but really he was a businessman. He traveled about Europe collecting maps, which he brought back to Antwerp to be engraved and printed. The artistic nature of his work was that he designed captions and legends for the maps, and hand colored the copies.

"Abraham," called Bruegel.

Ortelius's solemn face lit up with a crinkled smile. "Peter! And Martin de Vos. How remarkable to meet you here. Michelangelo paints like a god, eh? Those muscles, those colors, those men." The excited Ortelius threw his thin arms up into the air, as if the frescos were still overhead. "I could talk about it all day! You must join us for tea. Oh, Peter, let me introduce my friend Scipio Fabius. He's a fine geographer; he came all the way to Rome from Bologna to sell me some maps." He switched briefly into Latin, so that Fabius could understand. "Scipio has made wonderful maps of China and Africa. This man alone has made my trip a success! Scipio, this is Peter Bruegel, who's destined, I'm sure, to be one of our great artists. Were you inspired by the frescoes, Peter? Or discouraged?"

Before Bruegel could say anything, de Vos spoke in rapid colloquial Flemish. Here it came. "What's so wonderful about a bunch of naked men hanging from the ceiling like hams? All his women are really men, you know, just take a look at their tight little bottoms. It's typical of the Italians to have a sodomite decorate the Pope's chapel, eh? And meanwhile a whoremaster celebrates the mass. The noble Luther fought in vain."

Ortelius seemed shocked and even personally affronted. He stopped stock-still and stared at de Vos in something like horror. "This won't do," he said softly. "You can't speak that way here, Martin. If those are truly your feelings, I think we'd better part company at once."

"Fine," said de Vos. "I don't like you anyway. Let's go, Peter."

"I'm staying with Abraham," snapped Peter. "Idiot."

"Bugger all of you," said de Vos. "Bugger each other." He stormed off across the square. Staring after him, Bruegel saw de Vos kick over one of the tables full of religious statues and take off running, with two nuns and a priest at his heels. Despite himself, Bruegel began to laugh.

"Your friend Martin—he has a worm in his head?" inquired Scipio Fabius in dry, careful Latin. "The St. Vitus dance?"

"He's frightened," said Bruegel, composing himself. "He worries that because of Michelangelo he cannot paint." Saying this he looked within himself. He was far from frightened. He'd never felt more ready to paint in his life.

"De Vos is a stupid pig," said Ortelius. "I've never liked him either."

"My cousin works in an inn near here," said Scipio Fabius. "Let us repair there for refreshment."

The inn had a pleasant courtyard with leafy vines and the open sky above. Bruegel, Ortelius, and Fabius sat comfortably drinking fine Ceylonese tea and eating a flat round yellow cake that Fabius's cousin brought out. Soon the cousin sat down to join them, and the four of them ate the whole little cake a slice at time; it tasted of eggs, nutmeg, and vanilla bean. While Fabius and his cousin conversed in Italian, Bruegel and Ortelius talked Flemish.

"So let me ask again what you think of Michelangelo, Peter," said Ortelius.

"The work is sublime," said Bruegel with a smile. "I'm lucky to have seen it. I can spend a lifetime learning from what I saw in the chapel." He didn't know Ortelius well enough to say more.

"I'm very excited," said Ortelius. "Never before have I so clearly seen Man's place in the cosmos. We're like the scale mark on the corner on a map; the unit by which God measures His creation."

"Perhaps that's too much to expect of us," said Bruegel slowly. A swarm of little insects hovered over the crumbs of their cake, somehow reminding him of the crowd before St. Peter's. Tossed about by the weakest breeze. "Every creature is a part of the whole," he added. "The butterfly grows his wings, the bird weaves her nest, I'll paint my pictures—de Vos feeds the worms in his head. Perhaps in God's eyes we're all equal. We don't need to be classic and noble, and neither does our art."

"Well said," said Ortelius with a thoughtful smile. "And what are you painting?"

"I'm nearly finished with a landscape that our host Clovio will sell to a patron. De Vos is to add some figures to it. We're working for our room and board."

"De Vos is fortunate to have you as a traveling companion," said Ortelius.

"And I less fortunate," said Bruegel. "I tire of his folly."

"That was an ugly thing he said about Michelangelo," said Ortelius. "Whether it be true or not. The great old man still lives in Rome, you know. He's turned his hand to architecture. He's designing a dome for St. Peter's."

"The endless labor of the Tower of Babel," said Bruegel slowly. A lovely idea was dawning on him. "I promised to paint a miniature for Clovio, and now I have the theme. The Tower of Babel! I've seen it here today. I'll make the smallest painting of the biggest church. *Massimino!*"

At the sound of the Italian word, Fabius got back into the conversation, and they limped along in Latin for a while. After lunch, Ortelius urged Bruegel to come visit him at his lodgings near the Colosseum.

"It's the Albergo della Putti," said Ortelius. "Think of me if you need anything at all. If you're short of money, you can sell me some of your drawings and I'll resell them for engraving in Antwerp. Perhaps a landscape with something classical in the sky. I'll be here for another twelve days, scouring the city for maps, coins, medals, and antiques. And then I get a ship home."

"I'd thought you dealt solely in maps," said Bruegel, regarding Ortelius with interest. He'd never realized before that Abraham could help his career.

"I have a wide range of interests," said Ortelius. "I deal, I trade, I collect. I have some cabinets at home to display my favorite pieces. I call it my museum. I know all sorts of people, and reselling some drawings for you would be no trouble at all."

De Vos didn't return to Clovio's that day, nor the next. Bruegel was worried enough to ask the others to make inquiries, but Clovio and Giampietrino didn't seem very interested in getting de Vos back. His absence meant one less mouth to feed, and less noise in the studio. Quite early the following morning, Bruegel finished his part of the landscape painting. It hadn't turned out at all well, but he didn't want to work on it any more. It was high time for de Vos to show up and do his part, to slap on the stupid whey-faced Apostles, and damned if Bruegel was going to do that himself. It was time to start something new, to start the *Tower of Babel*—if only he could think of the right way to do it. He hadn't told Clovio about his plan yet. Later that morning, he walked over to Ortelius's inn, hoping his friend could help him find their fellow Low-Lander. And he was eager to discuss the possibility of selling Ortelius a couple of drawings.

The Albergo della Putti was a louche little dive with a tavern at street level and perhaps a dozen rooms upstairs. Apparently Ortelius wasn't as wealthy as Bruegel had begun to hope. The barkeep, a plump beardless youth with red lips, introduced himself as Beppo. Beppo's breath was sweetened by a clove that he jiggled with his tongue as he talked. He smiled and shook his head when Bruegel asked for Ortelius. He said something in Italian, but Bruegel couldn't make out what it was. As he spoke, Beppo made ambiguous rubbing motions. Was he asking if Bruegel wanted to take a bath?

Bruegel left the unwholesome atmosphere of the inn and continued down the streets to the Colosseum, which he hadn't yet seen. It was love at first sight. His eyes had seldom been so happy. He spent the rest of the day exploring the ancient stadium, sketching its arcades of arches, nosing around its subterranean halls, drawing it from below, then clambering up the fins of the inner buttresses and drawing it from above. Although St. Peter's was the underlying inspiration for his *Tower of Babel*, it was the Colosseum that gave him the actual image he'd use to start the work. He stayed with the Colosseum till dusk, and walked back towards Clovio's through dark bustling streets with his new picture like a beacon in his mind.

He'd quite forgotten about de Vos and Ortelius, and when he bumped into de Vos in the street, it took him a second to connect back to reality. De Vos was just crossing the square by the flower market, carrying a loaf of bread under one arm.

"Martin!"

"Oh, hello, Peter. Are you angry with me?"

"Not at the moment. I'm glad to see the priests didn't catch you. Where have you been sleeping?"

"My little friend from the flower market has been letting me bed down on the straw in her stall. If I play my cards right, she may join me there one night soon."

"A beautiful dream, I'm sure," said Bruegel. "What about coming back to Clovio's and finishing your part of our picture?"

"I can't paint," said de Vos wretchedly.

"You can't paint *like Michelangelo*," said Bruegel, getting annoyed all over again. "But you can damned well paint some figures onto this piece-of-shit pic-ture we signed up to do. I've finished my part on it, Martin. If I had my true wishes, I'd start afresh on the other side of the panel and do it right this time, but Clovio wants the damned thing sold this week, and with my name on it. And meanwhile he wants me to start painting the miniature to pay for our trip to the Sistine Chapel. You've got to do the figures now."

"It's all right if I paint badly?" said de Vos softly.

"The picture's a complete botch," said Bruegel. "I mixed my oils too fat in places and they ran; I had to touch it up all over with flat egg-tempera patches; it's like a poxed trull with a painted face. Especially if you see it from the edge in the light. But Clovio claims it doesn't matter, he says this particular patron has no eye and that nobody visits his collection. To tell you the truth, it makes me sick to think of signing the thing, but Clovio says the time's run out and I owe him the favor. You can think of it this way if you like, Martin: the poorer your work, the worse Bruegel looks."

"Say, I like that," said de Vos, cheering up. The old smile lit up his snub-nosed face. "All right, Peter, I'm coming with you. It'll be nice to have a chance to get a bath." Bruegel briefly thought of the unsavory youth at Ortelius's inn, but he certainly wasn't going to mention this to de Vos. No yelling or arguing for now. All he wanted to think about was his vision of the Tower of Babel, the plan as nicely balanced in his mind as a stack of delicate plates.

Clovio seemed happy enough to have de Vos back, now that it was time for the young Low-Lander to finish the *Tiberias* picture. At dinner, Bruegel told Clovio about his plans for the miniature. It would more than redeem the botched panel. Clovio was delighted at Bruegel's audacity in wanting to creating a Tower of Babel in so tiny a form. The peculiar Francesca was excited about the idea too and she even got out the family's heavy printed Bible to read them the Tower of Babel story in Latin. "Come, let us build ourselves a city, and a tower with its top in the heavens, and let us make a name for ourselves," repeated Francesca when she was done, and then she spun around the room chanting the word "Babel." De Vos and Giampietrino jumped up and spun with her, the cook hoarsely shouted "Babel," and for a few minutes everyone was in a festive humor.

The next morning Bruegel selected one of the newly polished ivory blanks, one of a goodly size, and borrowed a few of Clovio's miniature brushes. The smallest brush had only three hairs. He decided to paint in watercolors, in fact he'd use the glue-based pigments, called distemper paint, that he brought along in his satchel. This way there wouldn't be any bad surprises, like with the *Land-scape with Christ Appearing to the Apostles at the Sea of Tiberias,* which de Vos was busy making even worse.

Bruegel spent the first day painting a spidery outline of the shapes he wanted: a tower like a broken cone, a harbor on the right, a city on the left, and some figures in the foreground. On the second day he got down to the real work. Rather than executing any additional preliminary steps he painted *alla prima,* with no underpainting, working to immediately bring the picture into its finished form, one feature at a time. The more he painted, the more clearly he could see his vision of the Tower of Babel. It was as if the paintbrush were scraping the frost away from a clouded windowpane. On the third day the tower's galleries were finished. Where the Colosseum had two unbroken galleries, Bruegel's Tower had seven. On the fourth day Bruegel filled in a wonderful ruin for the Tower's top, and set men to work among the Tower's galleries. On the fifth day he shaded the hills of the background landscape, let a cloud drift across part of the Tower, and fleshed out the tiny figures in the foreground: a king and his servants. To Bruegel's delight, the king seemed to be none other than Cardinal Farnese: fat, lustful, and greedy as life, though his face was no larger than the head of a pin. On the sixth day boats appeared in the harbor, red roofs covered the houses of the city—and on the seventh day the picture was done. Bruegel felt as happy as he'd ever been.

"A little world," said Clovio, who'd been savoring Bruegel's progress. "This one, I'll keep." He turned to de Vos, who'd just finished up his work as well. "As for the *Tiberias,* well, you boys are still learning. In any case I'm quite sure the patron will take it. He's thickheaded. The main thing is that your work here is finished and tomorrow you can continue on your way. It's been getting a little crowded. Though, Peter, if you want to come back and work on another miniature sometime that would be fine. Maybe we could do one together."

De Vos was downcast at getting no praise from the Master, and now Giampietrino began chaffing him about his awkward, weakly limned figures, which sat upon the ungainly landscape as if pasted there. Bruegel tried to say a few nice things to de Vos, but it was hard not to just keep going back to stare at his little *Tower of Babel* some more. There was a near-perfect match between his vision and the painted image. In fact the image was *better* than the vision, thanks be to God. The little ships bobbing in the port looked so inviting.

Bruegel had learned that Rome had a port, a few miles to the east. Why not go there and take a ship to the tip of Italy's boot? All afternoon he weighed the thought in his mind, though without telling the sulky de Vos. Perhaps it was time for a parting of the ways.

Clovio served them a fine farewell dinner with roast pigeons, a cornmeal mush, and a sauce of port wine and porcini mushrooms. As on the first night, de Vos drank to excess, but this time Francesca stayed warily out of his reach. She was very taken with the *Tower of Babel,* and she bestowed many lingering smiles upon Bruegel. An hour later, the house was quiet and de Vos and Bruegel were safe in their guest room, getting in bed by candlelight. The evening seemed to have ended without disaster. But just then there was a delicate scamper of footsteps and a little note slid under their door. De Vos snagged it.

He was drunk enough that he had to squint one eye shut in order to read. It was in Latin. "I tremble," he intoned. "Come to me. Francesca." De Vos gave a low, gloating chuckle. "You hear that, Peter? She wants me after all."

"Perhaps the note was for me," said Bruegel mildly. "Not that I'd go to her. She's half-mad."

"Mad with love," said de Vos, already leaning over the basin and washing his face and his private parts. "This will teach that fool Clovio a lesson for belittling my work. I'll swive his daughter."

"Don't, Martin." Bruegel began inching towards him.

"Jealous, eh? Yes, you bungled the landscape and sabotaged my picture, but you're not going to cheat me out of my little roll in the hay." De Vos raised a fist in the air. "If you take one more step towards me, I'll lay you out flat, Bruegel."

"You're serious?"

"I am."

"Then I'm coming with you." Bruegel pulled his breeches back on, laced up his shoes, put on his jerkin, and picked up his satchel.

"You want to come to her room?" asked the befuddled de Vos.

"No, I'm leaving Clovio's. I don't want to be here for the shit storm. Wait." Bruegel found a scrap of paper and wrote a brief farewell note of thanks that he put on his pillow.

"Should—should I come with you?"

"No," said Bruegel firmly. "You're going to Francesca."

"Right." De Vos's familiar smile lit his face. "Good-bye then, Peter."

Once again Bruegel felt pity for de Vos—but enough was enough. "Goodbye, old friend. I'll see you back in Antwerp, God willing."

So Bruegel let himself out of Clovio's front door as de Vos padded off down Clovio's hall. Just as Bruegel got down to the street he heard Francesca start screaming. Chuckling despite himself, Bruegel headed towards the Colosseum. He'd sell Ortelius a couple of drawings to get money for the rest of his trip.

The tavern at the Albergo della Putti was quiet, with a few men drinking and talking intimately to each other. Ortelius was nowhere to be seen. Bruegel addressed a muscular fellow with a cleft chin who was pouring out wine for the customers. "Abraham Ortelius," said Bruegel, pointing towards the stairs. He attempted some words of Italian. "*Paisano mio.*"

The muscleman pursed his lips and said something incomprehensible about Ortelius, then gestured for Bruegel to go on up. "*Stanza sette.*" As a kindness he showed Bruegel the room number with his fingers. Seven.

Ortelius came to the door holding a little illuminated book of hours in one hand. "Ah, Peter. I've just finished my evening meditations." But the book was a prop. Behind Ortelius the red-lipped barkeep sat on the edge of a disordered bed, his clothes askew. Beppo. Ortelius said something to him in Italian. The youth got to his feet and stood there pouting until Ortelius handed him a gold coin.

"You must be very lonely," said Bruegel after Beppo had departed. It had occurred to him before that Ortelius might be a sodomist. "To seek out companions of this sort."

"A sinful urge which I occasionally indulge," said Ortelius. "I hope you don't think the less of me. Nobody else in Antwerp knows of my vice."

"Not your confessor?"

"To tell one of our Spanish priests that I've buggered an androgyne?" said Ortelius. "It would be an open death warrant. But here in Rome, yes, I've dared confess. The padre said lust is the least grievous of the seven sins, even if the lust is unnatural. I wish I could interest myself in women, but it doesn't happen. Do you despise me much?"

"What you do with your cock is your own affair, Abraham," said Bruegel, meaning it. He'd grown up on a farm, and nothing humans ever did could top the ribaldry of the pigs. "Stick it where you like—I'll treat you the same as ever. It's just a cock. Speaking of which, de Vos went after Clovio's daughter tonight. I left just as matters came to a head. I'd like to catch a ship to Naples tomorrow." Bruegel paused meaningfully. He sensed Ortelius would be all too glad to change the subject.

"And so you came to sell me some drawings," filled in Ortelius eagerly. "Let's have a look."

Bruegel got out the sheaf of landscape drawings which hung heavy inside his coat. He didn't want to part with his favorites, but he and Ortelius agreed on two likely candidates for resale to an engraver: landscapes of broad winding rivers amid mountains and plains.

"Not to tell you your own business, Peter," said Ortelius, "but do you think you could add something classical to them? Then they'd sell better."

"Here we go again," said Bruegel, and took out his pen. A few minutes later he had drawn an embracing pair of statuelike figures in the corner of the first landscape's sky. "You and Beppo," said Bruegel. "See how he reaches between your legs?"

"Peter!"

Bruegel squinted at his drawing and made some tiny adjustments with his pen. "Ah, I had it wrong. It's the lovely Psyche, borne aloft by Mercury's strong arms. Now for the second one." He scratched away in silence for a few minutes, happy to be drawing. "Recognize them?" he asked Ortelius when he was done.

"Daedalus and Icarus," said Ortelius. "Icarus has flown too near the sun. His wings are melting."

"Remember him when you're back in chilly Antwerp, Abraham," said Bruegel.

"Of course. Here." Ortelius got out his purse and gave Bruegel some gold. "These pictures will move well. Do you want to spend the night? My bed's wide enough. It's quite safe—though I admire you, Peter, you're not one of my types." Ortelius made an extravagant hand gesture and babbled on. "There's the alluring little hermaphrodites like Beppo, of course, but they're not my true heart's desire. What I'd really like would be a vigorous manly man. Older than I, tall and dark, passionate and strong enough to defend me as if I were his wife."

"Perhaps a soldier," suggested Bruegel with a yawn. Other people's love affairs interested him but little. He sat down and began pulling off his boots. "I'll take you up on your kind offer, Abraham. And, God willing, tomorrow's tide will carry me forth from this Tower of Babel."

Once they were bedded down, Ortelius dropped off to sleep right away. Bruegel lay in the dark for quite some time, thinking.

In his mind's eye he saw Italy as if from a great height, with the Mediterranean sun beating gold upon the wrinkled sea. There was a little ship far below, its sails puffed out with wind, and on the ship was an artist, Bruegel himself, alert to the patterns of the rigging and the waves. Yet even as he saw himself upon the ship, Bruegel's envisioning eye flew higher—so high he could see the verdant curve of Mother Earth, that unimaginable globe upon which he and his fellows played out their lives. Far below, the little ship sailed on.

Tomorrow he'd sail south to Naples, he'd make friends among the local artists, he'd paint and draw and sail about some more, to Sicily, to the hot, dry, rocky south beyond south. And then, full of pictures, he'd return, across Earth's haunch to the cold, wet, flat Low Lands. His home.

※ ※ ※ ※ ※ ※ ※ ※ ※ ※ ※ ※

THREE

THE BATTLE OF
CARNIVAL AND LENT
ANTWERP, FEBRUARY 1556

Standing at the top of the Our Lady Cathedral's white stone bell tower on the last day of February, Abraham Ortelius regarded the view.

In the middle ground was a swollen, estuarial river, spotted with ice floes and glinting in the weak afternoon sun: the river Scheldt. On the far side of the Scheldt lay flat lands with cows nosing for grass beneath the patchy snow, and beyond the fields was the stormy North Sea with little ships tossed upon it. Ortelius the mapmaker mentally embellished the waves with a gaping whale, its mouth a tiny dot of red.

On the river Scheldt, barges swung at anchor, alive with tented living quarters and men smoking pipes. Low fish-laden ketches tacked across the icy, roiling stream, and scores of merchant ships were coming in on the tide. The trading ships were two- and three-masted caravels and galleons. With their raised poop decks, they looked like a navy of high-heeled shoes.

On the near side of the Scheldt lay Antwerp, filling the foreground of Ortelius's view. It was shaped like half a disk, a semicircle attached to the river along its cut edge. Wrapped all round Antwerp was a thick new city wall that included a solid little castle right down in the water. There were hundreds of ships anchored along Antwerp's long riverfront; and still more of them floated in the city's larger canals. The smaller canals were frozen over. The docks were alive with porters and sailors from every land; Ortelius could pick out Turks, Africans, Indians, Malays, and Moors among them—a turban here, a nose-ring there.

Seen from above like this, Antwerp was a mass of stone and brick buildings topped by spires and turrets and by pink and gray roofs. The moldings and ornaments upon the walls were made vivid by a dusting of snow. Most of the houses had a stairstep outline along the edges of their gables. Ortelius could see people in many of the windows. They stared, gesticulated and beckoned; some leaned out and emptied their chamber pots into the damp cobblestone streets.

Peering directly down, Ortelius regarded the focus of the scene: the great cathedral square crowded with people celebrating the Carnival season. It was high time for him to join them. He liked crowds. He descended the stairs.

Down in the square, night was coming on rapidly. There were fires and bagpipes, with people running this way and that, many of them drunk on beer. One fellow had fallen on a patch of ice, or had been clubbed; the back of his head was partly crusted with dark dried blood, with some spots a wet, bright red. He was screaming like a seagull and two of his friends were attempting to close in on him like peasants cornering a maddened pig. A melancholy sight. The trio passed near the huge door of the cathedral, and the bloodied youth heavily jostled a lean Spanish priest who was keeping an eye on who came in and who went out. The priest raised his chin to peer through his spectacles at the cawing bloody man, who favored him with a curse—was it "Stink maggot"?

Ortelius watched the little encounter, watched as the injured man and his companions disappeared around the corner of the cathedral. The priest wrapped his wool cloak a little tighter against the damp, chill air. Ortelius turned his attention to a waffle vendor: a lively old woman with a gaping, thin-lipped mouth, aided by her son and two daughters. She was wielding a long-handled waffle iron, baking the treats over a crackling fire that her slackly grinning son, evidently a half-wit, was stoking with icy brushwood from the banks of the river Scheldt. The woman's hair was a straight, gray shock; her motions were quick and businesslike.

After Ortelius's long day decorating maps, the woman reminded him of a pen point drawing shapes on a page—her motions were written only upon the air, and invisibly written at that—but even so Ortelius felt that she *was* very like the tip of a goose-quill pen.

He watched the woman until she shot him a glance and demanded how many waffles he wanted or was he just going to stand there soaking up heat from her fire? Ortelius sometimes had a tendency to stare at people, speculating upon their thoughts, forgetting that they were going to start wondering why he was look-ing at them—it was one of the habits his mother nagged him about, not that his mother was anything like this strident ink pen of a waffle woman.

"I'd like two, please," said Ortelius with a polite nod of his half-bald head. He'd had no supper, and indeed no food at all today, save for the porridge his maid Helena had made him that morning. Perhaps he was a bit light-headed from hunger. He'd been embellishing prints of Mercator's map of Flanders all day in the workshop on the top floor of his family's house, with his sister, Eliza-beth, working with colors at his side. Just last week he'd returned from buying two hundred prints of the map from Mercator in the German town of Duisberg. Getting out and making deals was more to his taste than laboring over a table of papers.

Ortelius loved maps, he took pride in moving them from city to city, spread-ing the new God's-eye worldview far and wide. There was a kind of alchemy to a map. First the mapmaker refined the ore of travelers' and surveyors' reports into numbers on an ideal mathematical globe—even if some reports were given only as sun positions and hours of travel. Next came the mysterious algorithmic transformations that projected the curved patch of Earth's ideal globe down into a flat rectangle. And then came the illumination of the map.

As well as copying the map's topography, the artist-engraver incised calli-graphic labels, thickened the rivers into tapering curves, placed small buildings to represent the cities, decorated the seas with ships and leviathans, and finally con-structed a grand caption in a cartouche that looked like the work of a stonema-son wrapped round in straps of fine leatherwork. Once his maps were printed, Ortelius colored them in and added still more flourishes, a fairly trivial though time-consuming task. Since the mathematically minded Mercator's prints had been printed plain, Ortelius's work with them was considerable.

Bringing the printed paper of a map to life was tedious work, and Ortelius was glad his long day was past. It was good to be here with the Carnival crowd. Two waffles and a pot of beer would set him right. He planned to have a mild lager, and not the strong sweet lambic ale—but a beer in any case, for in these times, to drink plain water was to ensure days of intestinal flux or even the dreaded sweating sickness. He'd sit in the bustle of a warm inn with handsome men to smile at and think about, yes, he'd play, as usual, the kind and sociable bachelor. He dared not indulge his deeper passions within the small, gossiping half-circle of Antwerp—though more than once he'd been tempted to go and have a look at the male brothel so temptingly situated in the wharf district's Street of Stews.

The waffle woman took a large goose egg from a basket held by her younger daughter, who kept the eggs safe from the loose pigs that wandered about eating whatever they could find. Before Ortelius could stop the woman, she cracked the big egg in two. He would have preferred to have her drain the egg through little holes in its ends so that he might use its surface for sketching a map of the whole earth; it was a fancy of his to try and draw the known globe upon every egg he ate. This particular goose egg was a fine, nicely rounded specimen but now, alas, its shell had already been tossed onto the dirty, slippery cobblestones and had been snouted up by a passing piglet.

The old woman mixed the egg with some flour and milk in a wooden bowl and, *zick-zack,* she made two waffles, sprinkled them with powdered mace, and gave them to Ortelius. He paid her, or rather her older daughter, who favored him with a sly-looking simper. Women could sense that he was an odd fish, a permanent bachelor. Even though he was still twenty-eight, Ortelius's hairline had drastically receded. His chin was covered by a close-cropped beard, and a thick mustache hung over his lips.

He wandered off, biting into his waffle, enjoying the crisp surface, the sticky dough, and the aromatic mace, smiling at the costumed people in the teeming square. Glancing down at his waffle, the long day's labor caught up with him, and a set of grid lines seemed to spring out of the waffle, covering the whole square with a cartographer's graticule.

Ortelius squeezed shut his eyes to make the lines go away, then opened them and focused on the first human thing he saw: a tall, young, full-bearded man with a long straight nose and shoulder-length hair, kneeling to look at something on the ground. The man had a striking nobility and vigor to him; he was laughing in a way that made Ortelius smile, ignorant though he was of what the jest might be. He drew closer.

The laughing man was playing dice against a fat man. The two were decked out for Carnival. The fat man wore an executioner's black hood over his head, and the longhaired man wore a tight green cap and something like a crown, no, it was four waffles, held tight against his head by a leather thong. He wore gray tights and a woolly white tunic beneath a dirty dark leather jerkin, with a strange object strapped across the jerkin to his back. Ortelius had to look twice to make out what it was, then understood that it was a convex mirror set into a hexagonal wooden frame. The mirror held within its bulging surface the whole cathedral square, held all the festively gathered humanity, held the spire of the cathedral and indeed the last bit of the setting sun. How wonderful.

In a sudden shift of perception Ortelius recognized the man with the mirror.

Of course! It was Peter Bruegel, back from his long trip to Italy, and with a new beard.

"*Yaaah!*" cried Bruegel, looking at his dice. "Seven! I lose, Hans!" He handed one of his waffles to the stout executioner, who lifted his hood up far enough to feed the Carnival treat into a wide, thin-lipped mouth, crunching the delicacy down in two bites.

"Hello, Abraham!" said Bruegel, noticing Ortelius. "Well met, old friend. Care to game for your other waffle? To chance your sweet, grid-pressed dough against the fortunes of fat Hans Franckert, chief executioner of beer pots?"

"No thanks. When did you come back, Peter?"

"Months ago, busy bee! I got as far as Palermo—I rode a ship thither from Naples. It was wonderful in Sicily, a fairyland of beautiful processions and bright seashells upon the shore. I wandered the south of Italy for another whole year. But one morning I woke with a feeling of having stayed too long. Do you know the fairy tale where a milkmaid falls into a well? She finds a wonderful land down there at the bottom, she spends a day and a night, but when she comes back, she's been gone for a hundred years. I was starting to feel like that was me. So I started home, and that took another year. I crossed the Tyrolean Alps this summer, and made it back to the Low Lands by harvest time, my jerkin stuffed with drawings and my head filled with more."

"Joris Hoefnagel etched and published those two drawings you sold me in Rome," said Ortelius. "In fact I made a little money on the deal."

"Good man," said Bruegel. "I've seen the prints for sale in Jerome Cock's shop."

Their eyes met, and Ortelius silently asked Bruegel the question foremost in his mind. Did Bruegel still think well of him? Or was he disgusted by the knowledge of Ortelius's forbidden passions?

"I'm sorry not to have looked you up sooner, Abraham," said Bruegel, reading the moment. "I've been remiss. I have only my work for excuse. You do know Hans Franckert, don't you?" Bruegel got to his feet, extracted one of the waffles from his headband, and bit into it. "Enough of our gaming, Hans. Abraham Ortelius is a sound and sober man. Like him, I'll draw sustenance from my holdings, rather than gaming them away." He took another bite and, mouth full, gestured broadly with his half-eaten waffle. His long hair flopped about with his gestures. The bitten-off corners of the waffle made Ortelius start to think of islands set into an ocean's grid—but now Bruegel distracted him, saying, "Eating is transubstantiation. This low dough fuels the wonder of human thought. Yes, my gut burns this waffle so that my eyes can touch the colors of the world."

"Is that transubstantiation too?" said Franckert, pointing. "What that *varken* is doing?" The *varken,* or pig, was eating something unspeakable, and Ortelius silently questioned the delicacy of Franckert's commenting upon it, especially just now while they were enjoying their waffles.

"I see it," said Bruegel, calmly regarding the pig. Ortelius remembered once again how much he enjoyed Bruegel's skewed view of things. "A pig eats what he finds," said Bruegel. "I've missed our Low Lands."

"I'm for another pot of lambic," said Franckert. "How about it, boys?"

"We'll see you later," said Bruegel. "First Abraham and I must catch up on each other's lives."

Franckert wandered off, linking his arm with a little man dressed in fool's motley: a costume that was split down the center, yellow-blue stripes on the left and solid red on the right, with soft tiny horns sewn onto the top of his hood. A crowd of children ran past, swinging clattering noisemakers built from wooden gears.

"Have you ever seen the Alps, Abraham?" asked Bruegel. "Or do you know them only as little lumps upon your maps?"

"I've seen mountains," said Ortelius with a smile. "I travel a lot, as you know. I just got back from Germany last week. But, no, I've never traveled straight through the Alps like you."

"You must see my new drawings of them. I'm getting better all the time. Jerome Cock has engraved seven of my Alpine Large Landscapes for his Four Winds press. I've published some drawings of ships as well, and next we'll print some local landscapes. Or perhaps something in the style of Bosch. In return for a steady stream of drawings, Jerome gives me room and board and a bit of money to live on. If I could just get some commissions for paintings I'd be quite comfortable. But there are so many painters in Antwerp. Any chance I can sell you a painting, Abraham? You can pick the size and the subject."

Ortelius felt a slight pang, wondering if Bruegel's only interest in him were financial. "I'm afraid not," he demurred. "My map business and my trade in antiquities have to support my sister and my mother as well as myself, not to mention our maid. Where did you get that marvelous mirror on your back?"

"From Franckert," said Bruegel. "He brought several of them from Venice for our own mirror makers to copy. I traded him a drawing for it." Despite Ortelius's refusal to buy something Bruegel still seemed eager to talk. Raising his eyebrows in a friendly way, he slipped the hexagon-framed mirror off his back and stared into it, tilting it so as to reflect as much as possible of the church square. "This mirror is the very emblem of what I want to do in my painting, Abraham. To carry off the whole world upon my back. Look in there; see how the fires flicker! If only I could paint that. Yesterday Anja and I took this glass out into a snowy field with some trees and I was walking around staring into it. Eventually I fell into a ditch. Anja laughed and laughed."

"Anja?" asked Ortelius.

Bruegel took another waffle down from his head and began eating it. "We grew up together. She's just come to Antwerp from our village: Brueghel near Breda. She did something to disgrace herself, and when her family asked her to leave, she thought of coming to me. She's always been a scamp. I helped her find a position working as a maidservant for the Vanderheyden family, though I don't think it's going to last. Anja keeps giving herself extra holidays; she tells the Vanderheydens she has a sick aunt. She's here tonight, come to see the street plays. Let's find her!"

There was a little show taking place in front of each of the square's two taverns. Ortelius and Bruegel headed towards the closer tavern, which was named the Blue Boat, a place Ortelius frequented to see the sailors and soldiers.

In the street, six players were putting on a performance of *De Vuile Bruid*—which meant something like "The Dirty Bride" or "The Hillbilly Bride." The play was a standard, quite familiar to Ortelius. It featured a vagabond couple named Mopsus and Nisa who were putting on a wedding for themselves. The bridal suite was a patched cloth draped over dirty sticks with pennants on them; the wedding musician was a man banging a knife on a metal coal scuttle; and the bride's two attendants were women with gauzy white cloths tied around their heads like veils. The attendants had wrapped their bodies in white sheets, and they wore conical straw farm hats atop their heads.

"*Youchhiie!*" hollered Mopsus—which was Flemish for, roughly, "*Yee-haw!*" He kicked out his legs as he danced a fancy jig around Nisa. "Come along, little oyster, and I'll polish your pearl!"

Nisa's unkempt hair hung so far down into her face that all you could see was her nose. She had brown weeds woven into her locks in place of flowers, and she wore a colander as her wedding crown. Her clothes were layers of dirty rags. She took Mopsus by one hand and tried to keep up with his frantic dancing, but her broken-down slippers kept falling off.

"Slow down, big boy," she called in a coarse accent that set the viewers to laughing.

"Spin with me, Nisa!" said Mopsus, twirling her in a clumsy pirouette.

The *vuile* musician redoubled his efforts. He made a screeching sound by dragging the knife blade across the little shovel, and he drummed on the shovel with the handle of the knife. The two attendants had hollow, rattling gourds that they shook to the beat. Nisa kicked off her slippers and danced in her socks, which had great holes in the heels. Her garments flapped with abandon.

"City folk got nothin' on me," said Mopsus, crouching down and starting to dance his way into the makeshift tent. "Time for bed, Nisa!"

"Hold on, thar," cried Nisa. "I gotta talk to my bridesmaids."

The shapeless attendants bounced over to Nisa, swaying their veiled heads in a rhythm syncopated to the screeching and banging of the coal scuttle. Nisa and her bridesmaids put their heads together, briefly dancing as one.

"Not enough wedding loot yet, Mops, my lad," exclaimed Nisa, tossing her head so that her dirty hair writhed like a nest of snakes. "We gotta dance up some more coin before you can think about opening my oyster."

Nothing daunted, Mopsus continued his jigging, leading Nisa in a circle around the ragged tent. The attendants reached out into the crowd, waggling their gourds, which had coin-sized slits in the tops.

The screeching of the coal scuttle was annoying Ortelius, but when he looked over at Bruegel, everything seemed redeemed. Like the mirror upon his back, Bruegel's eyes contained the whole scene, they made it wonderful and whole. Just then a girl with thick blond hair and a plump, pleasant face appeared at his side. She wore her hair with the ends cropped off at shoulder length, an unusual style that gave her a playful, rakish air.

"Peter! Isn't this fun? That musician is a wonder. All he uses is a knife and a shovel! I can't get over how many people are here!"

"Hello, Anja. This is my friend Abraham Ortelius. He deals in maps. Would you like a waffle?" Bruegel took the last waffle from his headband and handed it to Anja.

"Thanks! Hello, Abraham." Anja nibbled off a corner of her waffle and smiled. She had a chipped front tooth. "I've never seen a map—well, I've seen maps, but I've never held one in my hands. It shows the world as a stork sees it, eh? Have you lived in Antwerp all your life, Abraham?"

"Yes," said Ortelius. One of the head-wrapped attendants danced forward to shake a gourd in his face; he dropped in a coin. "Should we go inside the tavern and get a pot of beer?"

"I want to see Mopsus and Nisa go in their tent first." Anja giggled. "I'll find you later in the Blue Boat."

"Oh, we can wait here with you," said Bruegel. "There's no great hurry." It was almost night, and Ortelius was cold, but he waited too, not wanting to leave Bruegel's company.

By now the attendants had gotten all the money the crowd seemed willing to give. They crossed their arms, hiding their gourds deep in their sheets, and stood before the tent, rocking from side to side.

"Have we raised enough dowry?" called Nisa.

The attendants bowed three times and the musician played even louder.

"Let's celebrate the splice!" whooped Mopsus, taking Nisa by both hands. "The bridal chamber's ready!" The filthy tent looked too low and awkward to hold the pair of rubes, but the attendants took hold of the ridgepole and raised the whole tent up off the ground, its cloths and pennants waving crazily. Mopsus and Nisa danced on under there; the attendants dropped the tent; the poles fell loose; and everything collapsed to the ground, with the *vuile* bridal pair orgiastically flopping beneath the cloths like two great fish.

"Finis coronat opus!" called the musician, and stopped his racket. The players sorted themselves out from the collapsed tent and looked to see how much money was in the gourds.

Inside the fire-lit Blue Boat tavern, Bruegel, Ortelius, and Anja settled down in a corner with three pots of beer, which Bruegel insisted on paying for. The serving maid brought the foaming pottery mugs and laid the copper and silver coins of Bruegel's change upon the table. He slipped off his mirror and his travel-stained jerkin, looking hale and robust in his wool tunic. Franckert was nowhere in sight, which was fine with Ortelius. If he had to share Bruegel, then Anja was more than enough.

"Are you married?" Anja asked Ortelius, sizing him up. She smiled flirtatiously, and her big cheeks squeezed up under her pale blue eyes.

"I'm a confirmed bachelor," said Ortelius, raising his voice to be heard. "I have my mother and sister to take care of." A guitarist had just begun to play. The musician was a sensitive-looking, long-legged man with slick red hair and a tidy goatee.

"Abraham is not a ladies' man," added Bruegel, fingering his green cap. "His mother, his sister, the Virgin Mary, and Mother Earth are the only women he cares about." He gave Ortelius a friendly, reassuring smile as if to show he thought no ill of him.

"Oh," said Anja, not really understanding. "It's a fine thing to be religious." She glanced around the room, perhaps sizing up the other available men. A few people had started clapping along in rhythm with the guitarist, whose voice was surprisingly loud in the small room. He was singing in Flemish about a soldier who shits in his pants—it was understood by all the locals that this was a reference to King Philip, a Spanish Habsburg who in October had become the new ruler of the Netherlands, taking over from his father, the Emperor Charles. This was understood, that is, by all the locals except Anja.

"Is that song actually about—" she began, but Ortelius cut her off.

"Don't talk politics," he cautioned, and drew his finger across his neck. More than one of Ortelius's acquaintances had been hung, beheaded, or burned at the stake by the occupying Spanish rulers. Some had been executed for sedition, some for what the ecclesiastical courts called heresy.

"To Michelangelo!" said Bruegel, raising his pot of beer. "As above, so below. It's wonderful to see you, Abraham. And don't worry about me trying to sell you pictures. It's more than enough that I'm able to talk with you."

Ortelius felt warm all over. The three companions drank; it was a fine sweet bubbly ale, not a thin lager.

"What was Peter like as a boy, Anja?" said Ortelius, smiling at his friend. "Was he always cheerful?"

"Not always cheerful," said Anja. "But always drawing. It was wonderful to watch him work on his lessons. The things he'd show me on his slate! It was like a magic window. Once he drew a picture of his teacher pissing at the moon, eh? My big brother, Dirk, stole the slate and brought it to school to show around. I think Peter got a whipping."

"The teacher only *said* he was going to whip me," put in Peter. "But after school he asked me to draw a picture of you squatting in the grass, Anja."

"He did not!" Anja reddened and laughed. "Peasant!"

"No more," said Bruegel with a smile. "Now I'm a cultured man. I live in Antwerp, the greatest port in the world. I'm a member of the St. Luke's Guild of artists. I'm friends with the scholarly Abraham Ortelius."

"You were raised a peasant, Peter?" asked Ortelius. "I remember you said you grew up on a farm. I'd like to hear more about your childhood."

"Can I tell him, Peter?" asked Anja.

"All right," said Bruegel. "But don't spread this around, Abraham. And don't tell anyone else but him, Anja."

"It was my family that raised Peter," said Anja. "And, no, we're not peasants, not really. Papa didn't have any education, but he was such a good animal doctor that the old Graaf de Hoorne deeded him a little farmhouse free and clear—Papa had saved the old Graaf's favorite horse. And pretty soon Papa started doctoring the tenant farmers as well. We were on the de Hoorne Ooievaarenest estate in the village of Grote Brueghel, not that the de Hoorne family was there very often. Mostly they just came for the harvest." *Grote* was Flemish for "great" or "big," and *Ooievaarenest* meant "Stork's Nest."

"Ooievaarenest," murmured Bruegel, savoring the word.

"Peter was a foundling," continued Anja. "One June morning when I was three, he appeared on our doorstep. Squalling his head off. My mother was going out to milk our cow and there was Peter. I heard the noise and I ran to see him. He was so cute." Anja rocked over towards Bruegel and kissed him on the cheek. "I thought God had brought Peter to be my baby brother. My mother couldn't have children anymore. But Peter wasn't a brother, he was a boarder. The old Graaf de Hoorne happened to be on the estate that month—though actually it was no coincidence—and he stepped forward to tell father he'd pay to see the foundling well taken care of. My parents didn't formally adopt Peter, as they didn't want to dilute my brother's inheritance. I think it was my mother's idea to call him Peter, and my father's to name him after our village. Peter Brueghel from Grote Brueghel."

"They spell it with an *H*," put in Bruegel unexpectedly. "But I might drop it to look more cosmopolitan."

"The *GH* cluster is Flemish indeed," said Ortelius. "Coming from the Low Lands, one gets more respect with a Latinate name. My Flemish name is Ortels, for instance. You could make a clean sweep of it and drop the *E* as well, Peter. Brugelius. But we were discussing genealogy, not philology! Do you know anything of your blood parents?"

"Ortels?" interrupted Anja. "Your name is Ortels? I know your maid. Helena. I met her at the laundry. She's fun. And now you're asking who's Peter's real father? It's Graaf de Hoorne, I'm sure of it."

"Everyone always thought the father was someone from the de Hoorne household," put in Bruegel. "Anja and I often discussed the question; she likes to think it was the old Graaf himself. The King Stork of the Ooievaarenest. My mother seems to have been one of the de Hoorne servant girls, a woman named Maria Verhaecht. She was buried on the estate the same week I was born, dead in childbirth, a poor stork-pecked frog. I often visited her gravestone."

"Little Graaf Peter," said Anja. Though he didn't think anything of it just then, Ortelius noticed that Anja was toying with the coins of Bruegel's change, sliding them about on the table.

"It's not at all certain the old Graaf was my father," said Bruegel. "Although he was very good to me over the years, it's possible that was only because my true father was some member of his retinue. The Graaf was an exceedingly honorable man. It's just as likely that my father was Jan Vondel, the tutor of the Graaf's son Filips, a boy nine years older than me. Vondel was known to be given to dancing with the maids and the peasant girls. And I think he was even a bit of an artist. Of course Anja always preferred the idea of me being bastard nobility."

"Did you ever ask de Hoorne or Vondel?" said Ortelius.

"I didn't want to repay the old Graaf's kindness by seeming to press any claims. In any case, he died when I was sixteen—shortly after I became Master Coecke's apprentice. And as for Jan Vondel, well, he was killed by a peasant woman's jealous husband at a harvest dance the same year that I was born, the rake. Of course I could ask the new Graaf Filips de Hoorne about it, but he might not even know. As I say, he was only nine when I was born. And this way Anja's still free to think I'm gentry. Her secret Viscount." Bruegel reached over to tousle Anja's thick mop of blond hair.

"Don't forget that every year, Graaf de Hoorne stopped by the house to see how you were doing," said Anja. "And it was the Graaf who paid to send you off to school with the Brothers of the Common Life in s'Hertogenbosch after Father said you had to leave."

Ortelius smiled at Anja. The girl was a fount of information. "Why did Peter have to leave?"

"For one thing, Anja's brother, Dirk, hates me," put in Bruegel.

"Dirk always said that *vuile* vagabonds left Peter on our stoop," said Anja. "He claims he saw them. Even though Peter wasn't adopted, Dirk was always anxious that Peter might somehow interfere with Dirk inheriting the farm. But that wasn't the real reason Father threw you out, was it, Peter?" Anja nudged Bruegel and giggled.

Bruegel looked embarrassed and changed the subject. "Well, now that Dirk's finally got the farm, he must be satisfied."

"That's right," sighed Anja. "Poor Father. He died too young."

A fight suddenly broke out at the next table. A red-faced, bare-shouldered woman had started screaming at one of the two men she was sitting with, an olive-skinned Spanish Moor with a downturned mouth and a pointed, scraggly beard. He cried out a curse in Spanish. A beer pot shattered against the wall: the Spaniard had thrown it at the woman. A black-toothed Flemish sailor at the next table grabbed hold of the Spaniard's ear and dragged him down to the floor. The Spaniard had his hair tied in a high ponytail with two long curling feathers in it; he wore a white tunic and baggy black silk pants. He was a tough character, and he was giving as good as he got. Ortelius shifted a bit to one side to avoid the flailing limbs. He was anything but a pugnacious man. The innkeeper appeared and emptied a bucket of dirty, greasy water onto the combatants, but they kept going at it.

A quick little movement of Anja's hand momentarily distracted Ortelius's eye. With everyone's attention focused upon the fight, the girl had slid Bruegel's coins off the edge of the table and into her lap. She was a sneak. Before Ortelius could try to decide how to react, the cultured-looking guitarist across the room stopped playing and the barroom brawl's drama entered a new phase.

The guitarist set down his instrument, unfolded his grasshopper legs, walked across the floor, and kicked the Spaniard very hard in the ribs. "That's for interrupting my song," he said after the first kick, and then he landed another one. "And that's for threatening a woman of the Low Lands." The Spaniard's companion rose to join the fight. The companion was one of the Rode Rockx—or "Red Shirts"—the French-speaking Walloon mercenary soldiers in the employ of Spain. In addition to his red jersey, he wore a brown leather jerkin, baggy leather pantaloons, red socks, and had a smooth blue cap pulled low down over his round head. By now Ortelius had forgotten all about Anja's petty theft.

Tilting back his head to see out from under his cap, the mustached Walloon looked stupid, nearsighted, and implacable. He lunged forward, intent on punching the guitarist in the side of the head, but the musician gracefully ducked the punch, quickly turning to slam his elbow into the face of the Walloon, who fell back against a table full of beer pots, flipping the table and drawing the angered drinkers into the melee.

"I don't like this," said Anja, frowning at a wet spot on the hem of clean gray dress. "Let's go outside. I want to see the other street play, anyway."

"Sound idea," agreed Ortelius, standing to leave.

"The street plays are over for today," said Peter, who was staring into his bulging mirror again. "This is a good enough show, isn't it? Look over there, the woman they were fighting over is leaving with the guitarist, there they go out the back way." Anja poked him. "Oh, all right, Anja—we can go outside, and, come to think of it, we can still watch them burning Old Man Winter." He shrugged on his jerkin and slung the mirror across his back. "Don't leave your mug half-empty, Abraham. I paid for that! Drink it down. Fuel for the fire of the mind."

Ortelius gulped the rest of his thick, sweet beer. When he stepped away from the table, his foot hit a wet spot and he lost his footing, falling onto the pile of men thrashing about on the floor. By the time Bruegel and Anja had pulled Ortelius free, he'd caught several pokes in the ribs and a sharp box to the ear. A rush of low-class anger made his temples pound; he felt a mad desire to plant his boot in the contorted, angry face of the Spaniard. Shocking how easily one could sink to the level of the rabble. He managed to keep the unworthy urge in check. Anja and Bruegel helped him outside. The fresh air cleared his head like a tonic.

They passed a group of people holding hands and dancing in a circle. A few homeward-bound churchgoers jostled past, carrying the three-legged chairs that they brought along to sit on during the mass. Ortelius moved aside to give the churchgoers room.

"Look out—" began Bruegel, taking Ortelius's arm, but he was too late. Someone had grabbed hold of Ortelius's leg, high up above his knee. It was, damnation, the repulsive beggar Floppy Jan who could be seen every day near the cathedral, dragging his inert, twisted lower limbs along on a little board with wheels. Floppy Jan normally rested his hands on a pair of wooden props like tiny sawhorses. Right now one of the little props was digging into Ortelius's thigh, dangerously close to his testicles. Floppy Jan gave off a mephitic stench; his upward staring eyes rolled loosely. "I hurt terribly," he whined. "Give me alms or I'll crush your balls." Ortelius grunted in dismay. As a religious man, he routinely gave alms. But he despised the unclean touch of the afflicted.

Floppy Jan's beggar companions pressed forward, none of them more than waist-high. One wore a soldier's red fez and had legs that stopped at the ankle. He had wooden clogs strapped along his shins, and walked in a kind of kneeling shuffle, aided by two little crutches. Another footless man had fox-tails pinned all over his back—the sign of a leper. His wooden shin pads had spiky projections that propped him somewhat erect. A hunchback with a gaping, drooling mouth pressed against Ortelius's other leg, his vacant face turned up towards him like a flower towards the sun. Still more of the loathsome shapes were lurching closer, calling out for Carnival largesse.

"*Pfui*," said Anja, looking alarmed. "We don't have so many of these in our village."

"*Cruepelen, hooch, dat u nering bern moeg*," recited Ortelius, which meant "Cripple, may it go better with you." It was the traditional thing to say. What a grip Jan had upon his leg. Damn the man! Ortelius handed a coin apiece to Jan and the hunchback, and threw a third coin towards the others. "Bless you, Mijnheer," said Floppy Jan, using the Flemish word for "Mister." Not that he sounded the least bit grateful or respectful. In fact he made a point of giving Ortelius a nasty jab in his privates before releasing him.

The strong beer and the agitation of the tavern fight must have been working upon Ortelius, for now he committed an uncharitable act. Leaning forward a bit, though not so far as to bring himself back within Floppy Jan's reach, he spit directly into the beggar's face, and told him to go to hell. The cripple spat back and dragged himself on his way.

Meanwhile the two men with no feet had begun fighting savagely over the third coin, repeatedly knocking it out of each other's hand. Their combat seemed to know no measure; they bit and scratched and hit each other with their crutches. And then, at an opportune moment, a little boy with a hat pulled low over his face darted in among the beggars and made off with the disputed coin.

"Two dogs, one bone, and the magpie takes it," said Bruegel, using a broad peasant accent.

"The boy runs like his ass is on fire," added Anja. She and Bruegel seemed to revel in Flemish folk-sayings.

"Be careful they don't catch hold of us again," warned Ortelius, still breathing hard. He was already starting to feel guilty about having indulged the sin of Anger.

Before they'd walked much farther, Franckert popped out of the square's other tavern, the Dragon. He'd removed his executioner's hood; and he had a bagpiper and a handsome woman in tow, the slender Hennie van Mander, who was a tapestry designer and a member of the artists' Guild in her own right. The bagpipe squealed and droned. Franckert and Hennie capered about, hands on their hips, shoulders swaying, feet twirling. Like so many fat men, Franckert was exceedingly light on his feet. He wore skintight breeches with a codpiece that contained— and emphasized—his genitals. The triangular flap of the codpiece was fastened to his trouser legs with buttons at the corners. The codpiece was a fashion that Ortelius found to be of some interest, though not as modeled upon this man's tun-belly. He wasn't particularly fond of Franckert. Ortelius had a sense that the loud and hearty Franckert thought him unmanly.

Several more couples joined in the dance, Anja drawing in Bruegel. Ortelius watched from the side. He ached all over from his tumble in the tavern, and he felt worse and worse about having spit upon Floppy Jan. He'd have to confess it tomorrow morning. Oh, how nice it would be if he could turn off his endless worries and dance like the others. If only a kind, strong man would step up and draw him into the merriment as easily as Anja had done with Bruegel.

As if conjured up by the thought, a striking, solitary man appeared at the other side of the dancers. Ortelius had seen this fellow around Antwerp before, sometimes in the company of the financier Anthonie Fugger, but he wasn't sure who he was. An exotic-looking character indeed. His eyes were like a falcon's, fastening on the people around him one by one, as if searching for prey. For a dizzy instant the man looked straight at Ortelius and, seeing his gaze returned, his lips twitched with the slightest of smiles. But then his attention moved on, drawn to bouncy, singing Anja. Of course. Why would a man of such beauty be interested in Ortelius?

Ortelius sighed, and tried to think of higher things. At lonely times like these he could sometimes distract himself with thoughts of work. He made a half-hearted effort to see the dancers as an archipelago of moving islands.

Just down the block a crowd had gathered to light the big damp straw effigy of Old Man Winter—more a pile than a semblance of a man. A slender stick with a white pennant protruded from the mound of straw; this was Winter's soul. The dancers stopped to watch as the straw flared into life. A gust of wind swept a drift of the smoke their way and—what a reek! The straw was from the stables. Ortelius moved out of the pissy, billowing fumes—and now the mystery man was gone.

"I'm going home to bed," Ortelius told Bruegel as the bagpiper paused for a drink.

"I'll walk with you," said Bruegel, dropping the country accent he'd been using with Anja. "I've never been much of a dancer. I saw you watching. That's me too, most times. You'd better come with us, Anja. The Vanderheydens are going to be angry if you stay out too late."

"I'm staying anyway," said Anja. "This is too exciting. Why hurry back to be a stupid maidservant? I'm better than that."

"I'll be the knight for her ladyship," said Franckert with a bow. Hennie had already started dancing with a different partner. Franckert took Anja's hand. "Let's kick up our heels, Anja."

"Good night, Peter," said Anja. "It was nice to meet you, Abraham. Sleep tight and dream about *me*!" She gave Ortelius a flirtatious hug, flattening her big breasts against him, and even favored him with a wet kiss. She was clearly in the market for a man to take care of her. Gently Ortelius pushed her away.

"I don't live so far from you," Bruegel told Ortelius as they walked off down the Meir, which was Antwerp's broadest street. "Come by and see me tomorrow. I think I told you I have a room above Jerome Cock's shop of the Four Winds? You only need ask for me at the shop. I'll show you my engravings of the Alps." His voice trailed off in thought, then resumed. "Did you notice that little man in the main square wearing yellow and blue motley with his right side all red? I'd like to paint him. May the dear Lord God bring me some patrons!"

Ortelius was still thinking about the feel of Anja rubbing herself against him. Absurd. Women weren't for him. What a curse it was to be so unlike the mass of his fellows. Not that he wanted to change. As long as he never discussed it with the priests here, it didn't even feel like a sin—and if it were a sin, then surely his loneliness was penance enough. It was good that Bruegel knew and accepted him.

"Look up ahead of us," said Bruegel, pointing to a tall man carrying a package. "It's Christopher Plantin! Hello, Christopher!"

"Happy Carnival, Peter," said Plantin, waiting up for them. "And Ortelius too. Has Bruegel got you out carousing?" Plantin was a tall, civilized fellow with slick red hair and a trim goatee. He had a shop selling books and prints; he was a bookbinder and a leatherworker as well.

"Hans Franckert is the spirit of Carnival, not I," said Bruegel. "Though Franckert has kept my landswoman Anja, I soberly follow the good Ortelius to my early bed. Have you got that new shipment of paper from Lyons, Christopher?"

"Indeed," said Plantin. "I've set some aside for you at the shop. And you, Abraham, I haven't seen you since you got back from Germany. How was that?"

"It was wonderful. I stayed with our friend Mercator. He sold me some beautiful new maps I can market. There's a very good one of Flanders."

"Mercator paid dearly for that map," murmured Plantin. "Remember how the Inquisitors pretended to think Mercator was out in the fields practicing witchcraft, when all he was doing was surveying the land?"

"Yes, and that led to his heresy trial," said Ortelius, lowering his voice as well. "Mercator told me the details. Is it a sin to show our land as God must see it? Mercator now thinks the Spaniards persecuted him because of a passing fear that our people might use his maps to plan a rebellion. It's a blessing that, in the end, his maps weren't proscribed, and that I can sell my copies in freedom. Mercator sends his greetings to you, by the way. He likes it much better in Duisberg. A man can breathe there."

"The stink of the Inquisition fills our streets like the shit in Philip's pants," murmured Bruegel, and then raised his voice back to normal. "And what keeps you out this late, Christopher? Have you been in the taverns?"

"Nothing so Flemish as that," said Plantin, looking a bit abashed. "No, as it happens, I was home with my wife, putting the final touches on a gilded leather satchel for our new King Philip's minister, one Bishop Granvelle, born Antoine Perronet. I'm shamelessly ingratiating myself with the new regime. I made a special book for King Philip, you know, and he liked it so much that Granvelle requested a tooled pouch for his state papers. A rush job. I'm bringing it to the royal villa. We three can walk a ways together."

"What kind of book did you make for the Foreigner?" asked Bruegel incredulously. Since Philip had hardly ever been in the Low Lands, and spoke no Flemish, the locals often referred to him this way.

"A poem of praise, translated into Spanish and set in beautiful type," said Plantin shortly. "As long as Philip's here in Antwerp, why not make an impression on him?"

"Christopher wrote the poem himself," said Ortelius, giggling at the memory of it. This was the kind of conversation he enjoyed. "It's most fulsome."

"Anything for commissions, I suppose," said Bruegel. "The Spanish are taxing our local customers into poverty."

The Meir street was lined with houses locked up tight, some with chinks of light showing through the shutters. Drunken revelers straggled past, many of them in masks. The street was icy in spots, with mounds of gray, cleared-away snow along the sides.

"I'll be glad when Lent starts next week," said Ortelius. "Carnival is a dangerous time."

As if on cue, three men appeared from an alley: it was the Spaniard and the Rode Rockx soldier from the tavern, accompanied by a pale, puffy man in a thick, quilted jerkin. It was an ambush. The three men rushed at Ortelius and his friends with a terrible, drunken intentness. The pale man had a face like the pith of a rotten tree, and he moved in an odd, triangular fashion—he was missing an arm. The Rode Rockx raised his great ham fist and struck the back of Bruegel's head.

"Run!" yelled Ortelius, and took to his heels. But Bruegel and Plantin's footfalls didn't follow along. Ortelius paused at a safe distance and looked back. Bruegel was lying facedown on the ground, stunned by the blow to his head, his cap knocked to the side, his tights-clad legs lying very still. The red-shirted Walloon had the struggling Plantin clenched in a bear hug and the leathery little Spaniard had drawn a knife. The one-armed man was clutching Plantin's bundle against his chest. The four figures loomed nightmarishly within the round mirror on Bruegel's back.

"Help!" screamed Ortelius. "Murder!" A shutter overhead swung briefly open and slammed back shut.

"Keep yelling and you're next," called the Spaniard with the knife. "After I take care of your friend the guitarist."

"That's not him!" cried Ortelius, realizing that it was a case of mistaken identity. "That's Plantin the bookman! Let him go! Someone help us, for the love of God!"

One of the house doors opened, and a stocky little man appeared with a flintlock harquebus. But it was too late. The knife flashed, Plantin screamed, and the three attackers went clattering off down the Meir. The harquebus fired, there was a guttural shout of pain and the one-armed man lay felled in the street, Plantin's package ten feet behind him.

※ ※ ※ ※ ※ ※ ※ ※ ※ ※ ※ ※

FOUR

THE FALL OF ICARUS

ANTWERP, FEBRUARY 1556

The gunshot snapped Bruegel out of his daze. Slowly he sat up. His head was pounding. The attackers were gone. He felt the hair at the back of his head, thank God no blood. The memory of the blow was clearer than the street around him. A thump that he'd felt more than heard, followed by a pattern of lights in muddy colors. Then a singing in his ears and a jolting fall to the pavement. He felt over his body. The mirror was still upon his back, unbroken. What of the others?

Christopher Plantin was on his back, his tunic dark with blood. Oh no. Far-

ther down the dim street lay one of the robbers. Dead? There were people
around Bruegel talking, fixing things. He listened like a child, taking in what had
happened, still too numb to speak.

Ortelius was leaning over Plantin, consoling him. Plantin was alive, but he
was bleeding heavily from a deep gash in his right upper arm.

"There's a surgeon who lives upstairs," called a man with a harquebus. "Hey,
Gough! Wake up!"

"I'm here," came a quiet voice from somewhere above. "I'm Gough."
Bruegel peered up, moving his head very slowly lest a fresh flower of pain might
bloom. He saw a bald man silhouetted in a lit window.

"Cart him into my hallway, no need to bring him upstairs," said the man. "I'll
pour some spirits on the wound and sew him up. Maybe cauterize it too. Do you
have a fire going, Antoon?"

"Some coals," said the man with the harquebus.

"Then heat up your poker in them," said Gough. "Have your wife use the
bellows. I'll be right down."

"Is my leather case gone?" Plantin asked distractedly. "I worked on it for so
long. I embossed it and gilded it and—"

"It's over there," said Ortelius. "But that's nothing compared to your
wound." He burst into prayer. "Holy Mary, Mother of God, please help this
man. Peter—you're all right?"

"Yes," said Bruegel, putting his cap back on and carefully getting to his feet.
The pain in his skull was settling down to a steady throb. Nothing, really. He was
fine. "How badly is Christopher cut?"

"Please, Peter, take my leather case to the royal villa," said Plantin. "I worked
so hard. I don't want to lose their favor." And then he fell into a swoon.

Antoon stepped back inside to ask his wife to help get the poker ready. Just
about then Bruegel noticed that the pale puffy bandit down the street was up on
all fours. In the faint light, he looked like a demon in a grisaille. There was no
blood on him; the ball of the harquebus bullet had been stopped by his thick
jerkin. Bruegel walked over and scooped up Plantin's package, which lay on the
cobblestones between him and the enemy. The puffy, one-armed man glared,
reached for his knife, but then thought better of it and hobbled off down an alley-
way. Bruegel had no stomach to pursue him. At least he'd saved Plantin's case.

Bruegel helped Ortelius and Antoon to lug Plantin into Gough's town house.
An aged maid appeared, holding up a candle and clucking over the bright red
stains Plantin's blood was making on the black-and-white tiled floor. Though
Bruegel was sorry for Plantin, he was glad to see the vivid color of the blood.
He'd heard of men losing their color vision from a blow to the head. The maid
lit more candles, and then got a wet cloth to wipe up the blood. "If you let blood
stand more than a minute, it stains forever," she said, scrubbing away.

Now Gough came down the creaking stairs, carrying a little bag of surgeon's tools. "Who are you people?" he asked.

"You and I have seen each other before," said Bruegel, beginning to feel like his old self. "Don't you recognize me? I'm Peter Bruegel the artist. And this is Abraham Ortels, a dealer in maps. The injured man is Christopher Plantin, a bookseller and leatherworker. Surely you know Plantin. He owns a house with a shop called the Golden Compasses. In Steenhouwerstraat. We're all citizens."

"Very well," said Gough, kneeling down next to Plantin. "One of you should go to Plantin's house and fetch a carriage to take him home. And don't forget to bring the money to pay me. A gold florin."

"You go, Abraham," said Bruegel. "I'll wait here. I can help Gough. Remember, I was raised by a doctor. And after we sew up Christopher, I'll deliver his package to Bishop Granvelle." It might be a good thing to meet some powerful people.

"Very well," said Ortelius. "I'm quite ill from all this. Ask Granvelle for justice, Peter. One of our attackers was a Spaniard. The same fellow we saw fighting in the tavern. It was him and the same Rode Rockx. They thought Plantin was that guitarist. Brutes." And then he was off.

Bruegel watched Gough draw out a pair of shears and snip the cloth away from the wound, which was in Plantin's bicep. "Your Spanish friend made a nice clean incision," said the surgeon, wiping away the blood and splashing on some gin. "But the arm will heal up weak. Some of the nerves and tendons are severed. Is the poker hot yet, Antoon?"

"I'll bring it," said Antoon, and reappeared with a poker whose tip was a dull red. The unfortunate Plantin was awake again. Bruegel gripped Plantin's good hand, helping him to hold back his screams. Gough singed shut the bleeding veins and sewed the rent flesh together. The blood was lurid in the candlelight.

"Why did they stab me?" Plantin wondered weakly as Gough tidied up his work and dribbled on some fragrant oil of clove. "What did I do?"

"They thought you were someone else," said Bruegel. "A guitarist from the Blue Boat. Abraham and I saw two of the attackers fighting with the guitarist earlier tonight."

"My arm," moaned Plantin. "I won't be able to use my tools." His thoughts kept circling back to his new leather case. "Go now, Peter. Don't wait for Ortelius. Take the leather satchel to Granvelle. It's to be a gift. Granvelle and Philip are leaving for Mechelen at dawn to meet with the French ambassador. If you hurry, they'll still be awake."

"All right," said Bruegel. "I'll go now. And if I dare, I'll try to get some justice for you. It was their soldier who injured you. They should pay."

To reach the royal villa, Bruegel walked another ten minutes down the Meir. The farther he got from the city's center, the more snow lay upon the ground.

He scooped up some of the snow in his felt cap and pressed it to the back of his head. This softened the drumbeat of the pain.

Walking on, Bruegel pondered whether he could really ask for a payment on the injured Plantin's behalf. Did he dare speak up to so many assembled dignitaries? They were men in a position to do great good or ill.

The villa was the property of the Fugger banking family, but the accommodating Fuggers had temporarily turned this particular home over to Philip. Antwerp was a center of finance, and Philip's purpose in visiting was to negotiate fresh loans for Spain. Despite Spain's ravenous intake of taxes and New World plunder, the Spanish empire lacked sufficient gold to pay their hordes of mercenaries. And a war with France was in the wind.

The Spanish guards outside the villa were in a lively Carnival humor; they had a bonfire and a good supply of wine. With their metal helmets and cuirasses, they were a bit intimidating, but one of them spoke Flemish. Bruegel pulled his cap on tight and explained that he had a package for Bishop Granvelle from Plantin. The guard, a short man with a squint, accompanied Bruegel up the steps and into the villa's great hall, his armor clattering.

It was a handsome interior space, brightly lit by hundreds of candles and painted in an intricate trompe l'oeil fashion, the air scented with cloves, nutmeg, and mace. Bruegel had been here before, as a matter of fact he'd helped when his Master Coecke had decorated this villa for the Fuggers nine years ago. The walls of the hall were set with pilasters painted to look like marble columns, and the ceiling was decorated to give the illusion of a round vault with a painting in the style of Michelangelo himself. It was all very up-to-date. The hall floor was covered with the largest Turkish rug in Antwerp—like a field of gems. Bruegel was glad to see the room, he'd never been invited to see its final finished state.

Glancing up at the imitation Michelangelo, Bruegel remembered mixing the paints for it, as Master Coecke lay up high upon a scaffold copying the picture from an engraving. To think that now he'd been to the Sistine Chapel himself. There were better ways to learn from Michelangelo than to copy him.

The tart, precise tones of a harpsichord drifted down the hall. And now, padding across the rug, here came a red-liveried Spanish servant with dark, slicked-back hair. "This is for Granvelle," said Bruegel, holding up Plantin's package. The servant made as if to take the bundle, but Bruegel hung on to it. "I must give this to the Bishop myself." The servant shrugged and beckoned Bruegel to follow him down the hall.

They came to a music room with an intricately inlaid wooden floor, which was also the design of Coecke. The walls were hung with a legendary series of Habsburg tapestries called *The Conquest of Tunis*; apparently King Philip had installed them here for the duration of his stay. The tapestries brought back more memories, for they too were the design of Master Coecke.

The year after decorating the Fugger house, Coecke had traveled to North Africa as a court artist for Emperor Charles, commissioned to document Charles's victories over the Turks. Coecke's wife, Mayken, had been pregnant then. Yes, Master Coecke had gone off to Tunis leaving his blooming young wife alone with his apprentice in the house. Bruegel stared at the rich silks, at the gold and silver threads, briefly mesmerized by the glitter and by his memories of those days with Mayken. And then his eye roved on to the rest of the room. Where were his prospective patrons?

Chandeliers and sconces gleamed; the blazing hearth was so big that a man could stand inside it. Grouped near the fire were satin-covered couches and armchairs, with an ornate Hans Ruckers harpsichord to one side and a punch-bowl upon an inlaid marble table. Sitting upon the highest chair was none other than King Philip II himself, a dark little man with thick lips and a bulldog's lower jaw. Bruegel stuffed his hat inside his jerkin and ran his hand across the back of his head, pressing down upon the steadily throbbing pain.

Philip was so thin as to look ill; he put Bruegel in mind of a sickly newborn calf. Thinking of all the ill that Philip and his family had already brought upon the Low Lands, it crossed Bruegel's mind how easy it would be to kick Philip to death. The memory of the physical violence he'd just undergone made the pos-sibility seem quite real. He imagined the broken ribs sticking from Philip's crushed chest. The intensity of the thought was invigorating.

The Foreigner was attended by two ministers and perhaps a dozen courtiers. The men were wearing suits of silk and velvet, with big round collars made up of yards and yards of folded Antwerp lace. The women were clad in breast-revealing gowns and their hair was twisted into fantastic, sculptural forms. Bruegel recog-nized some locals in the group, including the outspoken banker Anthonie Fugger and the financier Nicolas Jonghelinck, known as an intelligent connoisseur of the arts. A very good man for an artist to know. The servant went over to address a sensual-looking, blue-chinned man in bishop's robes of red and yellow silk. Pre-sumably this was Granvelle.

A Spanish noblewoman was playing the harpsichord; she looked up from her music and gave Bruegel a condescending glance. The woman was as thickly made up as a rose dipped into a pot of paint. Her large nostrils were holes in her face. Her black hair was stretched up high over two combs, like a pair of dog ears. For his part, Bruegel was still wearing his Carnival outfit: his gray tights and the fuzzy white tunic with the dirt-darkened leather jerkin. His bulging mirror remained slung across his back.

Bruegel's eyes flickered from the harpsichordist to Philip to the courtiers, tak-ing in the lineaments of the oppressors, letting his mind play with alterations of their shapes. He could see them as demons akin to foxes—or perhaps cats? What about insects? There was a sudden flash of black teeth in one of their faces, the teeth like the mouth parts of a beetle. It was Bishop Granvelle, smoothly gliding over to deal with the local craftsman.

"You come from Plantin?" said Granvelle in an indolent tone. "Let me see what he's done." He had something of a French accent.

Bruegel handed Granvelle the package. The Bishop unwrapped it and nodded with satisfaction. "Very cogent. Did you work on this, my man?"

"No, I'm merely a friend of Plantin's. I'm Peter Bruegel the painter. Plantin couldn't come because—"

"Yet another painter," interrupted Granvelle with a weary sigh. His breath was so foul that Bruegel stepped away. "Antwerp teems with your ilk. I suppose you're looking for patronage?" This was more than Bruegel had hoped for. The very heavens were swinging open at his advance. But he kept his head.

"I have patronage," he said loftily. "I've designed several series of engravings for Jerome Cock. But I suppose, yes, I could find time for a commissioned painting." Surviving the bandits' attack seemed to have filled him with reckless insolence. To a man who'd nearly been killed, the ordinary affairs of life were laughably small.

Philip had been idly watching them talk, and now he asked Granvelle a question in Spanish. The two conversed for a minute and then Granvelle turned back to Bruegel.

"Could you paint that lady's portrait?" asked Granvelle, indicating the harpsichordist. "If it comes out well, perhaps you might have the honor of painting His Royal Majesty." The woman tossed her head and displayed a tight little smile, keeping her lips closed to cover her teeth. The tense muscles around her mouth seemed to form a snout. And there were signs of whiskers beneath the powder. She was a badger or, no, a bat.

"You wouldn't like my portraits," said Bruegel, recklessly. "I see you too clearly." He caught himself. He was flying too high. "I could paint a Biblical scene for Your Worship. Or something classical. Or perhaps a fantasy in the style of Bosch?"

"Listen to the pigheaded Low-Lander," said Anthonie Fugger, who was sitting nearby with a glass of spiced wine and spirits. He was a ducklike old man with big eyes and a broad, flat nose. "Take no offence, my dear Granvelle. Our Bruegel's a competent lad. He helped Coecke decorate this house, and he's made a reputation for himself with his Alpine engravings. What kind of Bible scene might you pick, Bruegel?"

"How about *The Merchants Driven from the Temple*?" riposted Bruegel. The words were popping out of his mouth faster than he could think.

Fugger cackled and smacked his lips. "Just the thing for a financier. I'd like to see that one. In a cityscape with Moorish architecture. In fact, I'd like you to copy the architectural details from our dear dead Coecke's woodcuts of the

Turks. Yes, I'll commission such a painting from you, Bruegel. But, mind you, at no high price. See my secretary Williblad Cheroo about the details tomorrow. He can meet you at the Schilderspand. A little before noon."

"You never told me why Plantin is not here himself," said Granvelle to Bruegel. His voice had turned a bit cold.

"He was stabbed in the street by a Spaniard not one hour ago," said Bruegel, secretly astonished at his temerity. "And I beg the favor to inquire if Your Worship might know the assailant? The villain was Moorish in appearance, with a high ponytail that had two dark, curling feathers in it. He had a pointed beard, a white jerkin, and loose-fitting black silk pants. He was accompanied by a red-shirted Walloon and by a pale, puffy one-armed man." The description seemed to mean something to Granvelle, but for the moment he said nothing. "Allow me to sketch them for you and the others," continued Bruegel. He felt in his tunic for pen, ink, and paper. As always, he had drawing supplies with him. He had the feeling he was talking too much and too loosely. It would be good to quiet down and draw.

"Very well," said Granvelle with a negligent gesture. "Seat yourself and use this table. It'll be a bit of entertainment for the court to see an Antwerp artist draw. Like watching a dog wet down a tree. It's remarkable how prolific you people are." Granvelle explained in Spanish to the courtiers what was going on, lisping and showing his shiny black beetle teeth. Philip himself looked over with a flicker of interest.

Bruegel leaned to his paper, his three attackers floating before his eyes. The throbbing in his head came back with them, but he pushed it away. His little pen warmed instantly to his touch, the ink flowed as readily as thought. It was a matter of minutes to limn the Spanish Moor, the Walloon mercenary, and the puffy man. A few of the grandees sauntered over to watch Bruegel at work. One, who wore a small ring in his nose, leaned over, first to study his reflection in the mirror on Bruegel's back, and then to look at Bruegel's drawing.

Upon seeing the image, the man with the nose-ring grunted and exclaimed "Hernando!" The others quickly agreed. "Hernando Lopez!" Bruegel stopped drawing and looked inquiringly at Granvelle.

"I thought as much myself from what you said before," confirmed Granvelle. "Hernando Lopez is one of our quartermasters. He helps to organize the lodging and payment of our troops. Is the unfortunate Plantin gravely wounded?"

"The surgeon said that Plantin's arm won't be the same again," said Bruegel. "And Plantin had done nothing to Lopez! It was a case of mistaken identity. Lopez drunkenly mistook Plantin for a musician he'd been fighting with at the Blue Boat."

"Fie, fie," said Nicolas Jonghelinck, speaking up for the first time. He was an alert, thin-lipped man with a pince-nez perched atop his long nose. He wore his hair cropped short and he had very large hands. "Justice must be served. This man Lopez must answer to our courts. If Spain wishes to avail herself of Antwerp's financial institutions, she must respect our civic peace! Don't you agree, Anthonie?"

Fugger nodded, and Jonghelinck's pale blue eyes glared at Granvelle. As one of the Habsburg's chief creditors, Fugger was in a position of some power just now.

Granvelle raised his eyebrows incredulously, but Jonghelinck and Fugger didn't back down. So now Granvelle got into a brief discussion with King Philip.

"His Majesty requires Lopez's continued services," said Granvelle presently. "Lopez's duties preclude his losing any time to your creaking provincial legal system. But His Majesty suggests a reparation. We will pay a sum to your Christopher Plantin. Reckon it into our loan, Señor Fugger, and give Plantin the money yourself. Philip and the other Habsburgs will, as always, be good for the bill."

"I have enough Habsburg loans for now," said Fugger. "You take this one on, Nicolas."

"All right," said Jonghelinck with a little smile. He nodded his smooth, oval head towards Philip and picked up Bruegel's sketch with one of his large hands. "I fancy this, Bruegel. May I keep it?"

"Of course. You were good to intercede for Plantin." It was hard to believe how well things were going.

"Don't try being more of a skinflint than me, Nicolas," put in old Fugger. "It's impossible. Buy a painting from Bruegel instead of begging his scraps. I think it's likely to be a sound investment."

"Indeed," said Jonghelinck, still admiring the sketch. "How about something classical? I think I've seen an etching of Daedalus and Icarus by you, Bruegel, have I not?"

"That's right," said Bruegel. "Done as a river landscape and printed by Hoefnagel. You're well-informed, Mijnheer Jonghelinck."

"Call me Nicolas. I'd like you to paint me a *Fall of Icarus*. A fresh composition, though. The etching's design was a bit—opportunistic."

"Yes," said Bruegel excitedly. "Exactly! I'd like to paint it as a cosmic landscape, with a plowman on a hill in the foreground, a beautiful ship in the sea, and lots of blue in the sky and the water. I'll show the great world rolling on, with Icarus's fate very small."

"That sounds promising. Think it out a little more, and we can discuss it tomorrow. As you're going to the Schilderspand to meet Fugger's man, I'll be there at the same time." Bruegel was high in the sky, his wings finally warmed by the sun.

Granvelle caught the acquisitive fever and chimed in. "Listen here, Señor Bruegel, why don't you paint a Nativity for the court of Philip. Yes? Will you manage this matter for us, Jonghelinck? Arrange the payment for the painting from our loan, along with Plantin's stipend."

Dizzy with success, Bruegel bowed and backed out of the room. Three commissions! It was much more than he'd hoped. Get out while you can, Icarus!

He took away a final mental image of Philip and his court as toads and chickens. In the streets, sleet had begun to fall. For the first time in perhaps half an hour he remembered the ache in his head. He stuffed his cap with sleet and pressed it to the back of his head, singing and dancing a bit as he walked.

When Bruegel got back to his room above Cock's Four Winds, he was too excited to sleep. He hung his mirror on the wall, lit a candle, and walked over to his big drawing table, perching on a stool. He pushed his current drawings to one side and made some quick calculations, trying to estimate the costs and labor of suddenly producing three paintings.

There were two separate issues: first, whether to paint upon linen or upon an oak panel; and, second, what liquid medium to grind his pigments with. Thanks to Coecke and Mayken Verhulst, Bruegel was skilled in watercolors, egg tempera, and oil. Though egg-and-oil paintings produced finer effects, watercolor dried much faster, and it would be easier to quickly finish three paintings using it. Well, perhaps Icarus could be in oil. He'd do that one last and make it the best of the three. As for the painting surface, the supercilious Granvelle could settle for linen, while Fugger and Jonghelinck would get panels of fine, seasoned oak. Bruegel finished his rough estimates of the costs and then made a quick little test sketch for a *Fall of Icarus* as a seascape. He put a ship in the corner, with Icarus's little legs in a splash of water beside it. And on the horizon, a low blazing sun. Staring at the inked disk of the sun, Bruegel's mind blanked out, and he sat there motionless for a few minutes, grinning and bedazzled.

And then he finally got in bed, lying facedown so as to spare the tender spot on his head. He hadn't been asleep for more than an hour when there was a rapping at his door. It was Anja—cold, wet, and bedraggled.

"The Vanderheydens locked me out," said Anja with a timid smile. "And when I broke a window trying to get in, the housekeeper popped out of her hole roaring that I've been dismissed, eh?"

"Poor Anja," said Bruegel. "Not that I'm surprised. It wasn't the right job for you. But listen to my news! Tonight I got commissions for three paintings!" Telling of his good fortune felt like uncovering a golden treasure. Almost a dream, but really true.

"How wonderful," said Anja, stepping closer. "Can I share your bed, Peter? Like old times." She threw her arms around Bruegel and attempted to give him a kiss.

"You're chilled right through, Anja," said Bruegel, hugging her, but turning his head to one side. He wasn't sure he wanted to start up with Anja. Upon her recent arrival in Antwerp she'd made it quite clear that she'd be open to having sex with him. But Anja had always been a very practical girl, and Bruegel knew there'd be a price to pay for her favors. "Of course you can stay here. For tonight." His room was really too small for two persons. "Let me find you a dry shirt to sleep in."

"Why not nude?" said Anja into his shoulder, her voice very small. "It'll be warmer. Remember when we were young, Peter, how we'd play at Adam and Eve?"

"I remember," said Bruegel softly. He'd been wondering when she'd bring this up. "Our own Eden. Until your Serpent brother, Dirk, told the priest and the priest told your father, and Adam was expelled from the Garden."

Anja's father had sent Bruegel away to the boarding school of the Brothers of the Common Life, with his expenses funded by the ever-generous Graaf. All in all it had been for the best. Bruegel had learned a bit of Latin in s'Hertogenbosch, had seen some wonderful drawings by the immortal Bosch, and soon after that he and the Brothers had parted ways. Then he'd found a place as Master Coecke's apprentice—and thus his career. It had been for the best, but he could still remember how, all those years ago, he and Anja had wept. She was warming in his arms. She was very soft. His headache was gone.

Anja tugged Bruegel's beard, turning his face towards hers, and this time he let her kiss him. She smelled of beer. The kiss went on and on.

"I've missed you so, Peter," said Anja presently. "Why can't we live together now? We've no common ancestors. And we're well out of Papa's house. Let's finish what we started, all those years ago. We're free."

Perhaps Bruegel had been free a moment ago, but now he felt as if he were plummeting from the sky. He struggled to stay aloft. "I'm—I'm not ready to marry, Anja."

"We don't need to marry, Peter," said Anja in her sweetest tone. "You'll be a lusty master and I your willing housemaid—" Anja reached down to feel Bruegel with an intimate, familiar hand. "Oh my. How you've grown."

"Oh, Anja," said Bruegel, and they sank into his bed.

When Bruegel woke, it was well past daylight. The first day of March. Sleeping Anja was nestled against him: warm, naked, and womanly. It was good to have her here. He felt a great sense of peace. If this was how it felt to fall from the sky to the sea, so be it. He had three commissions and his head felt fine.

In the night the sleet had turned to snow. The snow was falling so thickly that Bruegel couldn't even see where the sun was. The sounds from outside were cozy and muffled. He lay still, staring out his little window at the falling flakes, enjoying how they swirled about with the puffs of wind. The closer flakes looked big and yellowish, the more distant flakes were smaller, with tints of blue-gray.

Anja stirred and her eyes flickered open. She smiled and kissed his bare shoulder.

"When I came to Antwerp I was hoping for this," said Anja. "Can I stay? We needn't tell the world about being lovers. For all they know, I'm just your maid!"

"I can't imagine giving you orders," said Bruegel. He hadn't yet given any thought to the practicalities of the situation, and he didn't particularly want to start.

"You won't have to. I know what to do." Anja looked around the room. "It's a mess in here. And too small. With your new commissions, you can afford more space. A second room. The new room can be your studio, and we could curtain off one end of it to be the maid's room. Anja's private corner. We'll make love as much as we like, but we'll keep some independence. Perhaps someday we'll marry others and move on. Say yes, Peter."

A second room! What a thought. Clever Anja. It was very pleasant to have her in his bed. Why fight it? "I'd like to have you stay," allowed Bruegel. "And as it happens, the room next door is vacant. A Calvinist lived there, the unfortunate Gus Groot. They burned him at the stake last week. A brave man. The Spanish soldiers came up the stairs for Gus and all he said was, 'It is finished.' Jerome Cock went to see him burned. Jerome wanted to bribe the executioner to strangle Gus before lighting the wood, but Gus said 'No, better to die by fire than by a murderer's hand.' Jerome said Gus sang hymns then, and he never screamed."

"Dreadful," said Anja, busy looking around. "Is his room the same size as this one?"

"Bigger. It has two fine north windows and, as it happens, a partitioned-off nook at one end." Bruegel smiled at Anja, touching his fingers to her cheek. "Where the titmouse can build her nest. Perhaps you can even help me a bit in the studio. Mixing the paints. I learned most of what I know about watercolors from a woman—from Mayken Verhulst."

"Then I can do it too. I'll do whatever you say, Peter. And more. Who's Mayken Verhulst?"

"Master Coecke's widow. She's an accomplished painter in her own right, a miniaturist. A wonderful woman." Mayken had been midway in age between Bruegel and her husband. For the second time in a day, Bruegel thought of the time when Master Coecke had been off with Emperor Charles's fleet fighting the Turks—but there was certainly no need to mention this.

"I'm jealous," said Anja, sensing something. "Where does your wonderful Mayken live?"

"In Brussels," said Bruegel. "Master Coecke moved there just before he died. He and Mayken and—and their daughter. She's named Mayken too." His voice softened. He'd helped care for little Mayken around the Coecke's household. He was fond of her—though certainly not in a lecherous way. She was cute and fresh, with a bright spirit, and perhaps someday—well, who knew.

In the raw emotion of Master Coecke's funeral, Bruegel had almost gone so far as to offer to marry the widow, but she'd forestalled him, patiently pointing out that she was just as happy to be without a man, to be her own mistress, to answer to no one. She was well situated, having inherited Coecke's workshop. She preferred to paint her miniatures in peace. And then she'd proposed that perhaps Bruegel could eventually join the house of Coecke by marrying her daughter.

The important thing, old Mayken had said, was to build her workshop into a dynasty, and she herself was past the age of wanting to risk another quickening. In her eyes, should Peter's career as an artist pan out, an eventual match between him and young Mayken could be auspicious. But for now, Peter was twenty-nine and all but unknown, little Mayken was but eleven, and only time could tell what would happen.

"You forget about those Maykens, Peter," said Anja, wriggling up to plant a kiss on his mouth. "Your Anja's right here. Your hot, dirty sister." She rubbed herself against him insinuatingly.

"No talk about brother and sister," said Bruegel, as sharply as if he'd been singed by a flame. He rolled away from her and rose up on his elbow to stare sternly down. "Don't you realize how savage the Inquisition is becoming, Anja? Any hint of incest could be reason enough for the ecclesiastics to have me executed, should something I draw offend them. From now on, you're just a woman from my village. Nobody but Ortelius knows more than that—and I can trust him to hold his tongue."

"Fine," said Anja, making a gesture as if locking her lips with a key. "I know perfectly well I'm not your sister." She held out her arms. "Let's do everything we did last night again, eh?"

So they did all of that, and then they sat up in bed together to look out the window, naked with the comforter pulled around their shoulders. The snow had stopped falling, but the heavens were still full of snow clouds. The clouds tinted the daylight a warm greenish yellow. What peace.

Bruegel's diamond-paned window looked out the back of the Four Winds building onto some small backyards with bushes and trees. The yards sloped down to a frozen canal with skaters scribing lines in the new-fallen snow. Lots of birds and people were out and about, taking advantage of the break in the weather.

"What's that door doing propped up in the neighbor's yard?" asked Anja. There was a heavy old wooden door in the yard next door, with a stick holding up one end of it. Fresh impressions of footsteps led to the door, and bread crumbs lay scattered beneath it.

"Oh, that's old lady Leyden's bird trap," said Bruegel. "If you look closely, you can see there's a string tied to the stick that holds up the door. And the string runs up to that little black hole in the wall? Mevrouw Leyden sits behind there squinting. When there's enough birds—*zack!*" *Mevrouw* was the Flemish word for "Mistress."

"The hole looks so *sly*." said Anja. "I hate it. What does Mevrouw Leyden do with the birds?"

"Eats them. But some of the birds never get caught. See that big crow there up on the branch watching? He comes every day. He's a deep one, that crow." As if to confirm Bruegel's statement, the crow flapped down to the ground, cast a sharp look at the hole in the wall, darted his head forward to snatch a crumb out from under the door, and hopped some distance away.

"The sparrows never learn," continued Bruegel. "Mevrouw always catches a few of them. The magpies and thrushes are as smart as the crows, but the robins and pigeons get caught too. Pigeons are what she really wants. I look out this window every morning. Isn't the crow wonderful?"

"There's so many people skating on the canal," said Anja.

"Birds and people," said Bruegel dreamily. "Something I always notice in this window is that they're the same size." He'd never tried to explain this fancy before.

"How do you mean?"

"For the eye," said Bruegel. He stuck his arm out towards the window, squinting along it with his thumb stuck out. "The crow's half the size of my thumb. And see the mother holding her child by the hand? They too are half the size of—"

"*Ow-wah!*" interrupted Anja. For just now the bird trap's string twitched, the stick popped out, and the trap fell down onto four or five birds. And at almost the same moment, the door to Bruegel's room flew open.

It was Ortelius, instantly beet red. "Forgive me! I brought Jerome Cock one of my new maps, and when I asked about you, he said I should come up and wake—" He turned to go.

"Hellooo, Abraham," cooed Anja, sliding the comforter a little farther down off her breasts.

"Wait for me in the shop, Abraham," said Bruegel, standing up. "I'll be right down. We have to talk."

The door closed and Anja let out a rich, triumphant laugh.

Outside in the snow, the bent old Mevrouw Leyden crouched to draw out the struggling birds from under the door, one by one. She broke their necks and stuffed them into a sack.

✶ ✶ ✶ ✶ ✶ ✶ ✶ ✶ ✶ ✶ ✶ ✶

FIVE

LUXURIA
ANTWERP, MARCH 1556

Going down the narrow little staircase, Ortelius was still blushing, though now he started to smile as well. What a sight! Bruegel and the brazen Anja made a handsome pair of lovers. Yet they'd grown up almost as brother and sister—might not the Church view their union as abominable? A sobering thought, that.

Jerome Cock was sitting on a high stool behind the long narrow table that served as the counter in the Four Winds, examining the newly colored Mercator maps of Flanders which Ortelius had brought for him to sell. To one side lay a fresh print of a landscape, along with an engraving plate and a burin, a tool like an awl with a crooked handle. Cock was a young stork of a man with a beaky nose and a cawing voice. A couple of artists and patrons were in conversation near the front of the shop, enjoying cups of coffee, the exotic new Turkish decoction which Cock sold from his kitchen. One of the patrons was none other than Hans Franckert, talking to the others about the stabbing of Christopher Plantin. The news was all over town.

"I like these new maps of Mercator's," said Cock to Ortelius, resuming their conversation from before. "I'll be glad to market them for you. The usual terms." He set the maps to one side and peered up at Ortelius questioningly. "So, where's our Bruegel?" Cock tapped the landscape print on his counter. "I want to show him the new state of our latest engraving. I sharpened up the walls of the castles and added some more leaves to the trees. It's called *The Belgian Wagon.*"

"He's coming," said Ortelius simply. He was determined not to betray any of his friend's secrets. Cock bent over the fresh print, studying it with a loupe, and Ortelius began walking around the room.

The shop's walls were hung with engravings. Among them were five of Bruegel's new Alp-inspired Large Landscape scenes. Ortelius examined them closely, marveling at the depths of the vistas Bruegel's images contained. In addition, there were many engravings by other artists: of saints, of animals, of national costumes, of architecture and of theatrical plays, not to mention the maps of countries and cities. The maps looked a bit flat and lifeless next to the landscapes, but Ortelius studied them with a professional's deep interest. Also on display in the Four Winds were a number of engravings after the paintings of the master Hieronymus Bosch. Dead forty years now, Bosch had come to be a great favorite throughout the Low Lands, Spain, and indeed all of Europe. Though Ortelius himself was partial to the more classical and Italianate kinds of art, he recognized that Bosch's images were a fitting reflection of the increasingly troubled times. With the Inquisitors at large, the most far-fetched torments had become all too imaginable.

Behind Cock's counter were clotheslines with prints hung on them to dry, and beyond the drying area was the cramped, inky workshop with its two presses. Cock's master pressman and his journeyman assistant were back there, maneuvering a large reddish plate of engraved copper into place on the bed of the closest press. The plate's grooves were black with ink. Now the men laid a damp piece of paper onto the plate, covered it with layers of felt, and started turning the big star-shaped wheels of the press, forcing the bed, plate, paper, and felt through a pair of rollers.

Instead of copying an image by the laborious process of tracing each line, the press reproduced a map or a drawing all at once—to Ortelius it seemed wonderful. What a curious thing is a machine, he thought. To duplicate a picture simply by arranging certain objects and manipulating them just so.

"We're pulling some more of Bruegel's Large Landscapes today," said Cock, noticing Ortelius watching. "In case you'd like to buy one. So where is the man, anyway? Did you find him still asleep?"

"No—he was just getting up."

"You look flustered, Abraham," honked Cock. "Was our Bruegel in an indecent state?" Not for the first time, Ortelius unhappily wondered if people could sense the oddity of his amorous humors. Was that what drove them to chaff him about any and all matters relating to venery? From the other end of the room, fat Hans Franckert guffawed at Cock's sally.

Ortelius cleared his throat and changed the subject. "Did you know that after the stabbing, Bruegel delivered a package from Plantin to the royal villa? I wonder if he had the opportunity to ask for justice?"

"Justice," said Cock laconically. "The rarest of the seven virtues." He bent his attention back to the fresh impression on the counter, comparing it to the copper engraving plate that lay beside it. After a moment he picked up his burin and began carefully scratching at the plate, holding the burin's square blade nearly level. Now and then he paused to clean away the curled copper shavings.

"Would you recognize the villain again, Abraham?" asked Franckert, walking over with coffee cup in hand. Though his voice was hearty, the big man looked bleary from last night's carousing. "Be he Spaniard or no, our city has the right to arrest him."

Franckert was proud of his acquired Antwerp citizenship, but the man's civic fervor sounded a false note in the ears of Ortelius, who'd been born here. He offered only a shrug in response.

But now, into the silence came Bruegel's voice. "The villain is one Hernando Lopez, quartermaster for King Philip," he announced, springing into the room from the staircase door. He was wearing what looked to be his best clothes: tight-fitting dark gray pants with a codpiece, a white linen shirt, and a dark blue velvet jacket with a matching dark blue cap that hung to one side of his head.

"And, no," continued Bruegel with a sweeping gesture, "Señor Lopez will not be arrested, for his time is too valuable for that." He smiled, savoring his bit of theater, and held up a hand to stay the angry murmurs. "At my instigation, Philip's minister Granvelle has authorized the payment of a handsome reparation to Plantin. It was, in the end, quite a successful evening. Did I mention that I sold three paintings?" His habitually solemn face was lit up as if by an inner sun. He swept his arm and bowed.

So now everyone gathered around Bruegel to hear his tale: about the stabbing, about Philip and his courtiers, about the money for Plantin, and about the three painting commissions.

"You're courageous to have spoken up for Plantin," said Ortelius when Bruegel finished. "And Jonghelinck is to pay both of you directly?"

"That's right," said Bruegel, adjusting his hat. "In fact, I'm on my way to meet him at the Schilderspand."

"Paintings for Fugger, for Jonghelinck, and for Philip's court," marveled Franckert. "More fool I, content with your drawings. Can't I order a painting as well, Peter?"

"No!" crowed Jerome Cock, his face going a bit red. "Bruegel is under contract to *me!* And, Peter, it's time to start some new drawings for me to engrave. Enjoy your three painting commissions, but no more for now. I need fresh images for my presses!" Cock dropped his voice to a more reasonable tone. "Now come here and look at the state of our *Belgian Wagon*. And then, fine, you can run off to the Schilderspand and play the master painter."

Now, to complicate things, Anja appeared in the staircase door, her broad face made all the wider by her smile.

"What's she doing here?" demanded Cock.

"Anja's lost her job with the Vanderheydens," said Bruegel with a forced air of calm. "And since I'm doing so well, I'm going to let her share my lodgings and work for me."

"You dog," said Franckert. "What kind of work do you mean?"

"Honest work," exclaimed Anja, tossing her head. "And as for the rest of it, well, a lady bestows her favors as she sees fit, Mijnheer Nose-in-Everything Franckert. Be that as it may, I'll have my own room. All quite proper. And if Peter and I visit back and forth it's no great sin. The country priests all sleep with their maids."

"Calm down," Bruegel cautioned Anja. "I haven't even asked about the room yet. She means the one next to mine, Jerome. Might I put Anja and my painting studio in there? It would be very convenient."

"You'd pay proper rent for it?" said Cock.

"Agreed. I hope you're not really angry about my painting commissions?"

"No, no, I'm happy for you. Both as a friend and as your publisher. But don't neglect to give me a new drawing this month. We need a big seller."

"I'll make you one in the style of Bosch."

"At last!" exclaimed Jerome Cock. "Oh, now I'm very pleased. All the customers want more Bosch. Why not a Bosch-style series on the Seven Sins? Avarice, Pride, Envy, Anger, Gluttony, Sloth, and—"

"*Luxuria,*" put in Franckert, using the Latin word for lust.

Cock dug in a chest beneath his counter and came up with a great key, which he handed to Anja. "For your new room, may poor Gus Groot rest in peace. Trot up and have a look around, my girl. I can give you a rag and broom to clean it up. And, Peter, tell me how you like the state of our *Wagon* today. Look at the foliage and the castles in the valley. Better, don't you think?"

"It's very fine," said Bruegel after a minute, standing back from the print a bit, lest he stain his fancy shirt with ink. "The farmhouse roofs are good. Perhaps you should hide the peasant's profile behind his hat? But you don't want to. Never mind. In fact he looks a bit like you. Let him stay. Your handling of the tree trunks is wonderful. Look at it, Hans, our wagon is modeled on yours. See the hoops holding up its cover?"

"Excellent likeness," said Franckert, leaning over the print. "And there's Max Wagemaeker astride the horse."

"These are the new maps of Flanders I got from Mercator," said Ortelius from the end of the counter, wanting some of Bruegel's attention for himself. He tapped upon the little pile of his maps. "See how I colored and decorated them, Peter? Jerome's going to sell them here."

"Very harmonious," said Bruegel, cursorily eyeing one of the maps. The lack of response was disappointing, as Ortelius had secretly hoped for an artist-to-artist discussion of his color choices. But Bruegel's next sentences restored his spirits. "Let's be on our way, Abraham. We can have a little discussion on the way to the Schilderspand. Good day, Anja, I'll be back in a few hours."

"I'll clean our new room and bring my things from the Vanderheydens," sang Anja. "And I'll fix us a dinner. Will I be able to get a brazier of coals to bring up to our room this evening, Mijnheer Cock?"

"God save me from this country bumpkin!" exclaimed Cock. "And burn down our whole quarter of the city? The common kitchen is right through that door." He pointed across the room. "We have a big hearth and a fine stove in there. Everyone brings their cook pots down in the evening. My wife, Katharina, will show you where everything is."

"I'll make us a fish and mussel stew with potatoes and cream," said Anja. "Perhaps I'll even find some nutmeg." She kissed Peter on the cheek. "You look very handsome today."

"Lucky man," said Franckert. "A hot meal from a loving maid. I'll accompany you and Abraham to the Schilderspand too."

"Well, if you don't mind, Hans, I have something rather personal to discuss with Abraham," said Bruegel. "But you can meet us over there in a bit, if you like."

"Putting Abraham ahead of me again!" said Franckert, slightly put out. "If our timid bachelor seeks advice about the ladies, he'd do better to ask me." He turned his attention back to Jerome Cock. "Print me a *Belgian Wagon* while I'm awaiting these gentlemen's pleasure, Jerome. I'll have the first impression of this new state! Hang it right here on the drying line, and mark it down as sold to Hans Franckert." He stepped towards the kitchen door and called to the maid. "Liesl! Another cup of coffee for me!"

Ortelius and Bruegel stepped around a pile of engravings packaged up for shipment and made their way out into the street. There was a break in the clouds with the sun peeping brightly through, making the snowy scene glisten. Bruegel's coat was a rich blue in the sun.

Most goods in Antwerp were sold at daily markets or at the great seasonal fairs, so there weren't so very many shops. Down the block was a combined barber and druggist, and on the other side of the street was a tailor. Just ahead of Bruegel and Ortelius, two men were pushing along a huge barrel of beer mounted on a freight sleigh, their feet slipping on the wet, trodden cobblestones.

As soon as they were out of earshot of the Four Winds, Bruegel whispered urgently to Ortelius. "Forget what we said at the Blue Boat about Anja and me being raised in the same home. I didn't realize that Anja would soon share my bed. I was blind to the strength of our old attraction."

"You can trust me," said Ortelius. "Just as I trust you with my secret." He felt a thrill at being on an equal footing with the artist. The two of them were sinners of the same stripe. "Anja came to you last night?"

"I welcomed her more warmly than I'd known I would," said Bruegel. "She's so comfortable and wanton. She even lets me watch her on the chamber pot. My village girl."

"Do others know you were raised together?"

"You're the only one in Antwerp, Abraham, unless she's blabbed it about, though she says she hasn't. I've told her that no one should hear of our past. I'm sure it's no sin for me to be with her, but gossip could twist things around. The new Spanish priests are so harsh."

"You're easy in your own conscience?"

"I think I am. Though perhaps it's sloth and lust that make me think this way. I'll pray and meditate upon it. In any case, I wouldn't want to marry Anja. Nor does she wish to marry me."

"How do you know that?" asked Ortelius.

"She said so."

They were on a wider street now, and a horse-drawn wagon of potatoes went rumbling past. The two men had to step lively to keep from getting splashed with icy slush.

"I've little experience with women," said Ortelius when they could speak again. "But I'd be surprised if Anja doesn't have some hope to wed you after all. Perhaps she knows better than to yank the line as soon as her fish swallows the hook."

"I really hadn't planned to have her move in," said Bruegel, fingering his cap. "In any case, I'm glad I can trust your discretion about her origins. It'll be bad enough when Mayken Verhulst hears I'm living with a serving maid, but if she knew that—" Bruegel sighed and changed the subject. "How do you like my Large Landscapes?"

"Very well indeed. They're honest, they show true forms. Seeing them hung near the maps set me to thinking about the similarities between the two. The shapes on maps are the same shapes that one finds in a landscape. River valleys are like the branches of trees, seacoasts are like the silhouettes of rocks. Nature rejoices everywhere in the same palette of forms."

"I feel a tree is more like a man's life than like a river valley," said Bruegel. "From moment to moment we decide what to do next, whether to do evil or to do good. We carry our own life history with us. When I look at the bends in a tree's trunk I see the whole past of the tree: its struggles as a sapling, its passion for the sun, its thirst for water, its—"

"But I'm talking about actual visible shapes," interrupted Ortelius. He stopped and pointed down at a puddle in the street. Snow was melting into it, and at one end the puddle was overflowing. "The shape of that rivulet of water, thick and bent near the puddle here, and sinuous and lean over there? It's very like the river Scheldt on the map of Flanders, is it not?"

"True," said Bruegel, squinting his eyes and cocking his head. "And if that's the Scheldt, then those chunks of ice in the puddle are the Zeeland archipelago in the North Sea."

"As above, so below," said Ortelius. "Your phrase, Peter. A rock is a mountain in small, and each woman or man is the world in miniature."

"Many worlds," mused Bruegel. "Many mirrors."

They were just crossing a bridge over a frozen canal. There were scores of people on the ice, most of them wearing long curving wooden skates strapped to the bottoms of their shoes. A wealthy fellow with a somber look had a servant towing him about by the hem of his cape. A tiny child sat in a little skate-sled poling herself along with sticks. Some boys and girls used bent sticks to play a game of hockey. An amorous man held a woman by the waist.

Across the bridge was the impressive pile of the new Stock Exchange, with its great stone columns. The St. Luke's Guild rented the second floor for the permanent painting market called the Schilderspand. As they drew close to the building, Bruegel grew quiet and thin lipped. Perhaps he was nervous about making his deals.

"I was here just last week," offered Ortelius to lighten his friend's humor. "I've been collecting small paintings of exotic animals to add to my curiosity cabinets."

"Ah, your 'museum,'" said Bruegel distractedly. "With your coins and your medals and your shells. I'd like to see it."

"Then come by this afternoon while there's still good light."

"I will, if I remember. Oh, Abraham. My blood's overheated. I can hardly believe I've yoked myself to Anja. What was I thinking? And now I'm to negotiate three commissions? Interrupt me if I begin gibbering like an ape."

"You'll do fine, Peter." Ortelius was starting to realize that Bruegel worried more than his calm appearance might indicate.

The Schilderspand, or Painter's Market, was a plain upstairs hall with white-plastered walls and an ordinary oak-plank floor. It was brightly lit by gable windows set into the slanting ceiling. Several half walls rose up some twenty feet towards the ceiling, dividing the space into galleries. Every vertical surface was completely covered with framed paintings by the local Flemish masters.

There were any number of cosmic landscapes with hills, rivers, mountains, and lakes. The scenes were all composed in three horizontal strips: blue at the top for the background, green for the middle ground, and brown for the foreground strip at the bottom of the canvas. The landscapes were populated by dainty figures from Scripture and myth, by saints and philosophers, by patrons and kings. They wore robes, togas, loincloths or, in the case of patrons, huge lace collars, and the folds in the cloth draperies were always clearly limned. The same cast of costumed characters appeared in the deep perspectives of the Italianate cityscapes that hung side by side with the landscapes.

Not all the pictures showed mundane fields and towns. There were a few Heavens and Hells: the Heavens featuring pink marzipan angels before the great white disk that stood for God; the blue-demon-filled Hells aglow with the evil light of burning cities.

But overwhelming every other category of paintings was an endless glut of explicitly religious art, a bright and meaningless diarrhea of Jesus, Mary, the Apostles and the saints, over and over and over and over again.

The Guild painters loitered beneath the thousand images, gossiping about their craft and keeping a sharp eye on the wandering patrons and connoisseurs.

Still at Ortelius's side, Bruegel looked very nicely turned out, his shirt and trousers still tidy, his dark blue coat falling in rich folds, his cap nicely adjusted. But his face looked a little wild, his gray eyes so wide open that the light made them almost blue. When someone suddenly spoke to him, he jumped.

"Hello, Bruegel!" It was Frans Floris, velvet clad and suave, his waxy face yellow against his enormous lace collar. The wall behind him was filled with smoothly executed paintings from his workshop, all the same size. It was like a crate of perfect fruit. Floris had art down to a system, and he was proud of it. Though he was only eight years older than Bruegel, he was quite the wealthy master. "Are you looking for a job?" he asked. "I need another landscape man. The orders are coming in too fast for us to paint."

"I've got commissions of my own, Frans," said Bruegel, perhaps a bit louder than necessary. "Have you seen Jonghelinck, or Fugger's secretary?"

"Commissions from financiers," said the expansive Floris. "Very fine. Be sure to ask them to pay you a third in advance. They can afford it. And Peter, when you deliver your pictures to them, get a look at their holdings. Both of them have some wonderful pieces. Jonghelinck has over a dozen of my paintings. And I recently did a marvelous *Last Judgment* for Fugger, fully classical in style. My

Satan is Pan with a harelip. He quite takes one's breath away." Floris twisted his face into an bizarre leer, demonstrating the physiognomy of his Pan. At the same time, he winked at Ortelius, including him in his audience.

Bruegel was listening so avidly that he imitated Floris's grimace. "What else does Fugger have?" he asked.

"Oh, he has Patinirs and Dürers and even a Bosch triptych. And cases and cabinets full of coins and medals. That's his secretary over there, the copper-colored fellow who glides about so smoothly. Calls himself Williblad Cheroo."

Ortelius felt a shock of recognition. This was the same exotic-looking man he'd seen at the Carnival street dance last night. Williblad Cheroo. He was even more striking by daylight than by firelight. Seeing him in the flesh, Ortelius dimly recalled that he'd dreamed of him in the night. Could Williblad and Ortelius be fated to meet?

"He's half-American," Floris was saying. "Would you believe? I'd love to paint what Williblad's seen. He's the orphan child of a New World Indian and the Spanish navigator Ponce de Leon. It seems Cheroo's mother died in childbirth, and when de Leon returned on a second mission a few years later, he was slain by the mother's tribe. The Indians must not have liked the looks of little Williblad, for they set him aboard his dead father's ship and sent him off to the Old World. That particular ship and its booty belonged to Anthonie Fugger, so Williblad came into the care of our Fugger, who made the boy his servant."

"Yet he carries himself like his own man," observed Ortelius, profoundly moved by Williblad's elegant appearance. The bronze-skinned man was beauti-fully dressed in dark green velvet: knee breeches with a bulging codpiece and a jacket with puffed-out sleeves with slits in them to show the jacket's yellow silk lining and the white linen of Cheroo's lace-collared shirt. Exquisite.

"He's his own man," agreed Floris. "A devil of one. I've lost more than one wench to him, too. Not only is he handsome, he's clever and highly educated. Yes, Fugger had him tutored and sent him on to the University in Leuven. He's a man of blood and choler, Peter, a refined deal maker, but prone to giving offence. If the House of Fugger were to fall, our Cheroo would be hard put to find another job. As for your strategy with him, my experience is that the second figure he offers you is as high as he'll go. If you try for a third, it's always lower. Have at him, Bruegel, and good luck to you."

"Thanks, Frans. Good Lord, but I'm shaky today. Stick with me, Abraham, and lend me strength."

Ortelius stood quietly at Bruegel's side while his friend began negotiating his deal with Fugger's exotic secretary. Williblad was tall like Bruegel and looked to be about ten years older. Save for the difference in hue, mused Ortelius, Williblad might almost have been Bruegel's older brother. But yet— what a difference.

Ortelius was so dizzy with infatuation that he missed the exact moment when Bruegel and Williblad began arguing.

It was about the money. They'd quickly agreed that Bruegel's painting for Fugger was to be *The Merchants Driven from the Temple*, watercolor on a wood panel, with a cityscape done Turkish style, completed and delivered in six weeks. But when Williblad named a figure, it was so much less than what Bruegel wanted that Peter quite lost his temper. And then Williblad lost his temper too, or pretended to. He turned his back and strode off, his gait as powerful and springy as a panther's.

Seeing Bruegel's desperate, unhappy face, Ortelius ran after Williblad and tapped him on the shoulder. Cheroo had dark, clearly delineated lips, sparkling hazel eyes and lustrous black hair. Though he spoke Flemish with no trace of an accent, there was a pleasant musicality to his speech. As a trader, Ortelius knew all about negotiations, and it was only a minute's work to clear things up. And of course Ortelius was thrilled to have had the chance to speak with Williblad Cheroo.

No sooner was this deal resolved than Nicolas Jonghelinck appeared. Pig-headedly enough, Bruegel barely introduced Ortelius, and once again began negotiating things on his own. In this case it was to be a Nativity in watercolor on linen for Philip and an oil *Fall of Icarus* on an oak panel for Jonghelinck.

But unlike Bruegel's stormy encounter with Williblad Cheroo, Bruegel's deal with Jonghelinck went smoothly. There was no need for Ortelius to jump in as a middle-man. The rich, successful Jonghelinck had no need to try and crush a mere artist with his bargaining skills.

Ortelius mused that the roughness of Williblad's dealing revealed a kind of awkwardness on the man's part, a certain lack of balance. Perhaps this orphan of the New World was unsure of himself. Perhaps he needed a friend. While Bruegel's talk with Jonghelinck flowed on, Ortelius watched Williblad Cheroo across the hall and tried to think of a reasonable pretence for going to talk to this alluring man again.

Meanwhile Jonghelinck and Bruegel had settled upon the sizes of the commissions: a very high price for Philip's Nativity and a goodly, though lower, price for the *Fall of Icarus*.

"There's no harm in gouging King Philip," said Jonghelinck easily. "Whatever his court pays you is as a gnat's egg beside their ravening eagle of a war loan. I have a clear conscience in telling you this, as it's I myself who's lending Philip the money in the first place! Though I misdoubt any Habsburg's willingness to repay a loan's principal, they do pay a wonderful rate of interest. This said, I have in fact sold most of my Habsburg loans to Fugger. But I'm sure this kind of thing means nothing to an artist. Let's talk some more about your plans for the *Icarus*, Peter."

"I'm planning to paint yours last," Bruegel told Jonghelinck in a friendly tone. "Because you're a fellow countryman. I'm always learning. Each of my pictures will be better than the ones before." Now Bruegel produced a scrap of paper and roughed out a cartoon of his picture. "The background will be a landscape with a sea, and I'll put in a beautiful ship. You like ships, don't you, Nicolas?"

"Very much," said Jonghelinck with a smile. "My father made his wealth by investing in Portuguese ships bringing spices to Antwerp from the Indies."

"I'll put Icarus in the corner, in the wake of our galleon; he'll be nothing but a splashing pair of white legs. A man dies—and the world doesn't blink."

"It's true," said Jonghelinck, extending one of his long fingers like a teacher. "But you should be faithful to Ovid. I reread the tale last night. 'Perhaps a fisherman plying his quivering rod, or a shepherd leaning on his staff, or a peasant bent over his plough—perhaps one of them caught sight of Daedalus and Icarus as they flew past and, seeing them, stood stock-still in astonishment, believing that these creatures of the air must be gods.' " Ortelius was impressed to see such erudition in a financier.

"That's rich material," said Bruegel, who'd doffed his cap to listen the more intently. "I'll put the witnesses in, but they won't be looking. I'll paint the plowman on a hill in the foreground looking only at his furrow. And down on a bank by the water I'll have the fisherman staring at his line. The shepherd stares into the air—but in the wrong direction." Bruegel threw back his head and made an imbecilic face, then let out an excited cackle. His humors had certainly changed from when he'd been all but screaming at Williblad just a few minutes ago.

"*De ploeg gaat over lijken,*" said Jonghelinck thoughtfully, meaning "The plow goes over corpses."

"Yes," said Bruegel animatedly. "You understand. In fact, I'll drive the lesson home by putting a dead body in the brush beside the ploughed field."

"I look forward to the picture," said Jonghelinck, counting out the coins for Bruegel's advance. He bowed and took his leave.

Ortelius was still watching Williblad Cheroo, who was quite nearby, talking to the landscape artist Herri met de Bles. Williblad's motions were like poetry, like music. It finally occurred to Ortelius that Fugger's "cases and cabinets of medals and coins" provided a perfect excuse for him to continue talking with Williblad.

"Excuse me now," Ortelius murmured to Bruegel. "I have something more to discuss with Fugger's secretary."

"About the cheap deal that fop gave me?" To Ortelius's chagrin, Bruegel said this loud enough for Williblad to hear. Although Williblad didn't turn his head, he stiffened a bit.

"Don't be a fool, Peter," said Ortelius in a low tone. "You've done very well today. I have other business with Cheroo." Williblad had parted with de Bles and was moving towards the stairs.

Bruegel gave Ortelius a thoughtful look. "Go after him, then. I understand."

"Understand what?" demanded Hans Franckert, who'd just appeared.

"Understand how fat and loud you are," said Bruegel, dropping his worries and ill-humor. He held up and jingled his little silk purse, plump with new coins. "I'm off to buy some materials now, Hans. Come along and help me carry the oak panels home. A taste of the artist's life for you."

"All right," said Franckert, lowering himself onto a stool. "And then we'll celebrate with a few beers. You can pay for once, Peter. But first let me catch my breath for a minute. See you later, Abraham."

Ortelius ran and caught up with Williblad Cheroo just as the beguiling half-American reached the street.

"I understand that Mijnheer Fugger collects medals as well as paintings," said Ortelius, managing to fall into step with the taller man.

"He didn't mean to, but he's had to accept a number of such miscellaneous objects in lieu of payment for failed Habsburg loans," said Williblad with a worldly grin. "The high nobles grow ever more unreliable." His clerkish choice of words made an odd contrast with his exotic New World appearance.

"Is it possible that Mijnheer Fugger might wish to dispose of some of his holdings?" asked Ortelius. "I collect and deal in medals myself. I would be ravished if you could show me the collection, Williblad." *Ravished?* Did he sound like a horrible importuning sodomite?

"I'm sorry, my good man," said Williblad, looking straight at Ortelius for the first time. His smile was gone. "Your peasant friend Bruegel never introduced us. What's your name?"

"I'm Abraham Ortelius," he gushed. "And my apologies for Bruegel. The artistic temperament. He's overexcited today, what with getting his first commissions, and having that maidservant Anja move in with him last night. As for me, I deal in maps, antiques, medals, and coins. Primarily maps, but medals are a great passion of mine. What kinds of things does Mijnheer Fugger have?"

"Dead things," said Williblad, seeming to tire of the talk about business. "Tell me this, Abraham, do you have a good map of the Americas? I'd like to try and pick out the place where I was born. It's in what you call Florida."

"I have an excellent map," said Ortelius. "It incorporates Magellan's findings as well as Columbus's. If you like, you can come back to my house with me and I'll show you the map. It has quite a prominent Florida."

Williblad glanced up towards the sun—or rather towards the brightest spot in the low, gray sky. A layer of clouds had blown in from the sea. "I don't have time right now," he said. "I'm on my way to meet a lady friend."

At the conscious level, Ortelius was relieved. It would be deadly folly to try and repeat his Italian escapades here in his hometown. But he was also disappointed.

Williblad read Ortelius's expression, or some of it. "You can come over to Fugger's this afternoon around teatime," he offered. "I can show you the medal collection and you can show me your map."

"Which of Fugger's houses do you mean? The one where King Philip is staying?"

"No, no, I mean his city house. It's just a block from here. In the Steenhouwerstraat. Handy to the Stock Exchange."

"I'll be there."

Ortelius felt quite dizzy as he walked home. Though the clouds were low, his soul swooped up through the gray mists, up into the bright blue sky. His thoughts were turned to an old dream: to map Heaven. On the walls of the Schilderspand, all was modeling and fancy, but a map—a map was reality made small, the world in a portable size. What would it be like to fly up and up into the sky, to pass the moon and the planets, to burst though the star-hung sphere of the firmament and to land at the throne of God—to sit with God and to chart what He could see; to draw the map of Heaven? Sometimes Ortelius could almost see the map: logical, clean, orderly, with everything in the proper place. But today his meditation was distracted by the face of God, so close, so very much like Williblad's.

At home, Ortelius busied himself with the maps in his workroom. His sister was out for the day, so he was alone with his thoughts of Williblad. As the hours went by, his desire for Williblad became more and more clouded by the fear that he might do something rash.

In the midafternoon there was a riotous pounding on his door. It was Bruegel and Franckert, drunk. Bruegel's white shirt had a Britain-shaped beer stain upon it and his floppy hat was askew.

"We got thrown out of the tavern," wheezed Franckert, his large face squeezing tight in mirth. "I was trying to teach Peter how to light farts with a candle and somehow—"

"He set the serving-girl's dress on fire," said Bruegel. "I had to pour beer on her to put it out."

"Who's there, Abraham?" It was Ortelius's mother's fine, thin voice, calling down the stairs. Though Mother was bedridden, she still tried to run the household from her room on the upper floor.

"It's two of my friends," said Ortelius. "Bruegel the painter and Franckert the trader."

"Show Franckert the great desk," piped Ortelius's mother. "A trader needs a desk with a lot of drawers in it."

"Show Franckert the great tun of beer," whispered Franckert. "A trader needs several."

"You've no need of more beer," said Ortelius, hoping Bruegel wouldn't think him too prissy. "Here, let's go where it's private." He led them into his study at the back of the house and closed the door. Books lined two of the walls and sat piled upon a long table with feet carved like a great beast's claws. Beside the table, an elegant pair of globes rested upon matching wooden pedestals, each with six elaborately shaped legs. The globes were a creamy white with beige and brown markings; one of them mapped the earth, the other showed the heavens.

Another wall was covered with paintings and miniatures from Ortelius's collection, lit by windows filled with small round panes of greenish glass. Finely worked cabinets of small drawers held Ortelius's collection of coins; and there were two glassed-in cases to show off his finest medals, seashells, and zoological curiosa. More than a study, this room was Ortelius's museum. A small fire glowed in a deep fireplace with an embossed panel of iron at the rear to help hold the heat. As always, he felt safe and happy in here.

"Would you two like some tea?" asked Ortelius.

"I would," said Bruegel, blearily rubbing his eyes and flopping down into a soft chair. "I'm quite fuddled."

"You've already had time to get your supplies and to get so drunk?" wondered Ortelius. "The two oak panels, the linen, the pigments?"

"It's easy to buy things when you have money," said Bruegel deliberately. "The supplier's not far from Cock's in any case. How many pots did we drink, Hans?"

"You had one more than me," said Franckert, struggling to unwind himself from his tangled cloak. "But I had four more than you." He staggered and fell down on an antique couch with such force that both legs at one end snapped.

"Damn the man!" exclaimed Ortelius, but Franckert only settled himself the more, sprawling askew on the crushed couch like a large, powerful fish on a cutting board, staring up with his mouth agape.

"I'm all in," he sighed, and fell asleep.

Ortelius noticed that Franckert's codpiece was quite soaked with urine. "Lets move him onto the floor," he said to Bruegel. He rolled the carpet aside, and he and Bruegel slid the great merchant off the smashed couch and onto the bare wood floor. Franckert protested, but didn't open his eyes. And then he began to snore. Bruegel sat back down in his chair.

"I'll get the tea," said Ortelius, and stepped into the kitchen to ask the maid to make up a strong pot. It was almost the time when he'd planned to go to Fugger's house. He could leave Franckert sleeping on the floor, but what to do about Bruegel?

Back in the study, Ortelius found Bruegel staring into the glass case next to his chair. "That's a nice medallion," said Bruegel, pointing to a large bronze disk, a low relief that memorialized the Dutch man of letters Erasmus. "I like the four-cornered hat."

"The medal is by Quentin Metsys," said Ortelius, always ready to discuss his medals and his books. "I got it in Rotterdam at the same time I bought Erasmus's *In Praise of Folly*. Have you ever read it? An ironic catalogue of the mad fancies we're prey to."

"I'd like to see it," said Bruegel. "Folly being an occupational interest of mine, you might say." He glanced over, his pale gray eyes frank, and let out a weary chuckle. He no longer seemed so drunk as he had before.

"I'll lend you my copy," said Ortelius, stepping across the room to find it. "Here it is."

Bruegel took the proffered volume of Erasmus and tucked the book into an inner pocket of his blue velvet coat. "Folly to piss away my time in taverns," he said, gazing around the room. The green windows were dimming with the waning of the afternoon light. "I should be getting home to Anja, I suppose. There's folly for you. God help me."

"I'll be off on an errand myself in half an hour," said Ortelius, not quite wanting to tell Bruegel where he was bound. "Ah, here comes Helena with our tea. Thank you, Helena. You can set it down here on the table. Don't worry about the man on the floor, that's Mijnheer Franckert, much the worse for drink."

Though Ortelius had hoped Helena might leave them without comment, he also knew this was too much to expect. Helena had come in from the countryside only last year, and she never missed a chance to milk excitement from the events of big city life.

"He's wet himself," observed Helena. She was a round-faced young woman with curly brown hair. "Begging your pardon, Mijnheer Ortels, if you're to entertain friends of such low caliber, how's a girl like me to meet any prospects?" She moved the furniture a bit further from Franckert, then darted a grin at Bruegel.

"It's nice to see you, Mijnheer Bruegel," said Helena. "Did I tell you that I know your friend Anja? She says you're a wonderful man." Helena was forever gossiping with the other maids about the city's supply of unattached men.

"That's good to hear," said Bruegel. "What village are you from?"

Helena managed to stand there chattering for several minutes before Ortelius could get her to leave the room. She was clearly fascinated by the fact that Bruegel had taken up with a maid.

"She loves love," observed Bruegel after Helena left.

"We all do," said Ortelius. "Each in our own way."

They sipped tea in silence for a minute and Bruegel wandered back to the case of medallions.

"Oh, look, you've got a medal of Dürer right next to your Erasmus!" he said, reading out the inscription. "'Albertus Durer Pinctor Germanicus.' How long and wavy his hair is. I wonder if they'll ever make a medal of me." Bruegel slurped at his tea, then looked again into Ortelius's eyes. "I'm uneasy, Abraham. My good fortune frightens me. What if I can't really paint?"

"We know that you can draw. And you did a fine grisaille on the wing of that Mechelen altarpiece. I've seen it. Drink down the tea and have another. And then I'm off."

"Where are you going?"

"To Fugger's city house," said Ortelius after a moment's hesitation. "It's a block from the Schilderspand."

"I know where it is. But why are you going there now? My picture for Fugger's not even begun." Bruegel had a way of turning most conversations around to himself.

"This isn't about your picture. Williblad—Fugger's secretary—he said I could come over and look at some medals for my collection."

"Let me come too," said Bruegel unexpectedly. "I'm not ready to face Anja. And I'd like to see Fugger's Bosch. Even if it is guarded by Williblad Cheroo." There was more than a little venom in the way he said the name.

"But—you quarreled with Williblad earlier," said Ortelius. "I'm quite sure he heard you calling him a fop."

"I suppose you want to be alone with him?" said Bruegel. "He's the older-man type you once mentioned longing for, isn't he?"

"You see through me," admitted Ortelius. "But I'm all too aware that this isn't Rome. I wouldn't want to lose my head and—"

"You undid the effects of my Anger at the Schilderspand," said Bruegel, pouring himself a second cup of tea. "And now let my steadying presence guard you from Lust at Fugger's. My head is clearing. If I could wash my face—"

"Can you promise to be civil?" demanded Ortelius. "If so, I suppose I wouldn't mind having you along."

"I'll behave," said Bruegel. "I'll simply go and sit before the Bosch. It's a triptych, says Floris. That'll keep me out of your hair, you can depend upon it. But you'll gain a bit of steadiness from knowing I'm nearby."

"Very well," said Ortelius. It might even make him seem more interesting to Williblad if he arrived with his mad artist friend along. "You can wash in here." He showed Bruegel a cabinet that held towels and a basin of water. Bruegel soaked his face and much of his hair, then thoroughly toweled himself off.

"That gets the stink of the tavern off me. And a third cup of tea, yes. Are we off to Fugger's now?"

"Indeed," said Ortelius, rolling up the map of the New World that he'd selected for Williblad. "You're not afraid the Bosch will overwhelm you? I still remember how the Sistine Chapel affected de Vos."

AS ABOVE, SO BELOW 97

"Afraid? I've known Master Bosch since I was a boy," said Bruegel, adjusting his clothes. "He's like a friend."

"He was ten years dead when we were born, Peter."

"Ah, but he was a student in the s'Hertogenbosch school like me." Bruegel winked and wagged his finger. "He left his mark. He lingered. Yes, Abraham, in the attics of the school, I came across what must have been some of Master Bosch's boyhood drawings on the walls. One thing led to another and the priests made me erase them. I got so angry I quit the school. But never mind. I'm talking too much." He squared himself and felt around in his loose-hanging blue coat. "I've a good pen and a bottle of ink, but my paper got spoiled in the tavern. Can you give me a sheet of paper? I'll want to copy some of the demons from the triptych. Demons now, Anja later."

"Here you go," said Ortelius, handing him two sheets. "I'll tell Helena to keep an eye on Franckert." At the sound of his name Franckert muttered and shifted his position.

"All fat men look alike," said Bruegel, leaning down to adjust Franckert's cloak so as to cover more of his bulk. "Perhaps Hans is the divine archetype for them all. It's soothing to see his slumber, no? Like having a faithful hound curled upon the hearth. Sleep well, dear Hans."

It had started to snow again outside, and children were running around yelling. Bruegel had pretty much sobered up. He looked cheerful and animated; he opened his mouth wide to breathe in great draughts of the cold air, and stuck out his tongue to catch the flakes of snow. Ortelius was happy to be with his friend, and happy to be on his way to see the medals and the enchanting Williblad.

Fugger's city house was even grander than the one he'd lent to King Philip. It had overhanging ledges with elaborately carved triangular buttresses; the windows were framed in brilliantly painted iron; and there was a huge open courtyard within.

"I know this house well," said Bruegel. "Master Coecke worked on this one too. See the frieze of the grapevines and centaurs halfway up the wall? I helped the Master paint that."

The doorman went to find Williblad Cheroo. Williblad appeared, wearing a fresh change of clothes—maroon velvet over a striped yellow shirt this time. Although he looked a bit surprised to see Bruegel, he greeted them with a polite offer of food and drink. Ortelius accepted, but Bruegel said he wanted nothing more than to be with Bosch. Bruegel also made a point of confiding that he tended to get hotheaded when he was uneasy, that he was sorry to have gotten angry at Williblad during their negotiation, and that all's well that ends well. Williblad haughtily shrugged off the apology. Before Bruegel could flare up again, a servant took him off to visit the triptych.

And then Ortelius was sitting at a table knee-to-knee with the beguiling Williblad Cheroo, snacking on pot cheese, pickled herring, and brown bread from the Fugger kitchen, the food washed down by a caraway-flavored gueuze lager. Displayed on a velvet cushion before them was a shiny medal, one of the prizes of the Fugger collection. And what a medal it was: one of a kind, cast in solid silver, hammered and stamped into exceptionally high relief with crests around its edge, a gift from the city of Nuremberg to the Emperor Charles. The medal had been designed by no less an artist than Albrecht Dürer. Its center held a sharply limned representation of the Emperor. Ortelius craved the medal exceedingly. For the moment he wanted it even more strongly than the naked flesh of Williblad.

"And look at this one," said Williblad with a refined snicker. The next medal was a bronze, depicting Danaë and the Shower of Gold. It showed the moment in which, according to the myth, Zeus impregnated Danaë. The image was frankly erotic, with Danaë lying on her back with her legs spread and her skirt pulled up in her hands. She was smiling, and above her was a cloud like a jelly-fish, with droplets shooting out of it. "Do you like it?" asked Williblad.

"The Charles is much more to my taste," said Ortelius primly. "Do you have any other unique editions?"

"We have the Trinity medal as well," said Williblad, gliding across the room to open a small drawer. He produced a large silver medallion with a relief even higher than the Charles. This one showed the Crucifixion, with a dove lighting on the top of the cross, and with a haggard, bearded God the Father looming up as the background. It was so deeply carved that Jesus's bent knees stood free. "It's also called the Moritz penny," said Williblad. "It was a gift to Moritz von Sachsen in 1542. His holdings came to us last year."

"How much for the Charles?" asked Ortelius, his mind still focused on that first medal Williblad had shown him.

Williblad looked nonplussed. "What do you mean?"

"The medal of Emperor Charles. I'd like to buy it."

"We seem to be at a misunderstanding," said Williblad. "It's the whole collection that we'd want to sell. Seven hundred and forty-three pieces. Possibly with the Gonzaga cameo trays as well. Mijnheer Fugger's family owns silver mines, Abraham. They're hardly interested in selling individual coins."

"Oh," said Ortelius, feeling himself go pink with embarrassment. "Well, I—I brought you a map."

"Let's see it," said Williblad, walking around the table to sit at his side.

"The original was by the Portuguese cartographer Diego Ribero," said Ortelius, sliding the food and the medals out of the way and spreading the map on the table. His hands were shaking a bit. It was almost too much to have Williblad so close to him. "I copied it for engraving, and gave it Italic labels and a proper border," he continued, his voice seeming to speak quite on its own. "I hand colored this print."

"I was born on the west coast of Florida," said Williblad, leaning over the map. "It would be about—yes, here it is! The mouth of the Myakka River below the Punta Gordo. Home of my tribe, the Tequesta." He sighed and ran his finger across the spot. "I miss it. It was my home, and they expelled me."

"What was it like to come from the New to the Old World?" asked Ortelius, regarding Williblad's profile with fascination. The half-American smelled wonderful.

"I was seven years old. Your buildings surprised me the most. All the parallel lines and right angles. My tribe's huts and longhouses were more like seashells or swallows' nests. Right angles tire me as much as your Church. The works of man count for so little in America. The greatest monument built by the Tequesta was a mound of clamshells. I used to play on it."

"Hello, Mijnheeren." It was Bruegel, his expression exalted. He was carrying his two sheets of paper, completely covered with quickly inked sketches. "I need more paper. And a rest. Master Bosch's triptych is a treasure mine with shafts down into the deepest bowels of the earth."

"Williblad was just talking about America," said Ortelius. "It's fascinating."

"Did you have birds like this where you lived?" asked Bruegel, flopping down in a chair and laying his papers beside the map. With an inky finger he indicated a little sketch of an archer with a bird's head. The bird's beak was shaped like a long spoon.

"A spoonbill," said Williblad. "Oh yes, indeed. They're pink. I've seen so many of them in flight that the sky was as rosy as the inside of a woman's mouth."

"Tell me more," said Bruegel, who seemed to have set aside his antipathy towards Williblad. He took a bit of bread and cheese. "Help me imagine your landscape."

"I remember one day," said Williblad, leaning back in his chair. "I was standing on some dry land at the edge of a swamp. The water was green with duckweed and dotted with cypress trees—they're a bit like pines, but very bulbous at the bottom, with roots that came up high to make knees." He gestured with his long-fingered hand. "On every branch of every tree there was a nest as big as a wagon wheel. And in the nests were birds in incalculable profusion: spoonbills, white and gray herons, egrets, and ibises with down-curving beaks. The gaps in the branches happened to line up so that I could see a distant island in the swamp, it was like a peek at paradise. On the island were two egrets as large as a man and a woman, flapping their wings in a dance, first one wing and then the other, twisting their bodies and twining their necks. It was scene like you paint on the insides of your cathedral domes, a view of heaven. And down below lurked the dark bumpy form of an alligator like a priest in a side chapel—black and slimy as a turd."

Williblad stuck out his two long arms, one atop the other, and slowly moved one arm up and down, miming the biting of great jaws. Ortelius tittered, but Williblad's face remained serious. The story seemed to hold some profound meaning for him. "The beast barely showed through the surface, his nostrils and eyes were as knots on a sunken log, and he was covered over and over in vestments of duckweed. Alligators lie utterly immobile all day long, you know, waiting for that one unfortunate egret or heron or ibis or spoonbill to wander too close. And now, in their excitement, the mating egrets stepped off the island into the shallows and there was a huge, wallowing splash—it was the alligator, unbelievably fast. He caught the female bird; she screamed and died, her feathers red with blood. The other egret flew away."

"What a vision!" exclaimed Ortelius. As well as being as handsome as a god, Williblad was an enthralling storyteller.

"My Spanish father was that alligator," said Williblad evenly. "In the fullness of time, my mother's widower killed him. I saw it. He smashed his head in with a club."

"A cold-blooded way to tell such a thing!" exclaimed Bruegel with a frown. "I too was fathered upon an unwilling woman by a powerful man. But it never crossed my mind to kill him."

"You're not a Tequesta," said Williblad shortly. "You're an artist. We act, you scrawl. Did you say you needed paper? You'll find some in the drawer of that desk over there."

"Very well," said Bruegel, taking some. "You're quite rude for a clerk." There seemed to be no hope of him and Williblad becoming friends. "Send Abraham to fetch me when it's time for us to leave. Meanwhile I'll be mining Master Bosch's triptych." With a final glare at Williblad he marched out.

Williblad gazed after him for a moment, his eyes hard. And then he turned his attention back to the map of Florida. "I'll tell you what, Abraham," he said presently, his voice friendly again. "I'll trade you the Charles medal for this map— and to justify this to Fugger, I'd like copies of all your other maps. It makes good business sense to have a uniform map collection. Fugger will approve."

"That's—that's an interesting offer," said Ortelius, doing quick calculations in his head. "You'd be talking about quite a few maps, you know. Maybe a hundred."

"You want more than one medal?" said Williblad expansively. "Fine, you can have the Moritz penny, too. Fugger doesn't really care about the medals. He only likes paintings, and he's too fatheaded to notice what I give away. But, to be fair, in addition to copies of all the maps you have in stock, we'll want copies of all the new ones you produce. I like maps."

"Let's just say all the new ones for the next two years," said Ortelius.

"Agreed." Williblad pulled the two silver medallions closer and wrapped them up in a scrap of velvet. "They're yours."

"Oh my," said Ortelius, at a loss for words. His heart beat faster as he took the two precious medals in his hands. How heavy they were. "You're sure Fugger won't mind?"

"I myself would rather hold a medal than look at a painting," said Williblad. "But Mijnheer Fugger has the European infatuation with perspective. He thinks medals unworthy of his attention. He likes a painting with a fine lot of buildings and fields in it, an image that says, 'See how much I own!' Myself, I'd rather hold a clamshell."

How openly Williblad was speaking to him! As if they were old friends. Ortelius cast about for a topic to deepen the conversation. "What you said earlier about priests and alligators," he essayed, lowering his voice. "You're for the reform of the Church?"

"I despise the Church," said Williblad quietly. "I'd like to see it wiped off the face of the earth. There is no God, Abraham." Williblad stopped and smiled oddly, his lively eyes gauging Ortelius's reaction. "I speak these thoughts to keep from bursting. In so doing, I place my life into your hands. But I sense your readiness to be more than a passing friend."

"I'll not betray you," breathed Ortelius. "I have secrets of my own." Did he dare to lay his hand upon Williblad's? There was a chance that Williblad's frankness was but a ruse to draw him in. The Inquisition had agents everywhere.

"I saw you at the Carnival last night," said Williblad, as if to put him at his ease. "You were watching the dancers. You looked quite alone. Perhaps you have trouble finding the kind of company you seek?"

"I travel a great deal," said Ortelius evasively. Williblad's reckless candor was frightening.

"I noticed an attractive woman dancing with your Bruegel," continued Williblad, caroming from one subject to the next. "She's new to town. Did you say that her name is Anja?"

"She's from the country," said Ortelius, speaking carefully lest he say something about the incest, yet wanting to promote intimacy by sharing gossip. "Yes, Anja. She lives with Peter as of last night."

"Fast work," said Williblad. "No sooner does this little pheasant whir past, then your friend has her in his talons." He paused. "I'd like to taste her juices too. I wonder how I might meet her? Perhaps she'll tire of her artist and choose to seek out a—clerk." It seemed the word from Bruegel had rankled.

"I—that's not my affair," protested Ortelius, feeling quite over his head.

"You have a servant girl, no?" said Williblad in a silky tone. "Surely she'll be acquainted with the consort of your close friend Peter Bruegel. Your maid can mediate. Send her to me with the maps, and don't think of it again. I'll do the talking." Ortelius could all too well imagine Helena as a go-between. He opened his mouth to protest, but Williblad cut him off with a gentle, lingering pat on the cheek.

Just then a servant appeared with a message that Mijnheer Fugger needed to speak with Williblad. Their moment was over. "I'm glad to have met you, Abraham," said Williblad, getting to his feet. "I'll explain our arrangement to Mijnheer Fugger. Don't forget to send your girl with the maps. Your cantankerous friend Bruegel is down the hall in the second room to the left. You two can find your own way out?"

"Certainly, dear Williblad. I'm very grateful. I'll send the maps in a few days."

"A pleasure to know you. Antwerp holds so few civilized men."

"I'm thoroughly enchanted," said Ortelius, speaking from the bottom of his heart. Williblad gave a wicked smile, and then he was gone. A deep man.

Ortelius found Bruegel alone in a dim sitting room with the Bosch triptych. It was five feet tall, with the main panel four feet across, and each of the side panels two feet across. It sat upon a massive table, placed so that the waning light of a window fell upon it. On the left panel was a scene of Eden, in the center was a Last Judgment above a scene of Hell, and on the right was more Hell. The overall effect of the picture was of rumpled brown velvet strewn with jewels, worms, and beetles.

Ortelius barely knew where to begin looking. "Too much to see," he murmured. On closer examination, the jewel-colored things were fantastic buildings of rose red, pale green, and light blue; the worms were writhing pink humans; the shiny black beetles were Bosch's demons.

"You see it one bit at a time," said Bruegel, who was standing before the picture with pen and paper in hand. "Just like you'd paint it. Here's a spoonbill and a gryllos."

"Gryllos?"

"At the bottom edge. A head with no body. He—or she—walks on two feet. I think perhaps she's a nun, a vengeful Mother Superior. How did things go with Williblad? Did you get what you wanted?"

"Well—yes, I suppose so. Look." Ortelius held out his hand with the cloth-wrapped medals and uncovered them. "He gave me these for copies of all my maps. They're very rare and beautiful." And, thought Ortelius, Williblad had given much more. His confidence. Who knew what it might lead to? The one painful thought was Williblad's talk of starting something with Anja. Should Ortelius feel guilty over his possible part in this? But surely if Williblad didn't use Helena as his messenger, he'd only use someone else.

"Shiny," said Bruegel, taking a quick look at the medals and then turning his attention back to the Bosch. "Isn't that fat blue beast a wonder? His nose is a horn— no, a bagpipe's chanter—and he's playing it with his hands. Look at the shading across his belly, and the lively way his legs are dancing. Oh, yes, the good

Master Bosch is incomparable." Bruegel was busily sketching on his piece of paper. "I'll make up for the drawings of his I erased at s'Hertogenbosch. I'll spread more of his inventions into the world."

"That's good," said Ortelius, increasingly uneasy that they were overstaying their welcome. "I think Williblad wants us to leave now. I don't want you to start a fight with him again. Why did you have to call him a clerk?"

"I don't like him. You heard how shabbily he tried to deal with me at the Schilderspand. And then he brags about his father's murder? I've met his type before. All talk and no action. He's jealous of me for being an artist."

And he's after your woman, thought Ortelius to himself. And my Helena's to be the mediator. And I love Williblad too much to stop it. Poor Peter.

"I have to net a few more of these beasts," said Bruegel. "Look at the fish with legs. Look at the man playing the trumpet with his ass. See the lines of white light on the backs of those serpents."

All across the middle of the central picture were burning buildings. The tormented sinners made Ortelius uncomfortably aware of the propensity of flesh to be wounded and pierced. He walked around and peered at the grisaille images on the backs of the side panels. One of them showed St. Bavo beside a begging leper who had his detached foot sitting on his begging blanket. It occurred to Ortelius that perhaps Bosch was mad.

"Come, Peter, let's get out of here."

"Do you see Bosch's punishment for Gluttony?" said Bruegel, furiously sketching. "A man's ass is squirting into a funnel that goes into a barrel that pours into the glutton's mouth. And here's a lustful sinner in a barrel of toads, guarded by a fire-breathing newt with a knife through his neck. The punishment for *Luxuria*."

"Is lust really such a blameworthy thing?" wondered Ortelius. His gaze drifted uneasily to the Lord of Hell in the right panel. The Lord of Hell was a cage of fire, like a stove. The Lord of Hell's stomach, mouth, and eyes were windows of flame, and sparks shot out of the top of his head. His mouth had fangs like a cat mouth. Ortelius hated and feared cats. "It's too heartless, Peter. Too cruel."

"It's cruel, but it's wonderful," said Bruegel, unperturbed. "Look at his color effects: see the verdigris on the bronze cupola of the warriors and the moss on the toad-barrel. How does he do that?"

"Williblad expects us to leave now, Peter. And it's getting too dark to see."

"All right," said Bruegel and made some final scratches with his pen. He folded up his papers and let out a long sigh. As they left the Bosch room, Bruegel walked half-backwards, staring at the triptych till the last minute. Finally they were outside in the dusk, Ortelius with his coins and Bruegel with his new images. Snow was softly falling.

"Good-bye, then, Peter," said Ortelius. "I'm going home."

"Me too," said Bruegel. "Home to Anja and my paints. I'm ready."

SIX

THE PEASANT WEDDING
ANTWERP, SEPTEMBER 1560

"Up with the cock, Peter! We've beer to drink and maids to dance with."

Bruegel opened his eyes to see Hans Franckert bulking over his bed. It was quite early of a September morn.

"I'd expected to find Anja in your arms," continued Franckert. "Indeed, I was looking forward to seeing her. Where is the good woman?"

"Fugger's," said Bruegel softly. "She often sleeps over there with Williblad Cheroo."

Anja had taken to betraying him more and more often, with Williblad

Cheroo and with other men. It was Cheroo who'd been the first to corrupt her. Williblad had lured Anja away, using Ortelius's gossipy maid Helena as go-between. A sad side effect was that, in his anger over the betrayal, Bruegel had damaged his friendship with Ortelius as well. Franckert was presently his only close friend.

Bruegel sat up in bed, taking in Franckert's garb. Instead of his usual city clothes, Franckert was wearing enormously baggy green trousers tucked into high, muddy boots that had their tops turned down. He wore a brown jacket with a pleated skirt, and upon his head was a high-crowned shaggy hat, evidently made from the fur of a dog. Bruegel laughed despite himself.

"You look the perfect peasant," he said. "I remember now. The country wedding. But I never got my costume ready. Maybe you should go alone. God knows I don't feel like eating or drinking. I'm all choler and bile."

"And leave you here to brood?" cried Franckert. "Never. You're losing your sense of fun. No need for peasant clothes. Put on your finest garb and we'll say you're the owner of my farm. Poor Bruegel. Anja's brought you low. You took her in—it's been four years now, no? You've lodged her, gotten her one job after another, and now she covers you with the blue cloak."

"The blue cloak," agreed Bruegel. "The emblem of cuckoldry. It's at the center of my *Low Lands Proverbs*. I don't think you ever saw it. Look, it's right behind you."

Leaning against the wall behind Franckert were two great oak panels, nearly five feet across and four feet high, each of them painted with hundreds of little figures, too many to count. Bruegel and his patron Nicolas Jonghelinck called them *wemel* paintings. The word *wemel* meant "seethe" or "boil"; it was the word they'd used in Bruegel's village to describe the motion of a mass of insects: like ants, like the roly-poly bugs found under a rotten log, or like the springtails in a wet pile of duckweed at the river's edge.

One of the *wemel* pictures was the *Low Lands Proverbs*, the other was *The Battle of Carnival and Lent*. Although the panels belonged to Jonghelinck, he'd returned them to Bruegel for safekeeping while his wife had their villa renovated. Nicolas had been made a tax collector, and he was making more money than ever.

Ever since getting the pictures back last month, Bruegel had been spending most of his mornings lying in bed looking at them. He was in the process of starting a third one, an encyclopedic picture of children's games. In some ways it was relaxing not to have Anja around all the time. She'd grown more and more demanding over the years. What it came down to was that she wanted Bruegel to marry her, while he wanted to wait for young Mayken. So she was looking elsewhere. Understandable, but it was a hard thing to be known as a cuckold.

"Ah yes," said Franckert, examining the *Low Lands Proverbs*. "Here's the woman draping the blue cloak over her man's face. A doddering fool with a cane. What a sly hussy she is. And look at her breasts—say, she's the very image of Anja, isn't she?"

"The very," said Bruegel, collapsing onto his back with an exaggerated groan. It was good to have his companion here to complain to.

"What wonderful pigs you paint," said Franckert, leaning closer to study the *Proverbs* details. "One man shears a sheep, the other shears a pig. I love the way you paint the *varken*, Peter. Their ears look so alert. The pig is an intelligent animal. My father's tenant farmer kept several of them. He could never keep them in the pen. And see, here you have one pulling the bung out of a barrel. Clever *varken*. And here's a man feeding roses to them."

"Like me showing you my pictures," said Bruegel, rising up on one elbow. He enjoyed teasing Franckert; it dulled the edges of his saturnine humors. And Franckert seemed willing to tolerate almost any insult from his volatile artist friend. But it was best not to go too far. Casting about for a different topic, Bruegel picked up the worn little leather book from the table by his bed.

"Have you read Erasmus's *In Praise of Folly*?" asked Bruegel. "Ortelius gave me this copy, back when we were friends. Listen to this. It's like he's describing these two pictures." He slowly read a passage aloud.

"'If you could look down from the moon, as Menippus once did, on the countless hordes of mortals, you'd think you saw a swarm of flies or gnats quarrelling amongst themselves, fighting, plotting, stealing, playing, making love, being born, growing old, and dying. It's hard to believe how much trouble and tragedy this tiny little creature can stir up, short-lived as he is.'" It felt good to be reading Erasmus; it made Bruegel feel like a scholar, like a man of the world. Not for the first time, he regretted having alienated Ortelius.

"Who's Menippus?" demanded Franckert rhetorically. "I detest classical allusions. They make me feel stupid." Loyally he gestured towards the *Low Lands Proverbs*. "You've got the spirit of Erasmus here, Peter, without the pedantry. A kneeling man making his confession to a devil! That's worth ten of the late Brother's sly digs at Greek philosophers. What a masterpiece."

Bruegel set down the book and got out of bed.

"I wish I could afford one of your paintings," continued Franckert, looking away from his friend's nakedness. "But business hasn't been good at all. The Spanish taxes are crushing us. Every twentieth penny of every exchange goes to them. I think you told me you're working on a third *wemel* picture? Where is it?"

"It's next door in my studio," said Bruegel, washing himself off with a rag and a basin of water. "*Children's Games*. I'm painting it for my old Master Coecke's widow. Mayken Verhulst. I went to visit her in Brussels last month. Her and young Mayken. The daughter's fifteen now. A little woman, very nearly. But she's—"

Bruegel broke off, discouraged, as always, by the difficulty of his long-held plan of trying to form a liaison with young Mayken. She was in truth still a girl, and any romantic thoughts she had were most certainly not of Bruegel. The old Mayken was doing well at managing Master Coecke's estate; the four stories of their solid brick house were filled with activity. Yes indeed, mother Mayken made a good business painting miniatures and designing tapestries. And as for Bruegel, the old Mayken was impressed with his progress as an artist. The engravings of his Bosch-style Seven Sins were well-known and had sold widely. And, in Nicolas Jonghelinck, Bruegel had found a loyal patron for his oils. But when he'd tried to steer the conversation around to the old plan of having him marry into the family, old Mayken had only asked if he was still "living in sin with that peasant serving maid."

"Young Mayken's not interested in you?" coaxed Franckert.

"No." Bruegel sighed. "I've known her since she was born, and she thinks of me as a family retainer, or at best an uncle. That odd, paint-smeared fellow who always worked with her father. A suitor fit for her mother. To little Mayken I'm as exciting as yesterday's potatoes. It will take some effort to spark her interest. So I thought I'd give her and her mother a *Children's Games*."

"Little Mayken likes games?" asked Franckert.

"Well, it's something that came up last month," said Bruegel, drying himself off. "I often saw her at play as a child, of course. And on my last visit, young Mayken and I got to talking about games, seeing how many we could remember. Even though she says she's outgrown them, she has fond memories. So I put forth the idea of making a picture with all the games in it. Old Mayken gave me a nod and said she'd buy the picture, just like that. But I'm insisting on making it a gift."

"Shrewd business," said Franckert mockingly. "The Bruegel style." He'd tried, unsuccessfully, to counsel Bruegel about financial matters in the past, but Bruegel never listened to him. So he contented himself with digs.

As Bruegel pulled on his undergarments, Franckert's attention turned to the second painting in Bruegel's bedroom, *The Battle of Carnival and Lent*. "What is this?" he cried. "That fat oaf riding a barrel—the spirit of Carnival? You've painted him to look like me!"

"That's the risk of befriending me, Hans." Bruegel glanced uneasily at Franckert, trying to gauge the big man's reaction. "I draw what I see—with changes. I hope you don't mind." He hadn't really meant for Franckert to ever see this painting at all. People were sometimes annoyed or embarrassed to find themselves in one of Bruegel's pictures.

It was in fact one of Bruegel's engravings that had cast the final pall over his relations with Ortelius. Angered by the maid Helena's role in leading Anja astray, Bruegel had created an allegorical image of Ortelius as a foolish, bent dotard who compulsively searches with a lantern in broad daylight through sacks and barrels and hampers, greedy for goods and for knowledge, his face set into a self-absorbed, avaricious frown. The engraving, successfully published with the title *Everyman*, had so upset the normally mild-mannered Ortelius that he'd broken off relations not only with Bruegel but with the printer Jerome Cock.

So Bruegel was greatly relieved to see Franckert's surprise turn into laughter.

"You're a good friend, Hans, and I'm grateful that you came for me today," gushed Bruegel. "I sorely need an outing. Explain again how you're going to get us into this peasant wedding?"

"The bride's a distant cousin of one of my teamsters," said Franckert. "Max Wagemaeker. You've met him, a loud fellow with a weathered face? He's not going, he's off hauling a load of imitation Bosch paintings to Germany, but I'll say I'm Max's half brother from down on the farm. Hans Hoiberg. That's good, no? Hoiberg for haystack. And you'll be my landlord; you're just coming along for the fun. Look, here's a gold piece you can give the bride. Everyone will love us."

"I thought you said business was bad," said Bruegel, taking the coin.

"I always have money for a celebration," said Franckert.

Bruegel smiled. Franckert wasn't peeved at him, and they were going out for some fun. Enough of lying around here brooding over Anja and working himself half-mad on the latest painting. He was smiling now, and began picking out the best clothes in his wardrobe: light gray stockings, black knee breeches, a lace-trimmed doublet, and a round black felt cap like a walnut shell. He peered at himself in his good old convex mirror, assessing the effect of the costume. In the glass, Franckert hovered behind him like a merry patron saint.

"What should your name be?" asked Franckert.

"That's easy. Peter de Hoorne. De Hoorne like the Graaf of my old village. Who knows, he may really have been my father. Anja used to think so, though she doesn't see much noble about me anymore. We'll say we come from there, too. Grote Brueghel." There was actually a Klein Brueghel village as well. With a flourish, Bruegel produced a splendid black coat, subtly patterned and lined with white fur that peeked out from the cuffs of the velvet-trimmed sleeves. It had been a gift from Nicolas Jonghelinck.

"At your service, my Lord de Hoorne," said Franckert miming a peasant's awkward bow. He made sure to bend his head forward so far that his hat fell off, and then he stepped on it while picking it up. One reason Bruegel enjoyed Franckert's company was that Franckert was so good at miming buffoonery. Though his speech was a bit ordinary, his motions were eloquent.

Hearing himself referred to as Lord de Hoorne gave Bruegel a shiver of pleasure. Though he rarely admitted it out loud, he was indeed fond of the notion that the old Graaf might be his father. Those who didn't know Bruegel well thought of him as a mad, vulgar peasant—they mistook his recent images of the Sins for his essence. Little did they know that Bruegel was an educated man and quite likely a son of nobility. He nodded his head in grave acknowledgment of Franckert's bow.

"I'm ready, my lord, are you?" asked Franckert.

"Let me take a look next door into my studio. Wait here." Again the reckless desire to tease his friend came bubbling forth. "Point your snout at the *Low Lands Proverbs* and *The Battle of Carnival and Lent.* Count the pigs."

"I'd think you'd keep these pictures in your studio for inspiration," said Franckert imperturbably. He was inured to Bruegel's reckless teasing.

"Jonghelinck made me promise not to. He was worried I might change something. Not that I would. They're perfect. I'll be right back."

Bruegel had half hoped to find Anja asleep in the studio's corner, but her featherbed was smooth and cool. He missed the days when he'd find her there every morning, often as not in a humor for some amorous play. There was little of that anymore, thanks to Ortelius's Helena and Williblad Cheroo. It had all gone sour about a year ago. Though Williblad was no likelier to marry Anja than Bruegel, he seemed to fascinate her as much as he fascinated Ortelius. Damn the man. Bruegel's heart could only stand so many blows. For the hundredth time he told himself to end his relationship with Anja. Yet he knew that, once she returned, she'd use her wiles to win him back over. He sighed and shook his head. Enough thoughts of Anja for now.

The studio smelled of paint and walnut oil. Bruegel took a good long look at his *Children's Games.* It was always interesting to see his pictures fresh in the morning, easier to judge their qualities. He wasn't fully fond of this one. He'd used the same odd perspective as in his other two *wemel* pictures, setting it up as if he were looking down on the scene from a rooftop or a high attic window. But the angles weren't working so well in this one. And what a dull, dun background he'd given the *Children's Games.* Anja's sneaking and lying was upsetting him, there was no doubt about it.

It struck him now that hardly any of his playing children bore smiles. Children were, on the whole, quite serious about their play, but a few more cheerful faces wouldn't have been amiss. Could it be that his unhappiness was showing through? That was the thing about art: your fingers spilled the secrets of your soul before you knew them yourself.

The other day, for instance, he'd found himself adding to the panel a little image of a girl with her skirts hiked up, squatting to piss and looking at herself. An idle kind of play. Was this a fitting thing to have in his presentation picture for the Maykens? Perhaps not, but it was droll, and it cheered Bruegel to see it. With so many figures upon the great panel to choose from, who needed to focus upon this particular child and wave the finger of academic taste? Bruegel's goal was, after all, to show life as a whole, from the high to the low. He liked the figure, and he wasn't going to rub it out.

In any case, the figure that he hoped young Mayken would most attend to was the girl at the very center of the picture, the one playing at being a bride. She had her hair unbound and she wore a crown. Her pleasant face gazed demurely down. Bruegel had in fact modeled the lass's features after those of young Mayken. It was meant to be a suggestion to her, something for her to keep in mind as she grew towards her marriageable years. The dream of joining the prosperous Brussels studios of Mayken's family was never far from his thoughts. To have a wife, and a house, and then some babies.

But this morning, thinking about Anja and the Maykens put an ache into his empty belly. It was indeed time for a day off. Looking around his dirty little studio, his eye lit upon a valuable sword that he had there for a studio prop; he'd borrowed it from Ortelius two years ago for his drawing of the sin of Anger, and, thanks to their falling out, he hadn't yet given it back. It had an intricately engraved scabbard and a fine silver hilt. The sword would complete his costume. He strapped it to his belt on the left side, locked the door, and joined Franckert.

Franckert had brought two horses. It was a sunny Saturday, and the streets were busy. Many of the farmers had brought their harvest wares to town. Bruegel rarely rode horseback; it was odd to have such a high view of the familiar city streets. He could see right into people's windows. A woman was meticulously peeling and eating an apple, slice by slice; a merchant was counting his purse of coins; a youth and a maid were laughing and tossing an egg back and forth; a graybeard was reading a book held right up against his nose; two children were looking out a window, the bigger one staring at Bruegel, the smaller one gazing up at the deep blue sky. Seeing all this, Bruegel's heart lifted. What a wonderfully full world it was.

"Peter!" It was Anja. The sound of her voice sent Bruegel's spirit plummeting from the heavens to the turbulent sea. She was on the arm of Martin de Vos, of all people. Even though Anja had been out all night, she looked quite fresh and tidy. Evidently she'd found a place to undress and have a bit of a wash. Before Bruegel could ask her any questions, she pressed one of her own. That was always her approach. "Where are you going, dressed up like that?"

"I'm taking the Lord down to Berchem for my cousin's wedding," said Franckert in a thick peasant accent. "It's good dancing on another man's floor, eh, Martin?"

"What's that supposed to mean?" snapped Anja. "I'm sorry I didn't come home last night, Peter. Fugger's granddaughter Elise had the colic and I was sitting up with her. I've only met Martin at the market just now. Can I come along with you today?"

"I'm sure you're too tired," said Bruegel coldly. It hurt a bit to see Anja's disappointed expression. What if she were innocent, what if she were truly his friend? On the other hand, why give her a chance to ruin his day? It was a virtual certainty that, given the opportunity, she would. He hardened his heart.

"How's your work?" Bruegel asked de Vos to change the subject. De Vos had stayed on in Italy much longer than Bruegel; he'd only been back in Antwerp for a year. Their old friendship had never quite resumed.

"I've started painting clouds and cherubs for Frans Floris," said de Vos. "It pays the rent. And on my own time I'm doing some drawings of real-life scenes. The jape is that I always have one of my people be Jesus, with a little halo. I'm going to engrave them and have Plantin make prints. Maybe they'll catch on with the public like your *Seven Sins* series. How does it feel to be the second Bosch?"

"Oh, Peter doesn't like to be called that," said Anja. For all her fickleness, she knew Bruegel's feelings well. He didn't want to be the second anything. He wanted to be the first Bruegel. Having Anja speak up for him made Bruegel feel bad about rejecting her. But he could see so well how the day would go if she came along. She'd chatter away to keep him from asking her questions, and then, once the dancing started at the wedding, she'd start turning on her charms to attract other men. And then she'd start a drunken argument with him on the way back home. The more he refused to marry her, the more she pestered him about other things. No, no, he needed his day off.

"It's ironic that Floris has me painting in the Italian style," de Vos was saying. "It's like that shit we hated so much in Rome."

"I didn't hate all of it," disagreed Bruegel. He had no desire to be a provincial artist who only admires his fellows' work. And seeing de Vos with Anja made him more than willing to return the dig about Bosch. "Are you still scared of Michelangelo, then? Maybe working for Floris will finally teach you how to draw a human body."

"I know all about bodies," snapped de Vos, making a show of slipping his arm around Anja's waist. "Floris and I surround ourselves with beautiful women. Have fun with the peasants, Bosch the Younger." Bruegel clenched his teeth, biting back his rage. He needed so badly to get out of this constrained little town and all its tiny doings.

"Don't be too late, Peter," called Anja, pushing off from the crook of de Vos's arm. Her face was a mask of guilelessness. But he wasn't fooled. "Have fun," sang Anja, putting on a wistful tone. "I'll have a nice supper waiting for you."

Bruegel nudged his horse and rode off without answering her. "Yet another lie," he snarled when Franckert's horse fell into a walk at his side. "She's my worst enemy."

"How do you mean?" asked Franckert. "She seemed pleasant enough."

"Anja won't have supper waiting for me. She deceives me about every possible sort of thing. I don't know why I continue living with her." His unhappy voice sounded petulant and unworthy. Ashamed of himself, Bruegel let his horse drop behind Franckert's and fell silent for a time.

He knew perfectly well why he lived with Anja. She was a comfortable echo of the bygone village days. She was a creature of fire and air, an ideal counterpoint to his cold, saturnine humors. When Anja did actually cook him a meal, it was a good one. She often helped tidy up his rooms. And, above all, there was the pleasure they took in the intimacies of each other's bodies. It was his own folly to expect her to be faithful when he himself refused to offer her security. Maybe he should stop dreaming of improving his lot, settle for Anja, and get on with the business of making a family? Not yet.

They passed through St. George's Gate in the city wall. The gate was manned by Spanish troops and Rode Rockx Walloon mercenaries. They were there to watch for political agitators and to make sure that Spain got every possible bit of tax. Bruegel's fine clothes caught the attention of a little Spanish taxman, who requested a peek into their purses. After some back-and-forth, the taxman extracted a silver piece from Franckert.

Immediately outside the gate was a spot of marshy land and a stream that ran towards the Scheldt. A ruined windmill that had belonged to the bankrupt brewer van Schoonbeke stood next to the stream, and the brewer's abandoned land was overgrown with bushes and trees. They rode past van Schoonbeke's windmill into the open countryside, leaving the smelly city streets behind.

The village of Berchem was less than an hour's ride through the flat, golden fields. Many of the fields were already harvested down to stubble, but in some of them the peasants were still at work: cutting the wheat with scythes, binding it into sheaves, and carrying the dried sheaves off to the barn. They also passed orchards laden with fruit; it seemed as if every apple tree had a peasant in it, wriggling about and gathering the bounty. The peasants in the trees brought back memories of boyhood apple gathering, as well as of perching in the high branches to spy upon women doing their business.

Bruegel noticed that one of the peasant boys was hanging upside down, spiritedly waving his arms and swaying from the backs of his knees. It struck him, not for the first time, that from a distance a man looks nearly the same turned either way. Like a letter H. A man was an H with his plump stubs a-waggling.

He'd thought a lot about the letter H recently. Last year, after much discussion with Anja, he'd dropped it from his name once and for all, so as to distance himself from that young, second-Bosch, Hell-painter Brueghel who'd drawn the famous Seven Deadly Sins. With his career fully in motion, he wanted to be very clearly his own man. How would it be to let Anja herself go the way of the H?

Bruegel and Franckert kept overtaking early-bird farmers on their way home from the Antwerp market. Franckert had a hearty greeting for everyone. He was working himself into his role of merry peasant wedding guest. Near Berchem they drew even with a couple riding home upon a rough wooden cart scattered with a few leftover cabbage leaves. "Greetings to you two on this lovely fall day," boomed Franckert. "I'm looking for the farm of Lucas Wagemaeker. My Lord de Hoorne and I have come to dance at their daughter's wedding."

Instead of responding, the man glared at them suspiciously, his open mouth showing a few yellow teeth. But his wife was ready for conversation. "Little Tilde and her Hendrik Hooft!" she exclaimed. "Yes, yes, the wedding's today. Geeraard and I would have been invited too, I'm sure, but the Rode Rockx say there can only be twenty of us villagers in one room at one time. Only twenty at a wedding feast, can you imagine? We must have had a hundred at our Susanna's nuptials, eh, Geeraard? Those were happier times."

"Wagemaeker didn't invite us because he hates us," growled Geeraard. The wrinkles at the corners of his mouth were as deeply carved as grooves in a piece of wood. "Due to that business with our pig in his garden this summer. He's a man who bears a grudge. And furthermore I wouldn't want to go. Wagemaeker thinks he's better than us." The peasant shot a sharp look at Bruegel. "What are you staring at, cookie eater?" That was the slang expression for someone from Antwerp. It was reckless for a peasant to address a lord in this wise. The old man's choler had addled his judgment.

"You have an interesting face," said Bruegel. "I'd like to remember it." To Bruegel's eyes, the peasant's face was already almost a sketch; he was mentally simplifying and universalizing it so as to make it fully ready for use.

"We're loyal Habsburg subjects, Mijnheer," said the man's wife, alarmed to have attracted a gentleman's attention. These days no good came from that. "All power be to King Philip and his sister, our good Regent Margaret," she said, her chatty voice changing to an abject whine. "I didn't mean to sound unhappy with the Rode Rockx. It's good they protect us from those mad Anabaptist heretics. You'll find Wagemaeker's barn at the end of a little track to the left, just before the village. Good day, my Lord."

"God's blessings and a bountiful harvesttime," said Franckert as Bruegel and he rode on past the cart. The village drew closer—a spire, a watchtower, a market building, a granary, a mansion, a cluster of houses with stair-step gables, an inn, and on the left a gallows with three dark, ragged shapes suspended beneath it. Crows circled the gibbets, cawing and feeding. And on the other side of the road, red-shirted soldiers sat drinking before the inn. Seeing them filled Bruegel with a visceral fear. Thanks to the Blood Edicts of the foreign tyrant King Philip, the crime of heresy was to be punished only by death, with no lesser penalties to be contemplated. Out here in the country there were no limits upon what the occupying soldiers might do.

"I heard about these hangings earlier this week," said Franckert. "Two women and a man. Anabaptists. They preached that all property should be held in common, but in the end, these three rebels couldn't share things any better than the rest of us. It seems the two women came to a falling-out over the man, and one of them set the Inquisitors upon the other two. I suppose the Rode Rockx are staying on in Berchem to make sure there's no further trouble. Well, that's none of our concern. This must be our turnoff here."

Bruegel and Franckert followed a grassy track to a solid little house, stable, and barn. The buildings were built of low mud walls topped by great, slanting thatched roofs that rose up four times as high as the walls. A cluster of gay blue and yellow ribbons hung above the barn door, and the sound of bagpipes floated from within. It was a nostalgic sound for Bruegel, who remembered going to some country weddings as a boy. When would he have a wedding of his own?

The party had started. People were milling around in the barnyard, drinking, laughing, and talking. A pimply youth ran across towards the two riders, rolling a hoop with one hand and holding a wedge of brown bread in the other. He was dressed up for the feast, wearing white stockings darned at the knees, a feather and a spoon on his green velvet hat, plum-colored breeches, and a white shirt with gray stripes. Seeing him, it occurred to Bruegel that he hadn't yet put a hoop roller into his *Children's Games*.

"Shall I take your horses, Mijnheeren?" asked the youth.

"Thank you kindly," said Franckert, and handed him a copper coin. "Fresh water and some nice hay for them, if you please. Are you related to Tilde or to Hendrik?"

"Tilde's my big sis," said the youth, letting the hoop fall to the ground as he admired his coin. "I'll use this to buy sweets in Antwerp the next time we go to market. We've been going twice a week." His voice had the cracking quality of early adolescence, deep one moment and high the next. He reached out to touch the velvet trim of Bruegel's luxurious coat. "Are you one of the Hooft relatives, sir? I didn't know Hendrik was kin to gentlemen."

"I hate to disappoint you, but it's *me* that's the relative," said fat Franckert before Bruegel could say anything. Franckert dismounted and did his full peasant bow: he let his dog-fur hat fall into the mud, cleaned the hat by beating it against his backside, and then put the hat back on crooked. "Hans Hoiberg from the village of Grote Brueghel. I'm your cousin Max Wagemaeker's half brother. And this fine gentleman with me, why, he's my landlord. He likes to keep an uncommonly close eye on his tenants, he does. I present to you the Lord Peter de Hoorne. And your name, young man?"

"Joop Wagemaeker. Pleased to meet you, cousin Hoiberg. But why has Mijnheer de Hoorne come, really?"

"I'm here to get the stink off me," said Bruegel putting on an affected, lordly tone for the benefit of Franckert. "I've been suffering from melancholy, do you know the word, boy? An excess of black bile. You might say I'm in search of myself. My good man Hans promises me that a peasant wedding will set right my humors. I've brought a gift for the bride." He tapped his purse meaningfully, then glared at Franckert, who'd let out a snort of laughter. "Decorum, Hoiberg! You're giddy before you've even begun to drink."

"We'll see if we can make a place for you," said young Joop. "It's awfully crowded. We're only supposed to let twenty inside at a time, you know. That's why so many people are out here in the yard. Just give me a minute to stable your horses."

The peasants in the barnyard were in a cheerful party humor. Full jugs of beer and plates of porridge kept being handed out from inside the barn, with a stream of empties being passed back in. The bagpipe music was loud and lively; several couples had started dancing.

Every time someone would come out of the barn, a fresh peasant would push in. It happened that a couple were exiting just as young Joop finished with the horses, and the youth made sure that Bruegel and Franckert were the next pair allowed to enter.

The barn smelled of beer and animals. The dust of the hay put a tickle into Bruegel's nose and reminded him more strongly than ever of his youth. He and Anja had often played in the haylofts, peering down at the broad backs of the cows. For a moment he felt weak with homesickness: for his village, for his past, for his younger, happier self. Black bile indeed.

A beam of sunlight angled in through a high window. The shaft of light was alive with specks that seemed to jiggle with the rhythms of the bagpipes. The twenty people around the long cloth-bedecked table were seated on benches made from split logs. A few children sat on the floor. Two bagpipers stood playing at the near side of the table. Behind the table, a tidy pile of wheat straw rose almost to the ceiling, making a wall of summer gold.

The bride was a round-faced, red-cheeked woman seated before a green cloth draped from the wall of straw. A red-and-white striped paper lantern hung suspended above her like the canopy of a queen's throne. She wore her hair long and loose, with a red flower-bedecked wreath atop her head. As was the custom at a peasant wedding, she neither ate nor spoke, but sat there with her eyes demurely downcast—just like the little girl in Bruegel's *Children's Games*. It was easy to see that she was happy.

Next to the bride were her parents. The mother was a kind-faced, noisy woman with some teeth missing and a white cloth on her head; the father was a quiet, bright-eyed man with a short white beard and a black cap that came down over his ears. Franckert told them his cock-and-bull story about who they were, Bruegel handed the bride the gold coin, and then they were seated with the others at the long table, Bruegel at one end next to a monk, Franckert at the other end near the barnyard. The signs of respect that the guests gave Bruegel were a soothing balm to his sense of himself.

Two young men with spoons tucked into their caps were just carrying in a big board, or no, it was a door, laden with fresh bowls of porridge, some white and some yellow. The man on Bruegel's left, a handsome, fresh-faced fellow in a red cap and a light brown jacket, hopped to his feet and began passing plates to the guests.

"Plain or saffron?" he asked Bruegel.

"Saffron," said Bruegel. "Thank you." What with his worries about Anja and this constant overwork, his stomach hadn't been feeling well of late. The fire element of the saffron could be just the thing to balance his humors. The red-capped man handing him the plate had a dazed smile on his lips and an odd light in his eyes. Bruegel realized this must be the groom. "And congratulations on your marriage, young Hendrik! You're a lucky man."

"Thank you, my Lord. Hey, Joris, give Lord de Hoorne your spoon." One of the food bearers pulled the spoon from his hat and handed it to Bruegel. Bruegel dug into his porridge. The saffron gave it a delicate aroma as well as a pleasant yellow color. It was the first food he'd had today.

"You can call me Father Michel," said the monk on Bruegel's right. From the cleric's garb, Bruegel could see that he was a Franciscan friar who'd taken priestly orders. "It was I who helped Tilde and Hendrik celebrate the marriage sacrament today," he said. "It's an honor to have you here, my Lord. I hope you weren't expecting meat; we've no fowl, nor calf, nor pig, nor rabbits. You'll find only beer, bread, and porridge. When the Wagemaekers asked me to perform the wedding, we discussed the feast, and I advised that too rich a fare might draw unwanted hornets—the red-shirted kind. I myself am quite content with this simple provender. My cardinal sin is something other than gluttony."

There was a pause, and when no more information came, Bruegel said, "So now I wonder what is your besetting sin." He wagged his finger, deciding to make a game of it. "I'll warrant I can guess it after a few minutes' talk. Meanwhile can you cut me a piece of that bread?"

"Gladly," said Father Michel. He was young and beardless, with a cowl worn over his shaved head. His fingers were white and delicate as he handed Bruegel the bread. "I take it that you're an expert on human folly?"

"I know physiognomy passing well, and I happen to have thought deeply about the Seven Sins of late," said Bruegel, continuing to eat. "Avarice, Pride, Envy, Anger, Gluttony, Sloth, and Lechery." Without seeming to, he closely watched the monk's reaction to each of the names. Now he mopped up the last of his porridge with the piece of bread, and a foaming pot of beer arrived. "It's good," said Bruegel, tasting the strong gueuze lager. "My tenant who brought me—Hans Hoiberg, that's him down there at the other end between the two laughing women—he'll drink enough for three men. It'll be up to me to guide us home." The festive company had made Bruegel begin to feel merry.

Something poked Bruegel's thigh, high up between his legs. He leaned over to see what it was, and found the long white head of an animal.

"Don't mind him," cawed a sour-faced middle-aged man who sat to the left of Hendrik. "It's my dog Waf. A once-noble hound, he's become a beggar. My son gave him to me." *Waf*, pronounced *"vahf,"* was the onomatopoeic Flemish word for "bark."

"I've heard the other dogs talking about him," joked Bruegel, giving Waf's head a pat. The beast was a long-legged, thin-waisted wolfhound with curly white hair.

"Ho ho," chortled the sour-faced man. "The dogs should be talking about my son getting married today!" He slapped the groom on the shoulder. "I'll be a grandfather yet, Hendrik. Not so, Tilde?" From across the table, Tilde smiled vacantly at her new father-in-law, perhaps not understanding his words across the many conversations and the raging of the bagpipes. "I'm Gilbert Hooft," continued the man, leaning past his son to clasp Bruegel's hand. He was wearing a white shirt and a black coat; there were ink stains on his hands. The sourness of his face and the dissonance of his voice were misleading. He was actually very cheerful and excited. "My son's a huntsman with his own cottage. And I'm a clerk from Antwerp."

"I'm Peter de Hoorne from Grote Brueghel," said Bruegel. Keeping up his cover story was starting to feel uncomfortable. Here he was amid these happy, innocent people—and he was lying to them. But it was too late now to change. "Congratulations on a fine match, Mijnheer Hooft. And don't worry about Waf; I'm happy to have his head in my lap." Bruegel slipped Waf a crust of bread, which the dog ate with great, exaggerated chewing motions. His long jaws and thin waist gave him a comically famished air. It was a delight to see him chew; Bruegel gave him a second crust.

"Have you read Erasmus?" asked Father Michel suddenly.

"Why, yes, I have," said Bruegel. "I enjoy his raillery. Your abbot permits you to read him?"

"Erasmus was a sound Brother of the Augustinian order," said the monk. "He even spoke out against Luther, once the sausage was fully upon the table. Erasmus was a humanist, not a heretic. My abbot knew him personally." Father Michel suddenly tittered. "Do you remember Erasmus's jape about the gourd? Where he's making sport of the academic theologians?"

"I'm not sure," said Bruegel.

" 'Could God have taken on the form of a gourd?' " quoted the monk. " 'If so, how could a gourd have preached sermons, performed miracles, and been nailed to the cross?' " The monk's giggles grew into peals of laughter, reckless as a child's. Evidently the beer had mounted to his head.

"You think gourds are of a comical shape," said Bruegel. The party atmosphere had loosened his tongue. For once he felt free to openly speak his intricate thoughts. "Perhaps they resemble a woman's body, a form that no doubt makes you ill at ease. And discomfort is the wellspring of humor. Yet, looked at in another way, a gourd can be menacing. A rotten, pulpy gourd with one side eaten away and a long-pincered beetle or a plague-ridden rat within, it's no laughing matter. The gourd is an image, and it's a noble thing to be an image maker. Like God Himself, a painter of sufficient skill can make a gourd indifferently into the Christ or into the king of Hell."

"I poorly understand you," said Father Michel, his face grown cold. "Do you mock me, Lord de Hoorne?"

Bruegel eyed the swollen, aggressive cast of the monk's upper lip. "I have it! Your besetting sin is Anger, no?" The bagpipers hit a particularly high squeal just then, and the dog Waf pushed out from under the table, raised his head, and howled. Old Gilbert Hooft winced and got to his feet to drag his dog outside. At the same time a hubbub broke out near the barnyard door. Franckert was showing off his strength by holding a shrieking, laughing peasant woman high up over his head. "I better go see about my tenant," said Bruegel to the monk. "But am I right about you?"

"You are," said the monk, recovering his good humor. "I have a terrible temper. I was so angry when those soldiers hanged those three people this week that I very nearly got myself arrested. The abbot had me say three hundred Hail Marys to calm down. If only the Inquisitor and the Rode Rockx had let me pray with that man and those two women. I'm sure I could have brought them back into the Church. I knew them well. They called themselves Anabaptists only because they were hungry and in despair. The Spaniards and their Rode Rockx kill us as heedlessly as a butcher's boy swats flies. One fine day a fly will bite them back." As he said this, Father Michel's upper lip began sticking out again.

There was a crash; Franckert had slipped and fallen. Bruegel got up and went to see. Franckert was flat on his back with his head beneath the skirts of the dark-haired woman who'd landed on top of him. She seemed no worse for the experience, though she took her time getting to her feet. Hans rose up beside her, his codpiece noticeably distended. He beat his dog-fur hat against his buttocks, cocked it rakishly on his head, and asked the woman, "Shall we dance now, Veronicka? Oh, and let me introduce my landlord to you, the great Lord Peter de Hoorne." Franckert turned his big head to his other side, where another woman stood smiling. "Will you dance with Lord Peter, dear Betje? The four of us can do some special dance steps from the village of Grote Brueghel."

Nothing loath, Bruegel accompanied Franckert into the barnyard to jig about with blond Betje and the dark Veronicka. More and more peasants showed up, until there must have been a hundred guests in all. Most stayed out in the barn-yard, for the Wagemaekers made sure that never more than twenty or so entered the barn, lest the Rode Rockx arrive and accuse them of hosting a seditious cabal.

Bruegel was happy out in the open air. Betje soon left him for another part-ner, and he sat on an empty barrel to one side, peacefully watching the dancers. He had no wish to get entangled with another woman today. Nobody paid him much mind, though the dog Waf stayed at his side. Waf seemed to have taken a liking to him.

Bruegel noticed Joop's hoop lying beside the barrel, and thought to take out his pen and folded-up papers to make a quick sketch from memory of how Joop had looked coming across the barnyard. There was a nice vacant spot still free in the foreground of *Children's Games*; he could paint Joop and the hoop in there tomorrow. Once he'd finished his memory sketch, he turned his attention to the crowd around him, drawing the faces and costumes of some of the people who weren't in wild motion, and making written notes about the colors of their clothes.

Two of the most noticeable figures were a man and a woman just arriving, the man running ahead and dragging the woman by the arm, the two of them has-tening lest they miss a single minute of this rare afternoon of fun. The man had a hard, humorless face, a face like a root or a gnarled piece of wood. The woman in her starched white headgear resembled nothing so much as a plump-cheeked goose. How desperately they wanted some pleasure. The man kicked up his back leg and the woman followed his lead, her cheeks slightly wobbling. The squeal-ing rhythms of the bagpipe whirled them around, but still their faces showed no joy. It crossed Bruegel's mind that his constant labor on his artwork was a bit like this. But what else was there to do?

Suddenly the beer supply had run out. Franckert howled in comic dismay, then enlisted Joop to take him in a wagon to the village inn to fetch another keg. Before leaving, Franckert gave out that it was "the Lord de Hoorne" who'd pro-vided the money for the extra beer. The peasants gave Bruegel a cheer. Veronicka sashayed over to watch him draw. She was a handsome woman with full lips and sun-browned skin, well past girlhood.

"You're very talented, Lord de Hoorne," she said. "If you had to work for a living, perhaps you'd be an artist."

"It's the noblest trade," said Bruegel, curious to see what she'd make of this remark.

"Tell me about your tenant Hans," asked Veronicka. Evidently she had no interest in discussing art. "Is he really married? And how much land does he farm? His hands feel too soft to be a farmer's."

"Hans is indeed a bachelor," said Bruegel. "As for his hands, well, he's so prosperous that he hires men to do his hard labor."

"Can you draw a picture of his house for me?"

"Sorry, I'm busy drawing something else. That frog-faced man asleep against the wall. I like his clothes."

"Draw that old sot? Who cares about him. Excuse me for a minute."

Veronicka disappeared around the corner of the barn. After a minute, Bruegel gave in to lust and peeked after her. She was squatting on a patch of straw. Catching Bruegel looking at her, she flipped her skirt towards him, revealing herself. He withdrew to his perch on the barrel. And then Veronicka returned.

"That's a handsome sword that you have, Lord de Hoorne." She reached out to finger the hilt.

"Call me Peter." He looked down at the sword. "See, there's enamel on the hilt and a unicorn etched onto the scabbard. A very fine piece of work. Would you like to see the blade? It has gold chasing upon it."

"Oh, better not unsheathe it here. You might frighten someone. Where is Grote Brueghel, Peter?"

"A bit north of here, and to the east. A long day's ride."

"Do you think you and Hans will sleep here tonight?"

Bruegel looked up at Veronicka. Her cheeks were flushed beneath their tan. Was it him or Franckert that she was after? "What about you?" he asked. "Are you married?"

"Yes, but my husband wouldn't come to the party, the fool." For "fool," she used the Flemish word *zot*. "He stayed out in the fields to get the last of our grain in. He thinks it might rain. But I wouldn't miss this wedding. Tilde's like a little sister to me. And I love to dance. Oh, here come Hans and Joop with the beer. Would you like a pot of it, Peter?"

The thought of Veronicka putting the blue cloak over her *zot* of a husband rather spoiled the lustful thoughts he'd been starting to have of her. "Yes, thank you," he said evenly. "I'll have one. But there's no hurry. Don't worry about me until the first rush settles down." Bruegel watched her swaying her hips across the barnyard. What was Anja doing right now?

The afternoon slipped into evening, and then the bride and groom emerged from the barn to ride off together, the two of them mounted upon the groom's powerful horse. They weren't going far; the groom's cottage was in the woods beyond the village. Father Michel said a final blessing over them, and Gilbert Hooft cheered himself hoarse to see his son set out on his new life.

The bagpipers declared their work done and sat down to eat and drink for quite a long time. And then they, too, went on their way. A core of some forty guests and family remained, working to finish off the lees of the beer and the last scrapings of porridge.

Bruegel was ready to go home, but Veronicka was enjoying Franckert's lusty suit too much to let the big man loose. She kept luring him forward and then pushing him away, alternating her kisses and her protestations. She put Bruegel in mind of a goosegirl using a stick and a piece of bread to herd a hissing gander.

Night fell, a moonless night with low-hanging fog. The fog thickened into a steady fine drizzle, and the full company withdrew into the barn. Mevrouw Wagemaeker lit some candles, giving strict injunctions that the candles stay in the middle of the table and that nobody smoke. The barn was stuffed with hay and straw. It made Bruegel uneasy to see the candles in the barn.

Bruegel found himself seated between Gilbert Hooft and Father Michel, and again Waf placed his head in Bruegel's lap. Would this day never end? He'd eaten and drunk and sketched as much as he cared to, but Franckert and Veronicka were hidden somewhere in the shadows behind the piles of straw. Perhaps the matter between them was coming to a head.

"I remember my own wedding feast," Hooft told Bruegel, his grating voice quieter than before. "More than half of the people who were at that table are dead now, these twenty-two years gone. My wife too, God bless her memory. It was good of Tilde and my son to give us a fresh wedding. My wife would have—" Hooft broke off, ran his hands across his face, and resumed talking. "I'll tell you something, Peter. When I was young I thought there was only one life story: mine. I felt like a single arrow shooting up into the sky. But life's not solitary, it's something that everyone does. Always have done, and always will. It's like a forest with the old trees falling and the saplings coming up."

"No, no, no, it's like a wheel," interrupted Father Michel. His voice was slurred, but his tone was sharp. The beer seemed to have put him into a choleric humor. "The year is a wheel and so is a man's life. I've worked it out in detail. I have a sharp mind for figures, you know, much keener than you realize. Suppose that a man or a woman's allotted span is seventy-two years, which is twelve times six. This means that your life is like a year of twelve months, and each of these great months lasts six years."

"In what month does an infant begin?" asked Bruegel.

"In March, of course," rapped out the monk. "With the first shoots of spring. A man's midlife is his September and death comes in his February. I'm twenty-two, so I'm in the midst of my June. It's simple. How old are you, de Hoorne?"

"I'm thirty-three," said Bruegel. "So where does that place me in your cosmic year? September?"

"No, no, you're August fifteenth," shot back the quarrelsome monk. The beer seemed not to have affected his calculating abilities.

"But what if Peter's not going to live to seventy-two?" demanded Gilbert Hooft in a challenging tone. "What if, God forbid, he should be fated to die at, oh, let's say at my age. At the age of forty-two. What happens to your little wheel-year then, eh, Father?"

"Are you trifling with me?" said Father Michel, his eyes glinting pugnaciously. "You don't know what kind of prodigy you're dealing with!" He paused for a second, his lips moving. "Thirty-three out of forty-two years gone, would put de Hoorne in mid-December. With only January and February to come."

"Then I better practice my ice-skating, because I've still got a long distance to go," said Bruegel. He'd had enough of this gloomy conversation and in any case numbers bored him. "Excuse me now, but I want to find my tenant."

He got up and walked across the room to peer into the shadows of the barn. Waf followed him, curious to see what was up. "I'm ready to leave, Hans!" hollered Bruegel.

There was an answering shout, but not from Hans. The shout was in French, and it came from outside. There was a sound of men dismounting from horses, and then two Rode Rockx appeared in the barn-door, both of them armed with swords. Sensing the threat from them, Waf began violently barking.

"*Beaucoup de paysans,*" said one of them, a tall, gray-haired captain with a dissipated air. He wore a knee-length gray dress-coat over his red jersey. His face was stiff and resentful, the face of a cruel drunkard. His reddened eyes were preternaturally alert.

"Many, many peasant in one room," said his companion in heavily accented Flemish. This mustached Rode Rockx sergeant wore a stained brown leather jerkin atop his red blouse, and he had sagging leather breeches with red socks. His dark, rain-soaked cap was pulled so far down onto his forehead as to nearly cover his eyes. He looked oddly familiar; the sight of him filled Bruegel with foreboding. He tilted back his head to see out from under his cap—and now his gaze fell upon Bruegel, fixing him with his squinting eyes. "Many peasant and one gentleman," he said.

Bruegel suddenly realized where he'd seen the sergeant before: he'd been one of the three who'd attacked him, Ortelius, and Plantin after the Carnival. But the sergeant showed no sign of recognizing him. He didn't look to be the type who remembered anything for more than two or three days. Or perhaps he was nearsighted. Even so, it was a very serious thing to have this evil man here as a last uninvited guest at the wedding.

The mustached sergeant picked up a candle and held the flame high, using his free hand to make counting gestures in the air. "Thirty peasant," he said after a bit. And now he pointed at Bruegel. "Perhaps zis one tells zem to make a revolution. Zey make cabal by ze light of candle." His tone was mocking. Politics weren't really on his mind. "Quiet, if you please, your dog, *monsieur,* or I will kill him."

Gilbert Hooft came quickly to Bruegel's right side and leaned over to hold Waf by the collar, trying to shush him.

"*Demande qu'ils nous donnent a boire,*" said the captain.

"Ze *Capitaine* say you must give us two bottle of *jenever*," said the evil sergeant, lurching forward to hold the candle close to Bruegel's face. "Good Flemish gin, *n'est-ce pas*? And he forget to say that we would also like to have some peasant maiden to fuck." Bruegel made himself very still within.

"I can get the *jenever* for you," called Wagemaeker's wife, her voice shrill with fear. "One bottle is all we have. But it's a big one. Wait. I come directly." She hurried off to the house.

"Ze bride, I hope she is still here?" said the sergeant with a leer. "We can teach her ze French art of love. *Mon Capitaine*, he has been to Paris."

There was a sudden twitch at Bruegel's left side, and a slithering of metal. It was Father Michel, his face swollen with unreasoning rage. He'd snatched Bruegel's sword from its scabbard.

"Don't!" cried Bruegel. The image of the three hanged Anabaptists flashed before his eyes.

"Leave us in peace, you swine!" roared the monk, twisting away from him and stepping towards the Rode Rockx with sword held high.

"Stop it, you *zot*," cried old Gilbert Hooft, throwing his arms around Father Michel's waist. "You'll bring punishment upon us all!" The two men struggled, turning this way and that, with Waf snapping at the monk's legs. With Hooft upon Father Michel's back, there was no longer much chance of him harming the soldiers, which was all to the good. For even if both soldiers could have been killed, their deaths would have drawn more hornets from the same nest.

As Bruegel was the one garbed as a gentleman, it was his place to speak. "Forgive the Father," he called to the sergeant. "The man is intoxicated and half-mad. Please just go upon your way. Mevrouw will have the gin for you outside."

The sergeant spat in Bruegel's direction, then tossed the flaming candle onto the top of the great wall of straw that still had the bride's paper crown hung upon it. Almost instantly there came the terrible crackle of flame. Meanwhile the tall old captain lunged forwards and stabbed at the two struggling men, impaling Hooft in the back. The crowd moaned. Hooft dropped to the ground, mortally wounded.

Freed of Hooft's restraint and maddened by seeing the old man injured, Father Michel charged at the two Rode Rockx, making great sweeping slashes with his sword, the blade glinting orange and yellow from the quickly spreading flames. The battle-hardened veterans dodged him easily. And then the mustached sergeant caught the monk by the wrist of his sword hand and slit his throat with a single practiced motion. He killed the monk as easily as a butcher slaughtering a pig.

Face lit by the flickering flames, the evil sergeant looked up from his kill, his complexion gone quite red with blood-lust. Bruegel took a step backwards. He was next. The wall of straw had become a solid mass of flame. The guests were screaming and pushing their way out the door. Just as the sergeant was about to set upon Bruegel, the captain seized him by the shoulder and pulled him towards the exit as well.

The two Rode Rockx reached the door just as Mevrouw Wagemaeker appeared with the jug of gin. Whooping with exultation, the Rode Rockx seized the bottle and swaggered across the barnyard, guzzling.

For another moment Bruegel hung back in the barn, looking down at the bodies of Hooft and the monk. The monk's throat gaped like a demon's lipless mouth. His dead face wore an expression of extreme surprise. The whole blood of his body was puddled on the ground. How quickly a living man could be emptied. Numbly Bruegel took the sword from the monk's limp hand and returned it to his scabbard. If only he'd left the sword at home. The flames were raging out of control; the beams overhead were creaking. Meanwhile Waf nosed at Hooft's face, whimpering. Perhaps Waf's master was still alive. Perhaps Bruegel could save him.

"Help me get him outside," Bruegel called to young Joop Wagemaeker, who'd appeared at his side.

"All right, but let's hurry, Lord de Hoorne," said Joop. "The roof's going to collapse. And then you should run away. The Rode Rockx are talking about arresting you. To justify what they've done."

Bruegel and Joop got hold of Hooft's arms and dragged him out into the mire of the barnyard. The man's life was leaking out of him as fast as water from a broken pot. "February in September," murmured Hooft, his glassy eyes reflecting the barn's leaping flames, and then he breathed no more. The rain fell upon his still face: beading, running, and beginning to form a little puddle where the socket of his eye met the bridge of his nose. Waf flattened himself upon the ground at Hooft's side.

Bruegel seemed to see something brushing past him, barely visible from the corner of his eye. The bony, grim figure of Death. The horses in the stable began whinnying with a sound like human screams. Their hooves pounded the stable doors into splinters; they charged out and disappeared into the night. And then, with an upwards explosion of sparks, the ridgepole of the barn collapsed.

Meanwhile the peasants had organized themselves to guard the thatch of the house, lest it too catch fire. And there was big Franckert, passing a bucket from Veronicka to Mevrouw Wagemaeker on the roof. Spotting Bruegel, the farmwife paused long enough to shriek imprecations.

"You fancy piece of shit! This is all because of you and your prick sword! I hope they hang you!"

"She make sense," said the Rode Rockx sergeant, who suddenly appeared holding the bridle of his horse. "You should hang." He turned to consult with the captain, but the captain was momentarily busy with tilting up the big jug of gin.

Joop nudged Bruegel and mouthed, "Run!" Bruegel took off, but not down the track that led to the main road. He circled behind the house and through an apple orchard, quickly losing himself in the fog. After several minutes of frantic running, he tripped over some brambles and fell to the ground. He pressed himself into a thicket and lay there panting, straining his ears to hear if he were being pursued.

He heard the distant yells of the peasants, the pop and rumble of the conflagration—but nothing more. He sat up, pushed aside the thorns, and looked towards the Wagemaekers' farm. The drifting fog cleared for a minute and now the blaze could be clearly seen. Sparks and great chunks of burning straw were shooting up into the sky. The fiery chunks were like witches and demons. Then the fog came back, softening and dimming the fire like a finger on wet paint. The mist was suffused with a wonderful pink and yellow glow. Bruegel rested for a time, letting his mind go out into the colors. Gradually his heart slowed down. And now finally he had the time to weep for Father Michel, for Gilbert Hooft, for the shattered joy of the peasants' simple wedding day.

After a time he thought he heard the rustling of leaves nearby. Was someone following him after all? But the Rode Rockx would have been on horses, wouldn't they? Again a stealthy rustle. Could it be Death himself? Bruegel got to his feet and took off running again, the unlucky borrowed sword slapping against his leg.

He was looking for the road to Antwerp, but he couldn't find it. Was he heading in the wrong direction? Or perhaps he'd crossed the road without noticing? It might have been possible to mistake the road's muddy track for a patch of plowed field. He might have run right across it. Bruegel still kept thinking he heard something following him, which made it that much harder to get his bearings. Finally he decided to just head for the faint glow of Berchem and make a fresh start from there. He'd take his chances with avoiding the Rode Rockx.

Soon he could hear the drunken laughter from the inn, and with the hooting came a carrion smell, an evil, deathly stench. The fog was coming and going in thick blotches. Bruegel moved slower and more cautiously, and at the same time the ground underfoot grew slippery. Something bumped softly against his face—pale skin, ragged nails—a foot? Yes, the putrid bare foot of one of the hanged Anabaptists, slimy with the shit of the martyr's last evacuation and, it seemed to Bruegel, slightly phosphorescent with decay. His gorge clenched; and then he was bent over vomiting out all of the long day's beer and gruel.

When he could straighten up again, Bruegel backed off from the body and tried to peer ahead. The road ran right by here; he had only to reach it without running into another of the three stinking bundles that had been two women and a man. Over to the right seemed best, but as Bruegel turned that way a piece of the fog detached itself and grew solid. It came at him, low and white. He let out a low groan of terror, biting back the scream that might attract the Rode Rockx.

A long narrow white head poked at his crotch. It was Waf the dog, writhing and wagging his tail. Bruegel fell to his knees and embraced the beast, filled with fresh grief over old Hooft, dead on his son's wedding day. He clung to Waf till he could calm himself, and then he dried his face upon the dog's curly white hair.

"Waf," whispered Bruegel. "Good dog. You come home with me. I'll be your new master."

Bruegel walked back to Antwerp in the fog, Waf quietly trotting at his heels. He kept thinking about the monk's slit throat, about the puddle of rainwater on Hooft's face, and about the vile softness of the suspended foot.

Was there nothing to be done against the grasping tyrants whom blind history had placed in control of the Low Lands? Surely it was his duty to act against them. A direct fight was hopeless, but there must be some small thing he could do to help undermine the foreigners. Even as Bruegel thought this, the fog once more seemed to form the lineaments of Death. He walked faster, hoping this was a night when he'd find his Anja at home.

When the guard at the Antwerp gate asked Bruegel why he was out so late, he said that he'd been chasing after his new dog, Waf, who'd been in pursuit of a rabbit. Bruegel and Waf padded through the empty nighttime streets and made their way to the building of the Four Winds press. Waf followed Bruegel all the way up the stairs. Not ready yet to risk disappointment, Bruegel went to his room before looking in the studio for Anja. He washed himself, fed the dog some bread and water, and only then did he carry a candle down the hall into his studio, with Waf close at his heels. And there he found Anja, plump and rosy, tucked into bed and fast asleep, her hip a finely curved mound beneath the feather-bed. She looked wonderfully alive.

"I'm back," said Bruegel touching her face.

"What's that dog?" said Anja when she woke. "What a long thin head he has. Is he kind?"

"His name is Waf. He's come to live with us. They killed his owner, and they nearly killed me."

"Who?"

"The Rode Rockx. They came and burned down the barn with the wedding feast. And they were going to hang me. I have to do something to fight the Spaniards and their mercenaries, Anja."

"What a world." Anja's face was still on her pillow, with her hand pulled up next to her cheek. She crooked one of her fingers. "Come get in bed with me, Peter. You're not hungry, are you? I made us some potatoes and mussels, but when you were so late, I ate them all up." Her voice got a bit lower and quieter, as it always did when she was telling a tall tale. What a relief it was to see her— so fully herself, so fully of this world.

"Maybe Waf and I should devour *you*, little pig," said Bruegel, seized by exhaustion's giddy merriment. "Bring her to earth, noble hound!" He nudged Waf forward.

"What kind of silly name is Waf?" Anja reached out and touched Waf's back while the dog gently sniffed her face. "Waf waf waf. I'm glad you're home, Peter. I missed you."

"Where were you last night?"

"I told you. I was sitting up with Anthonie Fugger's granddaughter Elise."

"You were with Williblad Cheroo," said Bruegel. "Or with that idiot Martin de Vos. He can't paint at all."

"Maybe I was with both of them," said Anja with a shrug. "Bing bang, one after the other. Why don't you marry me, Peter? I'd be faithful to you then. But if you're not going to marry me, I need to keep scouting for a husband."

"You enjoy your intrigues so much I doubt if you'd ever stop." Bruegel sighed, taking off his clothes. "But never mind." He didn't have the heart to argue. "This day's knocked the wind out of my sails, Anja," he continued. "The feast was so happy, a crowd of faces and bodies in motion, everyone talking and looking and feeling things. And then—*zack*—all of a sudden two men are cut down by the sword. I saw Death brush by, he took a clerk and a monk. I'd just been talking with them. Can you imagine? I should do something against the killers, I say. At the very least, I should draw political lampoons."

"We die and then we burn in Hell," said Anja, her voice soft and oddly wise. "With the good big world all gone. All the more reason to dance while the music still plays. Hold me, Peter." She moved over to the far side of the bed, making room and pulling down the featherbed invitingly. Her pink-tipped breasts were wonderful to see. "What would you do for me if I stopped lying for a year?"

"Don't promise something impossible," said the naked Bruegel as he folded up some drapery by the door to make a bed for the dog. "Just try lying a little less. Keep it within some pardonable measure. Maybe I should find a way to count your lies. Sleep here, Waf. Good dog." He hurried across the room and hopped into bed with Anja. "Did anyone come looking for me today? Any business?"

"No," said Anja. But then she caught herself. "I mean, yes. That Mayken Verhulst and her daughter, Mayken Coecke, were here to look at your *Children's Games*. What an ugly pair of women they are. Very cold to me. Stuck-up *kieker-*

fretters." The word meant "chicken eaters," and was a common nickname for people from Brussels. Anja stretched her arms out towards Bruegel. "You like me better than them, don't you, Peter?"

"You're the one I have in bed. Oh, God, I'm so glad to still be alive. I wonder if you and I should make a baby. Before Death takes us."

"We'd have to marry if we had a baby," whispered Anja, molding her body against his.

"Maybe so," said Bruegel. "Maybe we should marry anyway." The real and present Anja seemed more important than his old dreams of joining the Maykens. Even so, a sense of caution held him back. "Would you stop lying to me then?" he murmured. Anja pressed against him wordlessly, reassuringly. He grew aroused. Sex was the only adequate answer to Death.

Yet even as he and Anja rocked together, with his eyes closed Bruegel could see Death, grinning and nodding and using a violin bow to saw little marks into one of his long, bare, white leg bones, keeping track of years and months and lies. Was it August or December?

Their lovemaking reached its climax. Death's jaws opened; a swirl of snow turned everything blank white.

SEVEN

THE PARABLE OF THE BLIND
ANTWERP, AUGUST 1561

Anja hurried down the morning streets of Antwerp, all in a sweat.

Against her better judgment, she'd let Williblad Cheroo cozen her into spending the night with him once again. He was such a handsome man: fine smelling, smooth skinned, most wonderfully shaped in his private parts, and vigorous far above what one might expect from someone well into his fourth decade. But now she'd slept with him once too often, and trouble was in the air. Peter's stick was full of notches.

Last fall, after Peter had nearly gotten himself murdered at that peasant wedding, his high emotions had led him to say that he wanted a child and that he might marry Anja. But immediately his long-cherished ambitions to marry that Mayken brat had flared up, and he'd started looking for a way to get out of what he'd promised. Like some hateful lean-shanked schoolmaster, he'd cut a long bare stick off a tree and begun notching it to track Anja's virtue.

Each time that, in Peter's high and mighty opinion, she lied to him or deceived him, he made a notch upon his stupid stick. He decreed that if the stick became full before a year was over, their life as a couple would end. If Peter was really so eager to find a way to duck out of his marriage proposal, why should Anja enslave herself to his whims? There were always special treats she wanted, and tiresome tasks she'd rather not do. And so the notches began.

This needn't have mattered, for if Anja were to bear Peter a child, he'd be honorable enough to marry her—and his whittled scrap of kindling could go hang. Anja dropped all the artifices she'd been using to keep herself from quickening—and waited for results. Yet all through fall, winter, and spring she remained barren. And the notches grew.

Anja visited a midwife to be bled and fluxed, but it failed to correct the disharmony of humors. The midwife said Anja and Bruegel's couplings were fated to remain without issue. Anja kept this to herself. Perhaps she could get pregnant just the same. With the coming of summer, she covertly got Ortelius's Helena to reconnect her with Williblad Cheroo, expecting this dashing man's powerful ministrations to swell her belly.

With the resumption of Anja's dalliance with Williblad, the notches upon the stick began to multiply in earnest. Initially she didn't notice the damage, for most of the time Peter didn't leave his precious stick out in the open. She'd foolishly imagined she was deceiving him about her visits to the Fuggers. But two weeks ago, with her belly still flat, she'd spied the nearly used-up piece of wood upon his bed and, in a sudden panic, she'd sworn off Williblad.

Anja walked faster. If only she could only get back to the Four Winds before Peter went into his studio then he might not notice that she'd been gone. Lately he'd been sleeping apart from her, always alone in his own room.

The problem was that yesterday the cheerful little Helena had greeted Anja in the market to press upon her a lovely fragrant magnolia blossom from Williblad. Anja had felt it only right to stop by Fugger's to thank Williblad—and the usual lustful venery had ensued. This final notch could finish her.

The street ahead was blocked by two peasants with produce-laden carts. It was a market day, and more than that, it was the day of the great fair and national theater contest known as the Landjuweel. Anja and her girlfriends had been looking forward to it for weeks. But if Anja didn't get home soon, Peter's anger would ruin the day.

The farmers' carts had locked wheels. But they were in a sanguine humor, and rather than arguing, they were laughing and taking their time, introducing their horses to each other, exchanging gossip, and now—oh, Lord—even taking out sausage and a jug of beer to share. One cart was filled with cabbages and carrots, the other with cheeses and cans of milk. The carts reached from literally one side of the narrow street to the other; they were touching the stone walls of the buildings and there was no way around them.

"Drunk bumpkins," said Anja, climbing up into the cart of carrots and picking her way across it to hop over to the milk cart.

"Little hussy," said one of the farmers. "I can smell your spice box from here."

"Pig," said Anja, and hurried down the street. She could hear drums and bagpipes in the distance. There were hundreds of musicians in town for the Landjuweel, some on their own, and some to back up the theatrical performances.

A printed piece of paper blew past. Despite her rush, Anja stopped to pick it up. Something about the shapes upon it looked familiar—yes, this was surely another of Peter's anonymous lampoons. Instead of working for money, her man had been wasting his time all this year drawing savage cartoons of the absent King Philip, of Philip's half sister, Margaret, and of Cardinal Granvelle. The Spanish Philip had appointed the Italian Margaret as the Regent of the Low Lands, and the Frenchman Granvelle was the Regent Margaret's chief adviser and the true ruler of the realm. The Low Lands was at the mercy of foreign murderers and thieves, nothing new, but this year Peter couldn't stop thinking about it.

Anja's hasty steps slowed and stopped as she studied the reckless lampoon. Granvelle was drawn in the shape of a fat, untidy hen, perched upon a nest of dark eggs. Hatching out of the eggs were—alligators like the ones Williblad spoke of?—no, these were bishops on all fours, their pointed hats like hungry snouts. A few of the bishop-chicks were up on their hind legs, pecking and scratching for—Anja looked closer—the scavenging bishops were eating little bags of gold, except for the one up in front, who'd just scratched open a burrow that held tiny people kneeling in prayer. This bishop-chick had his head cocked to one side; his cruel mouth was open in an expression of gloating triumph.

Hovering above the wattled mother-hen Granvelle was an imperial orb with a little cross on it, the cross pointing down, and poised upon the orb was a hideous, beaked Satan surrounded by buzzing, verminous demons who drizzled shit and piss upon Granvelle and the bishops. Satan held out two taloned fingers as if conferring a blessing, but instead of pointing towards Heaven, his fingers pointed down at the filthy chicken. A scroll above Satan was inscribed with some writing, not that Anja could read.

Most people thought the lampoons were funny, but seeing this one today made Anja sweat even more. Peter was flirting with death. Even to be caught with one of these drawings could lead to torture or execution. What might the authorities do to the man who took such savage joy in drawing them? Someone passed by Anja then, saw what she held, and snickered. She folded up the paper, stuffed it into her damp bodice, and hastened on her way, thinking.

The topic of the lampoon was something the coffee drinkers at the Four Winds had been chattering about for months. In January, everyone had been happy because the Flemish nobles had convinced King Philip to withdraw the Spanish troops from the Low Lands. But then the Foreigner had gotten the Pope to appoint a pack of new bishops to the Low Lands, twice as many as before. Ordinarily the local nobles were allowed to decide who became a bishop, dispensing these plum positions to family, to friends, and to the better-loved local priests. But Philip had chosen to select the new bishops himself from Spain, both as a deliberate affront to the nobles and to ensure that his new ecclesiastics would be coldhearted, fanatical, and cruel in pressing forward the madness of the Inquisition.

As part of the new order, Bishop Granvelle had become a Cardinal, the Primate of the Low Lands. Everyone hated Granvelle now, from the highest nobles down to the lowest tanners, dyers, and apostate priests.

The drawing of the praying people in the burrow had to do with the Edicts of Blood that King Philip was so zealous to enforce. One of the Edicts decreed that it was a proof of heresy for a Low-Lander to be found praying or reading the Bible with no priest present to watch over him. To pray alone was a capital crime, punishable by hanging or by burning at the stake. The less agonizing fate of hanging was for those sinners willing to confess their heresy while suffering their preexecution tortures upon the rack. Those unwilling to confess were burned. It happened to more citizens every day. Thus Peter drew the bishops clawing open the burrows.

But all this fighting and biting among the men and their laws meant less to Anja than a raisin in a pot of porridge. She'd always supposed that God, Christ, and the Virgin were too busy to notice her, just as she was too busy to worry much about them. As for the bishops and the heretics, Anja went to mass once a week, and that was enough. Why waste more time on it? What she cared about was how to hold on to Peter. And if Peter were to drop her, then where could she find another man?

A sweet little tune was coming towards her down the street. A bagpiper, a flutist, and three performers were on a cart being pulled by a pair of horses. A man stood in the cart, dressed in green and with his face painted yellow. There were flaps of blue cloth around his face and green streamers hanging from his arms. He was a flower. He swayed back and forth to the tune, looking foolish and gentle. At his side, a sweet-faced woman wearing a lady's fancy hat was pretending to pour water on him. The third actor wore a monk's robe, but with his waist stuffed with so many pillows that he was round as an apple. "Come," he called to Anja in a Brussels accent. "Come to the Landjuweel, little lady. See the Cornflower Chamber of Rhetoric perform the tale of Father Strontkop."

Anja stopped rushing and waved at the actors. Her basically sanguine temperament reasserted itself. It was going to be a fine day. She'd handle the business with Peter one way or the other and then begin the fun. She'd told Helena to meet her at the Blue Boat inn at noon. She covered the last two blocks to the Four Winds at a leisurely pace, catching her breath and letting her slick face dry. She felt more and more confident that she could bring Peter around.

There was a Closed for the Landjuweel sign on the front door of the Four Winds. Anja went in through the side door to the kitchen, which was silent and empty. Had everyone left for the festival? Beyond the kitchen lay the Four Winds gallery. As always, the sight of these walls filled Anja with pride. Peter's engravings took up nearly one-third of the space: his landscapes, his Seven Sins, his Seven Virtues, and his one-of-a-kind images like *Big Fish Eat Little Fish* and *The Ass at School*.

The engravings provided Cock with a steady income. These days there was no question of Peter having to pay rent for either of his two rooms, and they ate from Cock's kitchen, which was preferable to Anja's having to buy food and cook. Peter grumbled that he'd be in poverty forever with Cock not actually paying him any cash, but Anja pointed out that if Peter wanted money, he should find some commissions instead of frittering away his time on illegal lampoons. In any case, with free food, a place to sleep, and the occasional coins she got from her other gentlemen friends, Anja felt they had more than enough.

A floorboard squeaked by the printing presses. Jerome Cock was moving slowly about back there, seemingly not wanting to be noticed. He was greasy and disheveled, as if he'd been up all night and, come to think of it, the shop smelled of fresh ink. Of course. Jerome had been busy printing copies of Peter's new lampoon so that the Four Winds crowd could spread the seditious sheets through the full streets of this Landjuweel day.

"Where's my man?" Anja asked him easily.

"Already gone to the great square," Jerome said, grimacing and shaking a kink out of one of his long legs. "With Franckert and Waf. He's finishing up the backdrop for the Violets' performance. I wish we had a good script to match. But the plan is to make up the lines as we go along, and not to have anything written down. One never knows—a too-bold written script can end up as one's death warrant in a heresy trial. That's what happened to Peter Schuddemate after the Landjuweel a few years back, you know. Before your time as an Antwerper. Now excuse me, Anja, I have to finish tidying up so Katharina and I can join the rest of the Violets."

"Did Peter say anything about me?" asked Anja, her confidence ebbing away.

"If you want some coffee, you'll find a pot of it on the hearth," said Cock, pretending not to have heard her. He edged behind his printing presses.

Anja went around the counter and seized Jerome by the arm.

"Tell me now! Is it over?"

"He broke the stick," said Jerome, pointing to the farthest rear corner of the room, and, yes, lying there was the notched stick that had seemed so comical only a few months ago. The whittled markings covered the whole stick and it had been roughly snapped in two. Like Anja's heart. "He threw all your things out the window," Jerome was saying. "Katharina and Franckert picked them up for you."

Anja began sobbing. Her wails echoed in the big empty gallery. And now Jerome Cock was pulling a little sheet-wrapped bundle out from under the counter: her possessions, everything she owned, all she had in this uncaring city. It made a ball no larger than a pumpkin.

"I'm going right back up to my room," said Anja defiantly.

"You can't," said Cock firmly. "Peter doesn't want you here anymore. You have to move. I'm sorry, Anja. Stay with one of your friends. Or get the Fuggers to give you a room. They have plenty of maids' quarters in that great house of theirs."

"You'll pay for this," shouted Anja, looking around for something to throw. By now she knew she was defeated, but she didn't want to let Peter and this bossy stork Cock get off too easily.

"Don't, Anja. Just take your bundle and go. And here's some money Peter wanted me to give you."

It was a larger sum than Anja might have expected; the heft of the gold coins calmed her down. Cock gently but firmly ushered her out into the street.

The sun was blazing in a milky blue sky. It was starting to get hot and the streets were filling up. Anja decided to go to the Blue Boat early and have a drink. Thanks to Peter she had cash for once. This was a nice sum he'd given her. Maybe it meant he still wanted her. Maybe she could get him back.

As it happened, Ortelius's maid, Helena, had come early to the Blue Boat as well. The two friends sat together on a bench with a good view of the square. Helena hugged Anja and cried with her a little when Anja told her the sad news. After the cry, Helena shook her curls and dabbed at her great eyes. She was unworldly, sympathetic, and fascinated by the game of Love. She'd taken great pleasure in being Williblad and Anja's go-between. She imagined their affair to be the very stuff of legends. And now that Bruegel had cast Anja loose, Helena was certain that Williblad would make an honest wife of her.

Encouraged by her friend, Anja went inside the crowded Blue Boat and bought cheese, bread, and beer. Helena remained outside, guarding Anja's bundle and saving them a nice shady spot on a bench so they could watch the doings in the great square.

Present for the Landjuweel were more than a dozen amateur theatrical groups—the so-called Chambers of Rhetoric. Each group had its own colored tent upon the square. Right in front of the Our Lady Cathedral was a high wooden platform for a stage. The first performance was to start soon. Mingling with the crowds were jugglers, hawkers, groups of musicians, and scores of actors in their costumes. It looked as if everyone within three day's travel had come to Antwerp.

After the food, Anja began to feel a little better. "I bet I can move in for good at the Fuggers," she said. "Maybe you're right. And Williblad will marry me."

"My master talks about Williblad all the time." Helena giggled. "He's hopelessly in love with him. Like a schoolgirl. He'll do anything Williblad says. Williblad has only to hint that he wants to see Anja, and Master Ortelius sends me after you right away."

"Ortelius isn't interested in women at all, is he?" asked Anja. "I noticed that about him right away. Back when he and Peter were friends. Your Master's quite unnatural."

"I wonder what he'd do with Williblad if he had his wish?" wondered the innocent Helena.

"*Pfui*," said Anja. "Williblad's mine. I slept with him again last night, you know."

"What does the priest say when you confess?" asked Helena, curiously. She was still a virgin.

"He asks for details and then I have to promise not to do it again, and then he assigns me a lot of Hail Marys and Our Fathers to say," said Anja. "And I give him some alms, eh? The alms are the important thing. I never get around to saying all the prayers." What kind of God would really keep track of a little woman's slippery twitches, or of the mumbles that some panting old priest said the twitches were worth? In any case, Anja didn't fully believe in an afterlife, nor was it clear to her why Heaven would be more interesting than Hell. But she knew better than to say things like this.

Some actors draped a cloth backdrop upon the framework behind the stage, and now the first play began. The two women sat on their bench, happily watching. The Rose Chamber of Bruges was performing a play called *Elckerlyc*, or *Everyman*. The main character was named Elck, which was the same as the name of that cruel, mocking engraving that Peter had made of Ortelius.

"I've seen this play before," said Helena. "The Rose Chamber always does *Everyman*. They're a cautious bunch of stick-in-the-muds. Typical of Bruges. They're nothing like the Cornflower group from Brussels. The Cornflowers always make fun of the clergy. Two years ago they put on a play called *The Barefoot Brothers* and Granvelle himself ordered an investigation. Look, here comes Death to get Elck."

Elck was being played by a strong-voiced actor with carroty red hair. "O

Death," he bellowed. "Thou comest when I had thee least in mind!" Death was a lean-shanked fellow with his face painted white and black like a skull. He capered about, prodding at Elck like a cook testing a roast chicken. It was wonderful to see.

Now Elck was trying to get someone to accompany him on his journey to the grave. Actors representing his Fellow, Kindred, and Cousin begged off, and next he tried asking his Goods. Goods was played by a little woman padded and wrapped like a giant sack of money. She bounced from one side of the stage to the other, shrieking out her lines, and not missing the chance to give Elck a few pats on the codpiece. Perched on the bench next to Helena, Anja laughed so hard that tears came to her eyes.

But once the tears started it was hard to make them stop. She was an outcast and nobody loved her. Her parents was dead, and her stingy brother, Dirk, had inherited everything, and Dirk didn't want her back in Grote Brueghel because one of the village gossips had seen Anja sucking off the priest, who'd caught her taking a coin from the poor box to buy herself a ribbon from a peddler, and anyway the priest had been a young one, kind of cute. She was done with that Brueghel, and this Bruegel here wouldn't let her live over the Four Winds with him anymore. And as for Williblad—deep down Anja knew the half-American was too wild and sour to take her in. And so the tears came.

Helena put her comforting arms around Anja, but kept her wide round eyes turned towards the stage.

Goods went on her way, and a faint voice came from below the stage. Elck leaned over to pull someone up through a trapdoor. It was his Good Deeds, a boy wrapped all around in chains. Knowledge and Confession stepped forward to help Elck revive Good Deeds. The comedy was over, and now the play grew didactic.

"This part is a little slow," said Helena. "Are you better now?"

"Yes." Anja sighed, leaning down to dry her eyes on a fold of her dress. "Let's get up and wander around." There were a lot of men here. Time to get back to the hunt.

It was too crowded to get much closer to the stage, so they circled around the edges of the square, watching the jugglers and peeking into the tents of the different Chambers of Rhetoric. One actor had a great green dragon mounted on a pair of wheels like a wheelbarrow. It was an impressive beast, with red paper flames coming out of his mouth. Seeing Anja's interest, the man charged at her, waggling the dragon back and forth. Anja laughed and moved on. Soon they came to the tent of the Antwerp Violets, a blue-and-yellow striped affair nearly as big as a house.

The Violet Rhetoric Chamber was practically the same group as the Saint

Luke's Guild of artists, though Williblad Cheroo had become a member as well. Fortunately he wasn't here just now. The tent was filled with familiar faces: slim Hennie van Mander, fat Hans Franckert, prim Christopher Plantin, cheerful Peter Huys, Jerome Cock, and his Katharina, pretty as a tulip. And there in the corner was Waf, and next to Waf was Peter with a pot of paint, daubing at a backdrop cloth that lay upon the ground, the plump Huys working with him.

"Well, well," said Anja, walking over to Bruegel. Though her voice was hard, she felt all quavery inside. "Aren't you going to put Granvelle in?"

Peter gave her a mean look, but didn't say anything. Waf rubbed against her leg, as friendly as ever.

"I talked to Jerome," said Anja, holding up her bundle. "You're a coward not to have told me yourself."

"You saw the broken stick?" said Peter finally. "Yes? Then you know why. It's impossible for me to live with you, Anja. Jerome gave you the money, no? I hope we won't be enemies. There's nothing more to say." He turned away from her, pretending to stare down at his painting.

But Anja knew full well that Peter couldn't work when he was upset. Indeed, though she didn't like to admit it to herself, she was probably the main reason he'd accomplished so little in the last year. She felt a sudden rush of pity for him, and started to step towards him, only now her toe caught the side of one of his paint pots, and a puddle of green spilled out onto his backdrop. Oh dear, thought Anja hopelessly, everything I do turns out wrong. Waf sniffed at the wet paint to see if it might be food.

"*Stront,*" said Peter, meaning "shit." He sighed, picked up a thick brush, and began pushing the paint around, trying to work it into his picture. He wore the tired, sour expression he got when his stomach was aching. Anja hunkered down so that he'd have to look at her face, and now she could see that he was crying.

"I'm sorry, Peter," she said.

"Leave me, Anja. Please leave me alone."

"Greetings, fellow thespians!" Williblad Cheroo had just stepped into the tent, festively attired in an orange-yellow silk shirt topped by a pale blue jacket with slits in its puffy, silk-lined sleeves. "Did I miss anything?"

"Enter the whoremaster," said Bruegel, getting to his feet and drying his eyes with a quick rub of his sleeve. "She's all yours, Williblad."

Cheroo cocked his head quizzically. "Pardon me?"

"Anja's no longer living with me," said Bruegel, stepping forward, the dripping paintbrush still in his hand. "Thanks in good measure to your lechery and deceit. Aided by the message-bearing of Ortelius's nasty little Helena, and yes, I see you over there watching me, you chit." Helena scooted out of the tent, leaving Anja alone with the angry men.

"Why be jealous of me?" said Cheroo sarcastically. "You, Peter, you're sup-posed to be the great artist."

Though this seemed an odd thing to say, Anja knew why Williblad said it. In his heart of hearts, he really did wish he could be an artist. It was a secret side of Williblad that Peter couldn't understand.

"Bested by a pet monkey," said Peter cruelly. "By an intriguer and a fop."

This hit home. Like so many flashy men, Williblad had little self-confidence. His face grew flushed.

"Blind pig," he snapped, stepping closer to Bruegel. "If you'd paid more attention to your woman, she would have stayed at your side." Well said, thought Anja.

"Lackey," said Bruegel and made a quick motion with his brush, daubing a great green squiggle across Cheroo's fine raiment. The assembled artists burst into laughter at Williblad's shocked expression. Most of them were on Bruegel's side anyway, and they found it heartening to see one of their fellows do literal battle with his brush.

Anja clapped her hands in delight. It was thrilling to see two men fighting over her.

Williblad's pride was sorely wounded. His eyes blazed up in such a way that Anja feared deadly violence. He had a short sword at his belt, and she knew that he practiced fencing in Fugger's courtyard every day. Better act now before it was too late.

Anja pushed past the laughing onlookers to position herself between the two men. "Leave Peter alone, dear Williblad," she said. "He's not himself today. Come outside and I'll help you clean up." She took Williblad's hand and kissed it, hoping to salvage some of his shattered pride.

Though Williblad let himself be led outside by Anja, he had little to say. He was quite unmanned by the humiliation of being laughed at by the gathered company of the artists' Guild. And Anja's kisses and whispers did nothing to lighten his mood. Perhaps he didn't really care about her at all. Perhaps the greater part of his attraction for her had stemmed from the fact that she was paired with Bruegel. Offering but the surliest of farewells, he went hurrying back towards Fugger's house to hide his face and to change his precious clothes. It was all Anja could do to keep from joining the others yelling insults and mockery at his back.

Exalted by the rich storm of emotions, Anja and Helena soon repaired to the Blue Boat for another beer. Martin de Vos and Frans Floris appeared and attached themselves to the two women. De Vos was wearing leather pants with a plump codpiece, a green tunic with enormous sleeves, and a pointed little green cap with a pennant in it, the pennant bearing a picture of the Crucifixion. Floris wore shiny high-heeled shoes, white silk stockings, red-and-white striped breeches, a white silk jacket covered with silver brocade, and a huge floppy gold hat like a pancake.

At a fair like this, gossip rode horseback. The two men already knew about Anja and Peter's breakup and about the scene with Williblad Cheroo. They seemed bent on linking up with the unattached girls. Anja fobbed off de Vos on Helena and focused on Floris. The famous painter was gouty, married, and over forty, but he was still a man of some possibilities. Before they'd been talking five minutes, he'd asked Anja to model for him. After the beers were gone, they all drank some clove gin from Floris's silver flask, and then the foursome pushed their way closer to the stage.

The official theme of the plays for this Landjuweel was supposed to be *"Wat den mensch aldermeest tot conste verwect?"* meaning "What awakes a person the most to art?" The Rose theater group had simply ignored the theme and trotted out their *Everyman*, but the other groups had new plays more or less related to the topic. The Cornflowers of Brussels were on next.

The Cornflowers fully lived up to their reputation for irreverence. Their play was about a young man named Strontkop who wants to be an artist but whose father makes him become a priest. Nevertheless Strontkop keeps on drawing. His bishop tells him that his art is permissible only if he will paint religious scenes that the church can sell to pilgrims. But Strontkop wants to paint naked women. Unable to think of a way to find models, he hits upon the expedient of getting sinful women to undress for him inside the confession booth.

On the stage, the women and Strontkop were mostly hidden by the mock confession booth, but the priest's arm motions were clearly not those of a man drawing. He was pulling himself off. Complications followed, and at the finale, one of the women's boyfriends showed up in the confession booth and farted in the priest's face, the fart simulated by a great blast of bagpipe music. The audience became riotous with glee.

"They're crazy," wheezed Floris, wiping his eyes and weakly gesturing towards the Our Lady's bell tower. "Granvelle's watching from that window up there." Anja leaned back and, sure enough, framed in a window halfway up the tower was a red-robed dark-faced figure with two grim priests at his side. For the first time since this morning, Anja remembered the lampoon that she'd stuffed into her bodice. She wondered if Granvelle had seen it yet.

"It's time for you and me to get into costume, Frans," said de Vos. These two painters were members of the Violet Chamber as well. "We're the play after next."

"What's the Violets' play called?" asked Helena.

"The Blind Leading the Blind," said Floris. "I fear the title's an apt description of our process of composition. We're painters, not poets."

It was early in the evening by the time the Violets' play started. The backdrop was lovely, with a city scene on the left half and on the right a landscape with cattle, peaked barns, a little church, and part of a pond. Anja's spilled paint had been turned into a bush. The painted city was Antwerp, and the frontmost building was the Schilderspand, where the St. Luke's Guild painters showed and sold their work.

The first person on stage was Bruegel himself, dressed as a peasant cowherd with a spoon in his hat, glassily staring up into the heavens and moving about uncertainly near the painted pond. He was supposed to be blind. He walked right up to the edge of the stage and a few people shrieked, thinking he would fall off. But at the last minute he stopped and shouted out his line.

"Lost and afraid am I. Who can lead me hence?"

Franckert appeared from the right, also dressed as a blind peasant, with his felt hat pulled down to completely cover his eyes. "Poor man, I hear your cry. I'll help you to your goal." Like Bruegel he spoke a kind of blank verse.

"I seek to be a painter," said Bruegel. "Safe in the Schilderspand."

"I saw a painting once," said Franckert. "Or held it in my hands."

"Then be my guide," said Bruegel. He and Franckert felt around for each other for a minute, making little noises to aid themselves, and then, finding each other, they embraced.

"Badslow is my name," said Bruegel.

"Fatleg to your aid," replied Franckert. "I'll come and be a painter too." He paused, looking confused. "Dear Badslow, is it day or night?"

"I deem it day," said Bruegel, throwing his head yet farther back. "I feel God's sun. Fatleg, you are a blindling too?"

"As blind as you I'm not, Badslow. Or maybe more." Franckert groped about in the air. "Which way the Schilderspand?" Receiving no answer, he raised his voice. "Help these blind herdsmen find true art!"

Jerome Cock and Williblad Cheroo appeared from the city side of the stage, Cheroo in front and Cock following with one hand on Cheroo's shoulder. They too were blind. Each of them was carrying a stretched canvas.

"Foppiano I, a daub by craft," sang Cheroo, using the music of his voice to suggest an Italian accent. He held up his canvas so the audience could see it: a mostly blank rectangle with some fresh clumsy pink paint marks in the curved shape of a naked woman. "What think you of my work, Quickmake?"

Cock felt around for the other's canvas, then knelt and sniffed it. "You have employed good paint, my Lord."

"You see the Lord?"

"I see Him in the small."

Cheroo squinted sightlessly down at his picture. "Methinks it is a country scene of Venus."

Cock stuck out his tongue as if to lick the canvas, then stopped, thinking better of it. "I'll make a fake," he said, holding up his own canvas, which was blank.

Cock pressed his canvas face-to-face with Cheroo's wet canvas, set the two down on the ground and rolled back and forth on top of them with great kicking of his long legs. He pried the pictures apart and held them up; they were smeared in roughly identical patterns. Offstage a bagpipe made a low hissing sound.

"I hear some art!" cried Franckert, leading Bruegel over to Cheroo and Cock. "The sound of hue!"

"Instruct us in the painter's skills," said Bruegel.

Cheroo began gabbling a complicated theory of painting in his fake Italian accent; it sounded like a passage he'd memorized from a book, but it was coming out cadenced like the rest of the play. In the audience, Anja and Helena looked at each other and laughed. The four blind men began marching around on the stage, each with his hand on the shoulder of the man in front. Foppiano first, followed by Quickmake, Fatleg and Badslow last, the four of them walking and talking ever faster, repeatedly on the point of falling off the edge of the stage, finally coming to a stop before the city side of the backdrop.

"Are we at the Schilderspand?" asked Bruegel.

"I think perhaps," said Cheroo, groping around until his hand fell upon Bruegel's face. "Though this piece be indifferently flat." He gave Bruegel's nose a vicious tweak, and Bruegel kicked at him.

There was a flourish of pompous bagpipe music and Floris and de Vos appeared from the left, with Floris dressed like a bishop and de Vos dressed like a gentleman's servant. Both characters were, once again, blind. De Vos was leading Floris by the hand. Floris was staggering as if from drink. Anja had seen Floris finish off his flask of gin, so she couldn't be sure if his unsteadiness was real or part of the act.

"I robbed his church, my eyes were slit in two," said de Vos to the audience. "And now I lead the Primate."

"I'm Greatstink, patron of fine art," said Floris. "Ho, Sliteye, see what the new men do."

"His Worship needs a portrait limned," said de Vos to the four blind artists. "Who can agreeably oblige?"

"I show the inner man," said Franckert, feeling his way over to the backdrop and producing a stick of charcoal from his clothes. With a few quick motions, he sketched something upon a blank area of the Schilderspand wall. It was a fat face with horns.

Floris reeled over and pressed his nose against the backdrop. "You draw Beelzebub?" he cried in rage.

"Oh no, Your Worship," said Franckert. "It is a cow."

"Let's try another man," said de Vos. "You there, Foppiano, canst paint a mythic scene?"

"A chemist knows that gold is meet to make more gold," said Cheroo, holding out his hand. Floris presented him with two large, gold-painted paper disks. Cheroo stuck one to the wet paint of his pink-smeared canvas and held it up. "Behold Danaë with Zeus's shower."

"A mate to this fine work I'll make," said Cock, snatching the second gold disk from Cheroo and sticking it to his own canvas. "Your Worship has a diptych."

"Blind fools," thundered Floris after feeling the pictures. "Show me the life of Christ! You, Badslow, canst paint me that?"

Bruegel held out his arms. "The living God is with us now. Paint Him I would, Greatstink, could I but see." Bruegel knelt in prayer, and there was a sudden rippling in the backdrop, accompanied by a trill of flutes.

A radiantly clad woman appeared though a gap: Hennie van Mander holding an Earth globe from Plantin's shop. "Wisdom arrives!" she declaimed in a high, clear voice. Greatstink and Sliteye recoiled, but the other blind men reached out towards Wisdom. The backdrop rippled again. A second woman appeared, a thin blonde with her hair in a mass of braids, clothed in garments of floating white gauze. "Here's Truth at your side!" she sang. The blind men's faces were wreathed in smiles. They rubbed wonderingly at their eyes.

Out in the audience, Anja's own vision grew red with anger. The second woman was none other than Mayken Coecke, the snippy little daughter of Peter's old master. The one he'd done his *Children's Games* painting for. What was Mayken doing here? She lived in Brussels now, so what business did she have poking around Antwerp, worming her way in!

Bruegel was the first of the blind men to get to his feet.

"O Truth!" he cried. "You make me whole!" He stumped across the stage and embraced Mayken, who—let it be said—tried to wriggle away before Peter was ready to release her. He clung to her like a beggar after a merchant, the slobbering *zot*.

Mayken was the reason Peter had left Anja! For her precious estate! Anja's rage grew to a fever pitch. She had to do something! Looking frantically around the crowd, she spotted Mayken Verhulst, the little Mayken's big-nosed mother, smiling and applauding. Go and yank the old bitch's hair out?

The church bell happened to toll just then, drawing Anja's attention upwards. Granvelle and his two priests were still in the window of the bell tower. How would Peter and his Maykens like it if Peter were burned at the stake, eh? Anja thrust her hand into her bodice, pulled out the lampoon, and elbowed her way through the crowd, heading for the church, not letting herself think about what she was doing.

A young priest was guarding the tower stairs, but Anja was able to convince him that she had something important for Cardinal Granvelle. The priest led her up the stone steps and stayed to listen.

Granvelle was sitting on a chair by the window, his expression calm and insolent. "What is it?" he asked after looking Anja up and down. He had more of a French accent than Anja had expected. His teeth were black and his breath smelled bad.

"Have you seen this, Your Worship?" asked Anja, handing him the lampoon. Though she was all in a turmoil, her voice came out fluently. She was bound and determined to finish what she'd begun. Peter had scorned her for a silly little sixteen-year-old with a four-story brick house. He was going to pay. "I know who drew it."

Granvelle looked at the picture for quite some time, with the three priests goggling at it over his shoulder. " 'Behold, this is my son with whom I am well pleased,' " he read from the inscription above Satan's head. He gave a short laugh. "At least someone likes me." He gazed up at Anja, his face big and calm, waiting for the name.

"Peter Bruegel," said Anja. In her mind she heard the thud of a hanging, the crackling roar of immolating flames. "What will you do to him?"

Granvelle raised his eyebrows, his expression showing mild mockery. "You wish to see him punished? I wonder why?"

"He lived with me and he won't marry me," said Anja. "He's left me for another woman and he's put me out into the street."

Granvelle only smiled. So Anja played her trump card. "The thing is, Your Worship, we were raised as brother and sister. Peter told me it was all right, but I'm afraid it's incest, eh?"

"How do you mean 'raised as brother and sister'?" asked Granvelle in a weary tone. "Under ecclesiastical law, incest means that you have one or more parents or grandparents in common. Is that the case, my child?"

"No, Your Worship," said Anja, partly disappointed and partly relieved. For the first time since seeing Peter embrace young Mayken, she wondered about the wisdom of what she was doing.

"Peter Bruegel," mused Granvelle, studying the lampoon once more. He glanced up at the three priests and pointed out the window. "That's Bruegel at the left end of the stage with the young blond woman. The one who played Badslow. Go fetch him for me. Do it publicly and with force. It can be a sign to the citizens that they've gone far enough."

Anja turned to leave with the priests, but Granvelle stopped her. "Wait here and see what happens. Perhaps you'll be surprised."

"I—I don't want Peter to know it was me," said Anja softly. She was starting to feel more and more uncertain about informing on him.

"A little schemer, aren't you? When he comes, go a few steps higher up the stairs. You can eavesdrop from there. I'm sure you know how. Meanwhile let's watch out the window."

As the actors left the stage, the three priests appeared and seized Bruegel. In his drunkenness, Floris swung at one of them, so they knocked Floris to the ground and kicked him till he lay still. And then they dragged Bruegel through the angrily grumbling crowd. Peter looked anxious, bewildered, and sick to his stomach. By now Anja was truly regretting what she'd done. She crept up around the next turn of the tower stairs as Peter's footsteps approached.

"Mijnheer Bruegel," said Granvelle's voice. "We meet again. I was disappointed by the painting of the manger that you sold King Philip. But I see you are a man of diverse talents." Anja heard a rustle of paper. "An angry little sparrow tells me that you drew this lampoon."

Bruegel mumbled something indistinct.

"Oh yes, you did. Now that it's pointed out to me, I recognize the style. I've seen your engravings of the Seven Sins, of course. Fine work, that, quite collectible. Some might think it an honor to be lampooned by the new Bosch. Perhaps I'll spare you. But don't waste my time by having the Inquisitors torture you. Admit that you drew this."

"Very well," said Bruegel, his voice clear and strong. "I did."

"And your friend Jerome Cock was the printer, no?" said Granvelle. "Or was it Plantin?"

"I printed them myself," said Bruegel quietly. "I live above the Four Winds gallery. I crept down and pulled the prints last night. Jerome knows nothing of it. It's my crime alone."

"Hmm," said Granvelle. "A loyal man. Too bad you don't have loyal companions. I wonder—if I were to spare Cock, what might you do for me?"

"Burn at the stake, I suppose," said Bruegel in a flat, melancholy tone. "Life's a foolish jape. I'll be well out of it." It crushed Anja to hear him brought so low. Peter was a man of delicate humors, too easily brought to despair. A fine and sensitive man, an artist. How could she have handed him over to this torturer? She fought back a little wail of woe. Peter mustn't know that she was here.

"Despair is a mortal sin, my son," Granvelle was saying. "Don't consign yourself to Hell." He fell silent so long that finally one of his priests spoke up.

"Shall I take him to the dungeon, Your Worship?"

"I think not, Father," said Granvelle. "Our Bruegel is a valuable man. King Philip and his court love Bosch's pictures exceedingly well. Now that I have this Bosch-bird in my net, why not pluck him for the court? Could you paint for me, Peter?"

"Paint what?"

"Scenes of Hell, of course. Death, torture, and destruction. Things to the Spanish taste."

"I could do that," said Bruegel. "Although it's a style I grow weary of. I'm the first Bruegel, not the second Bosch." Anja smiled a bit to hear her Peter arguing his case. When it came to art, he'd press his views till Judgment Day.

"Don't quibble," said Granvelle. "Painting Hell is better than going there."

"Agreed," said Bruegel, readily enough. "But how much would you pay me?"

"Listen to the man," said Granvelle with a hard chuckle. "He's spared from execution and he wants to talk terms! I'll provide the very best in painting supplies, pay you something reasonable, and you'll have—free room and board." Granvelle chuckled again. It wasn't a pleasant sound.

"Do you mean a dungeon, Your Worship?"

"An artist needs light," said Granvelle. "And a bit of comfort. No, my fine fowl, you'll have a gilded cage. I'll give you a room at the Regent Margaret's provincial palace in Mechelen, halfway between Antwerp and Brussels. I'm there regularly to visit the Regent. I'll keep a close eye on your progress."

"I'm to leave Antwerp?" This seemed to disturb Bruegel more than anything that Granvelle had said so far. Anja knew him as a creature of habit who hated to break his rituals of work. "For how long?"

"Let's try something like a year to start with," said Granvelle. "And then— who knows. We might send you into exile, or keep you on as Margaret's court painter, or mayhap hang you by the neck until dead. It depends on your actions."

"I'll be quite alone," said Bruegel, musingly. To Anja's ears, he didn't sound all that sad about it.

"You made your last woman very angry with you," said Granvelle. Anja cringed and crept a step higher up the stairs. "Anger's a terrible sin," said the Bishop, raising his voice. "Come down here, little sparrow, and atone," he cried sarcastically. "Tell your Bosch-bird that he's forgiven."

Anja would have run up the stairs to the top of the tower, but one of Granvelle's priests darted after her, caught her, and dragged her down to the landing. Peter's expression when he saw her was unforgettable. Solemn and wounded and sad.

"I'm sorry!" shrieked Anja, and clattered down the stairs.

EIGHT

DULLE GRIET
MECHELEN, APRIL 1562

Bruegel leaned close to the great oak panel, highlighting the ribs of another killer skeleton. *Zack, zack, zack.* This one was holding up a sword, getting ready to cut off the head of a kneeling man. Beside the man a long pole rose up into the smoky sky, topped by a headless corpse set out for the crows. Bruegel drew his lips back into a cruel death's-head smile, imitating the skeleton the better to depict it.

He picked up a scrap of eggshell with a bit of umber pigment in it and added the color to his little brush. His expression changed to one of prayerful resignation as he brushed a spiky shock of hair onto the condemned man's head. Bruegel always merged with the subject at the other end of his brush, be it a skeleton of Death's army, a pig, or even a tree.

He selected another eggshell and dabbed some black pigment onto his brush. It was the finest, richest of ivory blacks, made from burnt walrus tusk. Granvelle had told him to spare no expense in purchasing his supplies. His pittance of an artist's fee was another story. Franckert would have laughed to hear how little Bruegel was being paid—not that Bruegel had seen Franckert since being seized by Granvelle. Franckert, Jerome Cock, and the rest of the Four Winds group had done their best to distance themselves from their friend, fearful lest they too be tarred with the black brush of sedition.

With quick little pecking motions, Bruegel painted the image of a wagon wheel onto the bottom of the corpse at the top of the pole, getting all the angles just right so that now the wheel seemed to be beneath the headless body, supporting it high above the observer's point of view. He was pleased with how the pole had come out, he'd played a little trick with the perspective, drawing the pole's bottom as if it leaned towards the viewer, and tilting the wheel at the top so that the pole seemed to lean away.

"Crooked," he muttered to himself, thinking of the odd, reversed-looking gallows that he and de Vos had passed in the Alps. Executions were part of a Crooked World.

He noticed that his lips were dry and cracked. He'd been working solidly since dawn, without a stop, trying to finish off his two big new pictures. His tongue was sticking to the roof of his mouth. He set down his brush and drank from a pitcher of water.

The shock of the cold liquid sent a shiver of pain through his belly, but he'd learned to ignore the familiar ache. He let his eyes range over the painting of the army of skeletons, probing for any slight weakness and finding none. *The Triumph of Death*. It was a wonderful piece, some five feet by four feet in size, with a fine arabesque flow to the dun, figure-filled landscape, his best yet, rivaled only by the other big picture he'd been working on. It had been nice having two paintings in progress, that way there was always some spot dry enough to paint upon. His other picture was by a window, facing outwards to catch the sun. He'd added the last touches to that one an hour ago. Waf was lying in the sun on the floor beneath it. Seeing Bruegel's break in concentration, Waf got up and walked over for some petting. Many days, Waf was the only soul whom Bruegel spoke with.

Last August, Cardinal Granvelle had taken Bruegel captive at the Landjuweel. Under the guard of Granvelle's muscular priests, Bruegel had been given the opportunity to empty out his rooms above the Four Winds, with the priests examining each piece of paper to see if it might be some form of lampoon. This took the better part of a day. There were a lot of papers, and the priests were intent on rooting out every evidence of free thought, setting most of the papers aside to be burnt.

Throughout this ordeal, Jerome Cock, his fellow artists, and the coffee drinkers had stayed in the gallery below, gossiping among each other. One would have thought they barely knew Bruegel. The one and only brave soul who'd come to stand by Bruegel's side was his spurned old friend Abraham Ortelius. Having heard of Bruegel's trouble, Ortelius mounted the narrow Four Winds stairs unbidden, presented himself to the priests, and offered to keep in storage whatever possessions Bruegel couldn't take to Mechelen with him. In the face of the prying questions the priests pressed, Ortelius had stood firm, describing himself as nothing more and nothing less than a devoted personal friend.

Shamed over his spitefulness, Bruegel had wept to hear it. He'd embraced Ortelius warmly, and it had soothed both their hearts. It made no sense for Bruegel to blame Ortelius for what Williblad had done with Anja, nor was it fair for Ortelius to harbor long resentments over a satirical engraving made partly in jest. The two swore to each other there could be no thought of ever falling out again.

Once the rooms had been emptied, the priests burned the bulk of Bruegel's papers in the street, then carted him and Waf away. Ortelius had been the only one to wave good-bye.

That same night Granvelle had installed Bruegel in a second-floor room in the Regent Margaret's provincial palace, a great red stone building right in the little walled town of Mechelen. And Bruegel had been set to work painting Hell.

For eight months now, Bruegel had lived and worked in the one large room. Its high windows looked out onto the market square, with a view of the stubby tower of the St. Rombold's Cathedral. He was allowed to roam the palace and its courtyards, and occasionally the streets of Mechelen, but for all of fall and winter and spring he hadn't been allowed out into the countryside beyond the town wall.

The Regent Margaret spent most of her time off in Brussels, running the affairs of state for her absent brother, King Philip, but once a month or so, she and her retinue would come to Mechelen for the hunting, and for special meetings with her inner circle of three, the so-called Consulta. The Consulta consisted of the Walloon Graaf Berlaymont, the viciously antiheretical Viglius van Aytta, and Cardinal Granvelle: Archbishop of Mechelen and Primate of the Low Lands.

The Regent Margaret and her ladies-in-waiting spoke only Italian. Bruegel had very little to do with them. This was fine with him; he'd disliked Margaret at first sight. She was tall, fruity-voiced, and imperious. She had a lantern jaw and something of a mustache. Bruegel gathered that her three main interests were collecting taxes, suppressing heresy, and killing foxes. It was hard to believe that so unwomanly a creature could be a wife; in any case her supposed husband was back in Parma.

For company other than Waf, Bruegel had the artists of Mechelen from whom he bought his supplies, the Flemish palace retainers and, best of all, occasional visits from Ortelius and from the Maykens. Nobody else had the courage to visit.

Mayken's ostensible reason for coming to the palace was that she was designing a tapestry for the armory hall. But she seemed equally interested in visiting Bruegel. As for young Mayken, well, she enjoyed the day in the country. She seemed to think of him as a comical older companion, something like an uncle. Despite her continued casualness with him, Bruegel was beginning to feel the stirrings of romantic love. Young Mayken had reached a womanly age. Now and then, she'd look at him a certain way, with her lips red and full and kissable, and he'd nearly burst with longing. But other times she seemed so uninterested that Bruegel wondered whether his own feelings were real, or whether he only imagined them, driven on by his ambition for a place at the head of the Coecke workshop. Certainly life would be simpler if he and young Mayken were truly in love, and Bruegel sincerely wished for his life to become simple. Every hour wasted on emotional turmoil was an hour taken away from his time to paint.

In all honesty, his hopes for Mayken were a goodly part of why he'd ended his affair with Anja. Yes, Anja's constant lying and unfaithfulness had been troubling. He'd gone so far as to map out his unhappiness as notches upon a stick. But the morning he'd actually broken the stick over his knee had been the same morning that old Mayken—stopping by the Four Winds on her way to the Landjuweel—had told Bruegel that he would not be allowed to court young Mayken at all if he continued to live in sin with a serving maid.

So he'd gotten rid of Anja, Anja had betrayed him to Granvelle, and the odd result was that, all of a sudden, his professional career was going very well. Yes, he was a prisoner in Margaret's palace, but he was painting better than ever before.

One of the interesting features of this palace was its Wonder Chamber which held a remarkable collection of imperial artworks. Thirty years ago, the palace had been the home of Margaret's great-aunt, another Habsburg Regent named Margaret, and this earlier Margaret had been famed for her art collection, including Jan van Eyck's flabbergasting *Arnolfini Wedding,* which was still here on display. Bruegel had spent many hours studying the century-old masterpiece: the little Bruges couple in their room full of worldly goods, the man in a great black hat and the woman with her hand laid upon her rounded belly, the intricate chandelier in mathematically perfect perspective, and on the rear wall of the room a convex mirror with a tiny image of van Eyck and a friend, enshrined within his painting forever. As it happened, Bruegel had brought his own convex mirror with him from his Antwerp studio; it was an ever-fruitful source of inspiration, a little horn of plenty.

It made him happy that his *Fall of the Rebel Angels,* the first picture he'd finished at the palace, was now on display in the Wonder Chamber with the van Eyck. Though Granvelle had been the one to commission and to pay (stingily) for this work, he'd left it on display here in the palace for the time being. The picture had been quite a sensation, and a few of the visiting nobles had approached Bruegel with requests that he paint their portraits, this despite the fact that *The Fall of the Rebel Angels* showed some hundred chimerical demons composed of fantastic mixtures of human and animal parts. Did the highborn really think that Bruegel would depict them any differently?

How ordinary were the intellects of most nobles. Though in the past Bruegel had sometimes resented his own lack of an inheritance, he was in some ways fortunate to have poverty goading him on. This said, he was indeed working much too hard. With no Anja to distract him, he worked from dawn to dusk every day.

Stepping back to his *Triumph of Death,* Bruegel turned his attention to a pair of lovers, a man playing the lute for a buxom woman in a revealing green gown. Behind them a skeleton was sawing at a fiddle. The woman seemed not to hear Death yet, but the red-haired lutist did; he was rolling back his eyes to look over his shoulder, visibly wondering at the source of the dissonant tones. A little spot of brightness was still needed. Bruegel added a fluffy feather to the woman's hat, delicately stroking in its fronds with paint of white lead. He liked returning to this woman; she looked like Anja.

Ah, Anja. Alone here in this cold stone room, he often thought of the women he'd known. First there was Anja, then some other girls from the village, then the business with old Mayken, then two artist's models he'd known in Naples, a cook's assistant in Antwerp, and then Anja again. His merry playmate. Had he been right to break the stick? Yes. Anja had gone about with other men, had betrayed him to Granvelle, had done her best to get him hung. He'd never go back with her. It was preferable by far to direct his desires into the future, towards a vision of a pliant young Mayken, bursting with the juices of life.

Even so, Bruegel did still think of Anja sometimes, and not always in a vengeful or a lustful way. Come what may, she was part of his past life, and he was somewhat concerned about her welfare. Yesterday he'd gotten particularly disturbing news of her from Ortelius.

For his pretext to visit Bruegel in Mechelen, Ortelius had sold the court a set of his maps, and perforce he had to come several times to get them installed in the palace library. Each time his day's short business was done, he came to Bruegel and the two of them went and sat in the Wonder Chamber, which Ortelius adored. The first time they'd been alone together, they went over all their apologies again, almost as if each of them were afraid the other might have returned to coldness. Ortelius expressed his remorse for having instructed his Helena to pass messages from Cheroo to Anja, and Bruegel for having harshly caricatured Ortelius in his *Elck* engraving. The affair with Anja would have ended in any case, and the engraving was but ink. It was enough. The wound was healed, and things were as comfortable as before.

Isolated as Bruegel was in Mechelen, it was quite an extraordinary delight to converse with his old friend. Yesterday Ortelius and Bruegel had comfortably chatted for several hours, mostly about Antwerp. It seemed that although Williblad Cheroo had initially found Anja a station in Fugger's employ, she'd too insistently pressured Williblad for a lasting commitment, and the slippery Cheroo had ended her job. She was presently working as an artist's model and living with Martin de Vos. Thinking about this made Bruegel terribly uneasy. Anja was, when all was said and done, something very like a sister. Modeling could be a risky business; some models ended up as trulls in the Street of Stews. And in a port town like Antwerp, loose women died young of the pox. De Vos was no prize, a drunkard with a violent temper—although he was a safer haven than none at all. Might he be induced to marry Anja? It would help Anja's chances if she had a dowry. Bruegel sighed, trying to think of ways to provide her with one.

His own purse was exceedingly thin. And, confined as he was to the city walls of Mechelen, there was little he could immediately do for Anja. It wasn't clear when he'd be allowed to move away from the provincial palace and get back into the great river of life. Granvelle was equivocal about how long Bruegel was supposed to work for him. Upon seeing Bruegel's first painting, Granvelle had mentioned the possibility of Bruegel becoming a permanent court painter here, which seemed a grim fate indeed. Hopefully Margaret would have enough of Bruegel once she saw the new painting drying by the window. He smiled to himself, imagining her expression when she'd seen it. Margaret was expected here later today.

Shortly after Bruegel had finished *The Fall of the Rebel Angels*, Margaret's interpreter, an epicene citizen of Brussels named Gustav Meerman, had told Bruegel that the Regent would like a portrait—with Margaret posed sitting upon her favorite horse, perhaps with a battle scene in the background. Bruegel had said that although he didn't paint formal portraits, he'd make some kind of picture of Margaret. Being something of an aficionado of Bruegel's work, Meerman had an inkling of how the picture might turn out, but he'd kept the negotiation going to see what would happen. A fee had in fact been agreed upon, although Bruegel misdoubted that Margaret would pay him even this small amount. The Habsburgs were notorious for failing to honor their debts. That had been all the more reason to paint the thing exactly as he saw fit.

There was a light footstep and a familiar figure appeared at Bruegel's door. It was William the Prince of Orange, accompanied by his bodyguard, Grauer. William was a slight, graceful nobleman who sat on Margaret's Council of State. He had short reddish hair and clean, manly features. Also known as William the Sly, he made a habit of coming up to Mechelen whenever Margaret did. William wasn't part of Margaret's inner Consulta, and he wasn't really welcomed by her at all, but he too had a spare palace in Mechelen, and he liked to dog Margaret's movements, the better to stay informed about what the rulers of the Low Lands were doing.

Prince William had the winning manner of a natural leader, and Bruegel had taken to him right away. It was no secret that William the Sly wanted the Habsburg rulers out of the Low Lands, indeed it was he who'd played the largest part in convincing Philip to withdraw the Spanish troops last year. William knew something about art—his family's palace in Brussels held a magnificent collection—not that the Prince spent much time looking at it. William knew of Bruegel's engravings and lampoons, and he relished the artist's reputation for unconventional thought.

"Ho, Bruegel," said William, looking at *The Triumph of Death*. "I'm back. What mad dreams you must have! You can wait in the hallway, Grauer." Grauer was a hard-looking man with short gray hair and a cropped gray beard that blended seamlessly into the hair upon his head. His sharp blue eyes examined Bruegel and the room, and then he stepped outside and closed the door.

"When I work this hard, I sleep quite soundly," said Bruegel. "Though, God knows, I grow weary of my daily descent into Hell. Care to have a seat and watch me paint, Prince William? I wouldn't mind some company."

"You've grown thin and wan," said William. "There's too much black bile and not enough blood in your humors. Work no more today! Come out to the polders with me. I'm going to fly my falcons. That's the sole attraction of this turnip town. The game birds are more plentiful than near Brussels. We'll bag some partridges, and we'll take a heron from the clouds. You can use the fowl as studies for your monsters."

"You can bring me outside the walls?" said Bruegel. "I'm your man. Can my hound come, too?"

"If he doesn't spoil the hunt."

"Oh, he's well-behaved. Aren't you, Waf?" Bruegel had become uncommonly fond of the dog. He washed the paint off himself, laid a wet cloth over the bits of shells with their egg-yolk-mixed pigments, and found his cloak. Meanwhile William lounged on the cushions of Bruegel's bed, looking around with noble ease. His gaze kept returning to *The Triumph of Death*.

"You devil!" exclaimed William just as they were ready to go. "I've been thinking that your painting reminds me of something and now I have it. The great tapestry in the palace dining hall! The battle scene with Margaret's father!"

"*The Victory of Charles V Against the Ottomans,*" said Bruegel blandly. "A handsome composition. I suppose it's possible that I was inspired by the handling of the figures in that landscape."

"You devil." William was one of the few nobles with the perception and wit to match his exalted station. Most of those who gathered at the palace were at the mental level of dogs.

Or perhaps not even dogs, thought Bruegel, smiling down at the prancing Waf, who sensed they were going for a walk. Bruegel himself could have barked with delight at the prospect.

William's falconer was a brown-faced man named Bengt Bots from the village of Valkenswaard. He carried a large, hooded falcon perched on a heavy glove, while his son, also named Bengt, carried a slightly smaller bird. The hoods were like little leather helmets, with green billiard cloth sewn over the eye holes. Each helmet had a tuft of cock feathers on its crown, garnished with colored wool and bound with fine brass wire. The birds were held firmly in place on the falconers' gloves by straps that hung from their legs; these straps were called jesses. There were little bells tied to the birds' legs as well. Waf looked like he wanted to sniff at the falcons, but Bruegel scolded him back, and the dog understood.

"Where do you get your falcons?" Bruegel asked the falconer as they walked through the Mechelen streets. Since he had quite a bit of time to pass until Margaret's arrival, William had decreed that today's expedition would be on foot rather than on horseback.

"I trap them," said old Bengt. "When they're migrating, my boy and I tie some live pigeons to the ground for bait. We rig up bow nets over the pigeons, you know what they are? No? A bow net is like a tunnel with a bow of wood holding one end open. You have a cord tied to the bow, and you tug the cord to flop the net closed. Now, to make sure the falcons notice the pigeons, you tether a couple of sharp-eyed, noisy birds nearby. Shrikes or crows. We call them the council. When the falcons fly over, the council makes such a shriek that the falcons notice the pigeons. And when *we* hear the council, we know it's almost time to pull the cord."

"These two are peregrines," put in William, gesturing at the falcons resting on the men's gloves. "A mated pair."

"One is smaller than the other," observed Bruegel.

"The tiercel," said William. "Falconry's word for the male. He's a tiercel because he's a third less in size. Like me compared to the Regent. Not that we're mates, thank God."

"Margaret's drunk every night, isn't she?" said Bruegel. "And she hobbles. She must have gout." He bobbed his head forward and backward, imitating the way the Regent moved when she walked.

"A close observer," said William with a chuckle. "Have you been painting her portrait, then?"

"After a fashion," said Bruegel. "In fact it's done. You didn't see it; it was the one facing the window."

They made their way through the gate in the city wall, with William off-handedly giving the captain of the guard his word not to let Bruegel flee. It was the first time in eight months that Bruegel had been outside the city walls. They crossed the moat and went out into the marshy fields, a group of seven including William, Bruegel, the two Bengts, Grauer, another of William's guards, and a kennelman with a tan spaniel and a black-and-white pointer named Getrouw. Waf trotted along with the other dogs, stopping often to sniff at things, delighted to be in the fields.

Bruegel was every bit as thrilled as Waf. It was a day of sun and clouds, the fresh air like perfume in Bruegel's nose. A flock of tiny meadowlarks swooped up from the ground and perched in the green-budded branches of a chestnut tree. As the others walked on, Bruegel paused to stare up at the larks, rejoicing in the world's beauty. You could spend a lifetime painting and never come close to the richness of God's world—all around, all the time, free for any man or woman to see. He'd been cooped up for too long, inventing dream worlds from within a stiff, stupid castle. Now a cluster of brambles caught his eye, the bowed thorny canes eared with the tiniest of exquisite green leaves. What perfection in every detail. His heart swelled with such love for the Earth that he dropped to his knees and kissed the ground. Nobody noticed his actions. He rooted about in the dirt with his fingers for a minute, filled with a sense of pity for himself. How hard he'd been working, and for so long, with never a day in the country. In the distance he heard Waf barking. Tingling with pleasure at his body's large motions, Bruegel ran across the fields to catch up.

"How goes your courtship of Mayken Coecke," the falconer's son asked Bruegel as he fell back into step. He was a pale-faced lad with a shock of long, dirty hair. "I see her around Brussels. A swift little fish. She's young for you."

"How do you know about me and Mayken?" asked Bruegel, uneasy to hear young Bengt Bots speak of her. The boy was very close to Mayken's age.

"Gossip's the great pastime in any palace," said the boy. "A maid told me that Mayken and her mother have come to visit you twice. She's seventeen and you're—"

"Thirty-five," said Bruegel. "Not so old. Next year when Mayken is eighteen—well, we'll see. I've known her all her life, you know. I was her father's apprentice. I carried her in my arms when I was your age."

"Painters have apprentices?" said Bengt. "I'd never thought about it. That's the way one makes it a career?" Unlike his brown-skinned father, young Bengt was pale skinned. His hair was so fair as to be nearly white, and his eyes were the lightest possible shade of blue.

"What did you think, then?" said Bruegel, puffing himself up a bit. "Painting's a subtle craft, a kind of alchemy. We gather up bits of dirt and rock, grind them with egg and oil, saw down a tree for a plank to paint on, and the end result is a magic window into a timeless world."

"I like to draw," said Bengt simply. "I wish I could draw as well as Mayken's mother. The old Mayken."

"You're certainly well-versed on the Maykens," said Bruegel, feeling a bit miffed. He wondered if this pale stripling might be a rival. The similarity of Bengt's age to Mayken's played upon his persistent fear that the girl would think him too old.

"They've come twice to Prince William's palace about his wife's new tapestries," said young Bengt quite innocently. "The old Mayken is drawing the cartoons and the young Mayken is searching out threads of the right colors. I brought out the falcons for old Mayken to sketch."

"She draws well," agreed Bruegel. To his relief, Bengt's thoughts seemed not to be focused upon the girl. Even so, he felt a need to assert himself, to crow and to shake out his peacock tail. "But I draw better. You can visit my studio here if you like."

By now Mechelen was but a spiky gray blur on the horizon. Their view was filled by a bushy meadow and a great marsh in a bend of the river Dijle. This was more like it. City far, nature near. Again Bruegel hunkered down to touch the ground. Waf trotted over to lick his face. Waf understood.

"As long as you've got him, tie him for now," the older Bengt told Bruegel. "He might frighten the falcons when I take off the hoods." Bruegel tethered Waf to a tree. From Waf's point of view this was quite an injustice. His whines followed Bruegel as he walked off. Bruegel ran back once to reassure the dog, then went out into the meadow with the others.

The Bengts took the hoods off their falcons. The blackish blue peregrines stared sternly, their eyes large and cold beneath their prominent brows. Their fiercely hooked yellow beaks had little black markings like mustaches. Their breasts and legs were dappled with fawn spots. Pale feathers covered their legs like comfortable pantaloons, but their feet were powerful weapons with long talons.

The falconers unwrapped the jesses from their gloves and tossed the birds up into the air. The pair circled, feinting at each other and letting out a few metallic *hek-ek-ek* cries. The tiercel was playful, circling around the larger peregrine and getting her to chase him. Slowly they spiraled upwards with their tiny ankle bells ringing. The bells had slightly different tones, making a clear and plangent sound up in the pale blue sky.

"Will they come back?" Bruegel wondered. He certainly knew that he wouldn't come back if Granvelle were only to throw him free.

"They'll be high up there circling and waiting," said young Bengt. "And once we flush some game they'll drop like stones."

The kennelman loosed the pointer Getrouw, and after nosing around the field for a while, Getrouw froze into position by a particular thicket, one paw raised and her nose and tail stretched out. Meanwhile old Bengt Bots stared upwards, gauging the position of his peregrines relative to the wind. When everything seemed right, he made a gesture, and the kennelman sent the other dog, the spaniel, crashing into the thicket to flush the game.

With a clatter of wings, half a dozen partridges shot out of the bushes. Bruegel shaded his eyes and peered upwards. The peregrines were already plummeting downwards, wings nearly closed, with the tiercel slightly behind. There was a *thunk* and a puff of feathers, and one of the partridges dropped to the ground. The falcons dug into the air with flexed wings, coming out of their dive. Old Bengt gave a sharp whistle, and he and young Bengt each produced a lure consisting of a dead pigeon at the end of a long cord. They swung the pigeons around their heads, and the falcons glided over, easily catching the lures. The falcons fed for a bit upon the pigeons' breast meat, taking their pay, and then the falconers withdrew the lures and cast them back up into the sky. Meanwhile the spaniel brought back the slain partridge.

"Look it over," William said, handing Bruegel the dead bird. "Not a mark on it."

"How does the falcon kill it?"

"With this," said old Bengt puffing out his chest and running his hand along a line down the center of his breast. "*Paff!* It must be like getting hit by a cannonball."

"And it doesn't hurt the falcon?"

"Not at all. Look, Getrouw's at point again. Unleash the spaniel!"

Again there was a whir of partridge wings and again the peregrines dropped from the sky. This time they each killed a bird, and old Bengt rewarded them by letting them crack open the dead lure-pigeons' skulls to eat the brains.

"That's what they like best," said young Bengt to Bruegel out of his father's earshot. "Frankly I find falcons a bit disgusting." He wiped a bright spot of pigeon blood from the back of his fine, pale hand. Clouds were blowing in from the east, covering the sun.

Watching a few more cycles of the hunt, Bruegel began to get the queasy feeling he sometimes had—the feeling that everything stood for something else, that the world was God's great painting, with each figure standing in for some quality or humor, as above so below. His first thought had been to see himself as the falcon and the partridges as paintings. But perhaps the falcons were Granvelle, and Bruegel a partridge. Or was young Mayken the partridge, and Bruegel the heartless predator from the clouds? It seemed particularly apt that a falcon struck its prey with its chest. To kill someone by striking her with your heart.

It commenced to rain all of a sudden, and they lost sight of the peregrines in the low clouds. Bengt whistled them down, and he and his son slipped the hoods onto them, feeding them bits of pigeon breast all the while. William's guards loaded some eight or nine dead partridges into a pouch.

"Now for our heron," said William. "We'll work our way down to the river."

"Can I fetch Waf now?" asked Bruegel. It pained him to imagine his sole regular companion tethered in the rain.

"It should be all right," said old Bengt. "We'll be flying the falcons right out of the hoods for this last flight, so they won't have a chance to get spooked. And if your galumphing Waf flushes a heron for us, so much the better. You may have to lead him off when it's time to lure my falcons back."

Waf was so happy to see Bruegel that he put his feet up onto Bruegel's shoulders and barked into his ear. Waf ran off across the meadow in joyful leaps, catching up with the other dogs. The falconers raised their hooded birds high while Waf romped past. The three dogs disappeared into the rushes, prancing and barking. There was a huge splash, and Waf's head appeared in the rain-pocked gray water of the river. He was swimming out towards a little sandbar. A minute later he was on it, hugely shaking. He disappeared into some rushes on the far side of the bar.

"Ready?" said old Bengt, his hand poised over his falcon's head.

"Ready," said young Bengt.

And then a great blue form came gliding up from the river rushes, a male heron with a six-foot wingspan, Waf beneath him barking. The falconers unhooded their birds and threw them free. The heron saw the falcons coming, and dove down into the shallows of the river. The peregrines circled, but didn't dare to attack the wise old bird, who stood cocking up his beak at them. Meanwhile the spaniel had flushed another male heron, not so large as the first one. This bird, less cunning, headed towards the men, and the falconers waved their arms to shoo him up into the sky. He disappeared into the low clouds and the falcons followed, crying *hek-ek-ek*.

The falcons' bells rang from the clouds, there was a hoarse screech, and the heron came dropping down like a fallen angel. He landed in a heap, with his neck folded back onto his body, not twenty paces from where Bruegel stood. The dying heron's wings shuddered a few times. The falcons came gliding down like buzzards, and the Bengts drew them off with the lures.

Grauer snapped the heron's neck. "What a fine fowl, eh?" said William the Sly. "Almost like a coat of arms, the way he's twisted round. They're quite toothsome, properly roasted, and the liver's a specific for gout. I'll present him to Margaret and invite myself for dinner. She should be in her palace by now."

On the walk back, William fell into step with Bruegel.

"Are you planning to draw any more of your lampoons?" asked William. "I'm entirely in favor of them. They give our people strength."

"No," said Bruegel. "Granvelle would recognize my pen. He said that if there were a next time, I'd go to the dungeons, or hang, or take a dagger in the back. It's bad enough to be exiled to Mechelen."

"You could flee right now, if you like," said William, watching his reaction. "I certainly wouldn't try to stop you."

He throws me into the air, thought Bruegel. Should I fly? But what kind of career could a fugitive hope to lead? Better to stay the course, to follow the path likeliest to end at the four-story brick studio in Brussels.

"I'm hoping to get Granvelle's permission to leave," said Bruegel finally. "So that I can live in peace. Perhaps he'll grant it tonight, after I hand over my two new pictures. Granvelle gets *The Triumph of Death* and Margaret gets the other one. I think she expects a court portrait." That was another reason not to flee. Bruegel had to see Margaret's reaction to the picture. He chuckled and began imitating Margaret's graceless, flat-footed walk again.

"What did you paint?" asked William.

"You'll see," said Bruegel, the laughter tumbling out of him. "Margaret can't say I'm not delivering full value. It's a very fine work in the style of Bosch, perhaps not as good as *The Triumph of Death*, but in any case a masterpiece."

"This sounds most diverting," said William. "All the more reason for me to be in the palace this evening. I'll be your witness lest Margaret do something rash."

"She's swallowed me, and if I pain her, let her shit me out," said Bruegel, growing serious again. That was his real plan for freedom. To goad Margaret into sending him away. He'd been here eight months, had made three large paintings for almost no money, and in all fairness it was time for Granvelle to let him go. He and William walked in silence for a while.

"I happened to mention you to my friend Filips de Hoorne the other day," said William as they drew near the walls of Mechelen. "He spoke well of you. He said he knew you as a lad, and that it was his father who first recognized your talent."

"Graaf Filips de Hoorne!" said Bruegel. "Yes, I was a foundling at his family's Ooievaarenest estate in the village of Brueghel." Not for the first time, Bruegel silently wondered if Graaf Filips might be his natural half brother. It seemed unwise to mention this speculation to Prince William, no matter how easy were the Prince's manners. Nobles had no sympathy for commoners who pretended to their estates. Were Bruegel to press a claim William's companionability would disappear in a flash.

"Graaf Filips's father was exceedingly good to me," continued Bruegel.

"When my foster family threw me out, the old Graaf sent me for three years of schooling with the Brothers of the Common Life in s'Hertogenbosch. The same school that Mercator, Erasmus, and Hieronymus Bosch went to, I'll have you know. I learned Latin and how to write."

"And did they teach you to draw?" asked William.

"Yes and no," said Bruegel. "The Brothers frowned upon drawing, particularly of the kind I like to do. So I used to crawl up to a certain high attic to practice; the Brothers were all too fat or old or lazy to get to it—or so I thought. The attic had a window and fine smooth plaster walls that were perfect for drawing upon. I wasn't the first boy to have drawn on those walls, indeed it was the old drawings that gave me the idea of inscribing my own there. Some of the drawings were by Master Bosch, I'm sure of it. Quite wonderful. Demons and bagpipes and owls—the man loved to draw owls. And there was a great fish lying on its side with smaller fish falling out of its mouth. I later used that for one of my first engravings. That attic was the best part of my schooling."

"Those Bosch drawings would be worth something now," said William. "I have a triptych by him in my palace, you know. Do you think his drawings are still in that attic?"

"I know they're not," said Bruegel. "The Brothers beat me till I erased them. One day there was a strapping young Brother who followed me up to the attic, and he didn't like what he saw—I'd covered one whole wall with drawings of my own, including the Brothers as a pack of shitting monkeys. The Brother beat me and I had to whitewash over all the drawings, even the ones by Master Bosch, a terrible loss to cover the Master's lines. I was so angry about it that I left the school. And this leads us back to the good old Graaf de Hoorne, for it was he who paid the fee for me to become Master Coecke's apprentice in Antwerp. Did you tell Filips about my new *Fall of the Rebel Angels*?"

"Um, that's your painting in the Wonder Chamber—of the big pile of demons?" said William. Though he did have the ability to see a picture when it was in front of him, most of William's waking thoughts were about politics. "I failed to mention it. But I told Filips about the lampoons. He said you should pay him a visit sometime. Say, look there, Margaret's flag is flying from her palace. She's arrived."

Margaret and her retinue had ridden their horses into the front hall of the palace to dismount. The gawky, sour-looking Margaret was just draining a tall stirrup cup of French wine. Margaret's favorite lady-in-waiting, a fawning little woman named Giulia, was leaning against the Regent's side, laughing merrily. Some grooms were leading the horses out, with Margaret's interpreter, Gustav Meerman, calling out Margaret's instructions in his mannered, high-pitched voice. He was wearing a foppish gold velvet suit with a great ruff collar. Meerman smiled and waved at Bruegel; over the months they'd become friends.

William the Sly made an extravagant bow and had his second guard carry the heron forward.

"A gift for Her Highness," said William. "The liver is an excellent physic."

Meerman put the words into Italian for the Regent. Margaret talked in Italian for quite some time, finally gesturing dismissively at William and saying something sharp. As she talked, one of her retainers took the heron and carried it off towards the kitchens.

"The Regent says her health would be best served by your absence, William the Sly," said Meerman, enjoying himself. "And it pains me to tell your lordship that the Regent says you're as persistent as shit on a boot sole." Meerman grinned and made some fluid, mollifying hand gestures. "The Regent is of course grateful for your faithful attendance, but she requests that you not stay on after dinner. She has important matters to discuss in private with the Cardinal."

As if conjured up by the mention of his name, Cardinal Granvelle popped out of a darkened doorway in the hall's paneled wall.

"Behold the voice and the eye of the Low Lands," he said, seeing William and Bruegel. "I was a bit concerned when I heard you'd left the city walls."

"Like a well-trained falcon I return to Your Worship's glove," said Bruegel. Over his months here he'd learned to adopt the manners that covered over the essentially hellish nature of life at court. "I have good news. My two new paintings are finished, one for you and one for the Regent. I pray that my patrons might view them in the day's remaining light."

Granvelle spoke to Margaret in Italian. She nodded curtly, held out her silver cup for a refill, then turned and stumped up the great staircase, with the rest of them following along. Bruegel rushed to get up ahead of the pack, wanting to put his studio in readiness. But when he drew even with Margaret, Meerman lightly caught hold of his elbow, lest Bruegel precede the Regent. In his eagerness for the coming climax, Bruegel had nearly forgotten protocol.

"Careful there, Peter," said Meerman. "Her Royal Highness is choleric. That's why she's walking so fast." Meerman was puffing a bit for breath and he made a show of swinging his arms. As always, his breath was sweetened by a clove. "You look quite used up, poor lad. I'm very keen to see your two new paintings. I've told you before how I admire your *Fall of the Rebel Angels*. You have such a refined way with surface textures. I've heard some call your work vulgar, but when all is said and done, we're Flemings, not Italians, eh? You show the world as we see it. You're worth any ten classicists."

"That's good to hear, Gustav," said Bruegel. To speak of art in Flemish here was like drinking water in a desert. When would he have his dream of a real studio in Brussels with a wife, children, an apprentice, and fellow artists all around? "You know, I thought of you while I was working last week. I added two chained monkeys to one of the paintings. You and me."

"How very true," said Meerman, quickly taking the meaning. "But unlike you, I find that chains agree with me." They were almost even with Bruegel's open studio door.

"Please bid the Regent to wait out here for a moment," said Bruegel, all but trembling in his excitement. "I'd like to turn my pictures to the light for the best effect."

"Very well," said Meerman.

So Margaret, Meerman, Granvelle, William, Grauer, and Margaret's court waited in the long palace hallway while Bruegel stepped into his studio and closed the door.

Alone in the studio for the last time with his new pictures, he felt a mixture of sorrow, relief, and exhaustion. These two paintings had been his life for these last few months and now—now they were to be handed over to a cold intriguer and to a royal ninny. Well, at least he'd be free of them. The paintings were, after all, windows upon an unhappy world, a place to be well out of. Not that the images were really what stuck in his mind. His sense of the pictures was rather a feeling of color and line and craft, a memory of ten thousand and ten careful decisions made. Although the pictures would go, the craft would travel with him.

He pulled the easels into place so that the setting sun would fall upon the great painted oak panels. There was another good-bye to say—not to these pictures but to the spirit of Hieronymus Bosch.

Although he hadn't mentioned it to Prince William, back in that high attic in s'Hertogenbosch Bruegel had sometimes had the feeling of being with Bosch's shade—and this feeling had been with him again for the past months. Yes, Master Bosch had been at his side, helping him paint *The Triumph of Death* and *Dulle Griet*. The Master was a dry, cool spirit, more passionate about edges and hues than about the affairs of men. In his long life, Master Bosch had come to know the folly of the world so fully that the knowing had turned his blood as cold and gray as watered ashes.

There was an impatient knock on the studio door. Though inspiring, Bruegel's months with Bosch's ghost at his side had been anything but pleasant. He was ready to get out and live again. Bruegel swung the door open and let his rulers in. "This is for Your Worship," he said to Granvelle, *"The Triumph of Death."* He turned to Meerman. "And this one is for Her Highness. It's called *Dulle Griet."*

Dulle was Flemish for "dull," or "slow-witted," while *Griet* was a nickname for Margaret. The picture was five feet by four feet, just like the *Triumph of Death.* It showed a fantastic Hell landscape with a large female figure in the foreground: a greedy dullard, face blank with stupidity, carrying a great basket of stolen treasure under her arm, and marching across the panel in search of more. Following in her wake was a small army of henchwomen, pillaging Hell and tormenting the demons. Though Bruegel had managed to stop himself short of making Dulle Griet look precisely like the Regent Margaret, everyone in the studio seemed to divine his intended meaning.

The hubbub was extreme; for a moment it felt almost as if the demons, rampaging skeletons, and plundering women had tumbled out of the paintings into the room. The Regent was shouting in Italian, and it was taking Granvelle and little Giulia's best efforts to keep her from striking *Dulle Griet* with a poker that she'd pulled out of the fireplace. Though Bruegel dared do nothing, to see this filled him with anger. What a common, witless lout is Margaret beneath her robes, he thought, standing by. What rash thing might I do if she succeeds in striking my picture?

William the Sly was doubled over with glee, and many of the Regent's courtiers were laughing as well. Margaret's rage veered now from the picture towards the artist himself. Gesturing savagely with the poker, she shouted a phrase at Bruegel over and over again. Meerman's face floated up to Bruegel like the apparition of an urbane, satisfied demon.

"She says something like, '*Kwaad ei, kwaad kuiken,*'" drawled Meerman. The Low Lands proverb he quoted meant "Bad egg, bad chicken." The *Dulle Griet* was a bad egg, and Bruegel was a bad chicken. Or maybe it was the other way around.

"Ask her if I can leave Mechelen now," said Bruegel coldly. This was what he'd been planning for. To so madden Margaret with anger that she'd throw him out. The delicate thing was, of course, not to be hanged. If only he could keep his temper and not push things too far.

The Regent's answer was quick and to the point. She wanted Bruegel out of her palace right away and forever.

"Ask her if I can have my fee," snapped Bruegel, his pulse pounding. It seemed that he himself was in a state of rage. These fools had imprisoned him for nearly a year, working like a slave with never a rest, and this ignorant scarecrow dared to threaten him and his painting with a poker?

"I'm not going to ask her that," said Meerman. "I'd as soon stick my prick into a meat grinder. Talk it over with the Cardinal. Whoops, it looks like Dulle Griet's about to leave. Good-bye for now, Bruegel. I'm looking forward to studying these magnificent works. But I didn't have time yet to find our two monkeys."

"Right there," said Bruegel, pointing to a little barred round window in a Hell castle in the *Dulle Griet*. Behind it were a pair of monkeys, one staring out the window at the viewer, and the other holding up a glass.

"That's me," said Meerman, raising his hand in a world-weary drinking gesture that was also a farewell salute. And then Margaret and her retinue swept out of the room.

Bruegel, William, Grauer, and Granvelle remained. William had flopped down on the cushions of Bruegel's bed, and Granvelle was attentively examining *The Triumph of Death*. Grauer stood quietly off to one side, his rough face as unreadable as a leather shoe. As for Bruegel, he simply tried to catch his breath.

"A masterpiece," the Cardinal pronounced after a few minutes. "The figures, the landscape, the deviltry. Ah, how brief indeed is our earthly span. I'm going to ship this one to the imperial court in Madrid. King Philip will be very pleased. He loves executions. Yes, perhaps we should hang you, Bruegel." The last sentence was delivered in the same level tone as the others. Bruegel's stomach dropped. Granvelle showed his black teeth in a grimace that was far from being a smile. Now he turned his attention to *Dulle Griet*.

"I'm sorry that the Regent doesn't like her picture," said Bruegel deciding that the only thing for it was to press on. Surely Granvelle had no real plan to execute him. Best to ignore the unpleasant remark about hanging and to play his own game as hard as he could. "Do you think you could pay me for both the paintings?"

From the bed, William let out a whoop of laughter.

"*Dulle Griet* is a good painting," persisted Bruegel, his importuning voice sounding strange to his ears. "Her Highness should like it. But I'm afraid she's taken it personally. Which of course is not at all what—"

"Money is the Devil's excrement," said Granvelle sententiously. He was looking at a demon in the *Dulle Griet* who was spooning gold out of his ass to rain it down upon the marauding band of women. He gave Bruegel a cold look. "Yes, I suppose I could pay for this one as well. I could keep it myself or perhaps send it east to the imperial court in Vienna. Or to Prague. Certainly the Regent doesn't want it in her palace. No more than she wants you here, Bruegel. It seems you've set yourself free." Granvelle opened the silk purse that hung from his waist and began counting out coins.

"I can leave?" said Bruegel. "I can travel?"

"Leave right away and travel far," said Granvelle, glancing up from the money. The act of counting out coins seemed to be making him more annoyed. "Good riddance to you. I granted you mercy and a measure of hospitality, and in return you chose to insult our Regent. If you linger here, I'll have you flogged. Stay away for six months at least, and by then the Regent Margaret will forget. She and her brother, King Philip, have more pressing concerns than the insolence of an artist. It would be too ridiculous to hang a clown."

"Thank you, Your Worship," said Bruegel in a small voice as Granvelle handed over the coins. He was stung to hear Granvelle speak so coldly. Somehow he'd expected quite a bit more praise. Yes, even though he'd knowingly been as outrageous as possible, deep down Bruegel had unreasoningly expected that Margaret and her courtiers would love his new works purely for their craft and beauty, with all quibbles about proprieties and meanings set to one side. It was painful to grasp his folly. The insides of his stomach felt blazing hot. "I'll leave the paintings here for you," he said wretchedly.

"One more thing," said the angry Cardinal. "Although I may continue to buy your work, you should harbor no illusion that we're friends. I wish that you continue to paint—but only so that I can collect your pictures. I have no interest in seeing you prosper or be happy. Far from it." His growing fury made the Cardinal's French accent stronger than usual.

"I meant no disrespect, Your Worship—" began Bruegel, hating the wheedling tone in his voice.

Granvelle cut him off with an abrupt gesture. "One last word of advice. When you do return, don't move back to Antwerp. The place is a quagmire of sedition and heresy, with many of the conspirators your close friends. I won't indulge you for a third time. Mock us again and, rather than the pomp of a public execution, you can expect the ignominy of an assassin's knife." And with that, the Cardinal left the room.

"What a sack of shit he is," exclaimed William from Bruegel's bed. "Why don't you paint a picture of me killing him? Like David and Goliath." From the corner of the room, Grauer gave a low chuckle.

"Are you offering me a commission, Prince William?" asked Bruegel, struggling to regain his wits. A true artist was always ready for business.

The proposal seemed to strike William by surprise. He'd been speaking rhetorically. "Me buy a painting? My palace is already full of them. I told you I inherited a masterpiece by Bosch. Buy a new painting? It's my wife who's the art lover; her taste runs to miniatures. Me, I've more of a head for practical things." Nevertheless, Bruegel could see that William was tempted. If nothing else, the scene with Margaret and Granvelle had leant Bruegel some glamour.

"But could you really paint David slaying Goliath?" mused William. "I'd like to see David wearing my colors and Goliath in a bishop's miter. Or perhaps the giant should be the Foreigner."

"That's too much like a lampoon," said Bruegel. "Weren't you listening to the Cardinal just now? He's on the point of hiring a footpad to slit my throat. Let me paint you something subtler, Prince William, with nothing so overt as to put either of us into danger." Bruegel paused, and inspiration struck. How wonderfully the recent fracas had stimulated his mind. "I'll paint you a picture of David victorious, yet with no David in it. But, never fear, should Granvelle see or hear of this new work, he'll feel most unwell."

"How do you mean no David?" asked William.

"I'll paint you the suicide of King Saul," said Bruegel. "He was David's greatest enemy."

"Will it be a picture with a fine great army in it?" asked William.

"More soldiers than you've ever seen," said Bruegel. "In a picture small enough to fit into my pouch. Your wife who loves miniatures will find it brilliant. And you can explicate the veiled meaning to your friends."

They worked out the terms of the commission for a miniature painting to be delivered in six months. Working at a small scale would be perfect, as Bruegel would be on the road. For his part, William the Sly undertook to give Bruegel some money and a horse from his Mechelen stables. As William was handing over the money, there was a knock on the door. Grauer opened it and let in young Bengt Bots.

"Is this a good time to visit, Master Bruegel?" asked the fair-skinned boy.

"The last chance," said Bruegel jovially. His fear of Granvelle had evaporated during his pleasant negotiation with William. And, best of all, he was free to leave Mechelen. On a horse of his own! "It seems I'm leaving the palace today. Come in, my boy, and I'll grant you a few quick words about how masterpieces are made."

"You painted that?" said Bengt, staring at the *Dulle Griet* in awe. "How long did it take? I'd give anything to learn to paint like you." Bruegel beamed at him. The boy had a good head on his shoulders.

"Easy there, Bengt," said William. "I need you for my assistant falconer! Let's go down to dinner, Grauer. I don't want to miss the table talk. It'll be rich. Bengt, when you're done with your art lesson, you can take Bruegel over to my stables and let him pick out a horse. Farewell, Peter, come see me in Brussels when your exile's done."

That evening, Bruegel rode north atop his new horse, with Waf walking along at the horse's side, now and then veering off to smell something. Though he was tired and shaky from his ordeal, he had a fat purse and a heavy sack filled with sketches and the fine pigments left over from his three paintings of Hell. Yes, Hell was behind him now, and he wasn't going to paint it again.

Although Bruegel's destination was Amsterdam, the road thither led right past Antwerp. Granvelle had warned him not to stop there, but as he approached his former home, he got the notion of spending a night. At first he wasn't quite sure why.

"Would you like to visit Antwerp, Waf?" Bruegel asked his dog. In his months of living alone with Waf, he'd picked up the habit of trying ideas out by way of these one-sided conversations. It was a habit he knew he'd have to drop now that he was out in the world again. But right now it was just him, Waf and the horse on the road together. So he talked to his dog.

"You answer, 'Ja, Mijnheer'?" said Bruegel, cocking his head at the dog. "Very well then, if you insist, we'll stop with Abraham. He has a nice back yard that you can lie in. And maybe I'll find Anja and give her a good talking to? Eight months I've been locked up thanks to her. That little Helena will know where to find her. And, how about this, Waf, maybe Anja cries and takes off her clothes and gives me a roll in the hay to make up for what she did." Saying all this out loud, Bruegel wasn't sure if he meant it. It didn't sound like a good idea. But even so, at dusk he found himself riding through the Antwerp town gate.

The familiar smells and echoes of Antwerp's streets brought back so many memories: of arriving here to apprentice for Master Coecke; of returning from Italy; of welcoming Anja from Grote Brueghel; of the Carnival evening when the robbers had attacked; of the time he'd walked home with Waf from the peasant wedding; of the Landjuweel. The sounds of his horse's hooves echoed off the walls like the months flipping by. The past was over.

Now he was approaching Ortelius's house. With a mixture of surprise and relief, Bruegel realized that the thought of Anja left him cold. His future lay with young Mayken. There was a certain smell about the girl, a certain look—she was the field he wished to till. Yes, he'd stay away from Anja tonight, he'd do his six months of exile, and then he'd wing his way to Brussels.

But, tying up his horse in Ortelius's stable, Bruegel's mind still wasn't quite at ease. Even though he didn't want to see Anja, he felt he had to do something for her. That no good de Vos would never marry her. Anja needed a sum to attract a man with a future.

So that night Bruegel entrusted Ortelius with a third of his new-gotten money as a dowry for Anja's use. And this was enough to free him from that particular Hell.

NINE

THE SERMON
OF JOHN THE BAPTIST
ANTWERP, OCTOBER 1562

Ortelius sat comfortably in his study, examining a Roman coin in the green-stained afternoon light that slanted through his round-paned windows. The coin showed Nero, the last of the Caesars, and dated from thirty years after the death of Christ. It was a fine piece, purchased in Rome. According to the dealer, the coin was from a treasure trove that a peasant had plowed up: a hundred gold and five hundred silver coins sealed into a little red pot. Holding the coin close to his face, Ortelius imagined the fingers that had touched it, the eyes that had seen it—the slaves, the merchants, the persecuted Christians, Nero's brutal legionnaires—perhaps this coin had passed through the hands of some aging soldier who'd seen the earthly face of the Savior. Deep in his peaceful reverie, Ortelius was wholly outside of time.

But now there was a distant clamor, a strange dog barking in the hallway. Rome began slipping away, and when curly-haired little Helena came twittering into the study, the talismanic coin had become but a worn disk of metal. "It's Peter Bruegel to see you, Mijnheer Ortelius." Her eyes were quite round with excitement.

Bruegel was lively and of a sanguine color, quite unlike the wrung-out pale wretch who'd passed through Antwerp six months ago. Waf pranced at his side, beating his long tail. Bruegel wore a broad-brimmed red hat and a brown wool cloak. A big square satchel hung from his shoulder. And if Ortelius had any lingering fears about the state of their friendship, Bruegel's broad smile allayed them.

"Amsterdam was good to you, Peter?" said Ortelius, springing to his feet to embrace his friend.

"It was fine," said Bruegel. "A peaceful city of deep canals. The Hollanders have wonderful veal dumplings. I sold some drawings to a fellow named Herman Pilgrims. Ate a lot. Painted. Looked at ants. And, as you suggested, I spent some time with the scholar Dirk Coornhert. He's going to write verses to accompany some of my engravings. I see you have my *Two Monkeys* well installed." On his way north, Bruegel had made Ortelius a gift of a little foot-square piece he'd done in Mechelen on a leftover bit of panel: an image of two chained monkeys with Antwerp in the background.

"Ah, and there's my convex mirror too," continued Bruegel. "I'll come back and fetch that as soon as I'm properly settled in Brussels. Easy there, Waf, you'll sweep everything off the shelves. How are things with Anja, Abraham?"

"I set aside the amount you gave me," said Ortelius, slightly miffed to have Anja be the topic of Bruegel's very first question. What about Ortelius's own travels to Austria this winter, his longings, the compromises he made to keep up his position in the world? Or what about the growing wave of the Reformation in Antwerp and Ortelius's role in it? Frankly, Ortelius cared not a fig about the slatternly troublemaker Anja. And talking about her stirred up all his old guilt about having indirectly helped her betray Bruegel. But of course he didn't mention any of this. "And I had Helena tell Anja a small sum is there for her dowry. To tell you the truth, I haven't thought about Anja in months. Helena!"

Helena reappeared so quickly that she must have been right outside the open door.

"Mijnheer Bruegel is worried about Anja," Ortelius told her. "What's the latest word?"

"It's all right for me to speak of Anja to you, Mijnheer Bruegel?" said Helena with a timorous air. "You're no longer angry with me?" Evidently Bruegel had at some point vented his choler at her over that tiresome business with Williblad. Couldn't it finally be forgotten? What had Williblad seen in Anja? wondered Ortelius, not for the first time. You'd think he'd want to be with someone more cultured.

"Never fear, Helena, I've had a good rest in Amsterdam," said Bruegel. "I'm glad to be free of Anja. But I do worry about her. Give me the news."

"She left Martin de Vos, you know, because he beat her," began Helena.

"Just as I feared!" cried Bruegel, beginning to pace around the room. So much for his calm state of mind.

"Did you tell me this before?" Ortelius asked Helena.

"Mijnheer Ortelius has a poor ear for gossip," Helena said to Bruegel, favoring Ortelius with a rude roll of her eyes. "I was about to tell you that Anja's moved in with another painter. A fellow named Peter Huys. His pictures don't earn so well, but he gets steady work as an engraver. The big news is that he's asked Anja to marry him."

"Peter Huys?" said Ortelius, still trying to be part of the conversation. "I can't quite—" He was always at a bit of a loss when it came to the changing details of Antwerp's mating dance.

"Good Peter Huys!" exclaimed Bruegel. "Bless the man! You know him, Abraham. A round fellow, a few years older than us. He paints imitations of Bosch; technically second-rate, yet exceedingly droll. I recall a fat naked egg-shaped man whose top half was a beehive with two eyeholes; the man was wearing black boots." Combined with the happy news about Anja, the thought of the beehive-man made Bruegel laugh out loud. "Dear Huys," he repeated. "Do he and Anja get along well, Helena? Did she tell him about the dowry?"

"Anja says Peter Huys is like you without the clouds and mountains, Mijnheer Bruegel," said Helena. "And, yes, he's satisfied with her dowry, such as it is. In fact he hadn't expected so much as a stuiver. He loves Anja for her merry self. They're posting the banns this week, and it's none too soon, as she's already carrying his child. Much of the dowry went for a cradle and some linens."

"Anja with child," said Bruegel in a wondering tone, and fell silent. It occurred to Ortelius that for all the years Bruegel had lived with Anja, her womb never quickened to his touch. No wonder he looked discomfited. Perhaps this meant he'd never be a father. Bruegel ran his hand across the round flank of Ortelius's terrestrial globe and stared vacantly down at Waf. "Lie down, boy, lie down by the fire."

Ortelius did what he could to break the mood.

"Don't stand there gaping at us, Helena, bring Mijnheer Bruegel some beer. Cheese, bread, and sausage, as well, whatever you can find. And a pot of tea for me. You're hungry, aren't you, Peter?"

"I am," said Bruegel, sitting carefully down on one of Ortelius's chairs as

Helena left the room. "I'll try not to break any furniture. Remember that time with Hans Franckert? It was the day I got my first commissions. How goes it with the great oaf? I trust he and the others won't be scared to be seen with me anymore. I'll never forget how you came to stand by me on the day Granvelle shipped me off to Mechelen, Abraham."

"Thank you, Peter," said Ortelius, pushing away his memories of having gotten Helena to be Williblad's messenger. "You deserve good friends. Franckert was married last month to Hennie van Mander. What a celebration they had. Four bagpipers and a roast pig."

"Franckert married, too!" said Bruegel with a sigh. "What a lot can happen in six months. I feel like a laggard, Abraham. All I do is to make paintings and think about how to sell them. I cark and swink and fiddle with pigments, but I've no flesh and blood to call my own." He sighed again. "Well, let's not linger over my failure to start a family. The game's not over yet, eh? Tomorrow I'll be in Brussels, and then we'll see. Oh, that little Mayken. What I'd give to have my arms around her. So is there any chance the good Franckert might finally buy an oil from me? I need some commissions so I can set up a proper studio. I'm tired of living from hand to mouth."

"I don't think he and Hennie have much left after the wedding," said Ortelius. "Hans has had some reverses. He started dealing in spices this summer, and he made the mistake of selling a large shipment of cloves to the Walloon army's quartermaster. They gave him damn-all in pay, and told him that if he wanted satisfaction he could go to the Foreigner."

"What of Anthonie Fugger?" said Bruegel.

"You haven't heard?" said Ortelius. "The House of Fugger's about to go under. Spain owes them five million gold florins, and everyone's come to believe there's no hope of the Fuggers getting it back. Their credit is ruined, and they've begun selling off their assets. I've managed to acquire a few of Anthonie's portrait miniatures. See them over there beneath your *Monkeys*?"

"I suppose you've been dealing through your friend Williblad Cheroo?" asked Bruegel, an edge in his voice.

"No," said Ortelius, his pulse quickening, as always, at the thought of the divine man. "Williblad left Fugger's employ to try and find a new station before the final collapse. But it seems no other merchant in Antwerp will have him. He's made too many enemies over the years." Unfortunately, Williblad hadn't approached Ortelius for a position. Ortelius would have hired him in a heartbeat. In fact, he'd wanted to tell Williblad this, but before he got the chance, his vision of beauty left Antwerp. "He moved to Brussels a few months ago," continued Ortelius. "It's said he found himself some kind of position there, though he doesn't want to tell any of us what it is. We still see him in town every few weeks. Perhaps he's again a secretary. I think he wishes he had a trade and a fam-

AS ABOVE, SO BELOW

ily of his own, the poor man. He's not happy. He's very taken with your picture of the *Two Monkeys*, you know. He visited here once, and I showed it to him. He quite took your meaning—about how hard a thing it is to be a pawn for the highborn and the rich. Williblad envies your artistic gifts, Peter, really he does."

"Am I to pity the man who stole my woman?" stormed Bruegel. "Forgiving your and Helena's roles in the business is one thing, but to forgive my archrival? I'm afraid I'm not that enlightened yet. Enough about the wretched Cheroo. And you say Fugger's fallen on hard times? I hope Jonghelinck's not bankrupt too?"

"No, he's doing well. He was smart enough to unload his Habsburg loans last year. He's still a city tax collector, and they let him keep a cut of what he brings in. He's also in a partnership with a Frenchman named Daniel de Bruyne, importing wine from Burgundy. They're making good business."

"I should have a talk with him."

"As it happens, I can take you to see Jonghelinck later this afternoon," said Ortelius.

"At his estate?"

"Not exactly," said Ortelius, enjoying the chance to act mysterious. A heretical "hedge preacher" was expected outside the city walls in an hour or two, and Ortelius and his friends were planning to go hear him. Hearing sermons by hedge preachers was an entertainment that had come into popularity while Bruegel had been out of town. Recently Ortelius had been going to one or two a month.

Of course Ortelius was as good and devout a Catholic as ever, but in these times, with the Foreigner using the clergy for his own worldly purposes, any reasonable man could feel the Church to be in need of reform. Heresy was, after all, a somewhat elastic concept when a man could be excommunicated and burned for owning a Bible. Many of the hedge preachers had useful and interesting things to say. And of course there was the pleasant excitement of sneaking out to see them—not all that mortally dangerous an act, either, as so many people had begun to attend, including intellectuals as well as the disaffected lower classes.

"Hush, I can't tell you more now," Ortelius told Bruegel. "Here comes Helena."

Helena pushed aside some of the piles of books on the long table and set out the victuals. Waf watched with interest from where he sat before the fire. There was a lull in their conversation while Bruegel did justice to his food and drink. Bruegel was a slow, thoughtful eater. It always seemed to Ortelius that his friend got more enjoyment out of his food than other men did.

"You say you were painting in Amsterdam, Peter?" asked Ortelius. "Is that the new picture in your pouch?"

"Indeed," said Bruegel, who held a pickle in one hand and a wedge of soft cheese in the other. "It's a commission that I got from William of Orange just before I left Mechelen. It was no small feat to convince so practical a man of affairs to buy a new work of art. Especially when his palace is already full of them. Like selling fleas to a dog. But I persuaded our William the Sly that my new work could serve the twin purposes of annoying Granvelle and impressing his new wife. He gave me a horse and a few florins to paint him *The Suicide of Saul.* We agreed upon a miniature, conveniently enough."

"Can I look at it?" asked Ortelius as Bruegel continued eating. Bruegel nodded, so Ortelius opened the flap of the square pouch and drew out a flat box, about two feet by one foot in size.

"Set it down on the table and take the lid off carefully," said Bruegel, biting into a piece of bread.

With gentle fingers, Ortelius lifted off the elegantly carpentered lid—and uncovered a miniature world: a cosmic view of a river landscape with a rocky bluff filling the foreground. Crawling up through a defile in the bluff was an army of armored soldiers bearing lances. The massed lances formed a swirl of lines like the spines of a hedgehog, like the stalks of wheat in a trampled field. So many men in such a small picture. It reminded him of a dream he'd once had about a map that had tiny moving people within its dots of cities.

"There was a flat stone in the garden of the inn where I stayed," said Bruegel. "One day this summer the ants crawled out from under it. It was their wedding day, with the new queens and their suitors in long, new-fledged wings, stiff and awkward. All morning they milled about, one on top of the other, drying their wings in the sun. And in the afternoon, one by one, they took to the air. They didn't know they were posing for my picture. As above, so below."

"I remember the suicide of Saul," said Ortelius, eager to show of his learning. "It closes the first Book of Samuel. Saul was an Israelite king, a suspicious tyrant, unloved by God. When Saul lost his last battle and was on the point of being captured by the Philistines, he fell upon his sword to kill himself, and his armor bearer did likewise." He leaned over the wonderfully detailed little painting. "And yes, there they are in the corner, Saul already dead, and his armor bearer following suit. How miserable they look. Explain again why William would commission this? I'd imagine a painting of a spaniel with a pile of partridges to be more his style." Ortelius permitted himself a little gout of venom. In truth he was a little jealous that Bruegel had managed to befriend Prince William of Orange.

"I suggested the theme," said Bruegel testily. "I led William to the thought that Saul is like King Philip, with Cardinal Granvelle his armor bearer."

"Aha. The death of the tyrant and his counselor," said Ortelius, peering closer. "But you paint them so sympathetically."

"Every man's death is terrible," said Bruegel simply. "The end of each man's world comes in his own lifetime. Mayhap in February, mayhap in September. In truth, the dead king is no more Philip than he is Saul. He's Everyman. I don't expect many men other than you to have the wit to grasp this, Abraham."

Ortelius's pleasure at Bruegel's compliment was slightly dampened by the mention of Everyman, which reminded him again of the mocking caricature of him that Bruegel had put into one of his engravings. Better to focus on the present. He looked at the little painting some more, wondering at the delicacy of Bruegel's brush. Nobody else could have interpreted the story of Saul in quite this way. A Bible verse was itself like an ancient coin, a token passed from hand to hand down the ages.

"So what's the mystery about our seeing Jonghelinck?" asked Bruegel presently.

"Some of us are going outside the city walls an hour before sunset to see a hedge preacher," said Ortelius, happy to finally tell his big secret. Things had been developing while Bruegel was off in Mechelen and Amsterdam. A revolution was in ferment, and Ortelius was in the thick of it. "Hendrik Niclaes from the Family of Love."

"A heretic?" said Bruegel looking uneasy. "After the trouble with my lampoons, I don't think I—"

"Niclaes is worth hearing," said Ortelius. "He preaches the message of salvation through love. The brotherly kind of love, mind you; he's something of an ascetic. I have a book of his that one of Plantin's men secretly printed."

Upon his recovery from his stab wound, Plantin had turned his full attention to producing books and was by now the most successful printer in Antwerp, with a dozen employees or more.

"The Land of Peace," continued Ortelius. "It's hidden beneath my floorboards, but I can easily—"

"No need to show it to me," said Bruegel hastily. "I don't want to dangle from the gibbet. I only stopped in Antwerp to check on my friends and to look for commissions. And then it's off to Brussels to court young Mayken. I had some encouraging letters from her mother while I was in Amsterdam. She's eighteen now, you know. If I can finally marry into that family, I'll be settled at last." Bruegel paused for a moment, contemplating his prospects. How very often Ortelius had heard him hold forth on this long-cherished obsession. Ortelius, for one, had nothing new to say about the Maykens. Sensing his friend's disinterest in the topic, Bruegel changed back to the subject at hand. "How is it that your Hendrik Niclaes hasn't been roasted over a slow fire?"

"He moves too quickly," said Ortelius. "And now I must be quick, too. It's time to go listen to him. Are you coming? Jonghelinck will assuredly be there. The meeting spot is the little wood near the van Schoonbeke windmill. It'll be a large crowd, Peter, you've nothing to fear, there's safety in numbers. The authorities have no choice but to turn a blind eye. And of course you can sleep here tonight."

"All right," said Bruegel slowly. He wiped the food off his hands and took a long last look at his new painting before safely boxing it back up. "Come, Waf. We didn't travel enough yet today. We're going for an outing." He put his hat and cloak back on. "Lead the way, Abraham."

It was the very end of October. They walked through the late afternoon streets, greeting the friends they ran across. Most of them seemed to be heading the same way. It was a bright day, though cool, with the sun low on the horizon. Long slanting shadows covered the streets.

"There's several hedge sermons a week now," Ortelius told Bruegel. "I've attended a number of them. It's fascinating to hear what the different preachers have to say. Two weeks ago, I heard a fellow talking about how it's been fifteen hundred years now that people have been adding things onto the teachings of Christ. Of course one likes to say the Pope is infallible. But is it so? We've been to Rome, Peter, we know what their Popes are like. What if Christ speaks to us in our hearts, rather than only through a Bishop or a Pope?"

"I wouldn't care to leave the Church," said Bruegel, uneasily looking around. "I was baptized, I go to confession, I attend mass, I'll be buried in the Church and, God willing, I'll be married there too. Why not? The Church is Christ's body on Earth."

"I agree," said Ortelius. "But the Church has become the tool of those who hate us. It's the body of Christ, but a body plagued with warts, wens, buboes, and all other manner of bilious growths. These hedge sermons concern freedom as much as they do religion. The Foreigner's Blood Edicts against heresy are simply an excuse for killing us as he sees fit. And his bishops enforce them. The hedge preachers are the surgeons for reform. It's our duty as citizens to support them."

"Tell me more about the preachers you've seen," said Bruegel. They paused at a street corner to wait for Waf to catch up with them. He'd been busy rolling in something, and as he drew near they could smell that it had been a dead rat. "*Pfui!*" Bruegel pushed Waf away with his foot, and now the dog ran on ahead of them.

"This summer I saw a little German Anabaptist who called for the murder of all the nobles and the priests," said Ortelius. "His audience was quite a rough crowd: beggars and thieves, the lowest of the low. I slipped away early. But the Calvinist preachers are almost respectable; any number of tradesmen and small gentry go to hear them. They say that religion should be entirely separate from the government. Very sound. Unfortunately the Calvinists are iconoclasts."

"Iconoclasts?" said Bruegel. "How do you mean?"

"The Calvinists say religious art should be destroyed," said Ortelius. "They say a house of worship is no place for paintings and sculpture. They liken a statue of Our Lady to the Golden Calf; they say that God commands us not to worship graven images."

"I've seen some paintings of Mary that are bovine indeed," said Bruegel, not taking this very seriously. "If the Calvinists should ever prevail, perhaps I'll be glad that I never receive commissions from churches." They were drawing near the city gate. "This fellow Hendrik Niclaes, what sect is he?"

"Niclaes insists he's a good Catholic," said Ortelius. "Though I doubt the Inquisitors would agree. He speaks strongly in favor of individual prayer."

"Oho," said Bruegel. "I heard much about prayer from Viglius van Aytta while I was staying in Mechelen. Aytta serves with Granvelle on Margaret's Consulta. Once at dinner I mentioned that I sometimes pray to God for help with my painting. Our man Aytta delivered himself of a memorable tirade." Bruegel cocked his head and drew back his chin, putting on the persona of the choleric Aytta. He shook his finger admonishingly at Ortelius, and spoke in a voice made old and cruel and thin.

" 'Those who pray in private have a contempt for all religion, and are neither more nor less than atheists. This vague, fireside liberty should be by every possible means extirpated; therefore did Christ institute shepherds to drive his wandering sheep back into the fold of the true Church; thus only can we guard the lambs against the ravening wolves, and prevent them being carried away from the flock of Christ to the flock of Belial.' "

"Hush now," said Ortelius, a little chilled to imagine such mad, cruel words being said in earnest. How terrible it was that God's own Church had become a cause for hatred. Perhaps Bruegel felt he could sit to one side and take his religion as it came, but Ortelius, for one, could not. "We're at the gate."

Ortelius told the city gatekeeper they were out for a sunset stroll, and the man asked no further questions. No doubt he knew perfectly well where they were really going, but there were few in Antwerp who supported the Spanish rule.

"How golden the light is just now," remarked Bruegel. "Look at the side of van Schoonbeke's windmill."

"We'll follow its shadow into the woods," said Ortelius. "Come on, Waf, don't tarry. *Faugh,* but he smells foul. In all honesty, I don't know how you can keep such a brute, Peter."

"Ah, but he's such a clever dog," said Bruegel, bending over as if to pet the big white dog and then, smelling him, thinking better of it. "Waf can say his own name." He picked up a stone and shied it into the woods. "Run after it, Waf, and we'll follow you."

Once they'd pushed through some bushes, they found a well-trodden path into the trees. And up ahead was a crowd of people.

"It's a real Antwerp mixture," said Bruegel, looking pleased. Like Ortelius, he enjoyed crowds, particularly those as diverse as this one. Looking at Bruegel,

Ortelius played a private game of trying to see the scene with the acuity of his artist friend's eyes.

Closest to them was a Chinese spice merchant with a skull cap, silk breeches, and a long pigtail. At his side was a bearded gypsy in a striped blanket reading the palm of a tall well-dressed man with a green-and-yellow silk scarf pulled across his face. The gypsy's wife wore a conical Chinese hat, and next to her was a Turk in a turban with a spike in the middle. To the right of this group sat three burgher ladies in fine silk dresses, and farther on was a pair of pug-nosed Flemish peasants wearing caps with earflaps. A whole council of dark-robed men in ruff collars stood beyond them. Overhead, some city boys wriggled in the crotches of trees. Ortelius and Bruegel pushed in as far as they could, ending up behind a short, blond youth with a red cap four times the size of Bruegel's. On the far side of the crowd the close-cropped head of Nicolas Jonghelinck was visible. His alert blue eyes noted Ortelius and Bruegel's arrival; he gave them a slight smile and a nod.

In the midst of the crowd, Hendrik Niclaes was standing on a stump preaching. He was a sinewy man with a kind, tired face.

"The Kingdom of Heaven is within you," he was saying. "Seek and ye shall find. This is what our Lord told us when he walked among men. God is in this grove as much as in the churches of the foreign bishops, Christ is in your heart as much as in the bread and wine of their mass. Pray with me now, my dear ones." Niclaes paused in silence, bowing his head and folding his hands against his chest. A late afternoon shaft of light illuminated him. Many in the crowd bowed their heads as well. Glancing over at Bruegel's folded hands and unbowed head, Ortelius couldn't decide if his friend were praying, looking at the faces in the crowd, or just waiting to talk to Jonghelinck.

Hendrik Niclaes preached some more, speaking of prayer, and then of love, of a brotherly love for one's fellow man. "The only way to know peace is to be peaceful," he said. "And love is the only path to love." As he spoke, the sun sank below the horizon and the sky grew pink, then orange, then gray. Niclaes ended by mentioning that he had a book of his teachings to sell; two peasant-clad assistants produced a great market basket with the books hidden beneath a layer of straw. The crowd broke up into conversing knots and Waf ambled forward to sniff at the basket.

Ortelius turned to say something to Bruegel, but his friend was off like a shot, pushing his way through the people. By the time Ortelius caught up with the red-capped Bruegel, he'd all but sold Nicolas Jonghelinck a painting.

"A large Tower of Babel, then," Bruegel was saying to the solemn, thin-lipped financier. "I painted a miniature of it years ago in Rome. It'll be a bit like the Colosseum and a bit like St. Peter's Basilica. The vanity of the human lust for power, eh? Ah, here's good Ortelius. Shall we three walk back to the city together? If you want to stop by Abraham's, Nicolas, I can show you my latest work. A miniature *Suicide of Saul* done for William of Orange."

"I'd love to see it," said Jonghelinck. "I've heard rumors of the three great Hell paintings you did for Margaret in Mechelen. They say one's still in her Wonder Chamber, but two were sent away. One to Madrid and the other to Vienna, I believe. It's a shame I won't see them."

"The Vienna one would be my *Dulle Griet*," said Bruegel with a smile. "Never fear, I have a watercolor sketch of that one stored with my things at Abraham's."

"Oh, thanks for telling me," said Ortelius, pretending to be put out, though secretly proud Bruegel trusted him. "A fine thing to be sitting on, the next time my house gets searched."

"There's nothing heretical or subversive in my paintings," said Bruegel cockily. "Cardinal Granvelle himself buys them. As for Margaret's dislike of the *Dulle Griet*, well, she's a cretin. And why would you worry about my paintings when you have a copy of Niclaes's book?"

"You've read it, Abraham?" said Jonghelinck, reaching into his cloak to draw out a little leather-bound volume. "I just purchased it myself. *The Land of Peace.* I liked what Niclaes said." He squinted at the book through his pince-nez spectacles, cradling the small volume in one huge hand. "No publisher's imprint on it, of course, but I'd swear it's Plantin's font."

Ortelius looked around to see if anyone were listening. Happy to be in the know, he indulged his love of gossip. "It's one of Plantin's assistants who's been running them off. Christopher turns a blind eye."

"Well, enough skullduggery for now," said Jonghelinck. "Let's head for town." On the way out they passed the shrouded man who'd been having his palm read by the gypsy. The figure struck Ortelius as uncommonly familiar. He walked another twenty paces and then it came clear.

"I'll catch up with you on the road or at my house," Ortelius told Bruegel and Jonghelinck. "I just remembered I have to talk to someone." The men continued onward, accompanied by Waf. Ortelius hurried back to the tall man with the scarf around his face, who'd just said something to the youths with the basket of books. One of the youths had turned white-faced and was hurrying away; the other youth was dragging the basket into a thicket and heaping leaves upon it.

"Williblad?" murmured Ortelius. "Williblad Cheroo?"

"Hush." A hazel eye glared at Ortelius from above the green-and-yellow scarf. "I can't be seen here," said Williblad—for it was indeed he. "It could make great problems with my new employer. Follow me." Williblad headed off into the woods, tracking a path that only he could see. Soon they were alone in a dim clearing and Williblad lowered his scarf.

"So who is it that you work for, Williblad?"

An odd smile played across Williblad's lips. "Don't tell your friends I was here or they'll attack me, Abraham."

"I promise to keep your secret."

"I work for Cardinal Granvelle."

Ortelius felt his throat go tight with fear. "You're an informer?"

Williblad's expression was of impatient contempt. "Do you think so little of me? That I would condemn my old friends to the Tyrant's Inquisition?" His breath smelled of cloves and gin.

"Although you work for Granvelle, you're against Spain?" said Ortelius uncertainly. He never quite understood Williblad's intricate, resentful allegiances.

"You want the truth?" said Williblad with a sigh. "I'm against everyone. That's why I'm so alone. You're a rare exception, Abraham. You have an outlaw soul."

The skewed compliment made Ortelius's head spin. "Why do you hate all the others?" he asked, eager to hear more.

"Give it some thought, man," said Williblad impatiently. "The conquistadors who raped my mother and murdered her husband were white men—Spaniards, yes, but I'm sure Low-Landers would have done the same thing. So I hate Europeans. My own tribe of Indians expelled me and put me upon Fugger's ship, so I hate them too. Fugger cared for me, but he took me lightly. I hate him. Granvelle is a swine and an intriguer. I hate him. Though I will say he was the only one to offer me a job commensurate with my skills."

"I would have given you a job, Williblad," said Ortelius softly. "But you never asked. You're sure you don't hate me?"

Williblad gave him one of his rare smiles. "No. You and some others in your circle are among my friends. Those of you who've treated me with respect. I would never inform on such as you."

"So why are you at a hedge sermon?"

"To warn Christopher Plantin. I'd expected to find him here."

"Plantin?"

"The Inquisitors will search his shop tonight. I heard Granvelle arranging to send them. Christopher must leave the country. Make sure that he gets the message. I mistrust those fellows who carried the basket of books. In their panic they could neglect to warn him."

Williblad's voice was low and calm. Ortelius stared at him, more fascinated than ever before. Williblad returned his gaze. For the first time, Ortelius was sure that Williblad knew he lusted for him.

"Come this way, Abraham," said Williblad, lithe as a man half his age. "We'll find the road. Take my hand."

They picked their way through the woods. Ortelius wished the brief walk would never end. Ah, to hold Williblad's strong, firm hand. And then they were out on the road. It was quite dark now, and Williblad left his face uncovered.

"How are things in Brussels?" asked Ortelius, just to hear his dream man talk.

"Good." Williblad dropped Ortelius's hand. "There's a new woman I'm seducing. Perhaps you know her. Little Mayken Coecke."

"But Bruegel wants to marry her!" burst out Ortelius.

"I know it," said Williblad. "As does Granvelle. He urged me to court her. I'm not quite sure why. Perhaps he wants to see Bruegel suffer. As do I. Bruegel insulted me at the Landjuweel. Remember how everyone laughed at me? I aim finally to show him who's the better man."

"But Williblad—" began Ortelius.

"Enough," said Williblad, placing a finger on Ortelius's lips. Helpless with desire, Ortelius pushed his lips out, wantonly savoring the touch. "Remember to tell no one you saw me here. Especially not Bruegel. I'll give him my news of Mayken at the proper time and in person—so I can savor the look upon his face. And, oh yes, make sure Plantin receives his warning. My horse is tethered behind this windmill here. Farewell, Abraham." As if to fully seal the secret, Williblad leaned forward and placed a soft kiss upon Ortelius's lips. And then he was gone, silently blending into the darkness on the other side of the road.

Ortelius walked dizzily back to town, over and over brushing his fingers against his mouth, trying to recall the sensation of Williblad's kiss. As he came in through the city gate, he saw a carriage just leaving. Plantin and his wife. So they'd gotten the message after all. Just as well Ortelius didn't have to give it himself. It would have been hard to explain how he knew the Inquisitors' plans.

Helena had already let Bruegel and Jonghelinck into the house; Ortelius found them in his study, looking at Bruegel's new miniature, with Waf lying on the floor beside the fire.

"There you are, Abraham," said Bruegel. "What's kept you?" Waf sleepily beat his tail against the floor.

"A—a fellow cartographer. You wouldn't know him. He's preparing a new view of Brussels. Are you two quite comfortable? A glass of wine?" With Williblad's kiss still fresh on his lips, Ortelius needed time to digest what he'd just heard. There was no rush to tell Peter the bad news.

"That would be just the thing," said Jonghelinck. "Would you heat up the poker to mull it with, Abraham?" Ortelius busied himself with positioning the poker, taking as long as possible, giving his mind time to spin. Why did someone as beautiful as Williblad have to act so evil? Why torment Peter in the same way for a second time? It was like a horrible recurring dream.

Meanwhile Jonghelinck drew his new book out of his coat pocket. The sight of Niclaes's little volume made Ortelius tremble, knowing as he did that the Inquisitors were even now raiding Plantin's print shop in search of it. He felt sick and dizzy with his secrets. Williblad after the young Mayken! Bruegel had spoken of nothing but Mayken for the last five or ten years! To lose her to Williblad would crush him.

"Put it away," said Ortelius to Jonghelinck, more sharply than he meant to.

"Indeed," said Jonghelinck, slipping the book back into his pocket. "Tell me more about your plan for the *Tower of Babel*, Peter."

Ortelius went to the hallway to call Helena for some wine and cake. Little of the next hour's conversation registered with him, and then he was seeing Jonghelinck to the door. He went upstairs and bid good night to his old mother, then made his way back to the study. Bruegel was sitting there, sketching some of the faces he'd seen at the hedge sermon. Ortelius could hardly meet his eyes.

"Is something wrong, Abraham? You don't seem yourself tonight."

Ortelius felt a wave of pity for his friend. He wanted to tell him the truth. But Williblad's kiss had enslaved him, at least for now. He hardened his heart and held back his secret. "I suppose I'm a bit chilled, is all. Let's have another glass of wine."

"Fine," said Bruegel, though he was already a bit red in the face. "It's such a joy to hear Flemish spoken properly again. I could sit here and chat all night. I'll be on my way early tomorrow, though. I'd like to reach Brussels before nightfall."

"Is the young Mayken aware of your plans?" probed Ortelius.

"That's still a bit of a problem," confessed Bruegel. "The old Mayken's all for the marriage. She and I—" He got to his feet and checked that Helena wasn't listening at the door, then poured himself a bit more wine and flopped back down upon the couch. "Can you keep a secret, Abraham?"

"Certainly," said Ortelius gloomily. He felt dreadfully unworthy of his friend's confidences. But the rush to confess was upon Bruegel, and he took no note of Ortelius's unease.

"I had sex with the old Mayken when I was seventeen. It was while she was carrying young Mayken. Sometimes I worry that the girl knows. It happened like this. Master Coecke had gone off to North Africa aboard the fleet of Emperor Charles the Fifth. It was when Charles went to war against Suleiman the Magnificent's Admiral Barbarossa. Charles brought Master Coecke along to depict his triumphs. And indeed, in the fullness of time, Master Coecke helped produce a colossal series of extravagant tapestries, *The Conquest of Tunis*."

"I've seen one of them at Fugger's," said Ortelius, hoping to change the subject. He didn't want to hear Bruegel's confidences. Why must the man be so thickheaded about the Maykens? Why did he need to long for them so? "All covered with gold and silver threads," continued Ortelius urbanely. "I believe the Habsburgs stuck the Fuggers with the bill for all twelve."

"Quite likely," said Bruegel, not to be deflected from telling his tale. And here it came. "Well, while Master Coecke was conquering Tunis, I was conquering his wife. Or rather, she was conquering me. She and I were alone in the house for six months with the maids and one other apprentice, a smeary twenty-year-old fellow named Cornelius who lived in the shed in the garden. Yes, Coecke quickened his Mayken's womb and sailed off to Africa for adventure. One night soon after Coecke left, I was walking down the hallway and Mayken called me into her room. It was lit by candles. She was lying on her back with her night-clothes pulled up and her legs in the air. I could see everything. I knew what a female looked like from my little games with Anja, but the sight of Mayken— well, I'd almost say it frightened me. She was a grown woman, you understand, waiting for me in full readiness. It was, in its way, a terrible sight. I still don't know why she approached me in such wise. Perhaps loneliness, or the action of her swollen womb upon her humors, who knows?" Bruegel paused, smiling rue-fully. "The old Mayken has never been the kind of woman to flirt with a man; if anything she's rather stiff and cold. Lacking in social graces. But there she was on her back with her legs in the air. A moment of folly. Very clumsy, very human."

Ortelius shuddered at Bruegel's coarse image. Why did Bruegel perpetually have to discuss—and depict—such things? Ortelius had never seen a naked woman and he didn't want to. "I've met Mayken Verhulst," he said finally. "A dignified personage. I can hardly imagine what you're describing. Did you run away?"

"Of course not," said Bruegel with a rueful laugh. "I was frightened, but I was seventeen. I stayed and swived her. She had me do it to her once or twice a day for the whole time that Master Coecke was gone. By the end her belly was as big as your Earth globe."

"Did the others know?" asked Ortelius.

"At first nobody said anything," said Bruegel. "But secrets don't last long in a household. The other apprentice, Cornelius, made it clear that he knew where I went when I crept down the hallways of an evening. Though he lived in the shed, he was in the house nearly every night with the cook. There was a kind of mad lewdness in the air. Cornelius was jealous of my success with the mistress of the house, I suppose. It was he who told Master Coecke."

"Oh Lord," said Ortelius, laughing weakly. Despite himself he'd been drawn into the tale. "What a life you lead, Peter."

"Soon after his return, Master Coecke called me into his studio, high on his house's fourth floor, an enormous, high-ceilinged attic with gable windows. He was dressed as a Turk, in a green silk caftan the color of moonlight, wearing a turban and holding a curved scimitar. A canvas and a mirror stood before him; he'd been using himself as a model for an image of Suleiman the Magnificent. The sword put me ill at ease, the more so when he closed the door and placed the blade against my neck. 'You've made merry company for my wife,' said Master Coecke. I backed away, but he followed me, always with that great sharp blade at my throat. I begged for mercy. I told him I would leave his house forever if he so wished. He handed me the sword, put his face in his hands, and began to weep. 'Kill me now if you plan to touch her again,' he sobbed. 'You're like a son to me, Peter. I don't want to lose you or my Mayken. But I'd rather die than be a cuckold.' In time we smoothed things over. Indeed, we grew closer than before. I stayed on as his apprentice for five more years. And, good as my word, I never made love to old Mayken again. Nor, for her part, did she again petition me."

"A happy ending, then," put in Ortelius, not wanting to hear any further talk about Bruegel's Maykens. "Perhaps it's time for bed."

"I'm not finished," said Bruegel stubbornly. "There's more to tell." He drank from his wineglass and continued. "After young Mayken was born, Master Coecke and old Mayken were busy with their work, and it often fell upon me to care for the girl. She was a delight, the joy of the household. I'd carry her on my shoulders when I went out to make purchases for Coecke, and at home I'd draw her pictures and tell her tales. She was fond of me." Bruegel sighed. "But now I worry that she thinks of me as an uncle. Or as her mother's lover."

"How would she possibly know that?" cried Ortelius.

"For the first months of her existence, I was drumming at her door!" exclaimed Bruegel. "More fool I. Mightn't a homunculus sense such a thing? There's knowing and there's knowing, eh? When a bird flies back from the South, she knows the nest where she hatched, without being able to tell any man how. Oh, Abraham, if young Mayken feels me to be her mother's lover, then I'm as odious to her as a lecherous, unnatural father. What if she rejects my suit?"

"But old Mayken backs you, no?" Ortelius felt even sicker than before at the thought of that seasoned rake Williblad seducing young Mayken. And at Granvelle's behest. Should he tell? Impossible, Williblad had asked him not to. There was no way he could tell. Bruegel would see the wolf in the fold soon enough.

"Yes, now that I'm free of Anja, old Mayken's all for the marriage," prattled Bruegel. "The union was always her and Master Coecke's wish. I was the best of their students and old Mayken bore no sons. They expected that in due time I'd come back into the house of Coecke. Old Mayken is doing well enough, but her trade is small, and she has, I believe, not so good a head for business."

"But you do?" said Ortelius, sadly smiling at his friend, at the Bruegel who refused to paint portraits, who turned his back on the Italianate style sought by the churches, who depicted people defecating, who drew seditious lampoons, who insulted the Regent, who recently gave away a third of his commissions for the sake of an unfaithful woman friend, and whose latest work was a miniature that had taken him six months to paint in exchange for a horse and a few coins.

Bruegel caught some of what Ortelius was thinking. "I get commissions," he protested. "I sell everything I can paint or draw. But, yes, I'll grant that I'm not the shrewdest of men." He shook his head. "I make enough to live on, and that's it. When will I, alone, ever own a house? When will I, alone, have a full studio, with apprentices to grind my paints? I'm tired of being a struggling artist, Abraham. I'm a master in my prime, and I live like a student. Who knows how much longer I have? Death comes when you have him least in mind. I hope and pray the Maykens will take me in."

"God grant that it be so," said Ortelius, on the point of tears. "No more talk, dear Peter. I must sleep." And so, for the second time, Ortelius betrayed his closest friend.

THE PEASANT AND
THE BIRDSNESTER

BRUSSELS, NOVEMBER 1562

The ride to Brussels took all of a long, wet day. Bruegel and Waf found lodging at an inn near the docks of the newly dug Willebroek Canal. The next morning they made their way to the Coecke house. It was a narrow, four-story redbrick building in the Marolles district, a busy but not so fashionable neighborhood of merchants and artisans, down the hill from the city's great palaces.

The house was much messier than it had been in the days when Master Coecke was alive. Old Mayken had always been a poor housekeeper. She met

Bruegel at the door, her hair in an untidy gray bun, her wise face wreathed in smiles at the sight of Peter. They exchanged a few quiet words about why he'd come. And then she kissed him on the cheek and sent him upstairs to see her daughter. Bruegel found young Mayken alone in a sunny studio on the second floor, sitting at a table sorting threads. His heart beat faster at seeing her, at scenting her breath in the room. For her part, Mayken acted quite unromantic.

"Peter Bruegel! Have they thrown you out of Amsterdam as well?" Mayken tossed her head and gave a little laugh. "Draw me a picture of a pig."

She'd often greeted him with this request as a girl and now, as in the old days, Bruegel sketched a pig in the air with his finger. The jumbled studio had Bruegel's *Children's Games* on one wall, paint-spotted Turkish rugs on an equally spotted inlaid wood floor, a brick fireplace with ashes all around it, a dusty couch mounded with skeins of thread, and two worktables, one covered with threads and tapestry cartoons, the other covered with paints. Three tiny easels sitting upon the second table held miniatures that old Mayken was working on. Two high windows looked out upon the Hoogstraat, the crowded, narrow street that ran the length of the Marolles. Waf circled the room, then lay down at young Mayken's feet.

"It's wonderful to see you," said Bruegel, stepping closer. "You're quite the young woman now." Mayken's long blond hair was in braids that she wore piled upon her head, exposing a pale, alluring neck. Her lips were full and kissable. He wanted to reach out and pet her, but just now his hands felt like clumsy paws. His grin felt stupid. It was finally time to press his suit, and he hardly knew how to begin. "I'm overcome by your beauty."

"Don't be silly. Sit down and tell me what you've seen. Draw me a real picture, of a Hollander. I know you've got a pen and paper with you. You always do. Inky Peter."

"What are the threads for?" asked Bruegel, not getting out his pen.

"Mother's designing a tapestry for William of Orange's new wife. Princess Anna of Saxony. I've met her, a gossipy, lecherous little thing with a limp. She wants a Hunt of the Unicorn, with fine strong huntsmen and a buxom virgin that looks like her." Bruegel recalled that the falconer's son, young Bengt Bots, had mentioned showing a falcon to the Maykens at William's palace.

"I went falconing with William while I was in Mechelen," said Bruegel, thinking Mayken might be impressed. "And I've just finished a picture for him. I left it back at the inn."

"I want to learn more about falconry. Why don't the falcons fly away? But why are you staying at an inn instead of with us?"

"It's not fitting." There. He was finally approaching the topic.

"Why not?" Mayken's voice was sweet and bright, yet artificial. She was deliberately making it hard for him.

"Because I'm courting you," exclaimed Bruegel. He felt his face burning. What an oaf he must seem. "As if you didn't know. Dear Mayken, I want to marry you."

Mayken fell silent for a minute or two, looking down at her skeins of thread, moving a few of them back and forth with the tips of her delicate fingers. The noises from the street drifted in: voices in discussion, the hooves of horses, the wheels of carts rumbling past, someone playing a hurdy-gurdy.

"Mother told me to expect this," said Mayken finally. "She wants it too."

"And you, Mayken? Will you have me?"

"Oh, I don't know. Maybe I'm not who you think I am. It's been forever since we've really talked. But now let's just be silly like the old days. Be my Inky Peter and draw me a falcon attacking a Holland pig."

"All right," said Bruegel, and took out his pen. Though Mayken's rebuff came as a severe disappointment, there was still room to hope. She had a point, after all. They hardly knew each other anymore. First they should get comfortable with each other again.

Bruegel and Mayken spent a pleasant hour together, chatting while he drew things for her, though every now and then he'd have to pause, quite overcome with longing for her. Every aspect of the girl seemed perfect to him: the curve of her bosom, the rhythm of her breath, the intimate scent of her hair and skin, oh, how she had ripened. Old Mayken joined them after a while, and showed Bruegel the cartoon for the unicorn tapestry, which indeed included some falcons. Old Mayken wasn't happy with her drawing of a falcon in flight, and at her request, Bruegel rubbed it out and used a bit of charcoal to draw in a better one. Few could limn birds as well as he. While he was at it, he added a heron. The talk about William of Orange reminded him that he should deliver his picture, so after a bit he took his leave, with nothing about his and young Mayken's future resolved.

"She's been filled with fantasy of late," old Mayken told him at the door. "She's not her old self."

"Do I have a rival?" asked Bruegel, speaking quietly lest young Mayken overhear.

"I don't know," said old Mayken. She was a large-nosed woman with a generous mouth. "People come and go at our house on all sorts of business. And we're out in the city all the time. Perhaps she could have met someone. I'm not sure what she's up to. Of late she's shown an uncommon interest in going to afternoon mass, but if I try and accompany her, she says she'd rather not go."

Lost in thought, Bruegel made his way to William's Nassau palace. Young Mayken was certainly pretty enough to have attracted another man. When she'd said, "Maybe I'm not who you think I am," could she have possibly meant that she was no longer a virgin?

The palace was a magnificent stone structure of arches and buttresses on a long hill near the Coecke house. A servant showed Bruegel and Waf into a vast wood-paneled dining hall with tapestries, stained-glass windows, and a long linen-bedecked table laden with steaming food redolent of cinnamon, garlic, and cloves. William the Sly was sitting at one end, chatting with two other nobles. His customary bodyguard, Grauer, stood alertly behind his chair. The gimlet-eyed Grauer was the first to notice Bruegel's entrance.

"It's our Bruegel," called William. "And the noble Waf. Peter, let me introduce you to Graaf Egmont." Egmont was a handsome man with dark hair combed down over his forehead. He acknowledged Bruegel with a curt nod.

"And I believe you know Filips de Hoorne?" continued William. It had been years since Bruegel had seen Filips de Hoorne. Filips had grown a spade-shaped beard and his head had turned bald. As usual, Bruegel wondered if Filips might be his half brother. Like Bruegel, he had gray eyes, but Bruegel could see little other resemblance to his own features.

"Peter," said de Hoorne, getting to his feet. "William told me of your adventures in Mechelen with our Regent Dulle Griet. I'm proud of you." He gave Bruegel a little pat on the shoulder. "Father did well to have this fellow educated," de Hoorne told the others. "He was a foundling at our Ooievaarenest farm."

"With his paternity quite unknown, eh, Filips?" said William, instinctively going to the heart of the matter. Bruegel dared not add anything. As a result of the old Graaf's many kindnesses to him, he'd always felt himself to be under an unspoken agreement not to make any claims. But he dearly would have liked for once to discuss his paternity. Filips merely frowned at William's sally and resumed his seat.

"I brought Prince William's new painting," said Bruegel, pulling the box out of his pouch. It would be nice to have Filips see what kind of man he was. William called a servant to clear a space on the table, and Bruegel set out the *Suicide of Saul*.

"It's small," observed Egmont. Evidently he was a dunderhead. In the echo of his ignorant slight, the picture looked very tiny in this great, arched hall.

"A gem," said de Hoorne, leaning over it. "What mastery he has. Father knew it when he first saw him drawing on the wall of our barn. Explain the picture to us, Peter." Bruegel's heart bloomed and enfolded Filips.

Smiling in Filips's eyes, Bruegel briefly summarized the story of Saul. When he was done, William pointed to the dying king and the dead armor bearer in the painting's corner.

"Bruegel doesn't like to say so out loud, but this is Philip and this is Granvelle," said William. Grauer stepped forward a pace to peer at the dying men. His hard face split in a smile and he winked at Bruegel.

"Very subtle," said de Hoorne approvingly. "And very daring. The Tyrant dies, to be replaced by—whom?"

"By me," said William confidently. "I'm the new David, out there on the horizon somewhere."

"Why you instead of me?" said Egmont, not quite jokingly.

"Because it's my picture," said William, playfully sidestepping the proffered debate. He raised his voice and called to the other end of the table, where a group of women sat. "Come see what Peter Bruegel's painted for us, Anna."

A dark-haired little woman came rapidly their way, with several ladies following along. She moved with an irregular gait; her spine was a bit crooked. She had a pretty face and a loud, gay voice. She liked the picture well enough, and complimented Bruegel on the way he'd painted the trees.

"A pity you're not known at the imperial court," she remarked. "My councilors in Saxony have never heard of you. And I wonder, do you ever paint women? I see nothing but soldiers in this little picture. Women, after all, are more than half the race."

"My last painting was primarily of women," said Bruegel ingratiatingly. "It was called *Dulle Griet*. It was sent off to Vienna, so perhaps your councilors will hear of me soon."

"How nice for you," said Princess Anna, maintaining her somewhat cutting manner. "What are you painting next, Mijnheer Bruegel?"

"A large *Tower of Babel*," he said. "As soon as I can set up a studio in Brussels. Perhaps you and Prince William would like to commission something else?"

"Maybe next year," said Princess Anna. "But not just now. I'm busy having Mayken Verhulst produce some tapestries for me."

"I've seen the cartoons," said Bruegel wanting to show himself to be at ease in the artistic circles of Brussels. "I'm a good friend of Mayken's. I helped her redraw the falcons just this morning."

"She has a pretty daughter with a sweet figure," said the lively Princess.

"Young Mayken," said Bruegel. Basking in the nobles' attention, he decided to push himself forward a bit. "I'm more than fond of her."

"You're not the only one," said Princess Anna with a caustic shriek of laughter.

Bruegel's stomach went hollow. It was as he'd feared! He had a rival! "How do you mean, Your Highness?" he asked, struggling to keep a calm face.

Princess Anna nudged one of her ladies-in-waiting and said something to her in High German, too rapidly for Bruegel to understand.

"Don't torment him with your gossip, Anna," interrupted William. "Take away his picture now, will you?" I feed roses to pigs, thought Bruegel, watching one of the Princess's ladies carry off his painting to who knew where. Six months out of his life, and William and his wife might never look at it again.

How selfish and idle were the nobles. Waf was nosing at the edge of the table, trying to get a good scent of the food. It struck Bruegel that in some sense he was doing the same thing here himself. Sniffing at the edge of the table.

"Where are you staying in Brussels, Peter?" asked William, taking a scrap of clove-scented gristle from off his plate and giving it to the dog.

"In an inn," said Bruegel, feeling numb from Princess Anna's news. "Eventually I hope to move—" He stopped himself, not wanting to mention his hopes to this worldly, mocking company. He started over. "I hope to rent a large room."

"I own some buildings in the Marolles," said William in a friendly tone. "Talk to Groelsch, my purser, and he'll find you a sunny loft at a reasonable rate. That's him down there bent over his plate. Be a bit cautious when you interrupt his feeding. Farewell, then. Come visit again when I've fewer guests. I'll show you my collection. Remember that I have a masterpiece by Bosch. It's called *The Garden of Earthly Delights*." Grauer shifted, and now William looked over Bruegel's shoulder at a new arrival. "Ah, Brederode, here you are. I'll send the steward for more wine."

Egmont became immediately absorbed in discussing some point of governance with Brederode, and ignored Bruegel's dismissal. But de Hoorne gave him a friendly nod. Bruegel spoke with Groelsch about his need for a studio, and left the hall with Waf. He felt himself every bit the impoverished, overworked, disinherited, and unmarriageable peasant.

In the palace courtyard, Bengt Bots, the falconer's son, came dashing after Bruegel, his colorless hair flopping as he ran. Though it was cold, the boy hadn't paused to put on a coat; he was dressed in brown breeches and a loose red jerkin. His blue eyes were shining with excitement and his pale cheeks were flushed. He was carrying a roll of papers in his hand.

"Master Bruegel! I was upstairs when they carried up your new painting. Are you going to live in Brussels now?"

"I am." The youth's joy at seeing him was balm to Bruegel's soul. "How are the falcons?"

"Cruel and greedy as ever." The boy paused to catch his breath, his eyes searching Bruegel's face. "Master Bruegel, everyone says I draw very well, and I was wondering—could I be your apprentice?"

The unexpected request brought Bruegel back to the day when he'd first approached Master Coecke with the same question. It was after Bruegel had run away from the school and found his way to Antwerp, the city of artists, and there he'd ended up on Master Coecke's doorstep, hat in hand, begging to be taken on as an apprentice. And now he said to Bengt what Master Coecke had said to him then.

"You seem a likely lad, but it costs money to be my apprentice. People don't value what they get for free."

"I don't have any money," said young Bengt. "And my father only wants me to be a falconer. But, here, look at this."

And just as Bruegel had done with Coecke, Bengt Bots handed over a roll of papers covered with drawings of people and animals. A November breeze rattled the papers as Bruegel looked through them. The years were moving on, and it was really time he had an apprentice. Perhaps there was a way. If the boy's skill was only moderate, he definitely liked to draw. There were dozens, no scores, of scenes of falconry and palace life. Young Bengt had the most important trait, the obsession to draw what he saw.

"I'd like to have you," said Bruegel, handing the papers back to Bengt and patting him on the shoulder. "You have it in you to be an artist, Bengt. I wonder if Prince William would help you with the apprenticeship fee." In his own case, it had been old Graaf de Hoorne who came up with the money. It was striking how the world liked to repeat itself. Like some vast and intricate clock. "But there's no great urgency to sign on with me," he continued. "I don't have a proper studio yet."

"Thank you, Master Bruegel," said Bengt ardently. "Thank you." He brushed his pale shock of hair back from his eyes. "Are you still planning to marry Mayken?"

"Did I tell you that?" asked Bruegel, back on his guard.

"You hinted," said Bengt. "I saw her here again the other day. She's so pretty. You should get her before someone else does."

"Is anyone else after her?" asked Bruegel, a little ashamed to be lowering himself to this level with the boy.

"I wouldn't know," said Bengt, his pale face unreadable. Evidently he did know something, but he didn't want to say. A damp gust of wind buffeted them.

I've heard more than enough unpleasant mystery mongering for today, thought Bruegel. "Come see me in a few months," he said, sourly closing off the conversation. "And see if Prince William will pay your fee. I truly won't take you on without it."

The next few weeks passed quickly. Groelsch rented Bruegel a good loft above a candle shop on the Hoogstraat, just a block and a half from the Coecke house. Using the money Jonghelinck had advanced him, Bruegel set up a studio and some spartan living arrangements. The *Tower of Babel* was clear in his mind from the miniature of it he'd painted years ago in Rome, and the work went quickly. In Mechelen he'd grown used to working on more than one picture at once, so he went ahead and started a second version of the Tower. The large one would be for Jonghelinck, and the small one for himself—or for Mayken.

Ah, Mayken. Try as he might to lose himself in his work, Bruegel was desperately in love with the girl. No longer was it the family workshop, the four-story brick house, or the solid social standing that he sought. It was young Mayken herself—the frisky rhythms of her walk, the cheerful clamor of her voice, the special tang of her breath, the pinks and yellows of her skin, the glowing warmth of her face, and the wise, funny, unexpected things she said. Bruegel wanted to live with her, to swell her with children, to care for her and love her for the rest of his days.

But the situation remained unsettled. Mayken refused to give a yes or no to his proposals, always saying she needed more time. It made Bruegel feel old and ugly to badger her. A growing sense of despair flooded around him like a swamp.

At least old Mayken was still his ally. She and Bruegel had any number of whispered conferences at her front door. She reported that her daughter was still going out on her own most afternoons. Bruegel went to mass a few times to look for her, but she wasn't there. He considered following her, but decided it would be too absurd and ignoble. Better to wait, and if Mayken wouldn't have him, well then, life would have to go on. Meanwhile there was nothing to do but paint.

It was mid morning of a rainy day in late November when Williblad Cheroo appeared in Bruegel's studio, well turned out as usual, this time in soft black leather, a white silk shirt, and a cloak and hat trimmed with white fur. His tall boots had silver buckles. His cloak dripped a little puddle onto Bruegel's floor.

"Don't attack me with your paintbrush again," said Cheroo, not quite smiling. Waf had started barking when Cheroo came in, but now the dog recognized the tall half-American and lay back down.

"I'd heard you moved to Brussels," said Bruegel, prepared to be civil. He remembered Ortelius's remark that Bruegel and Williblad should be friends. "Who are you working for?"

"An old patron of yours," said Cheroo. "He'd like another picture by you."

"Pleasant news," said Bruegel. "Have a seat. Which patron do you mean?"

"Cardinal Granvelle," said Cheroo, still standing. "He'd like something inoffensive this time. A simple river landscape with a biblical scene."

"Granvelle!" exclaimed Bruegel. Though he knew the Cardinal lived in Brussels, Bruegel hadn't seen Granvelle yet, and that had seemed for the best. At their last meeting, Granvelle had been so very hostile. Though Bruegel had indeed stayed in exile for the prescribed six months, who knew but that Granvelle might suddenly choose to punish him some more. Yet now here was Williblad with a fresh commission from the man. So be it.

Bruegel always had a few ideas for new pictures in his head. The constant churning of his life seemed to unearth the ideas quite unbidden. He now proposed the one that seemed likeliest to fit Granvelle's request. "A *Flight into Egypt*," said Bruegel. "Joseph in the foreground on a hill crest, leading Mary into—into who knows what. The future. A dark gully. And a great landscape spreading out beyond that." Speaking of the picture, he realized it would be an image of him and Mayken. He made a little sketch of it on a piece of paper as he talked. "So it's Granvelle you're working for, eh? No wonder you didn't want to tell anyone in Antwerp. Even your friend Ortelius didn't seem to know. Well, I'm in no position to chide you. I've worked for him before and now it seems I'll work for him again." He handed the sketch to Cheroo. "Do you think a *Flight into Egypt* will suit?"

"Indeed," said Cheroo, pocketing the paper after a cursory glance. "Let's work out the figures." They'd soon settled this, with a better payment than Bruegel had hoped for. But instead of leaving, Cheroo walked over to Bruegel's window and stared out through the rain.

"Mayken Coecke's house is just down the road," he said presently. "I can see it."

"That's right," said Bruegel uneasily. A spasm of pain shot through his stomach. Cheroo had made free with his Anja. Oh God. Could it be that—

"Young Mayken's very impressionable," said Cheroo. "A word from me and she'd let you marry her."

This was worse than anything Bruegel had feared. He took an uncertain step towards Williblad. The older man placed one hand inside his cloak, and his voice took on a warning tone. "Don't rush at me, Peter. I have a knife and I know how to use it. Hear me out. Don't try and wrestle with me like a peasant boy."

"You've seduced her?" groaned Bruegel. His knees felt weak. He felt like throwing up.

"Granvelle sent me to her house to discuss a tapestry. I followed her to mass the next day, and now most afternoons we walk in the park. She likes hearing about America. About the egrets and the alligators."

"What do you want from the poor girl?" cried Bruegel in anguish. "If you have an honest marriage proposal, and if she prefers you, well then, I'll step aside. But—walking in the park? What park do you mean?"

"Granvelle's estate's not so far from here. It's commodious and private. On the rainy days we might sit in his library."

Bruegel groaned again. "Granvelle put you up to this, didn't he? He hasn't forgiven me for the lampoon and for the *Dulle Griet*."

"There's more to life than paintings, Peter," said Cheroo with a dismissive gesture. "*Dulle Griet* is forgotten, and the *Flight into Egypt* is but a pretext for us to talk. Politics are what interest the Primate. Connections and introductions. Granvelle deputized me to pluck your Mayken so that I could ask a special favor from you."

Bruegel would have lunged at Cheroo now, but, anticipating this, the tall, experienced man had drawn out his knife. Bruegel sat down on the edge of his bed, his stomach a filigree of pain. Sensing his master's distress, Waf walked over and sniffed at him. Distractedly Bruegel petted Waf's thick white coat. He felt weak and stupid and beaten.

Blearily he thought of Mayken's bright, kissable face. If Williblad kept up his game with her, she'd suffer greatly. The gossip, an unwed pregnancy, a full-blown scandal—her reputation would be ruined. "What do you and Granvelle want from me?" he asked Williblad finally. "I'll do what you say."

"Very good," gloated Cheroo. "I'm satisfied to see you so humble. It's a fine bit of revenge for our business at the Landjuweel, when you made the others laugh at me. Even though you're an artist, you're no better than me, you see?" The very fact that Williblad had to say this gave the lie to it. The man's inner weakness gave Bruegel a bit of badly needed strength. "I'm about done with Mayken in any case," continued Williblad. "I'd rather not see her cast out of society, better she ends up settled with you. She feels bad about her deceit, you know. I've had to dry many of her tears. Now keep your temper, Peter! Yes, I'll break off with Mayken if you'll do the one small favor for the Cardinal."

Something odd was happening in Bruegel's head. The room had stopped looking real; it had started looking like a painting. Tall dark Cheroo, the bright window with the gray sky, the uneven grimy boards of the floor, the peeling plaster on the walls, the convex mirror, some combs of beeswax in the corner, the pots and bowls of paint, the two panels of the Tower of Babel, the bed, and he himself upon it with the dog at his side—all of it was colors and shapes. There were three people in the picture: Bruegel and Williblad with their tangled histories, and somehow Mayken in the room as well, perched pale and alert to one side, invisibly watching them. They were like three trees with twisting trunks, their past and present in the picture's eternal Now.

"Did you hear me?" Cheroo was saying querulously.

"What?"

"You're to take on one of Granvelle's countrymen as an apprentice. Just for a month. The Cardinal himself will pay the fellow's apprenticeship fee, and after a month you're free to let him go."

"A Frenchman?"

"A French-speaking Walloon from the province of Luxembourg. His name is Lazare. I believe he's Granvelle's great-nephew. He's interested in the arts; he wants to have the experience of associating with you and your clients."

"Yet he's not an artist himself," said Bruegel, mechanically thinking out loud. "I could ask what he really wants in my studio. Not that you'd tell me. I suppose he's an entrepreneur of some sort. Or a spy. But I only have to keep him for a month? All right, then, I'll do it. I have no secrets for him to ferret out. And you'll break off with Mayken?"

"I'll do it as soon as the business with Lazare is completed. Sooner than a month, most likely."

"How will I know when 'the business is completed'?"

"You'll know," said Cheroo, putting away his knife and drawing out a purse.

"Here's your advance for the *Flight into Egypt*. I'll send Lazare right up to you."

"He's outside?" Bruegel was beyond astonishment at Williblad's maneuvers.

"Indeed," said Cheroo, stepping to the window and waving his handkerchief. A figure detached himself from an entranceway across the street. "I'll be on my way now," said Cheroo, walking rapidly to the door.

But then, at the door, Cheroo hesitated, turned back to look at Bruegel. His face had taken on a pensive air. "You're the one fit for Mayken," he said softly. "You deserve the prize. And Bruegel—" Cheroo paused, as if debating within himself about whether to add something more. Heavy footsteps were coming up the stairs. "Have a care for Prince William," whispered Cheroo, and then he was gone.

Cheroo's footsteps crossed the others on the stairs, and then a swarthy fellow with oily skin was in Bruegel's studio. He had a pointed little mustache and a prominent jaw. He looked much more like a hooligan than like a connoisseur of the arts. "Maître Bruegel," he said, bowing and removing his wet, plumed hat with an extravagant gesture that scattered drops of water across the room. *"Je suis votre humble serviteur Lazare."*

This time it was hard to get Waf to stop barking. When the dog finally had been calmed down, it turned out that Lazare spoke no Flemish. But Bruegel knew a bit of French. Lazare asked what he might do to help. Bruegel made a halfhearted attempt to teach Lazare how to grind paints, but the fellow was both clumsy and unwilling to learn. And every time he came near Waf, the dog growled. Bruegel sent him down the street to buy an oak panel for the *Flight into Egypt*, but Lazare took two hours for the task and returned with wine on his breath and the money for the oak panel spent upon an inferior piece of alder.

Wearily Bruegel and Waf went out to get it replaced, and who should they meet on Hoogstraat but young Mayken, skipping along with a hood to protect her from the drizzle. The sight of her filled Bruegel with sorrowful longing—as for a homeland to which he might never return.

She greeted Bruegel cheerfully. "Hello, Peter, how's your *Tower* today?"

"I've just talked with Williblad Cheroo," said Bruegel, drawing her out of the rain into a doorway. He rubbed his hand across his face to get the raindrops out of his eyebrows. "He told me he's been courting you. He's not a good man, Mayken. I'm the one for you." He hadn't meant to say the last sentence, but there was no stopping himself.

"I'm sure you are, Peter," said Mayken, flaring up. "Everyone says so. And I'm to get busy hanging apples on the family tree before I've ever even had a sweetheart. Don't lecture me!" She twisted away from him and ran off down the street. Waf ran along after her, but, seeing that Bruegel didn't follow, he returned to his master. At the corner Mayken paused and looked back at Bruegel. Were those tears on her cheeks, or drops of rain?

Hopelessly Bruegel supposed she was on her way to Granvelle's to meet Cheroo. He could only pray that Williblad would keep his word once Lazare had completed his business, whatever that might be.

Bruegel was in a black humor when he and Waf returned to his studio with a fresh panel of oak. Finding Lazare looking through his papers, he strode forward and cuffed him. He hadn't imagined that the thug could read.

"I don't like having you here," Bruegel told him in curt French. "You're not fit to be my apprentice. Tell me frankly what you want to accomplish, and let's get it over with."

Lazare was unwilling to give a direct answer, so Bruegel set him to work finishing the new oak panel. Lazare was to assiduously polish the wood by rubbing it with a damp cloth and sand, after which Bruegel would paint on a thin coat of quick-drying gesso, which Lazare would sand off, followed by a fresh coat of gesso, a fresh sanding, and so on, through seven iterations, each time using a finer grit of sand. "I want the smoothest possible finish for the Cardinal. And once we finish the front of the panel, we'll start on the back."

"The back?" said Lazare with a puzzled frown.

"I see you know very little about the painter's craft," said Bruegel, grimly enjoying himself. "For the greatest works, we masters paint the sky onto the back of the panel. It adds a certain *profondeur*."

Bruegel turned his attention away from the villain and went back to his painting. Let Lazare sand until his fingers bled, and maybe then he'd talk. And meanwhile, yes, Bruegel would paint. What else was there to do?

Soon he was safe inside his picture, free of his worries about Mayken. The tower was like life, with layer upon layer, detail upon detail, and the unfinished top in the clouds. The joke of the painting was that the inner parts and the outer parts of the tower didn't match. You could see the insides up above, and the outsides down below. The structure was incompletable.

After an hour of sanding, Lazare began to grumble. The work was not to the tough's liking. Bruegel coldly told him that this was the only task that he had for Lazare this month and that, yes, seven sandings of the front and the back of the panel could easily take several weeks. He told Lazare that if and when the Cardinal's panel was smooth enough, he'd have Lazare start in on sanding some panels for the paintings to come. But if the work didn't suit him, well, then he could go home to his great-uncle with his mission incomplete.

Lazare continued to sand and complain for a while longer. Bruegel kept an eye on him, using him as a model for one of the stonemasons who knelt before King Nimrod in the foreground of the large *Tower of Babel*.

"I heard you sold your most recent picture to William of Orange," said Lazare finally. There was a sly glimmer in the man's small, muddy eyes.

Oho, thought Bruegel. The rat peeks out of his hole. "Prince William and I are great friends," he said encouragingly.

"Does he ever come to your studio?" wondered Lazare.

"Indeed," said Bruegel. "Would you like to meet him?"

"Very much," said Lazare, sanding savagely.

Bruegel painted on in silence, finishing off the details of a great mechanical hoist. The day's light was nearly gone, and it was time to stop.

"William owns all the land around my village," said Lazare from the gloom. "His agents took away my family's farm. If—if I could speak with him, then perhaps there would be justice."

"Speak with him?" said Bruegel, feigning indifference as he washed the paint off his brushes. "What would you say?"

"That's between me and him," said Lazare, sullenly throwing down his panel and his sanding cloth. "Once you introduce the two of us, I'll be off your hands. Why don't you ask him to come here tomorrow?"

"We'll see," said Bruegel, maintaining his careless tone. It had by now occurred to him that Granvelle had sent Lazare to murder William. Cheroo himself had suggested as much in those odd last remarks of his. It was hard to fully hate the mercurial Williblad. Now let Granvelle see that Bruegel too could play at intrigue. "Off with you, then, Lazare. I'll put some gesso on your panel to dry overnight. I'll expect you back for work quite early tomorrow morning."

"I thought I'd be eating and sleeping here," protested the Walloon. "Like a proper apprentice."

The long day's frustrations came crashing in on Bruegel. This cat's paw was to live here as his apprentice? Instead of some friendly, talented fellow like young Bengt Bots? Was Bruegel to have no control over even this tiny wretched studio? "Go to the Cardinal's," he roared. "God knows it's not far. Give the fat, conniving sack of shit all the latest news about me. Out with you!" He strode menacingly towards Lazare. Lazare was powerful enough to snap Bruegel's back, but he was cowed by the older man's rage, and perhaps a little frightened by Waf, who'd bared his teeth in a fierce growl. He clattered down the stairs into the rainy dusk.

And now Bruegel was alone. Gradually his pulse slowed and the steel entered his thoughts. He lit some candles and continued cleaning up from the day's work, and when that was done he began pacing back and forth across the room, with Waf anxiously dogging his steps. Normally he'd go to the Coeckes' of an evening, but today that was out of the question. Surely Mayken had seen Cheroo again today. Cheroo had only promised to break off the affair *after* Lazare had done what it was he'd come to do. It was conceivable that this very afternoon Williblad and Mayken had lain together in Granvelle's library. It would be unbearable for Bruegel to see her.

"Dye den nest weet, dye weeten, dyen roft, dy heeten," muttered Bruegel. It was a Low Lands proverb about taking a girl's maidenhood: "Who knows the nest, knows it, who robs the nest, has it." In his mind's eye he saw a placid, unaware peasant pointing back over his shoulder towards a tree with a nest he plans some-day to take. And there, wriggling in the crotch of the tree, as yet unseen by the peasant, was a birdsnester, the kind of fellow who takes a nest as soon as he sees it. The damnably smooth Williblad.

It was long past time for action. Bruegel found his cape and hat, and set out into the darkness, hurrying towards William's palace with Waf at his heels. He had the beginnings of a plan, and William the Sly could help him.

The next morning Lazare arrived early. It was another rainy day.

"Good news," Bruegel said over Waf's barking. He'd hardly slept, so intense was his anticipation. "We're going to Prince William's palace today. Don't bother taking your cloak off, we can leave on the instant. He's expecting us. We're to get a tour of his collection. That should help slake your curiosity about art, eh?"

"I'd hoped to meet him here in your studio," said Lazare. "In full privacy."

"Never fear," said Bruegel heartily. "You won't find any of his courtiers in the painting gallery; they'll be in bed or at his dining table. You'll have ample opportunity to speak with William as privately as you wish. It's my intention that today our mutual business shall reach its climax."

"You do me and my people a great service, Maître Bruegel," said Lazare doff-ing his hat in one of his extravagant bows. Waf snapped at the hat as it swept past. "Can we leave your dog at home?"

"Very well," said Bruegel. "He had a good bit of exercise last night."

As meddlesome Dame Fortuna would have it, Bruegel encountered Mayken as soon as he entered the palace. The way to William's private sitting room led through the palace dining hall. Mayken and her mother were sitting with Princess Anna at one of the endless linen-covered tables, studying the cartoons of the unicorn tapestry. Old Mayken gave him an oddly exuberant wave. Young Mayken jumped out of her seat and came hurrying across the stone floor. She had something to tell him; her face was shining with her news. News about what? After yesterday, Bruegel didn't care to know.

"Not now," said Bruegel before she could start. His face was a mask of ice, his belly a ball of flame. "I don't have time to talk with you." Her face fell. Some fierce part of Bruegel was glad to crush her. Perhaps this morning's little game would even end in his death. Let her taste sorrow. He pushed past Mayken and hurried up the palace stairs, Lazare close at his heels.

They found William in a wood-paneled sitting room before a fire, in conver-sation over white bread and spiced hot chocolate with his purser Groelsch. The room was cozy and warm, with a rich tapestry, an exquisite carpet on the floor, and finely carved chairs with silk-cushioned seats. On a bench by the velvet-curtained window sat a lute and a little pile of leather-bound books, and by the bench was a large celestial globe on a stand with legs twisted like climbing vines. A servant poured out the chocolate from a silver pot with a greyhound upon the lid, and the rich scent of cacao and cardamom filled the air.

"Ah, Peter," said William. "I was expecting you. You've come to visit my collection, eh? Just another minute and I'll show you up personally." Bruegel noted that Grauer was nowhere to be seen. All was proceeding according to the plan that Bruegel and William had worked out last night. How sweet it was to be, for once, the driver of the steeds of fate.

Bruegel smiled. "You're too kind, Prince William. I've taken the liberty of bringing along my new apprentice, Lazare." He switched into French. "Lazare is most honored to meet your lordship. He comes from Luxembourg." Lazare bowed and smiled unctuously, but Bruegel could see the emotions in his eyes. Granville had handpicked this man for his hatred of Prince William. Lazare was an assassin.

"Welcome to Brussels," said William in French, keeping well back from the Walloon. "So then, Peter and Lazare, we'll head up to the gallery. We'll take the spiral staircase over here; it's a handy thing, a bit of a secret passageway. It leads straight up from a little entrance down on the street. A good way for sneaking in and out of the palace when I've the need, eh? But, hush, not a word to anyone else about it, least of all my wife!" William winked and grinned, playing the womanizing braggart. Let Lazare believe he'd have a clear path of escape. William pushed aside a tapestry to reveal the low stone door in the wall. He popped through; Bruegel and Lazare followed.

William rushed up the stairs at a run, with Bruegel behind him, and with Lazare in the rear. Lazare made as if to push up past Bruegel, but the stairs were steep and narrow enough that Bruegel could easily block him with his elbows. He felt as powerful as a cat with a mouse. A minute later they were emerging from behind another tapestry into the gallery.

It was a long wide hallway with bare wood floors, chilled with November. One side of the hall was all windows, the other was a wall hung with pictures, interrupted by two dark, open doorways. William sped across the glossy floor like an ice-skater, finally stopping before a huge triptych, fully twelve feet by six feet in size. From this angle, the light glared off the picture so that Bruegel couldn't make it out.

Lazare brushed past Bruegel and pressed forward towards William, speaking rapidly in a low, penetrating voice. "A word with you, Prince," said the Walloon. "Do you know that your tax assessor took my father's farm? And that one of your soldiers dishonored my sister? Eh? Do you know how many you've ruined in Luxembourg?" Matters were coming to a head.

William took a step backwards, glancing anxiously towards the nearest doorway. But he gave no spoken response.

"Nothing to say, Prince William?" said Lazare, his voice tight with fury.
"Here in your fine palace with your silver and your spices, you've no worries
about a little person like myself, eh? Never give it a thought. Why would you?
Ah, but now, but now, but now the little person's here and, by God, you'll pay the
price."

Bruegel plucked at Lazare's cloak, trying to slow him down.

"Keep your distance or I'll kill you too," said Lazare, not even looking back.
He shrugged and his cloak fell free, making a velvet puddle on the floor. Lazare
was holding a dagger. He strode onward, tense and alert, stalking his prey.
Bruegel hung back, all gloomy desires for self-immolation fled from his mind. It
occurred to him that neither he nor William were armed. He wished he'd paused
to speak with Mayken. What had she wanted to tell him?

"I'm ready!" snarled Lazare, eyes fixed on William. "Are you?" He moved in
for the kill.

But as the assassin passed the darkened doorway in the wall, a figure sprang
out at him with a roar. It was Grauer, swift as a falcon. There was the thud of
flesh, a clatter, a shriek, and then Lazare was tottering about, his hands clenched
over his belly, trying to staunch a great spreading stain of blood. His face wore an
expression of surprise, reminding Bruegel of Father Michel, dead on the barn
floor of that peasant wedding. No man ever believed that Death would truly
come for him.

Grauer was holding Lazare's dagger as well as his own. Two more of William's
guards appeared from the darkened doorway.

"Finish him off, Prince William?" asked Grauer.

"Not quite yet," said William, his voice a little shaky. "Question him."

Lazare had slipped to his knees before the triptych. It was the masterpiece by
Bosch called *The Garden of Earthly Delights,* with Eden on the left, Hell on the
right, and the huge six-foot-square central panel filled with birds, fruits, and
naked lovers. Kneeling before the picture, the wretched, wounded Lazare seemed
part of the painting's Crooked World. The scene made Bruegel dizzy, and now, as
in Mechelen, he felt Master Bosch beside him, gibbering into his ear.

"Who sent you?" Grauer was saying to Lazare.

"Get a physician," groaned Lazare. "A priest. I'm mortally wounded."

"Who sent you, dog?" repeated Grauer, slapping Lazare across the face.

By way of an answer, Lazare spat at Grauer. The spit was red with blood.

"The Cardinal Granvelle sent him," said Bruegel, speaking loud enough to
drown out Bosch's voice. "It's as I told you last night."

"Is it true?" Grauer asked Lazare, pressing his knife so tight against the Walloon's neck that the blood began to flow.

"The Cardinal helped," whispered Lazare. "But it was my dead father who sent me."

Grauer glanced over at William. William nodded. And the knife swept across Lazare's throat. The blood spurted out, soaking Grauer's arm and splattering the bottom part of Bosch's great central panel.

Bosch's shade pressed forward, more solid and animated than ever before, as if drawing substance from the blood steaming in the frigid air. In the past the spirit had only murmured—of colors and forms and certain grotesqueries—but now he was speaking to Bruegel as clearly as the other voices in the room. "Clean off the blood!" commanded Master Bosch. "Clean my picture."

Bruegel stepped forward, drawing out his kerchief. He knelt down beside the twitching corpse of Lazare and began wiping the blood off the painting. He had to dampen a corner of the cloth with his spit to fully wipe the stains away. Lazare's hot, puddled blood began soaking into the knees of his breeches: a terrible sensation, a feeling from Hell. As Bruegel labored to wipe off every spot, splatter, and drop, Master Bosch's voice was excitedly twittering, but the words were hard to understand. At the same time, William and his guards were talking among themselves—talking about Bruegel. They thought his behavior odd.

"Not a glance for your unfortunate apprentice, Bruegel?" asked William dryly.

"He's dead," said Bruegel, pausing from his work to take a quick glance around. "If left to stand, blood stains forever."

Just then a pageboy came clattering down the hall, drawn by the commotion. His wide eyes took in the corpse and the crouched, bloodstained Bruegel. The boy fled downstairs to spread the news. What would Mayken make of it? Bruegel was eager to see. For the first time since Williblad's visit to his studio, he felt a measure of peace. His ruse against Lazare had succeeded.

With Bruegel's calm came a fading of his sense of Master Bosch's presence. Even so, he returned to his task of preservation, rubbing the bespattered image of a great pomegranate whose seeds spilled upon painted grass.

"The man cares more about a painting than a human life," said Grauer, amiably chaffing him. "A colder fish than I."

"It's not I who chose to kill Lazare," protested Bruegel, wanting to push away the blood guilt, although he knew some measure of the guilt was his. With the guilt came pity. Lazare had been a murderous villain, but he'd started as a village boy, the same as him.

But enough weak thoughts. Lazare had been sacrificed for Mayken. Was it enough? "What are you planning to do to the Cardinal and Cheroo?" asked Bruegel.

"I've no power over the Cardinal," said William. "But my men will take care of Cheroo."

Looking at Lazare's blood, Bruegel felt unable to hold something back. "You should know that Cheroo gave me a hint," he said. "I don't think he wanted the assassination to succeed."

"I know where to find Cheroo," rasped one of the guards, as if ignoring Bruegel. "I'll go for him today."

"Don't—don't kill him," said Bruegel. Despite everything, there was something about Williblad that touched his heart. But the man had to leave Mayken alone! "Just make him leave Brussels."

"He'll leave," said Grauer. "He'll want to leave."

"Let it be so," said William. "Is there anything else I can do for you, Peter?"

"Young Bengt Bots wants to be my apprentice," said Bruegel, dabbing a last few small drops of blood from two pairs of naked legs sticking out of a great hollow fruit. Two pale, two coppery. Mayken and Williblad. One way or another that was taken care of now. But would Mayken want Bruegel? Soon he'd see.

"Ah," said William. "Bengt mentioned the matter to me, but I didn't take it seriously. An unlettered boy like that—an artist? You actually want him?"

"He hasn't got the money for my apprenticeship fee," said Bruegel, marveling at his own aplomb. He was like a gambler coolly picking up another trick. "Will you pay it?"

"Of course," said William. "You've done me a great service in flushing this assassin."

There was a hubbub coming up the main stairs. News of the attack had spread throughout the palace. Finished with cleaning the picture, Bruegel got to his feet, stepped back and looked at it. Huge birds and pink lovers. A marvel. But yet, after all, only a picture of Hell, or of something like it. Master Bosch's shade was quite gone. Poor dead Lazare lay curled on the floor, his head thrown back and his neck sticky with clotting blood. Bruegel had led him into this trap, and if he had to, he'd do it again. For Mayken. And here she came, running out from the crowd coming down the hall.

"Peter!"

She ran towards him with her arms stretched out. Bruegel embraced her, marking her garments with his blood-wet trousers.

"We heard the screams," said Mayken. "The page said you were bloody on the floor. Oh, Peter, I thought you were dead."

"I did it to make Williblad leave you alone," said Bruegel.

"There was no need, Peter! Yesterday—after I saw you in the street—I grasped my folly. I broke off with Williblad. Oh, Peter. Forgive me."

Bruegel's eyes fell on the left wing of Bosch's masterpiece. Jesus stood between Adam and Eve, marrying them. In the central panel the nude figures writhed in lust, and in the right wing they suffered the torments of the damned.

Better by far to live in Eden. Any lingering anger he'd held towards Mayken melted away.

"I forgive you, Mayken. Everyone has a past. I—" He wanted to confess something to her, but he couldn't say it.

Mayken took a step back, looked him in the eyes, and plucked the thought out. "You were my mother's lover, weren't you?"

"Yes," said Bruegel, his face flushing red. "Years ago. I was a boy and she was lonely. Your father was off fighting the Turks."

Mayken gave a little nod, took a breath, and pressed on. "The thing is, I've been worried that—you're not my real father are you?"

"Oh God, no, Mayken. That would be monstrous. Your mother was already quickened when—when we had our affair. It ended before you were born. It was folly." Bruegel laughed giddily. Losing his secret was like shrugging off a stone.

"Folly like me and Williblad," said Mayken with a tremulous smile. "You'll still have me?"

"I love you, Mayken," said Bruegel. "Will you marry me?"

"Yes," said Mayken. "Yes. I always thought I would."

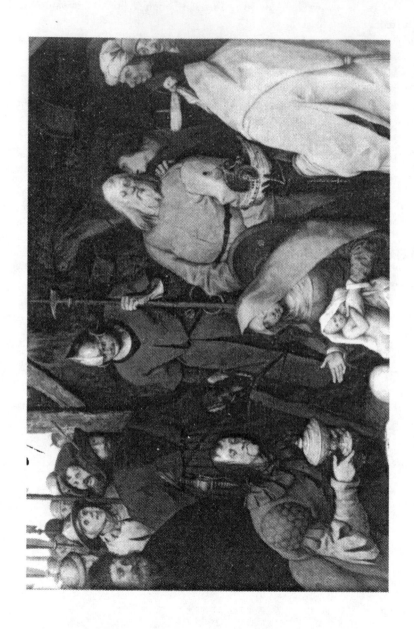

※ ※ ※ ※ ※ ※ ※ ※ ※ ※ ※ ※

ELEVEN

THE ADORATION OF THE KINGS
BRUSSELS, MAY 1563–
DECEMBER 1564

It was late of a balmy May evening. Mayken and Peter were in the little garden behind the Coecke house, standing beneath a flowering plum tree. Tomorrow they would be wed. The house was full of voices and candlelight; Mayken's mother had put on a preparatory dinner and some of the guests were still here.

"Look," said Mayken, taking hold of the plum tree and shaking it. She'd shaken this tree every spring for as long as she could remember. "It's snowing." The sweet-smelling white petals drifted down onto her upturned face and Peter kissed her. He was very affectionate tonight, every bit as excited as she.

"I love having them fall on me," said Mayken after the kiss. More than snow, the petals had always made her think of weddings. It was hard to believe her time was almost here. She and Peter shook the trunk some more; there seemed to be no end of blossoms upon the thickly branched little tree. Mayken felt open and happy, she felt as if the petals were falling right through her heart. Peter hugged her, his arms strong around her, his lips smooth and warm in the midst of his beard.

"Come on, then, Peter," came a voice from the kitchen door. "It's almost midnight. Let's go back down the street to your studio." It was Peter's fussy old friend Abraham Ortelius from Antwerp.

Ortelius had brought them a new wall map as a wedding gift when he came down yesterday, and had insisted on spending half of today getting it properly glued onto a wall, not that it had been easy to find the wall space in the stuffed old Coecke house. In the end they'd put the map in the kitchen. "It'll be good for Mienemeuie to see it," Mayken's mother had said with a laugh. "She still thinks the ocean boils below the equator." To which their cook Mienemeuie had responded, "And how do you know it doesn't, Mevrouw? You've never been there." Cocking her hands on her hips, the wiry old Mienemeuie had squinted at the big new map. "Doesn't mean a damned thing to me! What's supposed to be where? The only part that makes sense are the little pictures of ships and sea monsters."

"Peter?" repeated Ortelius.

"Wedding blossoms!" sang Peter. "Look." He gave the tree such a shake that the cloud of petals drifted as far as the kitchen door. Waf, who was out in the yard with them, raised his nose to sniff at the falling flowers.

"Lovely," said Ortelius. "My new house has trees like this, but they're not in bloom yet. I'll have to shake some petals for Williblad." Mayken and Peter groaned in unison, then burst out laughing. Nothing could dampen their gaiety tonight.

After the failed assassination attempt, Williblad had been driven out of Brussels by William the Sly's bodyguards. He'd ended up moving in with Ortelius back in Antwerp, where Ortelius had recently moved into a larger house. Ortelius gave him free room and board; in return Williblad helped a bit with Ortelius's antiquities business. With Ortelius's mother recently dead and his sister relocated to London, Ortelius welcomed the company.

Upon his arrival yesterday, Ortelius had been worried Peter might be angry with him for sheltering Williblad, but Peter seemed not to care—so long as Williblad remained in Antwerp. Mayken had trouble visualizing what Ortelius and Williblad did together. Did Williblad sexually penetrate the man-loving bachelor? An incongruous thought.

In any case, the love-smitten Ortelius seemed unable to stop talking about

Williblad; they'd heard about nothing else from him for the last two days. It had made Mayken and Peter uncomfortable at first, but Ortelius's constant repetition of Williblad's name had begun to have the effect of partly healing over the embarrassment. At least he hadn't brought Williblad here.

Mayken sometimes wondered what she'd seen in Williblad. Handsome, yes, but unhappy and empty-headed. Peter had more talent in his little finger than Williblad had in all of his beautiful body. And if Peter was a bit old—why, Williblad was a decade older. On the other hand, Williblad had been all hers. Mayken was still upset about Peter and her mother. Couldn't mother have had the decency to leave Peter alone for her daughter? And, aged or not, Williblad's face and body were lovely. It still made Mayken flush to think about their hours in Granvelle's library together. She kissed Peter again, pushing these thoughts away.

Another figure appeared at the kitchen door: Marcus Noot, a well-off widower who'd risen to the high political post of City Father. He was Mayken's mother's gentleman friend.

"The deflowering's in progress!" cried Noot, seeing the drifting petals and the embracing couple. He'd had more than his share of wine tonight.

"All you men get out of here," called Mayken's mother from the kitchen. "It's time for me to have a talk with my daughter."

"Yes, yes," said Noot. "Tell the girl about men."

Peter gave Mayken a last kiss good night, and then he, Ortelius, Waf, and Noot were on their way. Mayken and her mother sat in the candlelit kitchen sharing a piece of cake.

"I'm so happy for you, Mayken," said Mayken's mother. "Peter's a wonderful man." She had a glass of wine in front of her, and her smile was a little crooked. Once again Mayken felt a stab of anger about Peter and her mother. She felt a sudden need to lash out.

"I know about you and Peter," said Mayken.

"What do you mean?" said her mother, her face cautious.

"I know that you lay with him when you were pregnant with me." Saying it out loud forced Mayken to imagine it. It seemed she was always thinking about sex these days. She gazed at her mother's mouth, picturing Peter licking it.

"Who told you that?" said the mouth.

"I guessed. And I asked Peter just to be sure. I'd been worried he might be my real father." Mayken still had a lingering fear of this hideous prospect. "He's not, is he?"

"Of course not," cried Mayken's mother. "You're Master Coecke's daughter through and through. You've got his orderliness and his head for business. Not to mention his small nose."

"But it's true about you and Peter. Don't change the subject. How could you do this to me?"

"Cold old ashes," sighed Mayken's mother. "He was a boy. I was lonely and pregnant. You weren't even born! We were different people then. When your father found out, he nearly slit Peter's throat with a scimitar. The one that hangs on the wall in his old studio." She laughed ruefully. "Imagine this coming back again to haunt me! Sometimes I think life is too long. Don't even think about this ancient nonsense. I never do, and I'm sure Peter doesn't either."

"You're—you're not after Peter anymore, are you?" This was Mayken's biggest fear. To be overshadowed forever by her mother. She wanted a husband who was all her own. Not for the first time, she wished she'd been allowed to pick out a boy of her own age. It was tiresome to always be thinking about the future of the family studios. And if her mother was going to go around mooning after Peter it would be impossible.

"Perish the thought. Your happiness is so much more important to me than anything else, Mayken. And the grandchildren! Why would an old crone like me meddle in that?" In the candlelight, Mayken's mother looked both wise and sly.

"You're not quite a crone, mother. You have men visiting you all the time."

"Marcus is a bit of a fool, isn't he?" said her mother with a smile. "If the truth be told, I'd never link up with another man. I value my freedom too highly. That's the reward for marrying an older man, you know. By the time you're middle-aged you're on your own. Nobody to answer to, and you can amuse yourself by playing a few suitors."

"Marcus was drunk tonight," said Mayken. She herself had no head for wine. "Did you hear what he said about deflowering?" Mayken giggled. She was secretly glad she had her experience with Williblad to set off against Peter's affairs with mother and with that goose-faced peasant Anja. She couldn't tell if her mother knew about Williblad or not. But it was just as well to stop talking about the great issues. It was comfortable to gossip about the smaller things with mother.

"No matter about Marcus," said old Mayken amiably. "I'm glad I had some wine in me for this conversation. Peter is yours, and yours alone."

The service was at a neighborhood church called Our Lady of the Chapel, just a few blocks down the Hoogstraat from the Coecke house. The priest was Father Ghislain, a good old man, dear and familiar to the Coecke family.

The guests were wonderfully turned out. The men wore dark tights and jackets, with slits in the leg-of-mutton sleeves revealing yellow and red silk linings. Each of the men had a formal Low Lands ruff collar made of yards of starchy lace folded over and over in figure-eight loops. Peter's head upon his collar made Mayken think of an egg in a china eggcup—an eager, excited egg.

The women wore long-sleeved cottes with fine tunics. Mayken's tunic was of pale blue, and atop that she wore a sleeveless surcoat of yellow silk embroidered with gold brocade outlines of leaves and flowers. She too had a lace ruff collar;

hers was open in front and rose up behind her head like a low halo. As was the custom for a bride, her hair hung free, quite golden in the sunlight.

After the wedding, their party walked down Hoogstraat in their finery, with all the neighbors and shopkeepers smiling and cheering. Waf had escaped from where they'd penned him in the Coecke house garden, and led the way down the street, tail held high. Back at the Coecke house, Mienemeuie served a meal of oysters, wood snipe, and leeks, hares with a brown caper sauce, mountains of potatoes and onions, and cinnamon pancakes. Among the guests were Ortelius, Hans Franckert and his wife, Hennie van Mander, Marcus Noot, and some of Mayken's young friends, all very gay and cheerful. Rather than a rowdy peasantlike affair with bagpipes, they had civilized conversation and, after the meal, some harpsichord music, played by Mayken's friend Suzanna Smijters. Peter and Mayken danced together, Peter very handsome in his lace collar, though by now the folds were crumpled like the coastline on a map. Mayken wished she felt more swept away with love.

In the days before the wedding, Mayken's mother had moved down into a little room beside her studio on the second floor so that Peter and Mayken could settle into the great third-floor bedroom that Mayken's parents had once shared. In the mornings Mayken would wake up with Peter next to her in bed; sometimes he'd be asleep, but if he were awake he'd be on one elbow looking out the window down into the street. They'd kiss and talk and have bread and chocolate in their room.

The closer Mayken got to Peter, the more she liked him. Though he had the kindness and wisdom of maturity, he retained the fire and the playfulness of a schoolboy. Mayken's love for him began steadily to grow. She felt it to be like a fat winter turnip rather than like a spring flower that suddenly bursts into bloom. She tried once to explain her sense of this to Peter.

"Oh, not a muddy turnip," he protested. "Let's say your love is a fine orange pumpkin. I'll water you and polish you and see how big you grow."

Peter moved his studio into the Coecke house, setting up shop in Master Coecke's old workspace, the huge, open attic on the fourth floor, a lovely space with a smooth wooden floor, gable windows, a fireplace, and a great peaked ceiling that rose from eight feet near the walls to twenty feet at the ridge of the roof. His joy at occupying the studio was so great that Mayken had to wonder if her house were not, in the end, the real reason he'd married her.

She went ahead and asked him this. Peter insisted that, although he rejoiced in the studio, he'd live anywhere, so long as it was with her. In any case the studio was, he insisted, more hers than his. He suggested they enjoy it together, and that he teach her all about painting. Whether Mayken herself became a painter or not, if she was to be the lady of the house in a dynasty of artists, she would do well to know the secrets of the trade.

Peter hung his beloved convex mirror above the mantelpiece. And Peter's pale blond new apprentice Bengt Bots arrived along with the brushes and oils and paints. Bengt's father had been so angry with him for abandoning falconry that he wouldn't let him remain in Prince William's palace, so Bengt was to sleep on a cot in the studio.

And thus the new workshop got under way. Peter had finished up his two *Tower of Babel* paintings in his Hoogstraat studio, delivering the large one to Nicolas Jonghelinck, and making Mayken a gift of the small one. She liked it quite a bit, especially when Peter pointed out his joke that the outsides and the insides of the towers didn't match.

"Like the Church these days," he said, though he rarely spoke of religion. "Or like a person at disharmony with themselves. Life runs well only when what's above matches what's below." And he punctuated this by kissing Mayken and intimately pressing her belly against his. So far the new studio was seeming like fun.

Peter's first task in the Coecke studio was to make good on his commission to paint a *Flight into Egypt* for Cardinal Granvelle. Blandly pretending his ignorance of Lazare's plan to assassinate Prince William, the Cardinal had sent around a messenger to ask when Bruegel would deliver the finished work. As a second payment would be then due, it seemed as well to finish the picture. Peter had already started it in Hoogstraat, and he'd brought with him the pots of paint he'd made up for it.

In the mornings, after breakfast and some comfortable time in bed, Peter would head upstairs and rouse Bengt, who tended to sleep late. At first, Mayken felt like she still had to go downstairs to help in her mother's studio, running out to get paints for her miniatures or laying out threads for her tapestries. But being so dutiful made her weary, and then resentful. Was she to be her mother's girl forever? After a week of this, she snapped something angry at old Mayken, and her mother quickly relieved her of her old obligations.

"Don't worry about me, Mayken," said her mother, holding a tiny brush with a dab of red paint. She was working on a miniature portrait of William of Orange's wife. Somehow she'd gotten a bit of the paint on the tip of her big nose. "I can take care of things in my studio, really I can. Have fun getting to know your husband. That's more important. And how about this for a new job? Why don't you start running all our business affairs? I'd rather have you as a manager than an assistant. And then I can be the one to sigh and roll her eyes." She laughed easily, and Mayken's spirits surged sky-high.

So Mayken began starting the days by going up to Peter's studio with him. Peter decided to use Mayken as a model for the Mary in his *Flight into Egypt*. It was pleasant to pose, to sit and to be looked at by her lively new husband. It was remarkable to see how he could transform her into colors and curves. Just to train Bengt's hand, Peter set him to work trying to make a watercolor copy of

Peter's picture while he worked. As Peter painted, he talked to Mayken and Bengt, telling them the tricks and recipes of the painter's craft.

A few of Peter's phrases were familiar—though Mayken's father had died when she was only six, she still had some memories of hearing him teaching Peter. One of the familiar sayings was, "An egg is mostly water," to explain how egg-mixed paint could dry so fast. "Mix three shades of three shades," was her father's injunction for getting smooth colorings, and "Look through your painting like a window," was his old rubric for laying out a scene in perspective. Mayken had always wondered about that last one; as a child she'd practiced looking through all kinds of things as if they were windows, including the faces of her friends.

Peter had many other sayings new to Mayken, many of them relating to his uncanny ability to paint his lively little women and men. He sometimes called them his *pachters*—the Flemish word for "tenant farmers." If Peter's canvases were his estates, the pictures' painted inhabitants were his tenants. Among his teachings were these:

"A runner flies; a walker glides."

"Better too fat than too thin."

"A hat makes a head."

"See what your *pachter* sees."

"Objects are alive."

And—Peter delivered this one in a challenging tone—"The world is a parable."

"You mean the *painting* is a parable, don't you, Master Bruegel?" said Bengt, who enjoyed the give-and-take of discussion.

"That goes without saying," answered Peter. "No, I said the *world* is a parable. God made the world, and he made it a parable. The world's like God's painting."

"If the world's a painting, then who commissioned it?" demanded Bengt.

"You're the patron, the *pachter*, and the paint," said Peter. "The Trinity."

"How so the paint?" asked Bengt.

"The red is your blood, the black your bile, the yellow your choler, and the cool green is your phlegm."

The lessons and the logic-chopping word games mystified Mayken a little, and once Peter was through using her as a model, she began spending a bit less time in the studio. And a good thing too, as life in the Coecke house was going on as usual and her mother truly had abandoned all control over the finances.

So Mayken learned how to be a businesswoman. She gave Mienemeuie money for shopping, collected the fees from her mother's patrons, paid the taxman his share of what they earned, and so on and so on. Things were tighter than she'd ever realized—indeed the Coecke workshop was not so far removed from bankruptcy. No wonder mother had been so keen to have Peter join the family.

Every few months Jerome Cock would send down some undocumented payments for his sales of Peter's engravings, and Peter mentioned wondering if he might be underpaid. So Mayken got Jerome to give them a proper accounting, and ended up getting him a bit more money than before, which helped.

The one member of the household who doubted Mayken's acumen was old Mienemeuie. The day came when she tried to pooh-pooh Mayken's decisions and to go around her to her mother, but old Mayken stood solidly behind her daughter.

"Let her make her own mistakes," said mother. "They'll never be as bad as mine."

Before long Peter was finished with the *Flight into Egypt*, with Mary/ Mayken on a donkey and Joseph/Peter starting down the slope ahead of her, his head and face covered by a hat. The distant prospects of the picture showed a lovely, sunny river landscape. But for now, Joseph and Mary were heading down into a dark canyon they'd have to traverse before reaching their Promised Land. Mayken gasped when she saw the composition, so perfectly did it seem to express their situation. In the end all would be well between her and Peter, she felt sure of it—but in the meantime there were their financial problems, the growing political unrest of the Low Lands, and the lingering memories of her delirious affair with Williblad. Mayken still felt just a bit unsure of her love for Peter. Yes, the love was a fine big pumpkin by now, but why couldn't it be a bright thorny rose to pierce her heart?

Discussing his *Flight into Egypt* with her, Peter chose not to explore the meaning of the dark canyon. Instead he talked about a toppled pagan idol he'd painted in; it was sticking out from a little wooden shrine beside the path the painted couple trod. "That's the Cardinal," remarked Peter, pointing out the fallen idol with the end of his brush. "Sometimes a painting makes things so. Granvelle won't be in the Low Lands much longer."

Not wanting to see his tormentor Granvelle again himself—and perhaps not wanting to risk a tongue-lashing about the idol—Peter had Bengt deliver the panel to the Cardinal. Bengt reported that Granvelle had paid the remainder of the fee with barely a glance at the picture. Evidently the Primate had other things on his mind.

Indeed, the Low Lands were in great ferment. Politics was all that anyone talked about in the markets. The high nobles had presented King Philip with a petition that he lighten his edicts against heresy and end the slaughter of his citizens.

Meanwhile, the money from the final sale of the painting came in handy, though Mayken felt the overall price had been too low. She'd taken it upon herself to visit the Brussels Schilderspand to get an idea of the going prices for paintings the size and quality of Peter's. She urged him to let her help him negotiate his fees from now on, and he gladly agreed.

Politics and finances interested Peter much less than what he could see and think and paint. Mayken got her chance to serve as the negotiator for his next commission, which was to be his largest panel yet, done for Jonghelinck, who had been exceedingly pleased with his *Tower of Babel*.

The new picture was to be a *Bearing of the Cross*, a scene of Christ carrying his cross, but drawn as a Flemish crowd scene. It was a composition that had been done numerous times by other Flemish painters, indeed Jonghelinck owned a similar scene by Herri met de Bles. Jonghelinck paid a visit to Brussels specifically to ask Peter to do something like it. When he proposed a sum to Peter, Peter said neither yes nor no, but asked him to return on the morrow so he could discuss the offer with his manager, his Mayken.

As they discussed the painting that evening, Peter paced around his fine big attic studio with its many windows, telling Mayken that he was set upon making the biggest and best Flemish *Bearing of the Cross* yet, the one that would finish off this particular genre for once and for all. It touched her to see how high he set his sights. She fully believed he could attain his ambitions, and she wanted to see him properly paid. That night Mayken did some figuring from the going rates and from her estimates of the costs of making the work Peter wanted—and concluded that Jonghelinck should triple the figure.

To Peter's surprise, Jonghelinck accepted the counteroffer. His elation was extreme. Peter and Bengt ran out and purchased a huge, well-aged oak panel, the largest they could find, five feet by four feet in size. And now, before starting, he wanted to make up a fresh batch of paints. He insisted that Mayken be in on this. "So you can teach our sons and daughters some day," he reminded her. Mayken was getting to like this idea. The talk of their descendents had changed from being a burden to being a pleasant prospect. More workers to fill the accounts of the studio! And, truly, how sweet it would be to see a child who was half Mayken and half Peter.

The trade secrets of making paints were quite new to Mayken. Her father had died too young to teach her, and her mother had never had the temperament for fiddling with such alchemical processes. Instead, the old Mayken bought the paints for her miniatures ready-mixed from her artist friend Anne Smijters, who had a busy studio just a few streets away. Peter told Mayken they'd make pigments of white, yellow, black, green, blue, and red.

For the white and yellow, Peter, Bengt, and Mayken refurbished Master Coecke's "stack" for making white lead. The stack, abandoned for years now, consisted of a dozen clay pots arranged beneath the midden heap beside the shed in the corner of the garden. Some were cracked, and Peter replaced them. He poured a few inches of apple vinegar in each of the pots, and then he had Bengt and Mayken put a number of beaten sheets of lead into each vessel. The sheets, pounded to the thinness of paper, were separated by pebbles so that the vinegar would touch all the surfaces. They covered the stack of pots back up with rotting compost and household dung. Waf became so interested in this process that they put a fence around the stack to keep him from rolling in it or digging it up.

According to Peter, the decay of the offal released a fire element, which over the period of a few weeks would combine with the fire within lead and vinegar to turn the earthen elements of lead into an air element of fine, flaking white. Though his schooling had been quite brief, Peter seemed to have soaked up an uncanny ability to mirror the workings of the scholastic mind. Mayken chaffed him about it a little in private, asking him which element made his penis rise.

In any case, the point of the stack was that, washed and ground, the white lead would serve as the finest kind of white pigment, far superior in durability to marble dust or to ground egg shells. And once you had the white lead, you could heat part of it in a crucible, transmuting it into a fine yellow pigment called massicot.

"For the black we need bone," said Peter when the stack was done. "Or better yet, ivory." Something jogged loose in Mayken's memory. She ran and found a charred old walrus tusk from one of the basement closets; she'd occasionally played with the talismanic object as a girl, thinking of it as some eldritch northern Queen's scepter. Walrus tusk was, said Peter, the best possible source of black pigment. They heated the tusk over a fire, astonished by its fishy stench, and then scraped off a quantity of the blackened ivory.

"Now for the colors," said the busy Peter on the next day. "The water and air of our parable world." He produced a sack of special rocks: crumbly nuggets of azurite and malachite in shades of blue and green. The way to get the pigments from the ore was a process called levigation. Peter had Bengt crush the rocks and told Mayken to shake them up with water, the blue ore in one flask and the green in the other. The earthy dross settled to the bottoms of the flasks while the colorful powders swirled about in the fluid. Mayken liked this part, the dust in the water was pretty. They poured off the bright waters and levigated the mixtures again. The results were two heaps of fine, powdery pigment that were set out in the sunlight to dry.

Finally, for his red, Peter used a vermilion cinnabar that Hans Franckert had imported from Austria. This ore was said to be a blend of mercury and sulfur; it was a terribly dangerous substance with a lethal affinity for the blood humor; artists who carelessly inhaled cinnabar dust had been known to die within months: yellow, wizened, and smelling of urine. Peter implored Mayken to never handle the cinnabar herself; and he insisted that Bengt wrap a triple kerchief around his face before grinding it up on a table in the garden.

Rather than letting the powdered pigments wait, Peter deemed it better to mix them up into finished paint right away. They heated a mixture of balsamic turpentine with walnut oil and then melted a block of beeswax into the liquid. They split the smooth, sticky medium among four pots and folded in the bright dusts. And then, finally, there were four little vessels of paint: a black, a green, a blue, and a red, each with a layer of oil to cover it. Frankly, Mayken wondered if she could remember every step. But she knew she'd have many chances to see it all again. It was a little odd to think of her whole future life being already planned out for her.

"Remember, Mayken," said Peter, "white, yellow, and red are poisonous, while black, green, and blue are safe. It's the fire element that's deadly." Indeed, thought Mayken with a tiny inward sigh. The fire is what damages your heart. Better of course to be a safe old wife, working with water and earth.

While all the paint-making had been going on, Bengt had also been sanding Peter's new panel for him. Peter brushed the panel with a mixture of plaster and horse-hoof glue, giving it a firm white surface. And then he was ready to start populating it.

In these early stages of the picture, Peter worked with pencil and paper, first getting his *pachters* right, and then sketching them onto the panel. Just for the fun of it, Mayken took her own paper and began practicing drawing along with Bengt. But, even though her parents were artists, she didn't have the touch. While the lines sprang into life from Bengt's long, pale fingers, Mayken's drawings came out crooked and stiff. Peter encouraged her anyway, but soon she gave it up.

One day, to postpone having to go downstairs and work on the business accounts, she hit on the idea of helping Peter make up stories about the characters he drew. As Peter said, the more you knew about the *pachters*' lives, the better you could draw them. And Mayken was better than he at imagining other people's lives and minds.

So for the next few weeks, Mayken would go up to the studio in the morning and spend some time with Peter and Bengt telling stories about the people they drew. Here was a mounted soldier with two nose-holes in a face like an empty skull; Mayken said his family had died of leprosy and he'd gone into the army as a boy, sending part of his pay to cover the feeding of a single cow that he'd inherited on a cousin's farm, but that his cousin had long since butchered and eaten the cow without telling him. A workman with a shovel trudged along with four other workmen, one of them wearing a tight red hat with flaps. Mayken said they'd dug a tulip garden that afternoon for a lady who hadn't paid them, and now were trying to get good spots to watch the Crucifixion, with the hope of meeting someone there to give them more work, but it was hard to make plans as the man in the tight red hat was deaf from scarlet fever. A man ran across the scene with a heavy sack over his shoulder; Mayken said the sack was full of spoiled grain the man had stolen to feed his sick son Wim, who was home alone because his wife had followed Mary Magdalene to the Sermon on the Mount and had never come home, and that the man had been too busy with his son to listen to the gossip of the streets, so he was surprised to see Jesus here in the procession. Over by the fallen Christ and his cross, a fat man in chain mail blew a long, curving horn; Mayken said he liked to practice blowing it a lot during the daytime and even at night, and a neighbor had threatened to kill him, but the horn blower was friends with the local Inquisitor, and he'd had the complaining neighbor burned as a heretic. In front of him was a cart with the two thieves in it; one thief made confession to a sly, simian monk; the other thief stared white-faced into the heavens. Mayken said the confessing man had robbed and killed six merchants, and the staring man had murdered his mother, but that when hanging on their crosses, it would be the staring man who turned out to be the good thief, the one who asked the Lord to save him. The wheels of their cart were covered in mud, and the draft horse was knee-deep in water, his name was Paard, and he liked nothing better than rolling on his back in a sunny meadow, but he wasn't going to be doing that today.

In the foreground were a husband and wife struggling with three soldiers and a bald old Pharisee. The Pharisee had the husband by one arm, pulling him towards the fallen Christ. Two of the soldiers were pushing and pulling the husband as well, they wanted him to help carry the cross. The wife was hanging on to the husband. The third soldier, who wore striped tights, was threatening the wife with a pike. Her jaw was set and her husband's feet were braced.

"Put a rosary at her waist," said Mayken. "She says novenas, but she doesn't want her husband to help the Lord. And have the husband be looking to her for help. She's stronger than him."

The weeks turned into months before all of Peter's figures were sketched in. Mayken went up to the studio less and less often. There were too many people, too much to think about. How could Peter stay focused upon his little world for so long? Meanwhile Bengt harvested the white lead, cooked some of it into yellow massicot, and started a fresh batch in the stack. Finally the drawing was done. For the last two figures in the picture, Peter had drawn a skulking, anguished Judas, and beside Judas he had set a self-portrait of himself in profile, Peter standing there with his hands folded, calm and noble, gazing at the fallen little Christ in the center of the scene.

It was all quite lovely, but Mayken found that juggling the family finances interested her more—perhaps because this work was all hers. Mother had recently landed another tapestry commission, and to bring the money in faster, Mayken hit on the notion of patching together some of their old tapestry cartoons and having another studio take over some of the fabrication. Peter's advance from Jonghelinck was used up by now, and it was a daily balancing act to keep the House of Coecke solvent.

Even though she wanted Peter to finish his picture and get paid, Mayken would perhaps have liked it better if he'd spent more time in bed with her in the mornings. These days, no sooner was he awake, than he was running up the stairs to his studio.

"Come watch me start the underpainting," urged Peter. "That's worth knowing about too." So again Mayken started spending a bit of time in the studio each morning. It was in fact the one way to be sure she saw her husband before dinnertime. Peter dipped out bits of the red and the yellow, the white and the black, made up some shades of ocher, and thinned them with a mixture of egg and walnut oil. Inch by inch he went across the panel, creating a delicate underpainting in light tones that still let the drawing show through. And when, a week or two later, this was done, he went over the picture again, highlighting the bright spots with white lead. The intricacy of the process staggered Mayken. Her mother's miniatures took nothing like so long. But Peter seemed never to weary of his labors and, considering all that he set himself to do, he worked rapidly. Each detail of his picture seemed endlessly capable of arousing his interest.

In the afternoons Peter would quit work, wash himself off, and Mayken would take him and Waf out to walk the streets of Brussels. But even outdoors, Peter's attention seemed, more often than not, to be up in the fourth-floor studio with his little characters. His obsession with his work was beginning to make her jealous.

The town was in a ferment of gossip about whether the Foreigner might accede to the nobles' petition to soften the strictures against heresy. More and more people had become openly Calvinist. And then, in March of 1564, the word came out that Cardinal Granvelle was leaving. At King Philip's request, the Cardinal was to visit his mother in France for an indefinitely long period of time. People imagined that now King Philip would weaken his edicts and come to more reasonable terms with the citizenry of the Low Lands. Little did they know that the King was but biding his time, and that his persecutions would double and redouble in savagery over the years to come. But for a few happy months, the citizens could dream that their freedom was at hand.

The news of Granvelle's dismissal came out just at the start of Carnival, and the revelry was wild and unrestrained. Franckert and Hennie came down from Antwerp to visit; Mayken put them up in an extra room that was squeezed in on the second floor between her mother's bedroom and studio. Some wag had painted "For Immediate Sale" on the door of Granvelle's palace. Many dressed up like priests and cardinals for the riotous masking. Peter, the Maykens, and what seemed like half of Brussels were invited to a great celebration at William the Sly's.

At Franckert's urging, Mayken and Peter drank rather more than their custom. Fat Franckert could hold any amount of alcohol and still dance with his wife, but Peter grew more and more disheveled and stupid. He couldn't stop talking about having wiped blood from the Bosch in William's gallery, and then nothing would do but that he and Franckert disappear upstairs with candles to study *The Garden of Earthly Delights*. Mayken's mother and Marcus Noot were devouring pancakes at the long dining table, Hennie was deep in a discussion of tapestries with Anne Smijters, and for the moment Mayken was quite dizzy and alone.

"You look very lovely," said a familiar voice.

Mayken turned; the tall man behind her wore a Cardinal's cape and a copper mask shaped like the sun. His cape hung open to reveal a black jersey and tight breeches with a prominent red codpiece.

"Williblad!"

"Hush," he said, holding out his arm. "I'm not welcome here. Can we go off and talk in private?"

"I'm married now." Yet she found herself placing her hand upon his arm. A kind of shock traveled through her fingers. She took a quick, dizzy look around the room. Nobody was watching them. Peter had abandoned her and nobody cared.

"I think we might find a quiet parlor over here," said Williblad, steering her through the crowd. And then they were alone in a small book-lined room that made Mayken instantly think of the Cardinal's library. Well, not quite alone, as one of Lady Anna's ladies-in-waiting had fallen into a stuporous slumber upon one of the room's two couches.

Williblad took off his mask and closed the door. To Mayken's surprise, his fine straight nose had gone crooked.

"Oh, Williblad, what happened to you?" she said, raising her hand to her own nose.

"William the Sly's men gave me quite a beating the night they told me to leave town. They broke my nose and one of my arms. Perhaps your Peter told them to."

"Oh, you poor thing." Seeing the sadness in his eyes she stepped forward and gave his face a little caress. "You're still handsome, though."

"You're wonderful to say that." He seemed so needy for love. With a flourish, he removed his red cape and tossed it over the head of the inert woman on the couch. "To ensure that the parrot stays asleep," he said, with his old smile. He strode across the room and plopped down on the other couch. "Come sit with me, Mayken. Just like old times. I've missed your kisses." She sat by him and he pressed her hand. He was hungry for her touch.

Mayken had really meant to just talk with Williblad about how happy she was with Peter, but she felt so sorry about the broken nose that somehow one thing led to another and before long Williblad was on top of her, with her dress pulled up around her waist and his codpiece all undone. How he made her heart pound!

Suddenly the door to the parlor swung open. It was the pale young Bengt Bots. He flushed bright pink and quickly left, slamming the door behind him. The lady-in-waiting beneath the cape stirred and grumbled, fumbling at the heavy silk. Mayken twisted free of Williblad and ran out into the great, noisy hall. She found Peter, took him home, and made love to him like never before.

A month later Mayken realized that she was pregnant. Peter was thrilled to see Mayken's belly swell. For her part, Mayken was dreadfully uneasy. She and Williblad had stopped before he'd reached his climax, but perhaps that didn't make a difference. With these things one never knew.

"How does it feel?" Peter wanted to know.

"It feels strange," said Mayken. "There's someone tiny alive inside me, and only God knows what she—or he—looks like."

Summer and fall shaded into the hardest winter that any of them could remember, with the ground frozen solid from the start of November. It was bitter cold outside, with icicles hanging down off the eaves. A fire burned in every room. As Mayken swelled, Peter grew more romantic. He worked a bit less and chatted with her more. He was learning how to be a loving husband. And for Mayken's part, with the baby on its way, she appreciated more than ever Peter's ability to earn money with his labors. Sometimes, lying in a patch of sunshine on their bed, she'd imagine them coming out of the dark canyon and into the bright plain of their future. Mayken would become the matriarch of a great line of artists.

With Peter so affectionate, and Mayken's hopes so high, she no longer had any thoughts of any other man. The one shadow upon her pleasure was the apprentice Bengt Bots. The boy stared at her provokingly when their paths crossed. She did her best to avoid him. How could she have let herself get re-entangled with Williblad? God willing, he'd gone straight back to Antwerp. There'd been no sign of him since Carnival, and thankfully no visits from Ortelius. The business with Williblad at the palace was nothing but a half-remembered fever dream, and if Bengt would only keep his council, it need never have even happened.

Peter was on the home stretch with his *Bearing of the Cross*. He'd given the painting a low, cloudy sky that receded off into vast distances. There were any number of crows flying about; the closer Mayken looked, the more of them she could find. Peter loved crows, loved to draw them, loved the sounds of their caws, loved to speculate about their behavior, loved to point them out to Mayken whenever they were outside.

The wearisome Bengt, whose skills seemed to be coming along quickly, worked at Peter's side, painting a watercolor copy of the *Bearing of the Cross* on a large piece of paper. Peter had it in his mind that soon he'd have a proper workshop, producing multiple copies of his compositions. Bengt's copy would be saved for Bruegel's archives, to be used as the model for the finished copies to come.

Bengt's presence was becoming more and more of a burden for Mayken. Though the boy had said nothing to Peter yet, Mayken felt sure that he was constantly thinking about the sight of her beneath Williblad. She began to imagine that the quiet, bloodless lad had some hope of making love to her himself. He actually seemed to be making calf eyes at her. Did he take young Mayken for as great a goose as old Mayken? She treated Bengt with icy hauteur. She was a woman now, the manager of the family business, a wife and very nearly a mother.

When Peter finished his *Bearing of the Cross* for Jonghelinck in November, the snow lay very deep upon the ground. Jonghelinck had business in Brussels anyway, so he came to fetch his picture with a horse-drawn delivery sled. Bruegel made sure to have Mayken with him throughout their discussions.

As they'd been hoping, Jonghelinck loved the painting so much that he immediately commissioned a new one. With his strong, loving arm around Mayken, Peter suggested he paint an *Adoration of the Kings*, with Mary and her baby, painted as a winter scene. Jonghelinck gladly acceded. And once again Mayken was able to negotiate for Peter a much larger fee than he would have accepted on his own. And a good thing too, as the family coffers were all but empty.

"You've a good business head," Jonghelinck told Mayken, closing the deal with a squeeze of his large hand. "Peter's a lucky man to have such a helpmeet."

And then, at the very bottom of the year, Mayken's child was born in Brussels. A boy. To Mayken's enormous relief, the babe was pink like Peter, not copper skinned like Williblad.

They had a christening party; Ortelius came down from Antwerp to be the godfather—without Williblad, of course—and Peter invited William of Orange. To their surprise, William arrived accompanied by Graaf Filips de Hoorne. Mayken sat with the babe in her lap, and the three guests presented gifts, just like magi, each of them uncommonly interested in looking at what the others had brought, with kindly Father Ghislain to one side. William gave them a fine, gilded censer filled with clove incense, the Graaf had brought a large silver chocolate pot with his family coat of arms, the pot filled to the brim with costly nutmegs, and Ortelius presented a *nef*, a golden ship with an enameled seashell set into it, the shell filled with saffron strands, and a carved ebony monkey leaning out of the shell. Exquisite objects, of great virtu, and more spices than one could purchase with several months' work. But for Peter, the greatest gift was plainly the moment when the Graaf embraced him like a brother.

It would have been a perfect day if it weren't for Bengt. Yes, at the christening party, Bengt took it upon himself to lean over and whisper something into Peter's ear. From the jut of Peter's jaw, Mayken knew right away what Bengt had said. Peter glared at Bengt, then leaned over to pet the baby.

"My son," he said, loud and clear. "Peter Bruegel the Younger."

Later that evening before bed, dreading the moment when they'd be alone, Mayken heard Peter saying something odd to Bengt. "The attic's haunted," he was telling the boy. "The ghost of Master Coecke. I've seen him there once or twice. If you persist in your calumnies of his daughter, I don't like to think what could happen to you."

"I know what I saw," said Bengt stubbornly, the color rising to his cheeks. And then, seeing Mayken listening, he ran upstairs to his cot.

In their bedroom, Little Peter was lying in a basket, his bright eyes fixed upon the nearest candle. Mayken picked him up and began nursing him. How full and swollen her breasts were. Her husband sat silent off in the corner of the room, bending over something. Finally Mayken could stand it no longer.

"It's true Bengt saw me with Williblad at that Carnival party," she burst out. "It's terrible the way that boy creeps around. I only did it because I felt sorry for Williblad. Your friends broke his arm and nose."

"Does that mean you have to couple with the man? With my apprentice looking on? I'm glad they broke Williblad's nose. He nearly ruined you! That assassin friend of his could have cut my throat. Williblad's lucky that Prince William left him a nose at all. He shouldn't stick it where it doesn't belong."

Peter looked at her, his face wild and sad. For some reason he was holding some cloth and an old sword in his lap. What mad project did he plan? Certainly he was making no gesture to threaten her or the baby. "Aren't I enough for you, Mayken?" he pled.

"Oh, you're fine, Peter, you're wonderful," said Mayken, the baby nursing at her breast. "It wasn't really what Bengt thinks he saw. I don't know how it happened. Maybe at first—maybe at first I felt trapped. About having to be an old wife already. I didn't realize yet how much I'd come to like our life together. Oh, Peter, don't let this ruin everything."

"Trapped," said Peter in a gentle, musing tone. "I know the feeling, Mayken. I'm trapped by my career. We're God's flowers, planted only to bloom and die. But while it lasts—oh, Mayken, it could be so sweet to work and live together. You're my heart."

"Don't fret so, Peter," said Mayken, touched by his words. She glimpsed the broad, sunny plain of a happy future together. "Let's forget my mistake. And, yes, the baby is yours."

"I know," said Peter, holding up a piece of moonlight green silk. Now Mayken recognized it as her father's old Moroccan caftan. "But Bengt questions us," added Peter with an odd little smile. "I'm going to put a scare into him. Shut him up for good." He had her father's turban as well, and the sword in his lap was her father's broad, curved scimitar. Peter took out a whetstone and began sharpening the blade.

"Don't harm Bengt, Peter! You're frightening me!"

"I won't. But Prince William once advised me never to wield a sword that isn't sharp." The stone made a slithery sound moving up and down the damask steel. "I'm going to sit up for a few hours," said Peter presently. "To properly scare Bengt, I'll wait for the dead of the night."

"Oh, stop this foolishness and get in bed."

"I have to do this," said Peter, stubbornly continuing to sharpen the scimitar. He looked over at her, and now she could see there were tears in his eyes. "And you know, Mayken, as long as the sword's good and sharp, maybe you should go ahead and slit my throat if you don't love me." His voice broke, but still his hand moved steadily up and down along the curve of the sword.

Mayken switched Peter the Younger to her other breast. "You men and your dignity." She sighed. "Your swords and your codpieces. Look at me. I'm nursing your son. I'm your wife. What more could you want? You've enjoyed forgiveness—learn to forgive."

"Say you won't go with Williblad again," persisted Peter.

"Maybe you should be a better husband," said Mayken, suddenly annoyed by his doubts. "That means talking to me in the morning before you run upstairs. And it means *seeing* me when you stop work—seeing me and not your pictures." But now the pulling of the little baby's mouth on her nipple softened her heart. "Oh, don't worry, dear Peter. Of course I won't go with Williblad again. That time at Prince William's palace was a silly, drunken dream."

Peter set down the sword and came over to kiss her. "The Holy Family," he murmured, smiling at Mayken and Little Peter in the candlelight.

"Yes," said Mayken, feeling the moment realer than real, feeling herself as one with all the mothers up and down time. It was like being in a painting. How miraculous the baby was, how perfect in every detail. There was a tiny bubble of milk at the corner of his little triangle mouth. "Now come to bed."

"I will," said Peter.

Mayken drifted off to sleep in the strong arms of her loving husband. But wild shrieks awoke her in the dead of night. It was Bengt, quite mad with terror. Though she didn't see him, Mayken heard Bengt go crashing down all three flights of stairs, then heard the door open, and heard Bengt's light footsteps running off into the night. Downstairs Waf began violently barking.

An eerie glow appeared at their bedroom door, and Peter came gliding in, dressed in the caftan and turban, with the scimitar and a little green-glassed lantern in his hand. His face was pale green; he'd covered it with watercolor paint.

"That'll do it," he said, chuckling, and Mayken, comprehending the jape he'd pulled, began to giggle too.

"What's happened?" cried Mayken's mother from the second floor, and then Mienemeuie was calling out from her room off the kitchen on the first floor. "Have we been robbed?"

"It was young Bengt," called Peter down the stairs. "I think he had a bad dream."

"He didn't even close the front door," complained Mienemeuie's voice. "What a nonsense. Quiet down now, Waf."

Of course the baby woke up and began squalling, so Mayken changed him and began nursing him again. Peter cleaned his face, hid his costume away, and took the sword back up to its place upon the studio wall.

The next morning they slept late, waking only to baby Peter's crying. Mayken and Peter spent a friendly couple of hours in bed, chatting and watching the baby, enjoying the bread and chocolate that Mienemeuie brought up. As they were talking, Mayken came up with an idea for a commission big enough to pay their bills for the next two years. Peter should ask Jonghelinck to purchase a series of panels based upon the seasons or the months of the year. Why make a deal for only one painting at a time when you could sell four or even twelve of them? Doing a series was a common enough practice, so why not Peter? He liked the idea immediately, Mayken could see that it set him to dreaming great things.

Bengt appeared around noon, looking paler than usual.

"What was wrong with you last night?" demanded Mayken's mother. "You woke us all!"

"I—I saw a ghost," said Bengt uneasily. "I think it was your husband."

"I see," said Mayken's mother. Mayken could sense that her mother had guessed every bit of the whole story. "Perhaps you've done something to anger Master Coecke's spirit," her mother told Bengt. "If that's the case, you better not do it again."

"I won't," said Bengt abjectly.

"Then let's go upstairs," said Peter. "We have work to do. Mayken has a plan for our grandest commission yet when we finish the *Adoration of the Kings.*"

TWELVE

THE HUNTERS IN THE SNOW
BRUSSELS, JANUARY 1566

"It's possible that the Foreigner thinks of you, Peter," said William of Orange, looking down at the paper in his hands. It was a copy of King Philip's letter to his sister, the Regent Margaret, a much-copied-out epistle which, since its arrival in Brussels in November, had been spreading around the Low Lands like news of the plague. The letter treated of the King's refusal to soften the Blood Edicts, and of methods to best keep down the Low Lands citizenry. Prince William had brought a copy over to Bruegel's studio to share it with him. He smoothed his short, reddish hair forward and read the contemptible words.

" 'I cannot but be very much affected by the lampoons which are continually spread abroad and posted up in the Low Lands without the offenders being punished. This, of course, happens because the authors of earlier ones were not punished.' " William paused and gave Bruegel a worried look, then continued reading. " 'You should consider what remains of my authority and yours, and of the service of God, when it is possible to do such things with impunity in your very presence, Madame my dear sister. Therefore I pray you take the necessary measures so that this does not remain unpunished.' "

"I don't draw lampoons these days," said Bruegel, feeling very easy in his skin. "The Tyrant's fulminations mean nothing to me." It was a cold midday in January, with a few flakes of snow falling outside. Bruegel, Mayken, William, and old Mayken were sitting in his great attic studio, warmed by a crackling fire, the convex mirror shining reassuringly from the wall. Bruegel's son, Little Peter, lay on a cloak on the floor, pawing at Waf. His apprentice Bengt was at work with boards and a hammer, making up crates for Bruegel's six new pictures, three of them leaning against the walls, and three on easels. "Look around you, Prince William," said Bruegel, wondering a bit at William's blindness to anything except the latest doings of the court. "Look at my new paintings. They're very far indeed from being lampoons."

And what paintings they were. Bruegel's grandest commission yet, a cycle of six *Seasons* for Jonghelinck, who'd built himself a new house in Antwerp with the profits from his somewhat questionable dealings with the wine importer Daniel de Bruyne. Jonghelinck's house had a hexagonal salon waiting for Bruegel's *Seasons*. To make up six times of the year, Bruegel had split both Spring and Summer in two.

He depicted early Spring as a *Gloomy Day*,
late Spring as *The Merrymakers*,
early Summer as *Haymaking*,
late Summer as *The Harvesters*,
Fall as *The Return of the Herd*, and
Winter as *The Hunters in the Snow*.

Bruegel had been busy with the pictures for nearly a year now, working at the very limit of his powers, and, as of last night, he was done. He'd painted the wheel of life, the cosmic cycle of Man and Nature. His six panels showed people moving about as part of the landscape, as tightly knit into the world as trees or crows, the human lives a natural part of Earth's seasonal changes, as above, so below. His great work was finished. For once he felt fully at peace.

Today, he was sitting and resting while Bengt got the pictures boxed up, preparatory to hauling them to Antwerp on a great spring-cushioned wagon that Hans Franckert was going to lend him. The wagon was to arrive tomorrow morning, complete with two strong horses and a teamster.

"Now I know how you felt when you had Little Peter," said Bruegel to

Mayken, admiring the curve of her cheek. "I remember your expression so well. It's wonderful to give birth, to push your creation out. I'm empty."

"Not for long," said Mayken, giving him a loving smile and patting his head. "My horn of plenty." Despite his year-long immersion in the work, Bruegel and Mayken were on better terms than ever. He'd begun making a point of starting slow in the mornings, always allowing an hour or two for chat with Mayken and for playing with their growing baby boy. It was time well spent, and a relief for his frequently aching stomach. For her part, Mayken seemed more enthralled with the new works than anything Bruegel had ever done. "Aren't the panels a sight, Prince William?" urged Mayken.

"Indeed," said William, giving the miraculous paintings a cursory look. Politics meant so much more to him than art; like all the nobles he was eternally self-absorbed. As if their wars and edicts were as important as the truly real. But Jonghelinck would know how to esteem the work, as would the steady stream of cultured people who passed through Jonghelinck's house. Bruegel felt sure the *Seasons* would make his reputation once and for all.

"And listen to the part where he reaffirms the Blood Edicts against heresy," continued William, turning his attention back to his copy of Philip's letter. "It's very nearly satanic." Again he read aloud, his voice trembling with anger. " 'Since the men condemned to die advance to execution not in silence but as martyrs dying for a cause, you should consider whether they ought not to be executed in secret in some way or other—though it is true that a public execution also serves to set an example.' "

"I went to a public execution last Sunday," put in Bengt. "A torture jubilee." Bruegel's apprentice had matured over the last year. His voice had deepened a bit, his body had fleshed out, and he'd taken to wearing his hair cropped to a short blond stubble that matched the fresh growth on his chin. Bengt had been a tremendous help in finishing the six panels; he was nearly as proud of the work as Bruegel. By now Bruegel and the boy got along as well as uncle and nephew. It hadn't taken long for Bengt to figure out who "Master Coecke's ghost" had really been—and it had become a comfortable joke. Even so, Bengt had learned to treat Mayken with caution and respect.

"Their archheretic said very little once they'd ripped his tongue out," continued Bengt, who'd acquired a discursive, confident manner of speaking. "It was the velvet-maker Le Blas. Did you hear about him? A fanatical Calvinist. On Christmas Day he went to the cathedral, snatched the consecrated wafer of the Host, broke it into bits, threw the fragments on the ground and trampled them, crying out, 'Do you take this thing to be Jesus Christ?' " Bengt shook his head at the thought. "Why would a man to do such a thing?"

"You were at his execution?" said Prince William, eager for fresh news from the streets. "Tell me about it."

"It took all morning," said Bengt. "First they burnt three ordinary heretics—two men and a woman who'd done little more than read the Bible together. When called upon for last words, all three avowed their faith in the Church. In return, the priests granted them the mercy of having the executioner strangle them before lighting the faggots around them."

"And Le Blas?" pressed William.

"No recanting for this fellow," said Bengt. "He was yelling all manner of things, but, as I said, the executioners tore his tongue out by the roots. They waved it around and threw it into the crowd. It landed near me, in fact, still twitching. Horrible. Waf wanted to eat it, can you imagine? I held him back; another dog made off with it. And then Le Blas's right hand and foot were burned and twisted off with hot irons—the very hand and foot he'd used against the Host. They threw those into a slow fire they had left over from the three other heretics, a big mound of coals and embers. To finish Le Blas, they fastened his arms and legs behind his back and hung him by a chain over the fire to roast. His clothes charred away and then his skin began to brown and bubble. It was disgusting. Much worse than anything the falcons ever did. I made some drawings." Bruegel smiled at Bengt. He'd taught the youth always to carry pen and paper. You never knew what you might run across.

"Our Bruegel's making an artist of you, eh, Bengt?" said William the Sly. "Everything grist for the mill. That's one way to face these times. The Inquisitors grow more mad and evil all the time."

"What's going to happen, Prince William?" asked Mayken. Bruegel glanced over at his wife. She was a bit worried about tomorrow's trip. She was going to leave little Peter with Old Mayken and accompany Bengt and Bruegel to Jonghelinck's in Antwerp to see the new paintings installed.

Mayken had matured over the past year too; her face was firmer, a bit more rounded. She was enjoying motherhood and her stewardship of the finances. Bruegel's relationship with her had grown as sturdy as an oak table. Bruegel felt a rush of affection every time he looked at Mayken, every time he heard the music of her voice. He silently prayed that the storms of war would spare his family.

"The small nobles are banding together into a League," said William. "They've asked me to join, but I'm not ready to set myself so clearly against the Tyrant. There may still be some way to work with him."

"What will the League of Nobles do?" wondered Mayken's mother.

"Well, Philip resides in Spain, with no plan of returning here," said William. "The nobles still hope they can persuade the Regent Margaret here in Brussels to stop enforcing the Blood Edicts. And if she refuses—who knows?" He sighed and got to his feet. "But I did want to warn you not to draw lampoons, Peter. At least not for engravings. And having thus cleared my conscience, I'd also like you to consider privately doing another political painting for me. My friends have enjoyed your *Suicide of Saul* very much, and they admire how you've used a Biblical tale to so aptly present a telling allegory."

"I'm grateful to hear that, Prince William," said Bruegel. "I'd be honored to execute more paintings for you. But there's no current need for concern about lampoons. This year I've been taking the broader view. You might say I've crawled up to the summit of our angry anthill to have a look at the pastures around. Not that events aren't conspiring to draw me back inside."

William looked around, finally seeming to see Bruegel's new landscapes.

The tree-pruning, waffle-eating peasants of the stormy *Gloomy Day.*

The circle of dancing maids and youths beside the pond in *The Merrymakers.*

The three women calmly walking out to rake the field in *Haymaking.*

The dozy, picnicking peasants of *The Harvesters.*

The cows and the plain-faced landsmen of *The Return of the Herd.*

The bedraggled hunters and their pack of dogs in *The Hunters in the Snow:* the hunters passing an inn and heading down the crest of a hill into a vast snowy landscape filled with the tiny figures of their fellow humans.

"My heart flies right into it," said William, standing before the last picture. "It reminds me of—of childhood. When my world was new. God bless you, Bruegel." William looked around, his expression soft. Now *The Return of the Herd* caught his eye. "How different these are from your Hell paintings, Peter. Harmony replaces chaos. The birds, the peasants, the cows—all at one with the world."

"If you look closely at that particular picture, you'll see a gibbet in the middle distance," put in Bengt. "It's the only evil thing in all six pictures. Master Bruegel added it Sunday night after I told him about Le Blas's execution. If you look *very* closely you can even see Waf by the gibbet." Bengt shared Bruegel's love for fantastic elaboration.

"And perhaps you can find Le Blas's tongue at Waf's feet," said Bruegel with a rueful smile. It had a been a wonderful year, the best year of his life, and who knew now what would come next. "Yes, yes, I've a feeling you ants will soon pull me back into your tunnels."

"And let me be one of the number pulling at you," said William. "The Prince of Ants. As I say, I'd like you to consider doing something more for me with a political tone. The Princess Anna has been urging me to acquire another Bruegel painting, I might add. One of her counselors told her that your *Dulle Griet* made quite an impression at the Habsburg court in Vienna, and that now the Archduke Rudolph has carried it off to Prague. Our Bruegel of Brussels begins to acquire the cachet of imperial fashion." This was sweet music to Bruegel's ears.

Early the next morning Franckert's wagon arrived, big and strong with springs, enormous spoked wheels, and a cloth cover to protect the cargo. The teamster driving the wagon was none other than the same Max Wagemaeker who'd been with Franckert that time in the Alps. Fourteen years ago. Incredible how the years were mounting up.

Though thinner and more wrinkled, the leathery Max was as lively and loud as ever. "The famous Peter Bruegel," he cried when Bruegel opened the door to him. "I tell people I saw you sell your first drawing. I suppose this round-cheeked little vixen is your wife? Lucky man. I'm Max Wagemaeker, Mevrouw Bruegel, much honored to make your acquaintance."

"Tell me about Peter being famous," said Mayken with a smile.

"His engravings," said Max. "Everyone has seen them. I like that matched pair especially, *The Fat Kitchen* and *The Thin Kitchen*. Hans Franckert has those up in his dining room. The thin men are trying to drag a fat man inside the Thin Kitchen and the fat men are throwing a thin man out of the Fat Kitchen. He makes a face like this." Max bent over with an angry, openmouthed grimace and then burst out laughing. "I hope you folks run a Fat Kitchen. The inn didn't have any porridge ready when I got up. I wouldn't mind some hot chocolate and scrambled eggs and fried potatoes and plump sausages before I start helping you move your pictures. What floor is your studio on?"

"I'll tell you after you've eaten," said Bruegel. "Come on inside."

Later they got the crated panels loaded onto the wagon, and then Bruegel, Mayken, Bengt, Waf, and Max set off on the road to Antwerp, the two powerful draft-horses picking their way across the ice and snow. They moved along at a rapid clip, with Mayken and Wagemaeker sitting on a bench at the front of the wagon, and Bengt and Bruegel sitting on the wagon's back, where they could keep an eye on the crated pictures. Waf alternated between running alongside them and jumping aboard.

The road led through the open countryside towards Mechelen, accompanied for a bit by the newly dug Willebroek Canal, which eventually veered off to the west, taking a shortcut to the Scheldt. The bright, overcast sky was colored a shade of whitish green that bespoke more snow today. They rattled through little villages and past frozen marshes with skaters upon them.

"Have you thought what you'll paint next, Master Bruegel?" asked Bengt.

"Something for Prince William, I suppose," said Bruegel. "If not another piece for Jonghelinck. Right now, for once, I'm empty. Just a pair of eyes. It's a fine day, eh? Look how many birds are out and about." A flock of starlings fluttered up from some hawthorn thickets; three black-billed crows cawed from a pine tree; and now Waf flushed a whirring covey of quail. The damp black branches and twigs stood out against the snow like fresh-painted ivory black lines. But no man had labored over this exquisite tracery, God had put it here for free. Up ahead was a cluster of farmhouses beside a pond. The snow-covered roofs were yellow-tinted white lozenges; the pond ice mirrored the sky's pale green. Craning towards the front of the wagon, he could see Mayken happily chatting with Max. How wonderful it was to be alive.

"I used to dream I was a falcon," said Bengt. "In the most beautiful dream of all, I was flying through the snow, the big flakes coming at me."

"You're a born artist," said Bruegel, savoring the image. "Is your father still angry with you?"

"No," said Bengt. "We've made up. It helps that he's found a new assistant. One of my cousins from Valkenswaard. Do you think Little Peter will be a painter?"

"I hope so," said Bruegel. "He's my son." He emphasized the remark with an elbow to Bengt's ribs.

"No squawks from me," said Bengt with a smile. "I'd hate to face Master Coecke's scimitar again."

"Do you know anything about your own father?" asked Bengt after a bit.

"Most likely it was Filips de Hoorne's tutor," said Bruegel. "Though it could also have been Filips's father. The old Graaf was always so kind to me when I was young. And you saw how Filips embraced me at Young Peter's christening."

"Why don't you ask him straight out?"

"It could put him in an awkward spot," said Bruegel. "If he were to say that I'm his brother, then he'd have the worry that I might try to claim an inheritance."

"Every bastard thinks he's nobility," shouted Max, who'd overheard them. "Forget your dreams of glory and be glad you don't know your parents. Mine were drunken animals with seven children. I ran away when I was ten years old, and they didn't even notice. I grew up sleeping in the stables at the inn. Given the choice, I prefer living with horses."

It seemed that every village they passed had a gallows and some wheels on poles. The most recently hanged heretic was always left to dangle from the gibbet until a new one arrived, and then the old body would be placed atop a wagon wheel on a pole for the crows. Some villages had several wheels, and many of the wheels were laden with more than one body. This year had brought more executions than ever, and the coming year seemed likely to bring many more. Under Philip's edicts it took almost nothing to be executed for heresy. Not only was it proof of heresy for a solitary person to sing a psalm or to read the Bible or to pray, it was equally a capital offense to fail to report any friend or family member who indulged in such anathematized acts of piety. There was hardly a man or a woman in the Low Lands who wasn't technically subject to execution, and where facts were lacking, they could easily be made up. The Spanish rulers and their clergy were free to kill whomsoever they chose. Not only did they seek out the rebellious, the wealthy people and landowners were also being executed so that Spain could claim their goods.

When they approached Antwerp it was near dusk. Liberal, worldly Antwerp was the one place in the Low Lands were the Inquisition was still mild. For the benefit of trade, the Regent and her minions tolerated some freedom of thought in this rich port. The single gallows outside the city held a body that had hung so long in the sun and rain that it resembled a homely bundle of faded rags, the bones like clean, weathered wood.

The taxman at the gate knew of Bruegel, and, upon seeing the six crated pictures, demanded some pieces of silver. Bruegel paid him, and then they were rolling down the familiar streets. It was comfortable to see the spire of the Our Lady Cathedral once again. Fresh snow began to fall.

Nicolas Jonghelinck's house was on a fine big lot at the eastern edge of the city. Lights in the windows brightened the falling snow, and as they approached they could hear voices. In the front hall, Jonghelinck had gathered some guests to greet them: Jonghelinck's sculptor brother Jacob, Christopher Plantin and wife recently returned from their exile, the printer Jerome Cock, the painters Frans Floris and Martin de Vos, big Hans Franckert and his wife Hennie van Mander, good old Abraham Ortelius and—Williblad Cheroo. Bruegel hadn't seen Cheroo since his studio back in Hoogstraat. Cheroo's nose was flat and crooked—Grauer and his men had indeed broken it, most thoroughly.

When they were planning the trip, Mayken had wondered out loud if it would be too awkward for her to face Williblad. But Bruegel had urged her to come. It was Mayken who'd planted the germ of the *Seasons* panels in his mind, she who'd negotiated a proper fee with Jonghelinck, she who'd stood by him during this long year of creation, she who was his beloved, and Bruegel wanted her to share the glory of the final installation. And, despite any doubts, Mayken too wanted to be here for the great event.

"Hello, Peter," said Williblad, walking right up to Bruegel. "You're looking well. I can see that marriage agrees with you. You're a lucky man." Williblad himself looked not quite so finely turned out as in the old days. Though he was dressed in maroon velvet, the material showed some signs of wear. And, for the first time, there were silver strands in his smooth black head of hair. Bruegel went ahead and shook his hand. In the end, after all, it had been Bruegel who'd won Mayken. And today, of all days, he could afford to be big-hearted.

"And I'm pleased to see you as well, Mevrouw Bruegel," said Williblad, kissing Mayken's hand and executing a bow.

"You keep away from me," said Mayken with a disarming laugh. Williblad smiled rakishly, then drifted off across the hall to drink and talk with Frans Floris. Bruegel felt proud of how easily she'd handled him. He and Mayken looked at each other, feeling they'd weathered the initial encounter in good form. It seemed that all would be well.

Jonghelinck's footmen carried the six paintings through the hall and into a special hexagonal salon. With Bengt's help they uncrated them, with Waf very much underfoot. The guests came in to watch.

"Be careful not to shatter those boxes," called Jonghelinck as they worked. "I may need to use them again."

"What for, Nicolas?" exclaimed Bruegel. "You'll not want to part with these panels anytime soon!" But Jonghelinck didn't answer him. Bruegel felt a preliminary flicker of unease across his tender stomach. But what was there to worry about? The pictures clearly belonged here.

Bengt had prepared hooks on the backs of the panels, and before long the wonderful *Seasons* were on the salon's six walls. It was a noble room with cream-colored walls painted with green vines, a marble floor inlaid with pink alabaster roses, a great chandelier and any number of candle-filled sconces. A few standing chandeliers were brought in as well to increase the lighting. The air was perfumed by a great, heated silver bowl of red wine spiced with cloves and nutmeg. For an hour, the excited guests walked this way and that, exclaiming over the new works. Ortelius was particularly transported; he kept making notes on a piece of paper. Even the vain Floris could do nothing but call for a toast. They raised their glasses and Ortelius stepped forward to deliver an erudite, richly rhetorical encomium.

"Eupompos, the painter, on being asked whom of his predecessors he had chosen as a master, replied by pointing to a crowd of men: it is Nature itself that we must imitate, not an artist," declaimed Ortelius, reading from his piece of paper. "This observation so well applies to our friend Bruegel that he turns the maxim on its head. More than the painters' painter, Bruegel is the painters' Nature, and I mean by this that he deserves to be imitated by all. Our Bruegel paints the things that can't be painted. In these works around us there is as much thought as paint. Yet Bruegel adds no false elegance to his paintings; more than any other, he paints the world as it is. And in this wise, he achieves true beauty. Let us drink to our friend, the most perfect artist of his century."

Flushed with excitement, Ortelius raised both his arms high, then drank from his cup. The others cheered and drank as well. Bruegel was glowing, he felt as if his bones were made of light. How good it was to be here. Mayken was beaming, and even Williblad across the room was giving him a warm and friendly smile.

"I'm honored to know you, Peter," said Hans Franckert, standing at his side.

"What a nice speech Ortelius gave," added his wife, Hennie. She was a handsome woman with a kind, thin face. "You must be very proud, Peter."

"It's wonderful to have all of you here," said Bruegel, looking around the room. His eyes were wet from his emotion at Ortelius's kind words, and the many candles seemed surrounded by haloes. He laughed a little foolishly, at a loss for words.

238 🕷   RUDY RUCKER

"And how is Little Peter?" asked Hennie. "We've been meaning to get down to Brussels to visit you and Mayken. Is the boy walking yet?"

"Since Christmas," said Bruegel, for the moment too overcome to say more.

"He practiced by leaning on Waf and letting the dog lead him around," added Mayken with a laugh. "Waf's been very patient." Hearing his name, the white-haired wolfhound nuzzled her hand.

Still more guests were arriving, including none other than Peter Huys and Anja, who squealed and came running up to him, her big cheeks squeezing her eyes into slits. She'd grown rather stout. Anja was another person whom Bruegel and Mayken had been uneasy about encountering at Jonghelinck's.

"Well, well, Peter! We're both old married parents now!" Anja made an awkward curtsy to Mayken, not quite able to bring herself to say hello to her old rival—not that Mayken had ever thought of herself that way. What an unequal contest it had been. Bruegel thanked his stars for letting him end up with Mayken.

Anja mimed a quick look around the room. "What enormous pictures! We're glad to have a chance to see them. And what a palace your patron Jonghelinck has."

"Mijnheer Bruegel," said round Peter Huys with a formal bow that he punctuated with the sound of a fart. "I'm simply bursting with pleasure to see you." He fanned the air, clapped Bruegel on the back, and lowered his voice as if to a confidential tone. "I thought you'd broken in Anja for me, but she's as wild as an ass in a lion's skin."

"Did you want a wife or a cabbage?" said Anja, on the last word shooting a hard look at Mayken. "I'll go take a closer look at the pictures. Is anyone shitting, Peter?"

"Of course," said Bruegel, with a grin. "In the yard of the farmhouse at the back of *The Harvesters*."

"How common she is," remarked Mayken as Anja walked off. "What did she mean by that question?"

"Oh, when I was doing my drawings for the *Seven Sins,* Anja and I used to joke about what might be my artistic trademark. Bosch had his owls, I have my shitting men," said Bruegel calmly. If Anja was a bit coarse, she was still part of Bruegel's past. One's life was a seamless whole. Today it seemed as though everything could fit together. Even Williblad. He was still on the far side of the room, with Ortelius fluttering about to keep his wineglass full.

"Williblad's drinking too much," remarked Mayken. "I hope he doesn't make trouble. Do remember that you promised not to get into a fight."

"I've forgiven him," said Bruegel, almost meaning it. Williblad really looked quite pathetic. He was a drunkard with a smashed face making his living as something like a manservant. Bruegel squeezed Mayken's hand, and added, "I was sorry to see how badly they damaged his nose."

"Ortelius doesn't seem to mind," said Mayken, not liking the sight of the mapmaker's attentions to Williblad.

Now Floris and de Vos approached, Floris rather red in the face. Bruegel braced himself to listen to Floris brag about his career as usual. But in the presence of the six large landscapes, even Floris had to momentarily deviate from his customary torrent of self-regard. *"The Hunters in the Snow,"* he said. "Exquisite. The dogs against the glowing snow: their legs and curly tails." He glanced at Waf. "This beast is one of them, no?"

"Indeed," said Bruegel.

"I was just studying your *Gloomy Day* like this," said de Vos, making a little viewing frame by sticking out his thumbs and forefingers and joining them with one hand turned over. For the moment, even this friend of Bruegel's youth seemed to be in awe of him. "I was looking, looking, looking," continued de Vos. "And each little piece is a perfect composition. Worlds within worlds. It's as Ortelius says. 'Bruegel's work is like Nature herself.'"

"I like that idea," said Mayken, holding up her hands to make her own little frame. "I'm going to try it." She wandered over to look at the panels again, discussing them with the other guests and, Bruegel noticed, coincidentally moving closer to Williblad. He told himself it didn't matter if they talked. He trusted Mayken. But his stomach didn't fully seem to realize this.

By now Floris had heard enough talk about Bruegel's prowess. "Perhaps in a bit we can go look at my *Labors of Hercules*, eh?" he asked Bruegel. "Jonghelinck has the series installed in a slightly larger salon than this. And he's got my *Liberal Arts* series as well. Twenty pictures by me, all told. How many of yours does he own?"

"I thought about this on the ride up," said Bruegel, turning to this topic with satisfaction. "A pleasant topic. I make it sixteen. The *Fall of Icarus*, the *Merchants Driven from the Temple* that he got from Fugger, a pair of landscapes called the *Parable of the Sower* and the *Temptation of St. Anthony*, my *Low Lands Proverbs*, the *Battle of Carnival and Lent*, the *Wine of St. Martin*—that's St. Martin on a horse with a crowd of guzzling beggars—and then there's my big *Tower of Babel*, the *Bearing of the Cross*, the *Adoration of the Kings*, and now the six *Seasons*." While listing the pictures he'd been ticking them off on his fingers, with de Vos helping by holding out some of his fingers too. "Yes, sixteen in all," concluded Bruegel. To him it seemed like an amazingly high number, more pictures than he could hold in his mind at the same time.

"The greater part of your life's work, isn't it?" said Floris with a shake of his head. Here it came. The man never tired of doling out Olympian advice. "You paint too slowly, Peter. With fellows like de Vos helping me, I turn out twice that many pictures in a single year."

Bruegel resisted pointing out that all Floris's pictures were alike and that none of them were memorable. Instead he just said, "You should meet my apprentice," and motioned to Bengt, who'd been absorbed in talking to one of Jonghelinck's daughters, a lively red-haired girl with a weak chin.

Bengt was pleased to meet a famous artist, but when the overbearing Floris suggested that he might be willing to take Bengt Bots on as his own apprentice, Bengt demurred. "Master Bruegel still has so much to give me," said Bengt. "The world is a parable he's teaching me to understand." Bengt was learning well. For the moment Floris was silenced.

"Stout lad," said Bruegel, clapping Bengt on the shoulder. It was good to have this youth to stand by him. And now Mayken rejoined him as well. He truly felt like the master of his destiny. His wife, his apprentice, and this room filled with his finest paintings—it was all just as he'd always dreamed.

And then Jonghelinck walked over, with the storklike Jerome Cock at his side. "Nicolas tells me he's not going to order any new pictures from you for a while," cawed Cock. "So take a rest from painting and draw me something new to sell."

"Hush, Jerome," said Jonghelinck. "I need to give Peter and Frans the bad news myself."

"You don't like the new panels?" exclaimed Mayken, ready for battle. "How can you say such a thing!"

"They're exquisite," said the embarrassed Jonghelinck, awkwardly paddling the air with his oversized hands. "But the thing is—I'm in severe financial straits. The Antwerp City Fathers feel I was delinquent in not collecting excise taxes upon Daniel de Bruyne's wine. There's talk of malfeasance. I don't know who's been speaking to them. I'd hoped de Bruyne could help me set things right, but he's dropped out of sight. I'm sure he'll return from Burgundy in good time, but meanwhile I'm to give the city cash or goods worth—oh—tens of thousands of guilders. More than you can imagine."

"It's a shame you went in with a Frenchman," snapped Floris. "Filthy curs. But painters like Bruegel and I can find other customers, eh?" Floris's face suddenly darkened. "You *are* going to pay Peter the agreed-upon price for his *Seasons*, aren't you, Nicolas?" For all his self-centeredness, Floris was always ready to defend the rights of his fellow artists.

"Of course," said Jonghelinck, taking out a purse of gold. "I'll make good on it now. I just wish I would be able to enjoy owning your *Seasons* for a bit longer, Peter."

"What do you mean by that?" said Bruegel, the ground seeming to give way beneath his feet.

"That's what I'm trying to tell you. To make up for my debt to the city, I'm turning over a good part of my art collection to them next month. All sixteen of your pictures, Peter, and twenty by you, Frans—they're part of what the city will receive. They'll be crated up and kept in storage. If all goes well, I should have them back quite soon, but—"

Mayken said something, and then Floris interrupted with some other comment, but Bruegel had stopped listening. His stomach felt as if he'd been kicked by a mule. The better part of his life's work was to be boxed up and stored in an attic of the town hall? The fools! All in vain!

Jonghelinck tried to press a bag of gold coins into his hand, Bruegel pushed him away, Mayken took the gold for him.

Jonghelinck's bad news had spread quickly among the guests. What had begun as a christening had taken on the air of a funeral. With Bengt and Mayken trailing after him, Bruegel took one last sad walk around the salon, bidding farewell to his paintings. The paint was scarcely dry on the *The Hunters in the Snow*. This was the hardest one to let go of, this perfect picture, so like today's ride through the snow. *The world is a parable.*

"Hard news, Master Bruegel," murmured Bengt.

"It won't be forever," consoled Mayken.

And, yes, she was right. Today was gone, gone forever, yet his picture would live on. A crate was no coffin, and someday it would spring open again. His soundly constructed painting would be no worse for the wait.

To wait and to wait. Bruegel heaved a deep, weary sigh, a sigh from the bottom of his aching gut. The thing was—so much of his life had already been spent waiting. And who knew how much more time remained?

The party was breaking up. Jonghelinck had a bedroom prepared for Bruegel and Mayken, but in his anger at the financier's poor stewardship of his paintings, Bruegel haughtily insisted they had somewhere better to stay. Jonghelinck took the slight ungraciously. Mayken spoke with him for a bit to smooth things over, and while she was talking, Bruegel walked around the now-deserted hexagonal salon yet one more time. And then he, Mayken, and Bengt were bundled up and standing outside, the last glimpses of his pictures still swimming in Bruegel's eyes.

"Where are we going to sleep?" wondered Mayken. It was a bitter cold night with tiny dustlike flakes of snow falling. The other guests had already departed, with Wagemaeker and his wagon long gone as well. Bruegel, Mayken, Bengt, and Waf were alone in the mansion's courtyard.

"We can walk to the market square from here," said Bruegel. "It's not so far. We'll get a room over the Blue Boat tavern. Do you have Jonghelinck's gold in a safe place, Mayken? We wouldn't want to lose that too."

"Right here," said Mayken, patting her breasts. "But, Peter, the Blue Boat will have lice and bedbugs. I don't want to bring lice home to Little Peter. Most of the Blue Boat customers are soldiers and whores. We'll barely sleep at all."

242 ※   RUDY RUCKER

"It'll have to do," said Bruegel, barely stopping himself from adding a remark that Anja had liked the Blue Boat fine. In truth, he felt a little abashed at losing his temper with Jonghelinck. A minute ago they'd been inside the mansion, and now they were freezing in the snow. Thanks to Bruegel's pigheadedness. But how could Jonghelinck simply box up his panels and put them in storage with the city! He turned halfway back towards the mansion's door, almost wanting to go back inside and argue some more.

"Come on, then, Peter," said Mayken, tugging his sleeve. "I only hope we don't meet a cutpurse in the streets."

"You've got me and Waf," said Bengt, throwing back his head and blowing out a frosty plume of breath. "Lord, but it's cold. Mevrouw Bruegel's right. Let's be on our way."

As it happened, two figures were waiting for them in the darkness beyond Jonghelinck's gate. Waf yelped in fear, and Bengt started backwards so abruptly that he stepped on Bruegel's foot. But it was only Ortelius and Williblad. "Come back to my house, Peter," said Ortelius. "I invite you three to spend the night."

"Jonghelinck is a crooked bastard to do this to you," said Williblad Cheroo, throwing his arm across Bruegel's shoulders. The dashing half-American was quite drunk. "Come on home with Abraham and me and we'll talk about old times. I promise not to mention anything about fucking Mayken. Ah, damn me for a honking goose, I just did. Forgive me, Mayken. Throw paint on me if you like, Peter. I envy you. I'd like to be a painter."

"Scurvy fop," said Bruegel, with an anger that was partly feigned. In truth, he welcomed the distraction. It was better to be trading words with Cheroo than to be grieving over the loss of his pictures. "Mayken's lucky she escaped you. What is it you do for Ortelius now? Are you his valet? How far you've fallen!"

"Mayken lucky?" slurred Cheroo as the five of them walked down the icy lane together. The snow had stopped; the stars were hard, pitiless pinpoints. "It's you who's lucky, Peter. A twice-plowed field bears richer harvest. You should do me honor."

For all the sting in what Cheroo said, Bruegel sensed more despair than malice behind his banter. But even so, this was too much.

"Hold your tongue," he said, struggling to keep his voice even. "And no, Abraham, we don't want to stay with you."

The blood in Bruegel's temples was pounding. Mayken grabbed his arm, lest he do something rash. Towing Mayken along, Bruegel strode forward through the snow, seeking to leave Williblad and Ortelius behind. He had no wish to end this long day with a drunken street brawl.

Maddeningly, the besotted Cheroo kept pace. The man was beyond controlling. "You asked what I do with Ortelius?" continued Cheroo. "Well, most nights I let him unfasten my codpiece and he plunders the treasures of the New World—like so many others before him, eh? Whoops!"

In his haste to keep up with Bruegel, Cheroo had lost his footing. His feet shot out from under him and he fell jarringly to the ground. For the moment, none of the four others made a move to help him up. Only Waf seemed to have pity for the coppery man, stepping forward to give his side an encouraging nudge with his long white nose.

"Careful there, Williblad," said Ortelius, glaring down at Cheroo. "And tell Peter and Bengt you were joking about what you said before."

"About my codpiece?" asked Cheroo. "But in relation to you or to Mayken?"

"Damn the man," said Bengt. "Don't speak of my Master's wife that way, Cheroo. Let's kick his ribs in, Master Bruegel. I saw some soldiers do it to a sailor last week."

"Don't," said Mayken quietly.

There was a moment of silence. Bruegel looked down at Cheroo, moved by his evident despair and by his poor, crooked nose. He and Williblad were little gnats in the great, spinning world. Why make things harder for each other? Why not behave as if he were finally enlightened?

"The world's kicked us all enough," said Bruegel. He leaned over and held out his hand. "Come on, Williblad."

"All right," said Williblad, taking Bruegel's hand and slowly rising to his feet.

"And you'll stay with us tonight?" said Ortelius.

"I'd much prefer that to the lousy tavern," said Mayken. "And you behave yourself, Williblad. We've all heard more than enough nonsense from you."

"Agreed," said Williblad, his voice regaining its vigor. "Forgive me, one and all."

"All right, then," said Bruegel. "Yes, we'll stay with you, Abraham. Thank you." They walked on.

"Let me start afresh," said Williblad presently. "What I do for Ortelius is that I help him with his trade. I have a way of seeing things that other men overlook. The tracker's eye. This business with your pictures going to Antwerp, for instance, Peter. I wonder if Granvelle might be behind it? All the way from Rome?"

"How so?" said Bruegel cautiously. Was Williblad preparing to beard him once again?

"De Bruyne used to visit the Cardinal at his house in Brussels," said Cheroo. "And I've heard Granvelle mention that the Austrian Habsburgs have a passion for your work. Indeed, the *Dulle Griet* made so powerful an impression upon them that they engaged Granvelle to send them copies of all your engravings. Mayhap our departed Cardinal has intrigued to get your works away from Jonghelinck and into the city's hands, so that they can eventually pass to the Archduke. A grateful Antwerp's gift to its imperial rulers, don't you see? They're all thieving bastards."

Though Bruegel was somewhat intrigued by Williblad's theory, he didn't answer. Certainly it was an interesting thought to imagine that people might be machinating to get control of Jonghelinck's hoard of paintings by him. But he was too upset by the loss to want to probe the matter today. His stomach was greatly paining him.

"Just be quiet," Mayken told Williblad. "Don't rub salt in Peter's wound."

Ortelius's new house had a larger study, with a magnificent array of glass cases holding his treasured coins. A big fire crackled in a hearth surmounted by a marble mantelpiece. Bruegel and Mayken sat with Ortelius and Bengt before the fire drinking tea and chatting, with Williblad lolling on the couch with a glass of clove gin. For now Williblad was absorbed in his drinking, staring off into space. Waf fell asleep with his head upon Cheroo's feet. The dog seemed uncommonly attracted to him. Typical, thought Bruegel wryly. Anja, Mayken, and even Waf liked Cheroo.

The firelight glinted off the coins in Ortelius's cases, and on the wall hung his pair of Bruegel paintings: the *Two Monkeys* from Mechelen and a monochrome grisaille Bruegel had painted just before the *Seasons*. This was *The Death of the Virgin*, a detailed contemporary-looking image of Mary on her deathbed surrounded by the spirits of saints and martyrs from every period of history. A pious work, suited to Ortelius's love for the Church's finer traditions. Bruegel had expected to sell it to the Brussels Cathedral, in fact Mayken had arranged a commission, but upon seeing the work, the Bishop had rejected it as too strange. The image failed to be a composition that had been painted ten thousand times. Mayken raged to see her man's work go for nothing, but it had done Bruegel good to paint it. He'd made a gift of it to Ortelius, who'd been quite melancholic over the death of his mother.

"I love this painting so," said Ortelius, gazing into it. "In this light, the huddled figures look almost alive. How sweet and humble you've made them. And your tones of gray, Peter, for you gray is a color."

"I was thinking of our suffering people when I painted it," said Bruegel. "I'd just heard that three men back in my home village were burnt at the stake. Perhaps the Bishop sensed my sentiments, my unspoken questions about how our land can continue."

"Your *Seasons* are the answer," said Ortelius. "A fine refreshment from these evil times. It's an incalculable loss that Jonghelinck lets them slip through his fingers. You've caught the whole great world within those panels. A work never to be excelled." Ortelius stared into the fire for a while, evidently going over the works in his mind. Nobody else spoke. After a time Ortelius looked at Bruegel with a wry smile. "This is like petitioning the Lord on the seventh day," he said. "But I'm wondering what you'll paint next?"

"I think we can get some commissions from Prince William," said Mayken.

"It's back into the anthill," added Bruegel, feeling weary and bitter. "William delivered himself of a heartfelt warning that I not draw more lampoons, and then he turned around and asked me to paint him some Biblical scenes with anti-Spanish meanings. He's primed to pay a handsome price, don't you think, Mayken? His wife, Anna, has heard the same news that Williblad mentioned: that my work is known in the imperial court. Do you think they realize the *Dulle Griet* shows their cousin Margaret? Perhaps so, perhaps it makes them laugh. In any case, being known at court is the measure by which a petty noble like Princess Anna judges an artist's worth. Perhaps I'll take William's next picture a bit further than I did my *Suicide of Saul*." As rapidly as the cosmic harmony of the misappropriated *Seasons* was fading away for Bruegel, the desire to fight his oppressors was welling back up.

"Why not a *Slaughter of the Innocents*?" said Cheroo, suddenly breaking his seeming stupor. "Do you realize that under Philip's new dispensation they might execute sixty thousand citizens of the Low Lands this coming year?"

"How do you invent a number like that?" demanded Bengt, who seemed still to be spoiling for a fight with Williblad. "What do you even imagine it means?"

"I pay attention to your wretched native land's affairs," said Williblad tartly. "Viglius van Aytta was in Antwerp the other day, and he told the city council that the Inquisition plans to start 'saving' about two hundred men and women a day across the Low Lands. I learned to reckon at the University of Leuven, my rib-kicking little friend, and the way it works is that two hundred executions times three hundred days makes a schedule of some sixty thousands of executions for the year of *your* almighty Lord, 1566. A slaughter of the innocents, vaster and bloodier than King Herod with the babies." Cheroo paused and shook his head. "It's a filthy, bloody book, your Bible. Imagine if you will, my boys, a land with no God and no priests. I was raised in just such an earthly paradise. More's the pity I had to leave it for Europe's foul superstitions."

"You should go to bed, Williblad," said Ortelius. "You're much the worse for drink. Please, Bengt, don't repeat anything he says."

"He speaks against the Bible and God?" said Bengt, his contempt for Williblad tinged with surprise. "I've never heard talk like that. Not even from the heretics at the stake." He regarded Williblad with the expression of a boy teasing a mad dog. "No God, Williblad? Who, then, made the world?"

"There is no God, and the world made itself," said Cheroo, draining his glass and slouching back in his chair. "That's why I like Peter's *Seasons* so much. He shows people in landscapes without the burden of any religious flummery."

Bruegel was happy to hear a bit more praise, even from this source. With

Jonghelinck's celebration cut so sadly short, he hadn't gotten nearly enough. But he didn't quite agree with what Williblad was saying. "Religion's in those panels, just the same," said Bruegel. "Nature is God's body."

"And men the lice upon her," said Cheroo. "Why not leave us vermin out of your next picture entirely? Paint the land alone, and, once you've mastered that, paint a landscape with no land at all."

"How do you mean?" said Bruegel, smiling a little at Cheroo's fantasy.

"Paint something with no human name upon it. Paint a color or a shape or . . . something that's not a picture of anything. When I was a boy, there was an elder of our tribe who'd pour out different-colored sands to make wonderful patterns. Sunbursts and stars and whorls and zigzags." Cheroo's voice trailed off and his head dropped back against the cushions. He closed his eyes and smiled, perhaps visualizing the designs he described.

"Paint them yourself, you infidel," said Bengt. "And good luck finding a patron for your shit smears." But Cheroo didn't answer. He'd fallen asleep.

"Williblad takes advantage of me because I admire him so," said Ortelius. "He succumbs to dissipation." He ran his hands across his face and returned to the topic they'd been talking about before Cheroo's interruption. "It's a dreadful thing about your paintings going into storage with the city, Peter."

"I'll paint more," said Bruegel shortly. This crowning day to his year of work had ended in disappointment and strife. A sudden spasm seized his stomach. He was going to vomit. Not wanting to make too big a mess, he bent over the ash scuttle by the side of the fire and heaved up what seemed like a very large amount of sour, coppery-tasting liquid. Looking watery eyed into the scuttle he could see that it was quite red. At first he thought the color was from Jonghelinck's wine, but, no, he'd vomited blood.

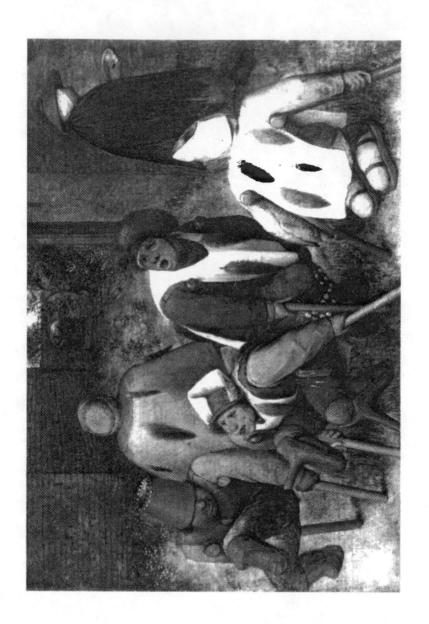

THIRTEEN

THE BEGGARS
ANTWERP, AUGUST 1566

Ortelius woke well after sunup, naked in his bed with Williblad beside him, the two of them filmed with sweat. It was late August, the air in the bedroom very still and close. Williblad was asleep, a peaceful expression upon the beloved face that was so often twisted in anger or contempt. Williblad had returned from the taverns very late last night, drunk and in a stormy, lustful humor. It had been pleasant work to soothe him.

The voices of Peter and Mayken floated up from the kitchen, where they were chatting with Helena. They'd arrived yesterday, come to Antwerp to deliver three new paintings to William of Orange, with the inevitable Waf at their heels. William had been in charge of Antwerp since April.

Ortelius slipped quietly out of bed, sponged himself off at the basin, and pulled on a silk shirt and some linen knee breeches. It was shaping up to be another beastly hot day.

"Do I hear Bruegel and Mayken?" It was Williblad, his reddened eyes wide open.

"They arrived after you went out last night," said Ortelius. "And we were all in bed before you returned. Do you remember how you woke me?" A smile stole across Ortelius's lips.

"I can't fathom the fact that I gave up Mayken to become a sodomist," said Williblad, his words as harsh as a slap in the face. He was unkind so much of the time. "I don't think I'll be staying with you much longer, Abraham." He rubbed his hands against his temples, ruffling his silvered hair.

Ortelius was used to this kind of thing from Williblad. Now he was supposed to beg and to say how much he needed Williblad. But today he didn't feel like it. For the first time it crossed his mind that he could in fact let Williblad go. The thought frightened him. And so he tried to smooth things over. "Please, Williblad. You say that every morning."

"Last night I met a woman like myself," said Williblad, staring abstractly at the wall. "Down by the docks. A fellow prostitute, also spawned by a Great Navigator. Well, not quite a prostitute, a laundress in a brothel. Niay Serrão from the Spice Islands. She says she came to Europe on Magellan's ship, the same year I arrived on Ponce de Leon's. She's as weathered as I, but perhaps we could make a life together. A decent, non-Christian life."

This was considerably further than Williblad usually took his morning complaints. Had he really found a woman? Imagining a female in Williblad's embrace made Ortelius quite ill with jealousy. "Have some elixir," he said shortly. Ortelius kept a decanter of gin and cloves in his wardrobe. Usually a few drams were enough to dissipate Williblad's morning melancholy.

Rather than waiting for any further response from Williblad, Ortelius left his room and started down the hallway. Williblad's mention of a "decent life" had set him to thinking. Was it truly a sin for Ortelius and Williblad to be living together? Williblad was far from being a prostitute, he was Ortelius's partner. The philosopher Plato taught that, in the earliest days of creation, humans had been androgynous. Perhaps the division into male and female resulted only from the Original Sin; perhaps androgyny was the true, pre-Adamite "decency."

But all this was vain logic chopping. Ortelius was profoundly glad, as he was every morning, that his mother and sister weren't here to see how he and Williblad lived. There'd be no use telling Mother about Plato. She was dead three years now, dear old thing, and his sister, Elisabeth, was married and living with her husband in London.

Thinking of London sent his mind's eye flying upwards to look down at the earth from a viewpoint where England and the Low Lands were both visible. Williblad's unpleasant remarks had jarred him into a loose, speculative state of mind. As he descended the stairs he imagined a viewpoint that flew yet higher and he dreamed—not for the first or last time—of mapping Heaven.

The new house's kitchen was a fine big room with a black-and-white tiled floor. Bruegel and Mayken were sitting at a square, wooden table with the morning light shining in from the garden window. A blue-and-white china vase with pink peonies stood on the deep windowsill, a little view of Antwerp upon the side of the vase. How clean and pleasant it all was, how decent.

"Hello, Abraham," said Bruegel, who was eating a plate of curdled milk with honey. Bruegel's face was lined; he'd begun to age. But he wore a smile. "Helena's balancing my humors. And most skillfully too. Is it true, Helena, that you've married?"

"I finally found the love of my life," said curly-haired Helena, standing by the shiny copper stove they used for summer cooking. "I just knew the day would come. It was love at first sight." She giggled deliriously.

"Where does your Prince have his castle?" asked Bruegel.

"My man Frans works for the merchant Gilles Hooftman, loading and unloading his ships, and running errands when all the ships are at sea. We have our own rooms at the warehouse. It really is like a castle, Mijnheer Bruegel. And I'm to be a mother soon as well." She giggled again.

"Congratulations," said Bruegel.

"To be sure," said Helena, patting her belly. "Oh, I forgot to put some ground nutmeg on your curds, Mijnheer Bruegel. Here we are then." She bent over his plate.

"Excellent suggestion," said Mayken. "Peter needs to eat better and to work less." She herself was busy eating smoked herring and fried new potatoes, her cheeks smooth and rosy from her night's sleep. "Good morning, Abraham. Where's Williblad?" The expected question. Williblad had long since told Ortelius all about his past escapades with Bruegel's wife.

"Just rising, I believe. But I warn you, it's not wise to speak with him too early in the day." And that was an understatement. How serious had Williblad been about that woman he said he'd met?

Waf appeared from under the table, wagging his shaggy white tail at the sight of Ortelius. Helena had already equipped the wolfhound with a beef bone, which he held clutched at a rakish angle in his jaws.

252 ※ RUDY RUCKER

"Helena says there's to be a great hedge sermon today," said Bruegel. "A Joachin Moded is preaching."

"Ah yes," said Ortelius, pushing Waf aside and sitting down at the breakfast table. Helena had thoughtfully set out silver forks and some good china with blue roses on it. "Moded of Zwolle. One of the fieriest of the Swiss Calvinists. He started preaching yesterday, and he's not done yet. I think half the city will go out to see him today. Ten thousand or more. These gatherings aren't so solemn as one might suppose—they've become almost like fairs, wouldn't you say, Helena? The enterprising Calvinists set up all manner of booths and games around the edges. It's the kind of thing you might like to draw or paint, Peter. We should go out there for the day."

"It's quite safe?" inquired Mayken. "With our William the Sly in charge of Antwerp, there's no more fear of heresy trials?"

"There hasn't been an execution since the end of March," said Ortelius, accepting a china cup of coffee from Helena. He prepared to launch into narration. Talking was a good way to keep your mind off your cares. "The Day of the Ill-Burnt. Perhaps you haven't heard the full story. It was Easter Monday. The Sheriff and the ecclesiastics had prepared a baker's dozen of convicted heretics to burn at the stake. It struck me as numerically fitting for Eastertide, you know, thirteen heretics to match the thirteen of our Lord and His twelve Apostles. Pythagoras taught that the numbers are even more elemental than the humors, you know. In any case, Williblad and I went to see the grim affair. One stays abreast. The heretics all had shaved heads, and their heads were bloody on top. It seems our executioners have been learning new barbarities from the Spanish, who make a ritual of scraping the scalps of the condemned with broken glass to remove, they say, the chrism oil of baptism. A most unpleasant sight for an Easter Monday."

"In Brussels they've started using a square on the hill above our house for burnings," said Bruegel. "Sometimes the wind catches the smoke and it blows right down into our windows. A smell like burnt hair and roast shit. It goes right down to my stomach."

"And to think men pretend to do this in Christ's name," said Ortelius with a shake of his head. "What savage folly. But, Peter, you haven't told me enough about how it goes with this unhappy stomach. You put a terrible scare into me this winter when you vomited blood. Last night you said your symptoms have abated? Did you consult a physician?"

"God forbid," said Mayken. "We asked one doctor's opinion and he prescribed salts of mercury! When every painter knows that mercury turns your blood to choler and bile. No, Peter's been listening to his insides, and they tell told him to eat only sweet and phlegmatic food. Lots of milk. And he's being more and more careful with his paints. He has Bengt brushing on most of the reds, whites, and yellows."

"Enough about my aching gut," said Bruegel with a sour belch and a wave of his hand. "Tell us more about the Day of the Ill-Burnt."

"Thank you, Helena," said Ortelius, as the maid set his breakfast before him: breakfast rolls with butter, a dish of fresh-picked cherries from his garden, and a single scrambled egg, the meat of the egg in a little mound beside the immaculate, blown-out shell. "Very well, then. On the Day of the Ill-Burnt, one of the condemned women was a thin girl like a peeled stick. She was the lover of a young monk, and the two of them had been found with a copy of Hendrik Niclaes's book *Terra Pacis*, dreaming of Love and Peace. As the executioner tied the girl to the stake, she kept screaming that she was afraid of the flames, and her mother ran forward and gave the man a florin so that he'd perform the rude mercy of strangling her before lighting the faggots. But as the executioner turned back towards the girl, a cobblestone struck him square in the back of the skull. It laid him out cold as a cod. And then the stones began flying like potatoes at a drunk peasant harvest festival. Two of the executioners were killed, and the three others resigned their posts on the spot; in fact they helped the crowd cut free the heretics. And the thirteen condemned men and women disappeared down the alleyways like rabbits into the thickets."

"But couldn't the constables still recognize the Ill-Burnt by their shaved heads?" asked Mayken.

"I'd wager that most of the Ill-Burnt ones caught ships for England before the sun went down," said Ortelius, finishing his egg and picking up the shell. As he talked, he took a bit of lead from his pocket and began sketching a world map onto the eggshell, starting with the view of England and the Low Lands he'd been imagining before. "England's all but Protestant these days, you know. I was in England last month to visit my sister. She has a fine son. I call him Carbo because of his father's name being Cole." Ortelius smiled at his little pun and glanced up from the egg. He did what he could to keep himself amused.

"I'm heartened by the tale of the Ill-Burnt," said Bruegel. "We can have our freedom if we take it. What manner of man cast the first stone?"

"None other than my dear Nature's nobleman, Williblad Cheroo," said Ortelius, warmed by his remembered pride. In the proper context, rash folly could be exemplary courage. He turned the eggshell in his fingers, and sketched the proud peninsula of Florida. "Not so much because he loves Calvinism, you understand, but because he hates executioners."

"That's Williblad all over," said Mayken.

Ortelius set aside this morning's sour words and smiled to think of Williblad. Having the man from Florida in his bedroom made it an exotic treasure chamber. How could Williblad speak of leaving? And how could it be that Ortelius sometimes welcomed the thought?

"And it was the Day of the Ill-Burnt that brought William of Orange to

Antwerp?" pressed Bruegel, not wanting Mayken's thoughts to linger over Willi-blad. Bruegel remained a bit uneasy about the other man's hold upon his wife's fancy.

"That's right," said Ortelius, coming out of his reverie about his partner. "The beadles and bailiffs had completely lost control. The lower elements were running riot. The mayor called upon the Regent, and she in turn deputized William to rule Antwerp for the nonce. One of William's hereditary titles hap-pens to be Burgrave of Antwerp, so he had a plausible claim to power. When he and his little army arrived, we all cheered him. Lord knows, any solid burgher like myself wants order in our town, preferably a rational and humanistic order such as our pragmatic William the Sly can provide. Many have taken to wearing wide-brimmed black hats like Calvin, and if you walk down an Antwerp street of an evening these days, you can hear Calvinist psalms being sung—but what harm does that do anyone? Does the Risen Christ care if a plate of collection money goes to Geneva instead of to Rome? Does our Savior care about a hat?"

"Well said," agreed Bruegel. "And what's the status of the Spanish taxes in Antwerp these times? Nobody asked me for the Twentieth Penny when I brought in my paintings yesterday." Ordinarily, one out of each twenty pennies exchanged in any transaction were to go to Philip.

"No, William hasn't been collecting taxes," said Ortelius, sketching away on his egg. With his years of practice, he could finish the whole world in a matter of minutes. "It's a way of ensuring his popularity. I'm sure the Regent and Philip are quite upset. But tell me about your three new paintings; I never got to see them."

"As it happens, one was of the hedge sermon you and I went to some years ago," said Bruegel. "I made it *The Sermon of John the Baptist*. I'm sorry I didn't show it to you, Abraham. But with everything in such disorder, I wanted to make sure I found William and got paid before something untoward happens. And I gave him a *Numbering at Bethlehem* and a *Slaughter of the Innocents* as well. I did these as a pair of winter scenes in a Flemish village, a place like my own Grote Brueghel. It was pleasant to paint snow in this heat. Not that I painted all of it."

"Bengt brushed on most of the white for him," said Mayken. "And it worked out very well. Prince William was pleased with them, no, Peter?"

"Not pleased enough," said Bruegel. "He looked at them for half an hour, then put them back in their crates to send to his estate in Germany. Dillenburg. At the very least, he could have sent them home to Brussels. All my roses go to pigs." He winced and pressed his hands against his stomach. "I can't be bitter. It hurts me. I'll say something nice. One of William's courtiers deemed the *Slaughter of the Innocents* a 'wonderfully apropos image for our times.'" Bruegel winced again. "Did I mention that it shows Spanish and Walloon mercenaries killing babies?"

"So you took my advice!" It was Williblad, standing in the kitchen door rubbing his eyes. He was wearing a curious costume: a shapeless gray robe with a cloth belt. "Hello, Mayken and Peter." Waf trotted over to lick Williblad's hand.

"Greetings, Williblad," said Bruegel. "That's right, it was indeed you who first suggested a *Slaughter*. I'm in your debt. Lie down and chew your bone, Waf."

"Good morning, Williblad," said Mayken in a honeyed tone. "Abraham told us of your heroism on the Day of the Ill-Burnt."

"Best not speak of it," said Williblad with a frown. "Mark my words, the executioners will return to their duties. As you well know, the Regent Margaret still refuses the League of Nobles and their requests to moderate the Inquisition."

"Her adviser Berlaymont called the nobles *gueux*," said Bruegel. "Beggars. Our Dulle Griet was frightened by the firmness of the League, and Berlaymont sought to comfort her. 'What, Madame, fear of these beggars?' The nobles took up the name for themselves, and ever since then, '*Vive les Gueux,*' has been the rallying cry all over Brussels."

"We know all about it," said Williblad. He gestured down at his loose gray garment. "That's why I wear a Beggar's robe. I have a wooden bowl that I carry with me when I go out." He wedged his tongue between his lower lip and front teeth, twisted his arms like a palsied rabbit, and lurched across the room, dragging one foot behind him. "I'm a Beggar," he said in a spitty, barely comprehensible voice. With great grunting and clatterings of the chair, he clumsily took a seat at their table. He worked his jaw, hunched forward, and stuck his face close to Mayken's. "Do you have something for me?" Ortelius winced. Williblad's fantasies grew ever more obstreperous.

"Don't mock the cripples," said Mayken. "It's cruel. They're men and women like you."

"She's right," said Bruegel. "A little more trouble with my stomach and I'll be so bent that I'll have to crawl around on a handcart. Be fair, Williblad, if Ponce de Leon's sailors had broken your legs, you'd be walking on kneepads too."

"I'm evil," slurred Williblad, sticking to his act, his breath fragrant with gin and cloves. "God hates me." Beneath the table, Waf whined uneasily. This was more than japery, it was a confession of despair. It made Ortelius's heart ache to know that life with him made Williblad so melancholic.

Williblad laid a theatrically trembling hand upon Bruegel's cheek, but Bruegel ignored him and shrugged off his touch. "What are you spending your time on these days, Abraham?" he asked. "Antiquities?"

"Maps," said Ortelius, handing Bruegel his globe-sketched egg. "Now do stop it, Williblad. You're upsetting everyone. Eat a proper breakfast and we'll have a nice day." Williblad cocked a fierce eye at him, but then relented, slouching back in his chair. "More maps than ever," continued Ortelius. "I don't know if you remember that Williblad once got me a contract to give Fugger a copy of each new map I made. Fugger's gone off to Augsburg, but I've been doing something similar for the merchant Gilles Hooftman."

"That's how I met my Frans," put in Helena. "He came here to pick up the book of maps for Hooftman. Here, Williblad." She set a plate of potatoes and herring before him. He mimed an extravagant gesture of thanks and began to feed himself with an exaggerated daintiness that made Mayken giggle.

"How do you mean, a book of maps?" said Bruegel.

"I gave him the idea!" exclaimed Williblad. This was something he was genuinely proud of.

"That's right," said Ortelius fondly. "Williblad and I were talking about the stack of maps I gave Fugger, and how hard it was to keep them straight, and then Williblad suggested I make all my maps the same design and the same size. And sew them together! I've started making up map books by hand for my best customers. And next I'm planning to publish them as a real book."

"A book with no words?" said Mayken.

"Who's to say what a book can be?" said Ortelius, full of the excitement that this new project gave him. "I've decided to call it the *Theatrum Orbis Terrarum*— that's 'Theater of the Earthly Globe,' Mayken. There's a Chamber of Rhetoric called the Globe Theater in London, you know. And no, the book won't be completely without words; we'll have labels and captions in Latin. Martin de Vos is designing the engravings for the caption cartouches. They're to look like leather and stone, you understand, it gives the book an air of solidity. De Vos is a competent fellow, grown marginally less annoying than in the old days. Remember when he flipped over the table full of plaster saints in Rome, Peter? Calvin would have liked that. Calvin hates art, and I rather think it's because he's a blockhead with no eye for beauty. A Swiss, can you imagine? Of course Calvin justifies his prejudice with the Second Commandment, and terms religious statues and icons a form of idolatry. It's a message that's well received by the rabble. For them, anything that they can't eat and turn into excrement is a waste of money."

"I'd smash a statue of a saint any day," said Williblad, slipping a bit of his herring to Waf. "When I helped Fugger dissolve his holdings, those were the least valuable of the items he owned."

"Ah, Williblad, you always rush to extremes," said Bruegel. "Certainly there is some grain of sense in what Calvin says. As Erasmus puts it, 'The stupid and thickheaded give their devotion to images instead of to the divinities they represent.' But one can't be indiscriminate. The best of images contain the divine within them. Any man who'd raise a finger against a van Eyck or a Bosch is a *zot*."

"How about the paintings of your Master Coecke?" said Williblad. "There's several of them in the Our Lady Cathedral, well varnished and most tediously

Italianate. Tempting targets." Ortelius wondered if Williblad remembered that Master Coecke had been Mayken's father. Probably so, but he'd say anything to get a reaction.

"Are you the first to think of a book of maps, Abraham?" said Mayken, side-stepping the quarrel that Williblad perversely sought.

"The Italians have made some attempts at such a thing," said Ortelius. "But they mix everything into a jumble with no two images laid out the same way. I discussed the idea of a uniform map book with Mercator not so long ago, and he said he'd been considering something like the same idea. He'd wanted to call his book an Atlas, after the mythical Greek giant who carried the earth upon his back. Be that as it may, he's being good enough to let me finish my version first. And Plantin is eager to see it into print. This will be my magnum opus."

"I do little on my own, but my illustrious friends learn from me," said Williblad equably. His breakfast was finally settling in. "Did I hear talk of a hedge sermon today?"

"What do you think?" said Bruegel to Mayken. "Maybe I should get back to the studio."

"Oh no, let's see the excitement," said Mayken. "Since Abraham so kindly invites us, we'll make a day of it and stay another night. It's good to have a change. Mother and Mienemeuie will be happy to have Little Peter to themselves. And Bengt can perfectly well gesso the two new panels on his own, Peter. It's best for your health if you're not around while he's putting on white lead."

"I only hope he's mixing in the proper amount of massicot. Too white a gesso kills a picture."

"Two new panels?" said Ortelius, marveling as ever at his friend's relentless productivity.

"I have commissions from some fellows I met in Amsterdam," said Bruegel. "A Herman Pilgrims and a Willem Jacobsz. And praise God for that. To tell you the truth, I've about lost my taste for selling paintings to my local countrymen. They underpay me and they box my pictures away. These Hollanders look to be worthier customers. I'm going to paint a little *Adoration of the Kings in the Snow* for Pilgrims. He's given me free rein, and I'm going to try something new. I'm going to paint the snow as it looks while it's actually falling. Big, blurred flakes in front, and smaller flakes farther away. Jacobsz wants a large painting of peasants, and I'm making him a *Dance of the Bride*. I'll have Franckert come and model for me in my studio while I'm working on it. Nobody swings a codpiece so well as he."

"Well, let's stir our stumps and go see some peasants in action," said Williblad. "Or, lacking peasants, we'll see the dregs of Antwerp. Wait while I fetch my wooden *Gueux* bowl." He headed up to the bedrooms, with Waf trotting after him.

"Can I tie up the dog in your garden?" asked Bruegel. "I don't want to have to worry about him in the crowds."

"You're just mad at Waf for liking Williblad so much," said Mayken, half joking.

"It's fine with me to leave Waf behind," said Ortelius, who wasn't overly fond of the beast. "There's a cool, shady spot under my cherry tree. Helena can give him a big bowl of water."

So Peter settled Waf under the tree in the garden. And then Ortelius, Bruegel, Williblad, and Mayken exited the city gate near the van Schoonbeke windmill, just like the time Ortelius had taken Peter to Hendrik Niclaes's hedge sermon in the woods. But there was nothing surreptitious about today's gathering. Jostling crowds stretched out halfway to the horizon, plain as day. French-speaking or no, many of the passersby greeted the gray-garbed Williblad with a call of *"Vive les Gueux!"* It was a blazing hot day, without a breath of breeze.

"Let's see who's the best shot!" said Williblad, pointing to the windmill. A pair of men in wide-brimmed black Calvinist hats were tethering bright red cloth targets to the end of a pole strapped to the windmill's lowest vane, which was angled towards the ground. "For a few stuivers we can take turns trying to shoot down one of the cloth birds with a crossbow," explained Williblad. "Be a sport, Peter, and treat us. I'm sure you've got pounds of gold from William the Sly."

"Fine," said Bruegel. "I learned to shoot a crossbow back on the Graaf's estate in Brueghel."

"They're not birds, they're Cardinals!" exclaimed Mayken, as they approached the windmill. And indeed the little red cloth objects were doll-like human figures, with paper miters and with eyes and mouths painted on.

"Bring down the Pharisees, good brethren," said one of the Calvinist-hatted men, a big-jawed fellow with several teeth missing. To Ortelius's eye, he looked to be an ordinary street ruffian who'd put on Calvinist airs to suit the day's activities. Two days ago there'd been a Church procession in town for the Feast of the Assumption, and likely as not this same fellow had been there wearing a medallion of the Virgin upon his cap and selling rosaries. "Three bolts for a stuiver," said the second man. He was distinguished by having one of his ears missing, with nothing but a little hole in the side of his head. "Take aim at the priests of the Golden Calf. I warrant this copper-skinned fellow in the garb of the Beggars can do the deed. Where are you from, my lad?"

"America," said Williblad, eliciting a whistle of surprise.

Bruegel gave the big-jawed man a couple of stuivers and received the loan of a crossbow and six of the special crossbow arrows, called bolts or quarrels. These were valuable items, with wide, sharp blades. A pair of boys stood ready to retrieve them, one fat and one thin. Ortelius smiled kindly at the boys, but they took no interest in him. They had eyes only for the crossbow and the bolts.

"Would you like a shot, Abraham?" asked Bruegel.

"No thanks," said Ortelius.

"I'd like to try," said Mayken.

"Very well," said Bruegel. "You go first. Here, I'll arm the bow for you." He put his foot in a stirrup on the bow, drew back the heavy bowstring with a special hook, and handed Mayken the weapon.

"Up, up, and up the Romish idolaters ride the wheel of Dame Fortuna," said the man with no ear, as his partner turned the windmill's vanes, sweeping the tip of the pole with the targets nearly a hundred feet into the sky. "Have a care when the quarrel falls to earth, little lady," he told Mayken with a lewd chuckle. "It could cut you a new slit. Let fly when you're ready."

Mayken's bolt shot off to one side and clattered off the masonry of the windmill. The fat boy scrambled up onto the crumbling stairs of the windmill to get the bolt. Bruegel re-armed the crossbow and shot. His quarrel shot up with a whir, rattled against the high vane, but missed the targets.

Ortelius was eager to see his Williblad do well, but Williblad notched the bowstring too far back, and his bolt sailed high over the vane and off into some bushes, sending the two boys scampering in pursuit. This time it was the thin boy who got the prize.

"I'll shoot again," said Mayken. Carefully she aimed her quarrel straight up into the still air—aimed it precisely so that when it began to drop, it would head straight for the man with no ear. "Look out," said Mayken as the bolt began to fall. "It's going to cut you a new asshole." Living with Bruegel seemed to have given her a taste for coarse wit. With a hoarse bellow, the man threw himself to one side, and the bolt slammed quivering into the ground where he'd stood.

Bruegel's second bolt hit one of the little red targets, but failed to cut it loose. Williblad targeted his last shot truly. The quarrel's blade sliced through the string holding one of the Cardinals, and the little doll came sailing down. With a lithe step forward, Williblad plucked it from the air. Ortelius was proud. Nobody was so graceful as his partner.

"It's yours to keep, brother Beggar," said the man with the big jaw. "Tie it to a stake and burn it in your stove when you get home. Let the Papists taste of their own special dish."

Beyond the mill was the public midden heap where carters dumped collected offal. The August sun had blazed without letup for three full weeks now, and the smell of the refuse was astonishing. Though Ortelius and his companions gave the dump wide berth, they noticed some sailors and prostitutes frolicking at the edge of the mound; they were spreading rotten garbage upon a wide flat spot in the ground and taking running slides upon it—just as if they were playing on the ice. Bruegel paused to watch for a minute.

"Hardly picturesque," said Ortelius.

"The postures are good," said Bruegel. "I might use one of them in my new *Dance*."

"Do you see your pictures before you paint them?" asked Williblad, who could never hear enough about the craft of painting.

"I see the outlines in my mind's eye, but not the details. I have to work to find out the details. It's a little like there's fog over the scene, and slowly it clears away. Or, no, it's more like a gold medallion that was buried in mud, and I'm clearing the dirt away with my brush."

"I wish I could paint," said Williblad. "I feel I've got it in me." It was an old obsession of his, never acted upon.

"You've told me that before," said Bruegel. "So why not start? You're ten years older than me, eh? That makes you forty-nine. We've still a bit of life in us. I'll give you some paints and, if you like, you can learn your colors by making patterns like your Tequesta shamans."

"You could be an artist's apprentice!" said Mayken.

"But not mine," put in Bruegel with a wry smile. "God forfend this randy savage from dwelling in my house."

Though Williblad smiled to hear his prowess mentioned, the thought of having to learn a craft from the start put him into a black humor. "The hell with being an apprentice," he exclaimed. "At my age, I should be the one in charge." Nobody said anything to this.

The crowd was growing thicker, and at the center of the crowd stood little Moded of Zwolle. He was perched like a rooster upon a pyramid of boxes, crowing out his teachings in a loud, angry voice. His head was bare and his face was quite red from the sun. It was a few minutes before Ortelius realized that Moded was preaching about religious art. He was for removing every trace of art from the houses of worship. And he wasn't speaking of a gradual process. He was talking about doing it today.

"It will be a small matter to destroy these graven images, which are only a species of idolatry," the Swiss preacher shouted. "For think, my Brethren, the Romish Church has done us a thousand times more hurt and hindrance through their persecutions. We propose to burn paintings and to smash stone statues, but the ecclesiastics have burnt and broken those 'statues' which God Himself has made, namely our dearest friends, fathers and mothers, sisters and brothers."

Ortelius and Bruegel exchanged a glance. This was nothing like the hedge sermon they'd attended years ago, nothing like Hendrik Niclaes's kindly preaching of tolerance and love.

"Do it tonight, Brethren, cleanse the paint from the Whore of Babylon's face!" shouted Moded, and pointed straight across the level fields to the spire of the Our Lady Cathedral. "Put an end to the horrible and abominable idolatries!

Sweep away the vile statues and ornaments; strip the altars and shatter the pagan stained glass! Purify the house of the Lord!"

"I don't like this," said Mayken. "He's a madman. His cure is worse than the disease."

"You're right," said Ortelius. He was sorry to have brought his friends here. The sun was beating down like a hammer.

"There's Niay," said Williblad suddenly. "Hey, Niay! Over here!" Some nearby listeners turned to shush him, their lips pursed with Calvinist strictness, but Williblad kept on hollering. A handsome Malay-featured woman pushed her way through the crowd to their side. Ortelius's heart clenched with jealousy.

"This is Niay Serrão," said Williblad to the others. "Niay, this is my friend Peter Bruegel the artist, this is Peter's wife, Mayken Coecke, and this is my landlord, Abraham Ortelius, occupation antiquarian and mapmaker." He was practically shouting so as to be heard over the baying of Moded.

"It's too hot here," said Niay. "Almost like Ternate. I was thinking to go sit in the shade." She had yellowish skin, high cheekbones, and a pointed chin. Like Williblad, her shiny black hair was threaded with gray. Yet she wore the bright face paint of a strumpet. Ortelius didn't like her looks at all.

"I'm with Niay," said Mayken, giving the woman a pleasant smile.

"Let's go," said Bruegel.

They wandered back out to the edges of the crowd, stopping to buy a basket of plums. It was too hot to walk any farther, so they sat under a tree by a slow stream, eating the plums and throwing the pits into the water. Two pigs lay nearly submerged at the edge, cooling themselves off. Nearby, six youths were practicing sword fighting, and chanting a Calvinist psalm as they went through their moves. Farther down the stream, some children were taking turns swinging out over the water with a rope and dropping in. Feeling excluded by Williblad's attentions to Niay, and unable to do anything about it, Ortelius stretched out on the grass and sealed off his senses. He thought of flying up into the air, of making a map of this field like a sea with each person an island in it. And then he was asleep.

When he woke, a cool breeze had risen to herald the onset of twilight. Niay had washed the paint off her face and was sitting cross-legged talking with the others. She had rough skin and very full lips. Williblad seemed fascinated by her. The memory of Williblad's morning unpleasantness came back to Ortelius. What if he simply let Williblad go? A few days of emptiness would follow, but perhaps it wouldn't be so long till he healed.

"Welcome back, Abraham," said Mayken. "Niay was just telling us her adventures. She comes from the island of Ternate in the Spice Islands east of Java and Borneo."

"The Celebes Sea," said Ortelius, sitting up. "I sell a map of it." He felt dizzy with possibilities. How strange to have this vivid woman here from a far dot on his maps. Ortelius's mind drifted back to the first time he'd sat at a table with Williblad, in that room at Fugger's, showing him the Florida map. What vast realities lurked beneath a cartographer's squiggles.

"I know all about maps," said Niay, pushing out her breasts. "My father was a Portuguese navigator named Francesco Serrão. He came to our island for the cloves. And it was one of your great Magellan's ships that brought me to Spain, years after when my father died."

"How did your father die?" asked Williblad, rapt with interest.

"My mother's family poisoned him," said Niay. "They were masters of the art. Mother's father, Almanzor, was the Sultan of Tidore, envious of Ternate for their Portuguese captain. In all the world, there are only two islands with clove trees, Ternate and Tidore, one mile apart from each other. The men of the one island partner with the women of the other, often by force. It's not uncommon for a man to be found stiff and blue after siring an heir upon a less than willing mate."

"We're two peas in a pod," said Williblad. "My father, too, was a raping navigator. My mother's husband killed my father with a club." He turned his head in a way that Ortelius knew was meant to show his features to their best effect. "It's too bad you and I are too old to have children together, Niay. What a lovely color they'd be."

Niay gave a whoop of laughter, planted a wet kiss on Williblad's cheek, and Williblad kissed her back, his lips sliding over to her mouth.

Ortelius's skin crawled to see this importunate woman sporting with his lover. "Did you actually meet Magellan?" he asked, to break things up.

"No, some islanders to the east had already slit his throat before his ships got to us," said Niay, after finishing her kiss. "It seems he was too strenuous in trying to convert our people to your One True Faith. He sailed to our Indies all backwards, you know, around the Americas and across the Pacific. The man was a fool. He deserved to die. Once his surviving sailors had loaded up their ships with our cloves, I got aboard one of the vessels and sailed along to Spain. I've always been one for adventure." She rolled her eyes to cast a fulsome look at Williblad.

This was really too much. Niay even dared to slight the great Magellan. "I say we go back into town," exclaimed Ortelius, getting to his feet.

"Yes, we'll go to the Our Lady Cathedral," said Niay, oblivious of his anger. "There's going to be a good riot. All the whores were talking about it this morning while I washed their sheets."

Back in the city, people were drifting towards the cathedral. Ortelius didn't want to go at all, and Mayken and Bruegel were hesitant, but Williblad and Niay urged them along. They found a sizable crowd inside the church, with a vocifer-ous knot gathered in front of Antwerp's little black statue of the Madonna, the same statue that had been carried through the streets two days ago for the Feast of the Assumption.

"She's had her last walk!" cried a man in a ragged tunic, his voice echoing off the stone arches of the church. *"Vive les Gueux!"*

"Smash the idols!" screeched a fiercely rouged woman with her front teeth missing. She glanced over at Ortelius and his group. "Well, hello, Niay," the har-ridan added in a conversational tone. "Have you come to lend a hand?"

"Sure, Beate," said Niay. "The Church has never done me any good. And meet my new boyfriend, Williblad. He'll help too, won't you Williblad? He's as old as me, but I'll warrant that he's nimble." How did this degraded person dare to claim Williblad as her boyfriend? Ortelius wanted to scream with frustration. He plucked at Williblad's sleeve to get his attention, but Williblad twisted away, drawn off by Niay.

"Mary's ruled for Rome long enough!" said another man, and began tugging at the grille that protected the Madonna. Niay and Williblad joined in, and all at once, with a resounding crash, the grille fell to the ground.

Ortelius looked around, hoping to see some priests or beadles to appear to put a stop to the disorder. But for some reason the protectors of the cathedral had all withdrawn. Were they afraid? Had someone paid them off?

With a wild shout, the crowd dragged the Madonna's effigy out onto the floor, tore off her vestments and hacked her to pieces—yes, some of the men turned out to be carrying axes, sledgehammers, and crowbars beneath their loose gray Beggar robes. More image breakers came streaming in the cathedral's side door, several of them bearing ladders.

With demonic agility, the iconoclasts clambered up to the heights, prying loose statues and letting them shatter upon the stone cathedral floor. The pictures were being torn down as well; those on panels were broken into kindling, while the linen ones were slashed to scraps. A pair of blond-haired, shock-headed ditch diggers began working their way around the perimeter, using their shovels to smash the cathedral windows one by one. More and more statues and pictures came tumbling to the ground. The mob systematically set upon the remains with sledgehammers and axes. A troop of harlots wandered about, carrying lit candles from the altar. A ruffian staggered out from the sacristy wearing a costly alb and carrying two great chalices filled with sacramental wine; the chalices passed around and were quickly refilled.

Ortelius stood off to one side, watching in sorrow, Bruegel and Mayken nearby. It was a scene like one of Peter's Hell paintings. But unlike a painting it was ear-splittingly loud, with hundreds of voices shouting at once. And where was Williblad?

264 ※   R U D Y   R U C K E R

"Look up there," said Mayken, pointing.

Williblad was dangling from a rope held by a group that included Niay. He was suspended high above the main altar, his face a mask of fierce joy, pulling at a life-sized statue of Christ upon the cross, a beloved image that Ortelius often stared at while praying at mass. *"Vive les Gueux,"* called the rabble watching him, and Williblad answered with a savage whoop, a guttural ululation from the New World. Christ popped free of his moorings and tumbled with his cross to crash upon the marble altar, thence to bounce down to the pavement of the nave. A lean man in a Calvinist hat darted forward to shatter Christ's head with a sledgehammer. The blow took with it some irretrievable part of Ortelius's feelings for Williblad.

Back on the ground, Williblad merged with Niay into the crowd.

The main part of the church was nearly stripped—the fruit of centuries had been destroyed in minutes—and now the image breakers turned to desecrating the cathedral's seventy side chapels, emptying out their little treasure chests upon a mound in the center of the nave. Anything like jewelry was donned as adornment, while the missals and illuminated manuscripts were fed to little fires built from the shattered strips of oak-panel paintings.

A stocky, mustached man sat by one of the fires, rubbing his leather pantaloons with the same sacred oil that had anointed prelates and kings. He wore a red shirt, red socks, and had a smooth blue cap pulled low down over his round head. He looked familiar, but Ortelius couldn't place him. Might Bruegel recognize him? But Bruegel's attention was occupied by his wife.

"Father's pictures!" Mayken was crying. She pointed towards the side galleries of the church. "We have to save at least one! Over there, the shoemakers' chapel, they haven't gotten to it yet. It holds Father's *Annunciation.* Help us, Abraham!"

The three of them ran over to the chapel, and Peter hopped up onto the altar to get the panel off its hook. It was too big for one man to carry easily, but small enough so that Peter and Mayken could handle it together. In truth, she was stronger than Ortelius. "Let's take it to your house, Abraham," said Mayken. "Lead the way."

Nobody paid them any mind until they reached the door of the church, but then a figure stepped forward to confront them. It was the stocky, mustached man who'd been oiling his leather pantaloons.

"Where you think you go with zat?" he asked in a French accent, peering nearsightedly out from under his low hat.

Hearing the voice, Abraham finally recognized the man. He was the same Walloon sergeant who'd attacked him, Bruegel, and Plantin in the street at Carnival some ten years ago.

"It's none of your affair," said Ortelius, acting braver than he felt. "Begone, you tub of guts." He hoped the Walloon would take him for a fierce iconoclast and give way.

The blow of the Walloon's fist in Ortelius's stomach was unexpected and quite devastating. "Ze Capitaine, he want you to smash up everything," said the Walloon, stepping over Ortelius and jostling Mayken loose from Master Coecke's panel. Bruegel held fast to the picture, balancing the rectangle of wood upon the top of his head. The Walloon squinted at the tall Bruegel rather than immediately launching himself at him. "The Capitaine have pay all ze church cats to go away, no? So you *Gueux* mice can play. Everyzing is to smash and burn, nothing to keep for souvenir." He rapped on the panel. "Now we put zis in the fire, monsieur, if you please."

At this point Bruegel finally recognized the Walloon. "You again!" he exclaimed. "Swine." By dint of main force, Bruegel twisted past the soldier and squirmed out the church door, single-handedly bearing the heavy panel.

"I break her if you no bring it back," shouted the Walloon, catching hold of Mayken and getting her neck in a choke hold. Still on the floor, Ortelius struggled to catch his breath, wishing he were a stronger, braver man. Mayken was letting out desperate, stifled cries. Bruegel threw down the picture and rushed back towards them, red with fury. The Walloon drew a dagger from his waist, Mayken shrieked, and—

Thud. The marble arm of a statue slammed against the Walloon's head and he fell to the ground beside Ortelius, bringing Mayken with him. It was Williblad to the rescue, using the language of violence that he so well understood. The redoubtable Niay was close behind him.

Mayken twisted free from the Walloon and got to her feet. The Walloon was struggling to rise as well; the blow to the head had only stunned him. Although his breath was back, Ortelius stayed on the floor lest someone hit him again. Niay drew a long, brown-stained pin out of her hair and lunged forward, stabbing her pin into the side of the Walloon's neck. He roared and caught hold of Niay's arm but then, in the twinkling of an instant, he fell silent and collapsed backwards, his head bouncing on the cathedral's stone floor. Ortelius reached out and touched his neck; there was still a pulse, but the man seemed paralyzed. Niay gave a satisfied nod and stuck her mother-of-pearl-headed pin back into her bun. The pinhead was, Ortelius noticed, the shape of a tiny skull.

"Well stung, Niay!" said Williblad. "My spider of the Indies! Now I'd better take my friends home with their painting. I'll catch up with you later."

"I want to loot something for myself," said Niay, and merged back into the hubbub in the nave of the church.

"A goodly number of these iconoclasts are in the pay of Spain, you know," said Williblad, grandly helping Ortelius to his feet. "I recognized this particular Walloon from my days with Granvelle. Now let's go!"

Ortelius, Williblad, Mayken, and Bruegel ran off into a side street, each holding a corner of Master Coecke's *Annunciation*. Ortelius was happy to have temporary possession of it. A fine piece.

"But why oh why does King Philip want our churches ruined?" wailed Mayken when they paused to catch their breath.

"If there's enough disorder, it gives him an excuse to bring in his troops," said Williblad. "When the burghers see the ruined church, they'll turn against the *Gueux*. They'll welcome Philip's army. I was a fool not to think of this before."

"Before you smashed Jesus?" said Bruegel angrily. "I can't believe you did that. Are you quite mad?"

"I thought you and I were agreed that religious statues are shit," said Williblad with a grin. "Note that I never laid a finger on any of the paintings. Save for this one. Lord but it's heavy."

"We're almost at my house," said Ortelius, looking away from Williblad. He didn't know how he felt towards him anymore. "The picture can live in my little museum, until such time as it's safe to restore it to the cathedral. You recognized that Walloon, Peter? He was one of the three who attacked us and Plantin years ago."

"Indeed," said Bruegel. "And Franckert and I saw this same man burn down a barn at a peasant wedding." He turned his attention to Williblad. "You and Niay did well to save us from the Walloon. I'm deeply grateful. But, you know, it's no good to blame the image breaking on Spain's provocateurs. It's our own Beggars and Calvinists who do this to us. And it's despicable. I ask again, how could you? You and your *Gueux* friends are cripples, if only on the inside."

"He has a point, Williblad," said Ortelius, trying to soften Bruegel's words. "You style yourself a healthy pagan, but the Catholic evil, the *Gueux* fever, and the Calvinist dysentery have fully infected you." In fact he felt as strongly as Bruegel. He couldn't forget the image of Williblad's fellow rioter smashing Christ's head.

"Niay and I saved your lives just now," shouted Williblad, resorting to anger as he so often did. "And this is how you thank me?"

"It's true," said Bruegel, his voice breaking in an odd, despairing laugh. "Your combat skills have put me in your debt. So I'll repay you—how? Christ with his shattered head tells me you must learn to paint. Yes, Williblad, preen yourself as would-be artist no longer, rather now do learn the hours and years of labor that we color-mad wights do varnish away. When would you like your first lesson, my liege?"

Williblad gave Bruegel a savage look, but seemed unable to formulate a response. Instead he turned to Ortelius. "I'm going to look for Niay," he said. "Farewell, Abraham. You and I are done." He turned on his heel and disappeared down the street.

A pang of grief shot through Ortelius, followed by relief. Losing Williblad was like pulling an aching tooth.

FOURTEEN

LAZY LUSCIOUSLAND
BRUSSELS, JANUARY–AUGUST 1567

As it happened, Williblad was one of the people whom William of Orange chose to single out when he went through the motions of arresting some people for the *"Beeldenstorm"*—as the orgy of image breaking came to be called. After the business with Granvelle's assassin, William had an abiding dislike for Williblad, and of course any number of witnesses had seen the half-American pulling down Christ and His cross.

The image breakers had stripped every church in Antwerp and the monasteries and nunneries as well, even going so far as to descend into the monks' cellars to stave in their barrels of wine and beer. Three of the ringleaders were hanged in September, but as the weeks and months went on there was still no word of Williblad's case. Mayken worried about him whenever she had a spare moment, which wasn't all that often, what with taking care of Little Peter and handling the business affairs of the family workshop.

And then, on a snowy day in January, Williblad turned up at Mayken and Peter's doorstep, with his friend Niay Serrão in tow. Niay carried a bundle of their possessions in a striped blanket slung over her shoulder.

"Williblad!" exclaimed Mayken and impulsively reached out to pat his shoulder. Her former lover looked more worn than ever. His spell in prison had given his skin a dull, silvery tone. "How did you get out?"

"William was too cautious to hang me straight off," said Williblad, shrugging off Mayken's friendly touch. He was here as a mendicant, unwilling to risk riling Peter. "I still carry a bit of royal protection from my days with Cardinal Granvelle, you know. And then the fact that I'd been seen saving your father's picture worked in my favor. In the end, Ortelius was able to pay a sum to get me freed. But I'm not going back to living with him. I'm settling in with Niay."

Niay greeted Mayken cheerfully. Unlike Williblad, she was strong and well. Mayken couldn't help but notice that Niay wore a gold and ivory necklace that looked to be a rosary looted from the Our Lady Cathedral.

Little Peter peeped out at the newcomers from behind Mayken's legs, and Waf delightedly jumped up to put his paws on Williblad's shoulders.

"Peter said he'd teach me to paint," said Williblad. "And Niay has plans to work for a Javanese fellow who owns a tavern."

"Let's tell Mother you're here," said Mayken, unsure what to say. Yes, Peter had, in a fit of emotion, said he'd teach Williblad to paint. But to have Williblad live under their roof was unthinkable. By now Mayken trusted herself, but she mistrusted Williblad. He'd be certain to stir up a fight, given the chance. On the other hand, it was freezing cold outside and Williblad looked a bit desperate. What to do? At times like this it was a relief to have her mother to turn to.

They trooped up to the second floor to find old Mayken at a table covered with scraps of paper, rolls of linen, and tangles of colored wool. She was designing a new tapestry for Marcus Noot, with Hennie van Mander busy with a charcoal pencil at her side. Marcus wanted a tapestry of the Brussels town hall with himself and the other City Fathers standing in front of it, a design which everyone in the Coecke house found ludicrously literal. But Marcus was adamant, and a friend, and had the money in his pocket for quite a rich tapestry, so old Mayken was executing the dull commission. Hennie was helping her translate some sketches of the City Fathers' faces into tapestry designs.

Neither of the women looked happy to see Williblad; they knew all about the troubles he'd caused. "The house is a bit full already," observed old Mayken, peering over her little spectacles. "You'll have to ask Peter." She liked to give the appearance of passing the hard decisions back to her daughter and her son-in-law. But in the end she always had her piece to say. And Mayken could see that her mother hadn't yet made up her mind.

In his attic studio, Peter was working on his *Dance of the Bride*, a big panel filled with dancing, carousing peasants, their legs and arms as fat as sausages, their codpieces bulging as never before. Peter's stomach had stopped bothering him, and he'd said he felt like painting something cheerful for a change. And indeed, whenever Mayken looked at this picture, she had to laugh. The fat Franckert figure was turning out particularly droll. Pale Bengt was painting a copy at Peter's side, and Hans Franckert himself watched from a chair, fully clad in one of his peasant costumes. He and Hennie had come down for a stay of three weeks after Christmas.

"Hello, Peter," said Williblad. "Will you teach me to paint?"

"The image breaker!" said Franckert, a half smile on his face. He was wearing a pink leather jerkin and skintight red breeches with the slit in front held together by a huge codpiece that Mayken knew from Hennie to be padded out by a rolled-up pair of stockings. Bengt regarded Williblad with a frown.

"You really want to learn?" asked Peter, pondering Williblad's request.

"I'm ready to try," said Williblad in a noncommittal tone. Niay squatted down to play with Little Peter; she made a pair of geese with her fingers and set them to quarrelling with each other, much to the boy's delight. "But the main thing is that Niay and I need a place to stay," admitted Williblad finally.

"Aha," said Peter. "I suppose I can ask around town."

"I thought perhaps I could stay here," persisted Williblad.

"There are limits," said Peter. "Even for a man who saved my life." Franckert had begun to smile.

"What about the shed in the garden?" suggested Mayken's mother, who'd come up to the studio as well. "In these times it wouldn't hurt to have an extra man around to protect the house. One of the apprentices used to live in the garden shed years ago. That fellow Cornelius. Remember, Peter?"

"It leaks," said Peter shortly. The memory of Cornelius seemed to pain him. Mother had found a weak spot, and Mayken sensed Peter's opposition giving way.

"I'm sure we can fix it up," said Niay, springing to her feet. "I'd love to try. I've never had my own house." She walked gracefully across the studio and looked out of the window. "That's it down there? It's sweet. In the Americas or the Indies, a *Sangaji* might live in a hut that size. A chief." She turned back and flashed Bruegel a bright smile that lacked a few teeth on the sides. "Let us stay, *Sangaji* Peter."

"I suppose it's God's will," said Peter with a half smile.

By the end of the day, Williblad and Niay had made the little wooden shed quite livable. Like old Mayken, Master Coecke had been something of a pack rat, and the cellar of the Coecke house was filled with damaged or unusable goods. Williblad and Niay lined the walls of their shed with stained carpets, covered their floor with cracked tiles, shielded the leaky spot of their roof with an oak panel too badly warped to paint upon, and made up some bed ticking from a great sack of odd-lot skeins of wool. Both Williblad and Niay were nimble with their fingers; they patched up two broken chairs and made a table from an empty barrel. To complete their homemaking, a rusted old armor cuirass was pressed into service as a stove. Little Peter ran back and forth, dogging Williblad and Niay's steps. The boy was fascinated to have these colorful new creatures in his garden.

During the first week, Williblad made an attempt to learn painting, but in his own fashion. Disdaining to work from a drawing, Williblad said he'd directly limn what he saw in his mind. *Alla prima,* as the masters said. He took thin and thick brushes, scooped some oil colors from Peter's paint pots and set himself up beside Bengt, daubing away at an oak panel several feet across. For Williblad, nothing but the finest materials would do.

Mayken peeked in at them, enjoying the sight of three painters in the family workshop, with Waf lying on the floor at their feet. She hoped it was a harbinger of the great family painting dynasty she and mother dreamed of.

On the first day Williblad said he was painting flamingos and alligators; he used a great deal of yellow, white, green, and red. But his birds and beasts were so smeary, that on the second day he decided they were flowers, and now the expensive blue paint came into play. The oils were rather more slippery than Williblad had expected; on the third day, his panel had become a murky, mottled gray. On the fourth day, Bengt scraped Williblad's paint off for him, and Williblad made a fresh start. He would paint a Tequesta shaman's magic snake. All through the fifth day, the shape came along tolerably well. And by the end of the sixth day, Williblad had created a jagged rainbow of colors that swooped from one edge of his panel to the other, with the shades blending from one to the next in quite a pleasing progression. The Tequesta design showed up nicely against the gray background left over from his first attempt. On the seventh day Williblad carried the still-wet painting around town fruitlessly looking for patrons, and after that he rested.

Meanwhile Niay found work as a scullery maid with her Javanese friend Raos. Raos's tavern was called the Pepper Berry; it was a little place in the St. Catherine's district near the docks at the terminus of the Willebroek Canal. This neighborhood was nearly as cosmopolitan as Antwerp, alive with the Turks, Moors, and Malay lascars who sailed upon the barges and ships.

Williblad decided not to be a painter, and began looking for work too. But his name was in bad odor among the merchants and nobles of Brussels, thanks to his old entanglements with Granvelle and his plots. As the well-loved Peter and

Mayken were sponsoring Williblad, he wasn't directly run out of town—but nobody would give him a job.

In the end there was nothing for it but that Williblad work with Niay at the Pepper Berry. He became Raos's barkeep and bookkeeper. Niay also enlisted him to help with some kind of show at the Pepper Berry; she called it a *wayang kulit*, and it had something to do with shadows.

Life ran on peacefully in this wise, and Williblad and Niay continued living in the shed.

Inevitably the day came when Williblad managed to catch Mayken alone and to try his old charms upon her. It was a rainy morning in February. Franckert and Hennie had gone back to Antwerp, both Peter and Mayken's mother were at work in their studios, and Little Peter was watching Mienemeuie make him a waffle. Mayken had put on a coat and a big hat to run across the muddy garden with two cups of hot chocolate for Williblad and Niay, barely avoiding getting tripped up by Waf, underfoot as always.

She found Williblad alone in the dim, cozy room, stretched out on his bed staring at the carpets on the walls. The rain drummed hypnotically upon the low roof. The room smelled faintly of Williblad's sweet breath, and of the musky tang of Niay.

"Little Mayken," said Williblad in a caressing tone. "You brought me chocolate."

"Where's Niay?"

"Off buying potatoes. Come sit here next to me on the bed, my angel."

"That's never going to happen again, Williblad," said Mayken. And, looking within herself, she realized that she meant it. Even so, her mugs clattered as she set them down upon the barrelhead that served as a table. "We're getting too old," she said, taking a step back towards the door, bumping against Waf, who was peering in after her. She noticed some odd-shaped pieces of filigreed leather lying upon the table.

"Yes, yes, you're all of twenty-two," said Williblad. "But I suppose it's me that you're talking about. Don't you want me to give you another baby?"

"Stop it!" said Mayken, laughing at his sally. "Little Peter isn't yours, you vain man. Haven't you looked at him? He's pink."

"As Peter tried to teach me, the mixing of colors is a subtle thing," said Williblad, his smile as long and beguiling as ever. "In any case, I'd be glad to help again."

"No," said Mayken firmly, and when Williblad made as if to get up from his bed, she scampered back to her house. She'd known the test would come, and was glad to see how easily she'd gotten past it. And if Williblad still wanted her—well, that was fine, that was a nice thought to carry around, a little flattering. And for that matter, there was some attraction between Peter and Niay as well, not that

Peter was likely to do anything about it. All his passion went into his art—and into his love for Mayken and Little Peter. Their family life was strong and solid, thanks be to God.

Though things were peaceful in the Coecke house, the world outside was seething. In the wake of the *Beeldenstorm* and its riotous image breaking, the Regent Margaret had made some concessions to religious freedom. In return, the *Gueux* and the League of Nobles had all but disbanded. Prince William remained in charge of Antwerp, Graaf de Hoorne was entrusted with calming the town of Tournay, and the Graaf Egmont began to pacify Flanders. Even so, many Low-Landers remained in open rebellion, and it was said that King Philip was planning to wreak some terrible vengeance upon the Low Lands.

Williblad still claimed that King Philip had instigated the image breaking to drive a wedge between the rebels and the middle classes. But Mienemeuie repeated a popular story that when the Tyrant heard of the image breaking he'd torn his beard for rage, saying, "It shall cost them dear! I swear it by the soul of my father! It shall cost them dear!" For some reason this tale greatly amused Little Peter, and he made it a habit, whenever the fancy struck him, to launch into an imitation of Philip: capering about, plucking at an imaginary beard, and crying, "It shall cost them dear!"

In the southern Low Lands, the Calvinists took over the city of Valenciennes, and the Regent Margaret sent an army to lay siege to them. To the north of Brussels, Brederode raised an army of rebels, who fought a series of battles with the Royal troops. The rebels met with some success, but in March Brederode's men were massacred—literally hacked into pieces—right outside the walls of Antwerp, upon the very spot where Moded of Zwolle had preached. Full news of the battle was brought to the Coecke house by William's falconer Bengt Bots.

"I'm back in town to help collect some things for the Prince," the brown-faced old Bengt told them, sitting on a chair in Bruegel's studio. He looked over at the original and the copy of the *Dance of the Bride.* "Big codpieces on these fellows," he observed. "Did you paint any of it, son?"

"That one's all mine," said young Bengt, indicating the copy. "We're shipping Master Bruegel's original off to Amsterdam tomorrow."

"Perhaps it'll ride on the same scow I'm loading up. Prince William's cleaning out the most valuable things from the Nassau palace. All the falcons, for one."

"He's not coming back to Brussels?" asked Mayken, feeling worried. Was Brussels abandoned to the eagles of war?

"Going to Germany," said old Bengt. "To his estate in Dillenburg. Wants to keep his head on his shoulders, he does. He saw a letter from Philip's envoy in Paris to Margaret, saying she's to shorten Prince William—chop off his head the first chance she gets. The Tyrant's out to kill all our high nobles: Graaf de Hoorne and Graaf Egmont as well as the Prince."

"De Hoorne?" said Peter, looking upset. Mayken well knew Peter's special feelings for Filips de Hoorne. She'd come to believe his notion that Filips was his half brother. Of all the men Mayken had known, few seemed worthier to be called noble than her wise, long-suffering, hardworking man. Her horn of plenty.

"Don't worry, he and Prince William are both heading for Germany," said old Bengt. "They'll be well out of it before Philip's army arrives."

"But it's not fair for the Regent to want to kill them," protested Mayken. "They've been helping to keep the peace." The world had grown so mad and full of hate.

"Damn right," said old Bengt. "Our William the Sly kept the Antwerp gates locked tight as a maiden's crack while Margaret's troops were killing off the rebel army. No sir, William wouldn't let his Calvinists and Lutherans run out to join the fight! So now the rabble's saying that if it hadn't been for William, the rebels might have won."

"I hadn't heard that," said young Bengt.

"Yes!" said old Bengt. "Prince William reckoned that if the gates were opened, the royal army and the vagabonds who travel with them would rush inside to pillage the city. Antwerp's the richest town in the country, and many's the idler who'd like to plunder her. There was no point in risking it for the sake of those raggedy-ass rebels. And by God, William was right. I watched the whole thing from the walls. Margaret's troops are a bloodthirsty lot of torturers and butchers. Walloons and Spaniards. They would have mowed those reformed Antwerp cookie-eaters down with the rest of them. But try telling that to a frothing Calvinist who thinks God helped him break the cathedral statues. So now the Calvinists and Lutherans are running William right out of Antwerp. And he's too sly to come back to Brussels. So we're packing up."

"What about the Bosch?" asked Peter.

"How do you mean?" said old Bengt with a veiled half smile.

"The big triptych of the *Garden of Earthly Delights!*" exclaimed Peter. "The painting with all the naked people in it, Bengt. It's the most precious thing William owns. Is he taking it with him?"

"I knew it!" said old Bengt, with a wheeze of laughter. "The Prince was right. Told me that would be the one thing Peter Bruegel would ask me about. The painting with the naked people and the giant birds. You artists are crazy. And, God help me, my son's one too."

"Maybe Master Bruegel should keep the picture for William," suggested young Bengt.

"Don't do that," said old Bengt, shaking his finger. "William says that when Philip's troops get to Brussels, they'll be looking for the Bosch. Don't sit on the manure pile if you don't want to get fly-bit. That big Bosch has Hell on one of the side wings, and they say there's nothing the Foreigner likes better. Now, don't tell anyone this, but one of the things I'm taking care of here is to get that damned picture sealed up inside one of the Nassau palace walls. It's too big to take to Germany."

"But is it really true that Philip is sending an army to Brussels?" asked old Mayken in dismay.

"That's what Graaf de Hoorne's brother wrote him from Madrid," said Bengt. "One of Philip's generals is to pull out four regiments from Spain's Italian provinces. Spanish soldiers seasoned by a few years in Sicily and Naples. The scum of the earth."

"Oh, what can we do?" cried Mayken's mother, sounding old and querulous. "God help us!" If mother was panicked, who could Mayken turn to?

"Maybe he's mistaken," said her good husband. "It's not too late to pray."

With the *Dance of the Bride* shipped off, Peter started work on his *Adoration of the Kings in the Snow*. He'd been thinking about it off and on all winter, periodically staring out the studio window to sketch the falling snow. But before painting the snowflakes, he had to paint the scene behind them, which was a humble and touching Nativity in a Flemish village, glowing with a snowstorm's yellow-green light. It was June by the time Peter reached the final stage of brushing on the snowflakes, bigger and blurrier in front, smaller and sharper in back.

The finished *Adoration of the Kings in the Snow* was Mayken's favorite picture yet, a thing of true enchantment, with none of the sarcasm and pain that Peter had put into the *Adoration of the Kings* he'd painted at the time of Little Peter's birth.

This new *Adoration* was just what Master Coecke had said a painting should be: a window looking into another world. Or no, more than that, it was a door. When Mayken gazed at the little painting long enough, she felt herself transported to the Nativity—not to an *image* of God's birth but to the actual event itself. With so much evil in the world, God had come to save them in the form of a newborn baby. The baby was a seed that would take time to grow, the start of a long and gradual salvation, but, yes, He had come.

When summer came, Mayken decided to give her beloved, hardworking husband a special party. It so happened that Peter reckoned his birthday as June 20, 1527, the day he'd appeared on the doorstep of Anja and her veterinarian father's cottage back in Grote Brueghel. So June 20, 1567, was his fortieth birthday—although it was more normal to celebrate someone's birth on the saint's day for their name. But June 20 was handy, a good day to celebrate! Though Peter welcomed the thought of a feast with his friends, he didn't have the bent of mind to organize one. Mayken arranged the party all by herself, keeping most of the details secret. The locale was to be at the port in the St. Catherine's district, on the other side of the Grand' Place that lay at the heart of Brussels.

Peter, Mayken, Little Peter, old Mayken, Bengt, and Waf arrived at the harbor basin near sunset to find among the barges a lovely high caravel bedecked with pennants and ribbons. Realizing the ship was there for him, Peter broke into a smile and gave Mayken a kiss. Peter loved ships. Lute music drifted down from the caravel's poop deck, which was crowded with festive figures silhouetted against the glowing horizon. At the water's edge, old Mayken's friend Marcus Noot was eagerly pacing the cobblestones, waiting for them. Mayken felt very happy. Everything was working out perfectly. Her hair was nicely arranged in a coiled braid, and she was wearing a new blue watered-silk overdress with a low-cut square neckline, and under that a white linen chemise.

"Come aboard the *Luilekkerland*!" exclaimed Noot. "And let me be the first to wish you a happy birthday, Peter!"

"*Luilekkerland!*" repeated Peter with a laugh. The name meant something like "Lazy Lusciousland"—it appeared in folktales as a magical place where food was everywhere and nobody had to work.

"Hans Franckert's name for the ship," said Marcus Noot. "His fleet of one. He's been using her to import spices and pigments from Lisbon, sending paintings and lace back in return. Usually she docks in Antwerp, but Hans brought her down the Willebroek Canal so we could celebrate your birthday on her! Getting that canal built is the best thing I've accomplished in all my years as a City Father. In fact, I've been meaning to make a suggestion to you about it, Peter. What if—"

"All aboard!" called Franckert, leaning over the taffrail with a great mug of beer in his hand. There was a weathered-looking sea captain at his side.

"It shall cost them dear!" piped Little Peter, stamping his foot.

"Up with you, my scamp," said big Peter, hoisting the boy onto his shoulders and carrying him up the gangplank to the *Luilekkerland*.

Franckert was already a little drunk, and now, as he continued to gesticulate, his flat green cap slid off his head and dropped into the harbor water. It had been some time since Mayken had seen Franckert hatless, and he didn't look good at all. He was bald for one thing, with only a few greasy scraps of hair at the sides. And the flesh he'd accumulated upon his neck looked pale and pasty, like sweaty curds of thickened bile.

"Shit!" shouted Franckert as his hat fell. And when it hit the water he added, "Leave it there, it's ruined now. I'll find another."

Mayken was suddenly struck by how bad the harbor smelled: like decay and human offal. Foolish of her not to think of this before. She prayed the air would be better on the high deck.

Just then Waf rushed past her and wormed through Peter's legs to be the first aboard, very nearly toppling her husband and her son off the plank and into the vile black water where, yes, some kind of dead animal was floating, a cat or a rat or a dog that—Mayken thought in momentary fit of choler—should really be

278 ■   R U D Y   R U C K E R

Waf himself. She ran up the gangplank to give the hound a good scolding. He grew more willful every year. And now of course he was the first one up the companionway to the high deck where their friends were gathered, Waf pushing himself forward, whining and thrashing his tail and nosing around for food.

With her humors addled by the days of preparation and by her concern that everything turn out well, Mayken felt almost like throwing the beast overboard, but bald Franckert handed her a mug of beer and a fresh radish and, yes, everything was fine on the high deck after all. Waf composed himself and lay down under the table. A sweet evening breeze came in from the woodlands across the water, and if you didn't concentrate on your nose, there was no smell from the harbor at all.

"We're on a ship, Mama!" exclaimed Little Peter, waving a big pretzel that the smiling Abraham Ortelius had handed him. "We're at sea!" Not that the ship was really going anywhere. They'd decided to simplify things by keeping her at the wharf for the party.

"Let the captain show you how to sail, my boy," said Franckert. Seeing him sweaty and hatless, Mayken realized for the first time that it cost the man some effort to play the merry reveler. A noble effort in its own small way. "Mayhap he'll hire you on as first mate!" Franckert told Little Peter. "Let me present Captain Adam van Haren to you. Captain, these are Mayken and Little Peter, the wife and the son of the greatest artist in the Low Lands." Adam van Haren had a brown, smile-creased face and a shock of blond hair bleached to near whiteness. He doffed his little black cap, gave Mayken a formal bow, and took Little Peter to look at the tiller.

Many old friends from Antwerp were present, such as Christopher Plantin and Jerome Cock. There were a few artists as well, including some youngsters greatly in awe of Peter, and one or two older men, also in awe, but less openly so. Among the artists were young Joachim Bueckelaer and his tall old uncle Piet Aertsen; they'd recently moved from Antwerp to Brussels to set up a new studio. The gregarious Joachim was playing lovely music upon his lute. Mayken had decided not to invite Peter Huys (because she didn't want to see Anja), nor Nicolas Jonghelinck (because he still hadn't redeemed Peter's sixteen pictures from wherever it was in Antwerp they'd been stored). No need to think about old worries today!

Williblad was in attendance, but in something of a professional capacity, for the drinks and food were being provided by the Pepper Berry tavern, which was only a stone's throw from where the *Luilekkerland* was docked. Soon after Mayken and her family arrived, Williblad hurried down the gangplank and across the wharf, returning with a little cask of wine on one shoulder, and followed by a procession of Niay and three more maids from the Indies, each of them bearing a steaming platter of food.

There was fish baked Javanese-style with cream and nutmeg, mussels and lampreys in curry, a fine red joint of beef studded with cloves, mounds of fried new potatoes with garlic, green beans shining with bacon fat, rounds of brown bread, fresh onions served nearly raw with shaved ginger, and, to end the meal, a huge bowl of berries and sour cream with chopped mint leaves. The aromatic spices quite covered the vagrant odors of the harbor waters.

As night fell, Bengt and Lange Piet (for "Long Pete") Aertsen moved about the ship, hanging and lighting paper lanterns with candles in them. Lange Piet was known for painting peasant scenes using live models. He and Peter had become friends quite recently; Lange Piet and his nephew, Joachim, had come by the studio to see the progress of the *Dance of the Bride*, and, just for the fun of it, Peter had gotten them to pose as peasant dancers. Lange Piet was dressed in full propriety tonight, complete with a ruffled lace collar, though the lute-playing Joachim was dressed more casually, in a loose linen shirt tied together with red ribbons.

Little Peter followed Bengt and Lange Piet around, fascinated by the colored lanterns. Up on the high deck, the guests were lolling back in their chairs, nibbling at the berries and sipping a little more wine. Mayken and Peter sat side by side. Captain Adam van Haren was passing around a long clay pipe of the newly popular American tobacco. Williblad in particular liked the stuff; he said his tribal elders had smoked it when he was a boy.

"This year's been good to me," said Franckert, presently. He'd found a sailor's hat to cover his scalp. Sitting here wreathed by smoke he looked at ease again. The scene he'd helped set was a success; this was the kind of moment he lived for. And now he crowned the moment. "And you know, Peter, I'm finally ready to buy a picture from you. Can you paint me a *Luilekkerland*?"

"Paint this ship?"

"No, no, paint me the fairyland of plenty, the place where a roast pig trots by with a knife tucked into a flap of skin on his side, where a roast goose flies down to your plate, where the roofs are tiled with pies, the fences are made of chains of sausages, and pancakes push out of the ground like prickly-pear cactus." Franckert gestured to sketch out his image of the picture. His joy in doing this was so palpable that Mayken felt like hugging him, sweaty neck-rolls and all.

"That sounds like good fun," put in young Joachim Bueckelaer, striking a chord on his lute. "I'd like to see this picture."

"I'll paint it," said Peter, smiling. "With some plump, lazy fellows lying on the ground."

"A fitting image for us in the Low Lands," intoned Ortelius. Mayken could tell that seeing Williblad happy with his Niay had put the old maid into a bilious humor. "We're like Nero," he continued. "We fiddle while Rome burns. Meanwhile the Duke of Alva is on his way to massacre us." Mayken felt like kicking him for spoiling the conversation.

"What?" cried Mayken's mother, who was alert for any hint of danger these days. "Philip's sent the troops?"

"The Spaniards are swine," said Captain van Haren, exhaling a cloud of tobacco smoke. "One day we'll have a fleet of Sea Beggars to bring them to their knees."

"The troops are coming?" repeated old Mayken.

"Yes," said Ortelius, "the Tyrant's finally picked our executioner, one Fernando Alvares de Toledo, the Duke of Alva, Viceroy of Naples. It's said that he dresses from head to toe in black. You hadn't heard? Last month Alva assembled an army of ten thousand Spanish foot soldiers and a thousand on horse; seasoned men from Spain's Italian provinces. They sailed to Genoa last week, and as we glut ourselves they're on the march to the Low Lands through the Alps." Mayken gasped. It was just as old Bengt Bots had warned. How she'd hoped it wouldn't come to pass.

"The lanterns are flying," said Little Peter, pointing out across the lower decks. "Look!" Some of Niay's companions from the Pepper Berry had come up to join the party, and their motions were gently rocking the ship. The slow swaying make it look as if the lanterns were moving about on their own. Off on one side of the deck, Bengt was involved in what looked like a romantic conversation with one of Niay's friends. Life is dear, thought Mayken, life is precious. Surely God would protect the Low Lands, this earthly heaven below.

"I want to commission some pictures too," put in Marcus Noot, who tended to lag a minute or two behind in every conversation. "It's what I was starting to tell Peter before. The city of Brussels needs a series of paintings to commemorate the construction of the Willebroek Canal. Wouldn't that be a plum of a job?"

Mayken knew her Peter's expressions well enough to see that the idea bored him to tears. But he gave the polite answer. "What an interesting idea, Marcus. Perhaps I could get to it next year. A project like that would take some proper study. I wonder if I might do a less demanding work for you first." He turned to Ortelius. "But what's this, Abraham, you say Alva's coming through the Alps? It's finally come to that? What are we to do?"

"Let's lie on the ground with shit in our pants and our stomachs swollen up till the Black Duke slits them open," said Williblad with a weary sigh. "Who's for more wine? It's very light stuff, really."

"Shit in our pants!" repeated Little Peter, cackling for joy. "Williblad said it!" Williblad grinned at the boy and gave him a wink. Little Peter relished the irresponsibility of the older man. "Shit in our pants!" cried Little Peter again.

"Stop it, or you won't see the show," Mayken told him.

"What show, Mama?"

"*Wayang kulit!*" said Williblad. "We're putting it on for your papa's party, Little Peter. Shadow puppets that are flat pieces of leather. Just wait! I'm going down to help Niay and Raos."

On the lower deck Raos, a small Malay man with a clear voice, had unfurled a large white sheet of cloth, suspending it from a convenient bit of the ship's rigging. He disappeared behind the cloth and lit a lantern to brightly illuminate the screen.

Clusters of shadow figures appeared on the left and right edges of the screen, and in the middle there was a shape like a conical tree, intricately filigreed and with some animals pricked out by dots inside the shape.

The guests trooped down below to get a better look, bringing their chairs with them. Perhaps twenty Malays and Indians had already gathered on the deck; some were sailors from the ship, some were patrons of the Pepper Berry. As many of them sat in back of the screen as in front.

"This is the *wayang kulit*," said Niay, standing in front of the screen to face the guests. "It means 'shadows of leather.' In the Indies we celebrate a great event like *Sangaji* Peter's birthday with a *wayang kulit* show. Relax and enjoy yourselves." She scampered behind the screen with Raos and Williblad, and the show began.

First there was a knocking sound, which set Waf to briefly barking, and then the tree danced off to one side. There was a gentle chiming of gongs, the tootling of a flute, and now two gnarled shadow figures vibrated out to the center of the screen and began to talk, though not in any language that Mayken had ever heard. They talked for a very long time, their slender arms bobbing up and down. Like the conical tree, their bodies were filled with perforations that sketched out lines of dots to limn their features. You could see their eyes and faces and the draped folds of their garments. The shadows seemed to breathe as the puppeteer turned the flat leather figures this way and that.

A new shadow appeared, a squat, farting creature named Semar. The conical tree floated to the center of the screen and Semar picked his—or her?—way around it, encountering a fresh set of shadow figures: pop-eyed beastly-faced fellows much larger than the first figures. Giants. On and on Raos's voice toned, accompanied by the piping and ringing of what amounted to a little musical ensemble.

Mayken looked at Peter, sitting at her side with Little Peter in his lap. The two of them were fascinated. Mayken was happy but exhausted. Her party was a full success. With a sigh she settled back in her chair, letting her eyes drift closed.

It was well past midnight when Mayken awoke. The *wayang kulit* show was finished, the Malays were gone home or belowdecks, and the guests were preparing to leave. The plan was to walk to the better part of town in a single large group lest any of them be picked off by waterfront cutthroats and footpads. They set off towards the Grand' Place, quietly talking. A crescent moon on the horizon lit their way. Peter walked at Mayken's side, their sleeping son cradled in his arms and Waf at his heels.

"Did you like your birthday, Peter?"

"It was wonderful, dear Mayken. Those shadows—a shadow's even less than a coat of paint. It's nothing at all. But even so we see it. And what life that man breathed into them. Raos. He told me that in Java, a *wayang kulit* show lasts till dawn."

"Did he tell you what the story was about?"

"The usual thing. Different men woo the same woman. Evil giants are defeated. Raos says the *wayang kulit* shows can be used to change the world."

"The *wayangs* teach many lessons," put in Niay, proud of the success of her countryman's performance. "At home we say the world itself is a shadow of something higher. We're *wayangs* of the gods."

"You sound like the philosophers at Leuven," said Williblad, and gave a rueful laugh. "It's damned rare I use my fine European education anymore. Not that there's much to learn from the kind of men who would take Florida and the East Indies for the same place. At least they brought us together, eh, Niay?" He gave his woman a little hug. "Did you notice that some of the *wayang* shadows were red, Peter? They use very thin hide with paint on it for those ones. Can you imagine a *wayang* painting that was all moving colors?"

"On a night like tonight, I imagine all sorts of things," said Peter genially, his fingers twined in Mayken's. "But I'm especially taken with the idea that *wayangs* can change the world." How comfortable his voice sounded in the dark.

They were passing through the Grand' Place, a great open square surrounded by showy stone buildings with ornate cornices. Many of them were occupied by guilds; among those guilds fortunate enough to have a building right upon this central square were the brewers, the tailors, the archers, the tallow merchants, the armorers, the boatmen, the gardeners, the coopers, the tapestry makers, the painters, the butchers, the bakers, and the cabinetmakers. The great town hall of Brussels was there as well, distinguished by the exquisite stonework of its tower, over three hundred feet in height. The tower and the ornamented parapets of the buildings stood out in crisp relief against the moonlit clouds. At night it felt a little spooky, like the backdrop for a Hell painting.

"The shadow play can be a kind of prayer?" said Mayken, wanting to keep Peter talking.

"That's it," said Peter. "So of course I'm thinking that a painting could do that as well. You know me, everything always comes back to my pictures. I'm a bore."

"Oh, go on and tell us what you're thinking, Peter," said Williblad in a friendly tone. He'd managed not to get too drunk tonight. "It's your birthday, isn't it?"

"All right, then," said Peter with a smile. "Remember when I painted the toppled idol in the *Flight into Egypt*? And then Granvelle left. An answered prayer! I'm thinking I should paint something to try and stop Alva before he gets here."

"Do it, Peter," said Mayken, feeling a flicker of hope.

"I will." Peter raised his voice. "Hey, Marcus!"

"Yes, Mijnheer?" Noot's voice was slow and sleepy. He and old Mayken were a few steps behind them, walking arm in arm.

"What if I painted you a picture to stop Duke Alva from coming?"

"That would be nice," said Noot. "With the canal?"

"I'll paint the canal later, Marcus. Right now I'm thinking—I have it! The

Apostle Paul. He persecuted the Christians until he saw a light on the road to Damascus. I'll paint a *Conversion of Paul!*"

"A Bible scene?" said Noot.

"It'll be soldiers in the Alps," said Bruegel. "Like Alva! Can you see it, Marcus?"

"I can't see anything but flat shadows," said Noot. "Ask me tomorrow. With so much food in me, I feel like that fat clown thing, what's-its-name. Semar. Ah, here's where I turn off. Give me a kiss, Mevrouw Verhulst." Old Mayken gave Marcus a warm embrace, and then the Maykens, the Peters, Bengt, Niay, Williblad, and Waf headed home to the Coecke house.

The next day old Mayken worked a little on Marcus, and he good-naturedly agreed to Peter's proposal. He owned a part interest in a stone quarry, and had made quite a bit of money from the canal construction. Peter was very pleased. He loved nothing better than to work on two paintings at once.

Bengt readied the panels for *Luilekkerland* and the *Conversion of Paul* while Peter feverishly prepared sketches for the two paintings. And then Peter got to work on the backgrounds, with Bengt hard put both to mix paints and to keep his copying work abreast of Peter's progress.

The *Luilekkerland* was a smallish panel, less than three feet by two feet in size. Peter incorporated all the features Franckert had described—the pancake bush, the fence of sausages, the goose on the plate, and so on. In the picture's center he placed a tree trunk holding a round table of extra food, the table circling the tree like a hub. Three men lay stretched out on the ground like the spokes of a wheel: a sleeping cavalryman, a stunned peasant, and a writer numb with idleness, his mouth slackly open to catch the last drops of wine dripping from a toppled jug upon the table. Nearby a dazed foot soldier lay propped upon a pillow, vacantly gazing at the tree, his mouth hanging open in hopes that a little roast bird would fly into it. A perambulating Luilekkerland pig with a slice out of his back was silhouetted between the four men and the background. And in the upper corner of the background, a purposeful man with a big wooden spoon was crawling out of a hole in a cloudlike mound of white porridge or pudding. Like some devouring worm, the newcomer had eaten himself a tunnel through the cloud; he'd made his way to Luilekkerland from a tiny, white Mediterranean city perched by the sea upon the horizon at the other end of the cloud. The invader was climbing down from the cloud to a tree to the ground—and who knew what he'd do to the paralyzed inhabitants of Luilekkerland.

Mayken wouldn't have noticed all these details on her own, but Peter was eager to point them out. In his maturity he was getting more and more voluble about his pictures. Joachim Bueckelaer had taken to stopping by the studio once or twice a week, and when he was present, Peter talked even more.

The *Conversion of Paul* was one of Peter's full-sized panels, some five feet by four feet in size. It showed an army marching through a high Alpine gorge, with the cliffs falling precipitously off to the left to reveal a distant sea and a heart-breakingly lovely stripe of lapis-lazuli blue sky. As always in Peter's paintings, crows dotted the endless heavens. The right part of the picture was filled with mounting pinnacles of rock, threaded by a trail that led to an oddly solid-looking bit of cloud in the upper right corner. In the foreground several horsemen looked in towards the middle ground of the picture, where a bearded little Paul was having a seizure in the middle of the trail, with a mild ray of light shining down upon him. The most commanding figure of all was a horsemen who sat with his back to the viewer. No fleck of color was visible upon him; he was clothed entirely in black, with even the back of his neck covered over. Alva.

"The pictures show the two ends of the journey," said Peter one day when Joachim Bueckelaer was visiting.

"How do you mean?" asked Joachim.

"This is where he goes in," said Peter, pointing at the cloud in the corner of his *Conversion of Paul*. "And this is where he comes out." He indicated the man emerging from the cloud in the *Luilekkerland*. "May Alva see the Lord's light before he gets here."

Above and beyond any hope of changing the events to come, the *Conversion of Paul* struck Mayken as Peter's finest masterpiece yet. Working at white heat, he added layer upon layer of detail, filling in the fronds of the sentinel-like ever-greens beside the trail to make each tree different from the one beside it, refining the soldiers' pikes and the horses' harnesses into an exquisite alchemy of lines, going over each cliff and boulder to model the pits and cracks and shadows of the actual world.

"When Peter walked to Italy through the Alps all those years ago, he swallowed up the mountains and rocks," said Joachim Bueckelaer with an admiring laugh. "And now he spits them out whole."

Usually when Mayken looked at anything, she tended to talk about it to herself in the privacy of her soul. But when she stared at the *Conversion of Paul* for a bit, her eye would take over and her inner voice would fall silent. Even the literal-minded Marcus Noot could feel something of the enchantment. Once again, Peter had outdone himself. What kind of painter might he become by the age of fifty?

But if the *Conversion of Paul* was meant to stop Alva from coming, it was a failure. On August 22, 1567, almost exactly a year after the image breaking, the Black Duke marched into Brussels with several companies of his troops. His route was to lead from the Leuven Gate to his lodgings in a house near Graaf Egmont's palace. Mayken and the rest of the Coecke household walked up past the gallows on the hill to a street corner where they could watch the invaders pass.

First came phalanx after phalanx of foot soldiers: olive-skinned, hard-faced Spaniards clad in finely engraved armor and bristling with weapons. They were

variously equipped with swords, crossbows, pikes, javelins, halberds, and harque-
buses. Some were armed with a new kind of gunpowder device much larger and
heavier than a harquebus; it took two men to comfortably carry one of these
seven-foot-long contraptions.

"What are those?" asked Little Peter from atop Peter's shoulders.

"Muskets," said a thin-lipped man next to them. "They can drop a horse."
He made a noise like a moan. Perhaps he'd meant to sound comical, but he
wasn't able to. "It's the chopping block for us poor *kiekerfretters*."

"Muskets for the chicken eaters!" echoed Little Peter, watching the parade
with simple pleasure.

Bringing up the rear were the cavalrymen. Their armor was gilded as well as
engraved, and their armaments included lances in addition to the other kinds of
weapons. Waf grew excited at the sight of so many horses and began barking.
Mayken took him by the collar and gave him a good shake. She'd wanted to
leave him at home, but as usual he'd wormed his way out and had come along
after them.

"There's Alva," said Peter just then, and yes, there in a hollow space in the midst
of the cavalry was a man dressed all in black, riding upon a spirited white horse. The
Duke was tall, thin, erect, with a small head, a lean yellow face, black, bristling hair,
and a silvery beard that hung down upon his chest in two waving streams.

"I wonder if I could hit him with a cobblestone from here," murmured
Williblad and, as if gifted with preternaturally sensitive hearing, the Duke
glanced over towards them. His eyes were dark and cold.

Waf chose that moment to twist free of Mayken's grip and to bound forward,
barking as if possessed. Alva called out something in Spanish, and the closest
cavalryman killed Waf with a single thrust of his sword, knifing in between two
ribs of the dog's chest. So smooth was the rider's motion that his horse didn't
even break stride. Little Peter shrieked and Mayken buried her face against her
husband's shoulder. Niay began shouting curses, but someone murmured a warning that made her stop. Mayken's mother was sobbing on Peter's other shoulder,
and Little Peter slid down to be in Mayken's arms.

Out in the street, the procession of horses stepped over or around Waf, who
lay stock-still, his white fur drenched with the cooling blood from his so easily
punctured heart.

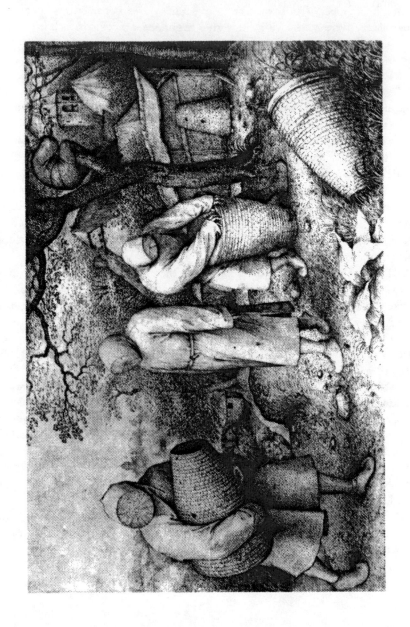

� � � � � � � � � � � � �
FIFTEEN

THE BEEKEEPERS
BRUSSELS, JUNE 1568

"*Vamos,* José!" called an aggrieved voice outside Bruegel's bedroom door. It was the wiry little Carlos, one of the two Spanish soldiers quartered in the Coecke house. Nobody but Niay, who knew some Spanish, was able to talk with them. The family had wanted to lodge the pair in the basement, but the soldiers had insisted upon a room with a window. Bruegel had tried the tactic of having Niay warn them that the attic was haunted by Master Coecke's ghost, and this had given fat José pause. But Carlos, a demanding man in his early middle age, had insisted that they needed a good view of the streets, so in the end the soldiers had ended up on pallets in a corner of Bruegel's studio. Bengt had moved to the basement rather than have to associate with them.

It made Bruegel terribly uneasy to have these unpleasant louts occupying the very core of his life. They viewed his craft as a buffoonery, pointing to and laughing at his new panels. Every now and then the bilious little Carlos would go so far as to snatch up one of Bruegel's brushes and to mime daubing at the paintings himself, clutching his crotch and chattering in his tongue.

Bruegel's stomach had been hurting all winter, and Carlos's japery brought the pain to a level he hadn't experienced since Jonghelinck had sent the better part of his life's work into storage. He began regularly seeing blood in his stool, sometimes fresh and red, sometimes congealed and brown like coffee grounds, sometimes black and tarry. A palette of inner decay.

To lessen the danger of Carlos actually defacing a picture, Bruegel, Bengt, and Williblad built an enclosure in a corner of the attic, a little room in which to store the paints and brushes out of sight. Although it wasn't practical to extend the storeroom's walls all the way up to the high, slanting ceiling, they were a good ten feet in height. Bruegel put a heavy lock on the enclosure's door and had Niay tell the soldiers that if they were to go in there, a formal complaint of theft would be filed with their captain. That had been over a month ago.

The stairs creaked and thudded as the fat, blank-faced José came rushing down the steps two at a time, his armor clanking. He was in his twenties, phlegmatic and dull.

"*Vámonos*, Carlos," said José, and then the two of them went pounding down to the kitchen where they always grabbed whatever food they could get their hands on before heading off for duty. A minute later their voices could be heard outside, José talking with his mouth full, and Carlos complaining.

"They're early today," said Mayken, sleepily pressing herself against Bruegel's back. The bulge of her pregnant belly was like a firm hassock. Bruegel rolled over, and Mayken rolled over as well, so that now they could spoon together more tightly. He breathed in her scent, running his hands over her swollen breasts and big belly. His treasure, his world.

"They're going to the Grand' Place for the executions," said Bruegel after a while. "Of Graaf Egmont and Filips de Hoorne. A full regiment of Alva's troops will be there."

"And you?" asked Mayken.

"It'll be my last chance to see Graaf Filips. Maybe I can bid him farewell as he walks through the crowd. You shouldn't come."

"I don't want to!" said Mayken. "In any case, it would be a dreadful thing to mix into my humors, what with the baby coming any day. If I saw a beheading, the child might end up as bloodthirsty as Alva. Or take it the other way and grow up a coward. Do you really think she'll be a girl?" Downstairs in the kitchen, old Mayken was scolding Mienemeuie about something.

"I can feel her moving," said Peter, pressing his hand tight against the taut dome of Mayken's belly. "Bip, bip, our little rabbit." It was good to have this life to balance against the death around them.

Their door creaked open and Little Peter came trotting in, still wearing his nightshirt. He hopped onto the bed and snuggled into his mother's arms.

"Mienemeuie said Carlos and José are going to chop off Uncle Filips's head," said Little Peter in a small voice. "She said he'll be dead like Waf."

"It's not sure that Filips is your uncle," said Mayken, trying to divert the flow of thought. "Papa just likes to say that. Filips's father was kind to Papa when he was young."

"Mienemeuie said they'll send the head to King Philip in a basket," said Little Peter. "And then Grandma got angry at her. Will they put Uncle Filips's head back on after he sees the King?"

"Not a pleasant way to travel, being a head in a basket," said Bruegel, reaching across Mayken to stroke his son's hair. "Did Mienemeuie give you any breakfast with her tales? No? Then let's you and me get something to nibble on, and fetch something for Mama, and then the two of us will go up and look at my new pictures, eh? We won't have them with us much longer."

Old Mayken was settling into her studio on the second floor, not that she really had any work to do. With everything in turmoil, nobody was ordering art anymore. Her motions were a little angular; she was still huffy from her fight with Mienemeuie.

Down in the kitchen Mienemeuie was silently serving Bengt some porridge. Bruegel and Little Peter joined him, and Mienemeuie slapped down two more bowls. She was smarting from old Mayken's tongue-lashing.

For a few minutes Bengt and the two Peters ate in silence. A gentle breeze wafted in through the open back door. It was a fine day in early June, with the sky pale blue and the trees covered in their vernal greenery. Out in the corner of the yard, Willibald and Niay were sitting on a bench by their shed drinking tea, Williblad enjoying the sun and Niay busy with her essences and herbs. She was something of a medicine woman. Normally Niay and Williblad went to work at noon, but Alva had decreed that all the inns and taverns were to remain closed today, lest there be riots after the executions.

"It's all done but the hammering," said Bengt presently. He was talking about the three new paintings he'd been helping Bruegel with. They'd spent quite a bit of time on these works, as there were no new commissions coming up—other than Noot's panels of the Willebroek Canal, which Bruegel didn't feel like painting. But now the new pictures were finished, and it would be the work of the next two days to crate them up and send them off.

"As it happens, Franckert's good ship *Luilekkerland* is in Brussels," said Bruegel. "We'll put our boxes aboard before they leave tomorrow. Franckert can collect his panel when he meets the ship in Antwerp. And he'll see that the two big ones continue on to Amsterdam. Can I have some more porridge, Mienemeuie?" His stomach felt better when he ate a lot. "And something for Mayken, too."

"And what does the little Mama want this morning?" asked Mienemeuie, setting aside her sulk. Young Mayken had always been her special pet.

"You decide," said Bruegel, happy to see the cook's humor lighten.

"If I myself were the size of a cow with a calf, well, I think I'd like a cup of tea and a bit of bread," said Mienemeuie. "I have a nice loaf that I hid in the oven where the pig and the monkey wouldn't think to look for it." That's how the Coecke household spoke of the two soldiers: José the pig and Carlos the monkey. "Trust a man to stay away from an oven. Are you and Bengt going down to the Grand' Place today, Mijnheer Bruegel?"

"In an hour or two," said Bruegel, not wanting to reopen the topic in front of Little Peter. "There's no rush." He, Bengt, and Little Peter headed upstairs, stopping off to give Mayken her breakfast.

At first everything looked fine in the studio. The disorder of the soldiers' beds and equipment was off in a far corner. A sweet-smelling pile of alder lumber stood ready to be made into crates.

In their walled-off corner, Bruegel's three new panels were calm in the morning light, with Bengt's linen copies to one side. His Amsterdam patron Herman Pilgrims had commissioned two peasant paintings, a *Peasant Wedding* and a *Peasant Dance*, each of them over five feet by three feet in size. At the same time, Bruegel had been working on a small panel for Hans Franckert, finally painting the image of the *Peasant and the Birdsnester* that he'd thought of a few years back.

It was the *Peasant and the Birdsnester* that the soldiers had vandalized.

The picture was a two-foot-by-two-foot panel. In the middle ground, a man in a tree was seizing a fledgling from her nest. The foreground of the picture held a peasant pointing back over his shoulder towards the tree with the nest that he trustingly assumed was still his. To achieve a new optical effect, Peter had modeled the peasant upon his own reflection in his convex mirror, which made it appear as if the peasant were about to fall right out of the picture and into the viewer's arms. To give the peasant a sufficiently guileless look, Bruegel had based his features upon Little Peter's face, a friendly pie with two big blue eyes.

It was of course the peasant's distended codpiece that had attracted the attention of the soldiers. Nearly every day, Carlos would point at it and say, *"Mas grande,"* each day laughing harshly as if he'd made a fresh joke. And this morning or last night Carlos the monkey had climbed over the walls of the storage enclosure, gotten out a brush loaded with white paint, and had inexpertly attempted to daub a man's prick atop the codpiece's bulge, leaving a ragged streak like pigeon shit on a window pane. The brush lay tossed onto the floor.

"God help me," said Bruegel, his stomach blooming with pain. He wanted to step forward and get to work fixing the damage, but for the moment his force was gone. He looked around for his chair; it was set against the storeroom's wall where Carlos had used it to climb up. With tottering steps, Bruegel made his way to the chair and sat down. How fragile everything suddenly seemed. His paintings were but the thinnest films of oils and pigments, easily scratched, easily rubbed out, easily smeared, upon wood panels so easily broken and burned. He himself was but a sack of blood and bile and choler, fit to burst and leak at any time. And out in the world, evil piled upon evil, with no end in sight.

"I'll clean it off," said Bengt, carrying the panels out into the main room and getting a palette knife and an oily rag. With calm, skillful motions, he scraped off the still-wet white paint and wiped its traces away. The picture itself had been quite dry already, and hardly any of the final coat was damaged. It would need only a few minutes of touch-up work. "I'll mix the colors you need," said Bengt, looking solicitously at Bruegel, who was bent over in his chair holding his stomach with both hands.

"Are you all right, Papa?" asked Little Peter, who hadn't even noticed the smear. He'd been busy looking out the one particular attic window he always liked to check. It looked onto a schoolyard. Little Peter's face was bright and clear. And to think Mayken was about to have a second baby. Yes, yes, still and all, life was good. One had to think that. Life was good.

"I'll be fine in a minute," said Bruegel, sitting up. "Maybe I ate too much breakfast. How are the little peasant girls today?"

Little Peter skipped over to the *Peasant Dance* and looked at the two girls Bruegel had painted into the lower corner. The smaller of the two looked to be Little Peter's age; she had a bell tied onto her arm so that she wouldn't get lost. Her older sister was holding her hands to teach her to dance. Sitting above them was a squinting bagpiper, with a happily drunken man leaning close to savor his music. It was unbearable to think of these precious images at the mercy of the soldiers, to have his unprotected panels in the hands of a monkey and a pig.

"I should be sleeping up here to watch over them," said Bengt, looking up from the paints he was mixing. "They wouldn't dare do it in front of me."

"But what if they did?" said Bruegel, slowly getting to his feet. "If you laid hands on them, they might kill you. Those men shouldn't be up here at all. We simply have to convince them to live in the basement. Niay can talk to them some more. Perhaps I could pay them something. A pity we're so low on funds."

"How about Master Coecke's ghost?" said Bengt all of a sudden. He nodded to the old scimitar hanging upon the wall.

"That's a thought," said Bruegel, taking the brush and palette that Bengt handed him. He looked down at the palette, part of his mind wordlessly comparing the new colors to those on the panel, part of his mind chattering along, comparing the situation with the soldiers to the time he'd dressed up to spook Bengt. "I like the idea," he said presently. "But we'll have to be careful. Best get Williblad and Niay in on it too. Niay can tell them about the ghost again before they go to bed."

"What ghost?" asked Little Peter alertly.

"Your grandfather Coecke," said Bengt. "He's been seen in this attic from time to time, waving a scimitar and wearing a green silk turban. Maybe he'll teach the filthy monkey and the stupid pig not to touch your Papa's paintings again."

"Could the ghost chop off someone's head?" asked Little Peter uneasily. The lad was hearing a lot of scary things today.

"He doesn't have to," said Bruegel. "When people see him, they run away."

He focused his attention upon his brush and palette, shoving about the globs of paint till he had the exact three or four shades of gray-blue that he needed to repair the peasant's codpiece. And meanwhile the planning, talking part of his mind was babbling like a waterwheel. But it wouldn't do to say too much in front of Little Peter.

"We'll try and finish as much of the crating as we can this afternoon, Bengt," said Bruegel, drawing a deep slow breath to calm himself down. "Before they come back."

"Good," said Bengt.

Steady now. Dab, dab, dab, and in a few more minutes Bruegel was done. He and Bengt leaned the panels against the walls to clear out space for the crating. And as a precautionary measure they turned the panels so it was their backs that faced out into the room.

Bruegel and Little Peter found the two Maykens at old Mayken's worktable on the second floor. Little Peter became absorbed in playing with a box of buttons, and Bruegel quietly told the Maykens about what had happened to his painting, and about the action he planned.

"His ghost again?" said old Mayken with a little laugh. "My poor dead husband, dug up over and over like a dog's favorite bone."

"Think it through, Peter," cautioned Mayken. "These men are armed. I'll never forgive you if you get yourself killed. Talk it over with me again this afternoon." How round and solid she seemed, how full of life. Bruegel kissed her cheek and caressed her curves.

Out in the garden, Bruegel and Bengt found Williblad and Niay. Those two had been living in Bruegel's shed for a year and a half now. Bruegel's old rivalry with Williblad was all but forgotten and they'd become true friends. For his part, Williblad had become less mercurial and more generous with his smiles.

The four of them walked down to the Grand' Place together, Bruegel explaining his new plan. In the excitement of his scheming, Bruegel almost forgot where they were going. But the sight of the scaffold dispelled all thoughts but of the executions. They'd arrived a little late.

The scaffold stood draped with black cloth in the middle of the Grand' Place. It was set up like a high stage; its sinister gravity reduced the massive and heavily ornamented buildings around the square to scenery. Several thousand Spanish troops dressed in full battle array were standing at attention around the scaffold, with half the town of Brussels crammed in around the edges of the square. Though the sun was bright, the square felt grim and dark. Upon the scaffold were a little table with a silver crucifix, a black velvet cushion, two wrought-iron spikes, a Marshal, a Bishop, and a lumpy shape beneath a dark cloth.

"That's Egmont," someone told Bruegel. "Already dead. Hoorne is next."

There was barely time! Bruegel furiously pushed himself towards the elaborate stone house of the Baker's Guild, where the two condemned men had been brought for the execution. And now the door swung open and Filips de Hoorne appeared, his bald head uncovered and his hands unbound. He wore a plain dark doublet with the collar cut off. His blue eyes seemed to be taking in every detail at once. How long might one's last walk seem to take? With a final effort, Bruegel wormed close to him.

"Bless me, brother Filips!" he cried.

The Graaf gave him a faint smile.

"Brother? Why not. Though Father always credited you to my tutor. Bless you, brother Peter. Pray for me."

The crowd lurched and the Graaf was swept onwards. Bruegel was able to push as far as the back row of the ranked troops. Filips ascended the steps of the black-draped scaffold. He glanced sadly down at the covered shape of Egmont's remains, then turned his attention to the Marshal, who held a placard with the de Hoorne coat of arms reversed: a deliberate dishonoring of the family escutcheon. Filips spoke to the Marshal so heatedly that the man took a step backwards and laid the placard down upon the table with the crucifix. Filips stepped to the edge of the scaffold and raised his voice to speak a few words to the crowd, but with all the troops between him and the citizens, he couldn't be heard. The Bishop held out the silver crucifix for Filips to kiss, but Filips refused him, kneeling down on the boards of the scaffold to pray on his own. In a few minutes he rose again to his feet, pulled a dark cap down over his eyes, and knelt upon the velvet cushion at the front of the scaffold, his head bowed, the bare nape of his neck exposed. There was a billowing in the material that hung from the scaffold's sides. The executioner stepped forth and ascended the stairs, a powerful red-haired, red-bearded man with a great sharp sword in his hands. He placed his left hand upon the top of Filips's head, raised the sword high in his right hand, and severed Filips's head from his shoulders in a single blow.

Blood from the severed neck jetted out onto the front row of troops. The executioner took the cap off the head and held up the bare head with both hands. Filips's eyes were open; his mouth was twitching. The executioner walked the circuit of the scaffold, and then with an abrupt gesture he impaled the head upon one of the two iron spikes.

Bruegel screamed. It was too horrible to imagine the sensation of the iron spike pushing up through Filips's neck, piercing the back of his throat, and blindly crunching through his skull's gentle filigrees of bone. In the shock of the execution's moment, the world around Bruegel had seemed soundless. But now, as he screamed, it was as if his own voice awakened his ears. All around him others were groaning and crying out as well.

The executioner retrieved Egmont's head from under the cloth and impaled it upon the other spike. Four soldiers carried up a pair of coffins, and the two men's bodies were laid within. The Marshal and the Bishop descended from the scaffold, leaving the heads and the coffins on display. The soldiers loosened the ranks, allowing the citizens to press close to the scaffold and fully absorb its lessons.

Bruegel stood rooted to the spot, numb to the jostling of the crowd, staring at Filips's head and praying for the dead man's soul. As he prayed, a kind of light seemed to grow behind his eyes until finally he seemed to see the kind face of Christ. Though the men of the Church were evil, Christ was still good. "Help Filips," prayed Peter. "Help us all."

"I love you, Peter," Christ seemed to say. "Don't be afraid." Life was a turbulent dream. The words fell away and Peter was alone in the Light, the divine light that floods every part of creation, on Earth as it is in Heaven.

Presently Bruegel's friends found him. "There you are." It was Williblad, Niay, and Bengt. "We should kill them," said Williblad.

"Who?" said Bruegel, blinking his eye, coming back to himself.

"Any of them we can get our hands on," said Williblad. "Carlos and José."

"That would make us the same as them," said Bruegel. "We'll scare them, and that's enough." But how small and petty his plan now seemed. Nevertheless, it needed to be done. He had to drive the soldiers from his studio. One step after another in the long winding tunnels of the human anthill. The Light was gone.

"Niay says she has fresh venom on her special pin," said Bengt. "It's from a mollusk that lives in the Indies, you know. They call it a cone shell. One touch of her pin, and your man is paralyzed for hours."

Niay grinned, showing her large, gapped teeth, and patted the knot of hair on the back of her neck. A pin with a mother-of-pearl head protruded from the bun, the pinhead worked into the shape of a tiny skull. The same pin she'd poked the Walloon with on the day of the image breaking.

"If needs be." Bruegel sighed. "But no killing!"

The show on the scaffold was reaching its finish. Three hooded monks climbed up onto the stage. Inquisitors. Their dark hanging hoods completely covered their faces. They had two woven rush baskets, each with a domed top and a round lid that fit over its open bottom.

"Beehives!" exclaimed Bengt. Yes, the monks were putting the two executed nobles' heads into beehive baskets. The baskets held purple silk cloths to cushion their terrible cargo.

"They'll be shipped to Spain for the Tyrant's delectation," said Williblad.

Looking at the shrouded Inquisitors with the baskets under their arms, Bruegel formed a sudden mental image of grim beekeepers in woven straw head covers. People sometimes spoke of the Church as a beehive, with the faithful the bees. The iconoclast bees had smashed up the insides of the hives because the beekeepers were evil and cruel. The horror of the faceless Inquisitors and their baskets made his skin crawl. He tried to summon back his image of Christ, but the fiery ache in his guts distracted him.

"Let's go home," said Bruegel. "Let's get ready for tonight. And I have to see about Mayken. She could have the baby at any time." It made his voice crack to speak of the baby. It was a sad world to bring new life into.

"So we want to frighten the soldiers from your studio?" said Williblad as they walked up the Hoogstraat. "They'll be in the right frame of mind for it after this grisly day. José should be easy. I think he preferred the basement in the first place. It's a better match for his Earth humor."

"I've heard Carlos talking about deserting," said Niay. "Apparently the troops aren't being regularly paid. I heard him say he wants to hop a ship and work his way back to Spain as a sailor. If we scare him enough tonight, he could be on his way."

"I just hope our ghost jape will truly spook them," said Bengt. "I hope I haven't sent you down on a false path. Not everyone's so great a donkey as me."

"It would be best to befuddle them first," mused Niay. "Do you have any nutmegs, Mijnheer Bruegel?"

"Odd you should ask," said Bruegel with a rueful smile. "Good Filips de Hoorne gave us something like a lifetime supply of nutmegs for Little Peter's christening."

"Give me a dozen of them," said Niay. "I'll extract the oil from them and mix it with some gin."

"Why?" asked Bengt.

"A sufficient quantity of nutmeg acts as a poison," said Niay. "It provokes a peculiar delirium that's like waking dream. Sometimes our tribesmen undergo a nutmeg ordeal for purposes of divination. Yes, when our little Spaniards return tonight I'll invite them to make merry—and I'll madden them with nutmeg gin. They'll grow flushed, they'll vomit, they'll drag themselves to bed, and then the show can begin. You do have gin, don't you?"

Bruegel gave her an appraising look. Niay had nearly so great a weakness for drink as Williblad. Was the gin for her or for the soldiers? Was it wise to plan on crazing two armed men?

"I know where they hide the gin," said Bengt, proud to be trusted. "Shall I decant a quart of it for her, Master Bruegel?"

"Don't you get so drunk that you let them have their way with you, Niay," cautioned Williblad. Despite his sorrow over the executions, Bruegel smiled to hear Williblad worrying about a thing like this. Williblad and Niay had grown quite domestic.

"They'll be too sick from the nutmeg to poke me," said Niay. "And if they did, what's the difference after the life I've led. It's just a stick in a hole. Anyway, once I think they're ready, I'll bring them up to the attic and—" But now she had to stop talking. They were in sight of the house and Little Peter was running down the sidewalk to them.

"Did they chop off uncle's head?" piped Little Peter as Bruegel raised him up in his arms.

"Yes," Bruegel told him. "It was terrible. Filips is in heaven now. I prayed for him." His son felt lively and whole upon his shoulder. Tears came to Bruegel eyes. "Let's not talk about it anymore, Peter. It's too sad. How's Mama?"

"She's lying down."

Bruegel found Mayken in bed with her mother at her side. "She feels dreadfully uncomfortable," said old Mayken. "I think the baby could come anytime. Did you see the execution?"

"The baby's almost come?" said Bruegel. "What a wonder, what a day. Filips went out with great dignity." He paused to run his hand across Mayken's brow. "I managed to get close enough to say farewell to him."

"Did you ask him if you were his brother?" asked Mayken. She knew how much this had been on her Bruegel's mind.

"I did. He said his father always credited the tutor. Jan Vondel. Maybe I'm not a secret noble after all." It made Peter sad to say this. He'd grown fond of the story over the years, it made him feel less like an insignificant part of the crawling human horde. It was well and good to think of mankind blended in with nature, but for oneself—frankly one wanted a slightly superior position. But of course he did have an elevated position, he was a successful artist with a career and a studio and a family and his head still firmly upon his shoulders, thanks be to God.

"Jan," murmured Mayken. "A good name. I feel too limp to talk, Peter. It's like I'm waiting for a storm to break."

"Should I stay with you?" The execution had left him itchy for activity and for vengeance. Mayken sensed his unsettled state.

"No, no," she said, distractedly waving her hand. "Do what you have to."

Whatever was to happen tonight, it seemed best to fully secure the new paintings. Williblad helped Bruegel and Bengt in the attic. By the time dusk fell, the panels were safely boxed, with a goodly amount of lumber left over. They made some preparations for the ghost show and then they went downstairs.

Niay was gaily busy in the kitchen with the gin and the nutmeg. She'd ground a dozen nutmegs into powder and was heating the dust in a little water. She'd also found time to paint her lips and to change into a very filmy and revealing yellow gown. Mienemeuie and Little Peter were sitting in chairs watching her.

"I thought you were going to press oil from them," said Bruegel uncertainly. She already appeared a bit drunk.

"I tried, but none came," said Niay airily. "I think the ones at home are fresher and wetter. This should work fine. See how brown the elixir is?" She swished around the liquid in the pan and decanted it into the glass quart bottle. A portion of the gin was missing. The mixture was now the color of tea, and turbid with the softened dust of the nutmegs.

"Don't look so worried," said Niay. "I won't drink any more. Or maybe just a little cup or two so the soldiers don't think I'm poisoning them." She cocked her head. "Hush! They're coming. You men get out of sight! You too, Mienemeuie. And someone put Little Peter to bed. I want our Spaniards to feel fully at liberty." She smoothed back her hair and pinched her cheeks. "How do I look?"

"Like a whore," said Williblad gloomily. He and Bengt ascended to the attic, and Mienemeuie went to join the Maykens in the bedroom on the third floor. Bruegel felt more and more dubious about their plan. Perhaps today was full enough, with the executions and with Mayken on the point of giving birth. Why carry out some crackpot scheme to scare the soldiers?

On the third floor landing he turned to start back downstairs, but now the soldiers were already in the kitchen with Niay, already drinking their nutmeg gin, their voices and laughter floating up the stairs. Hearing the voices and thinking of the prick scrawled on his painting, Bruegel steeled himself to carry through the evening's plan.

He peeked in at his fruitful Mayken, who was staring out the window breathing hard, Mienemeuie and her mother mopping her brow. She gave him a weak wave. He had Little Peter kiss her good night, and then he put the boy to bed in his room across the hall. Little Peter was excited, and Bruegel calmed him with a

298 ✖ RUDY RUCKER

long story about sailing to Lazy Lusciousland. Finally the little head was quiet on the pillow.

Back in the hallway he could hear Niay talking in Spanish, sounding solemn and drawing out her words for a spooky effect. Presumably she was telling the tale of Master Coecke's ghost. José interrupted with a question, Niay answered, and then Carlos went off on one of his resentful-sounding tirades. The three voices were slurred with drink. Niay would be bringing them up to the studio soon. The clock on the wall said it was near midnight, much later than he'd thought. Time itself seemed out of joint today.

Checking on Mayken again, Bruegel found her in an increased state of discomfort. "The birth pains have started," said Mayken, smiling wanly at him. He went and held her hand. Her hair was damp with sweat and her face shiny with oil.

"That's good news," said Bruegel. "How much longer will it be?"

"Could be an hour, could be twelve," said Mienemeuie. She and old Mayken had delivered Little Peter and they were ready to midwife again.

"Little Peter took six," said old Mayken in a lively tone. "But the second time might be faster. Isn't this exciting? Go downstairs and fetch some clean cloths and water, Mienemeuie. What's all that stupid noise? It sounds like a ship of fools."

"Niay is feeding the soldiers nutmeg and gin," said Mienemeuie. "Remember? To make it easier for Mijnheer Bruegel to spook them out of his studio."

"Do you have a worm in your head, Peter?" said old Mayken with a frown. "You're doing that silly nonsense today? While your wife is having a baby?"

"We—well, we got started on it before we realized," said Peter. He felt foolish indeed. On this portentous day of death and birth, he and his friends were playing a childish game.

"Well, get them out of the kitchen," said old Mayken. "We need more hot water from the stove, and less drunken cretins underfoot. Tell them they have to go up to the attic right away. The baby's about to come!"

"Can you go tell them, Mienemeuie?" said Bruegel feeling doubly foolish. "I have to go up to the studio first so I can hide in the storeroom. So I can play the ghost."

Old Mayken let out a wordless little shriek of impatience.

"Do you mind if I leave you, Mayken?" said Bruegel, wanting very much to edge out of the room.

"Be careful, Peter," said Mayken.

"Bless you, darling," he said, and kissed her forehead. The finger of God was about to touch down into this room, about to incarnate a fresh human life. Bruegel imagined the tiny new soul hovering nearby, ready to pop into the baby at the moment of birth. Mayken felt another pang, she closed her eyes and moaned.

"Go wave your silly sword," said Mienemeuie, shoving him ahead of her towards the door. "That's men's work. Meanwhile we'll be doing women's work. Bringing a new person into the world." She clattered off down to the kitchen.

Up in the darkened attic, Bengt and Williblad were idly staring out the window, watching the passersby on the moonlit Hoogstraat. Williblad lit his lantern to help Bruegel see. It was a clever affair with a sliding, light-proof shutter. In the faint light, Bruegel quickly daubed green watercolor paint on his face and put on the old green silk caftan and turban. Bengt handed him the scimitar.

"Careful with the blade," said Bengt. "While we were waiting, I sharpened it, just in case. Do you think you could take off a head with a single blow, Master Bruegel?"

"If those soldiers disappear, their sergeant's going to come looking for them," said Bruegel. "And if the sergeant finds bloodstains on our floor, we'll dangle from the gibbet. We're only going to scare them."

"They better not go too far with Niay," said Williblad.

"*Now* who's the peasant and who's the birdsnester?" said Bruegel unable to resist the dig. The old rivalry was never quite dead. He heard himself letting out a nasty chuckle.

"Fie!" said Williblad angrily. "How do you know that Mayken didn't—"

"Hush," said Bengt, cutting him off. "They're coming."

Downstairs Mayken began letting out rhythmic cries of pain.

The three men retreated into the storeroom. Williblad slid the dark shutter over the lantern's single pane, completely hiding the light. Mayken was silent again. Steps came up the stairs and into the attic. They heard José stagger about the studio and stop in the middle of the room to vomit onto the floor. There was a thud as the oaf collapsed onto his pallet, abruptly followed by snores. This was followed by whispering, giggling, and a quiet rustling that was Niay and Carlos lying down as well.

Everything was quiet for a few minutes and then came another of Niay's low giggles and the sound of Carlos's boots coming off and hitting the floor. Williblad opened the shutter of the lantern by a hairsbreadth so that he and Bruegel could see each other. Williblad still looked angry, and the sight made Bruegel want to burst with laughter, and now, seeing the glee in Bruegel's face, Williblad himself began to grin. This was madness. Downstairs Mayken let out a long, wavering moan.

A slight tremor began pulsing through the floor, accompanied by wet noises. Carlos and Niay were making the two-backed beast. A giggling snort escaped

Bengt. Willibald stamped loudly and pulled open a goodly chink in the lantern's shutter. The floor's shuddering ceased and Carlos let out a questioning grunt.

Williblad was beaming the ray of light down upon Bruegel's convex mirror, which lay at the ready upon the storeroom floor. Holding the lantern in one hand, Williblad took a flat leather cutout in his other hand. It was the shape of a dog-headed demon with dangling arms, great rows of teeth and a long, forked tongue. Slowly he moved the *wayang kulit* puppet back and forth above the mirror. Looking up at the ceiling, Bruegel saw a warped, shadowy demon floating in the midst of a faint glow.

"Una sombra fantasmal!" cried Niay, her voice most convincingly filled with terror. Carlos said something. Williblad intensified the light and passed the lantern to Bengt so as to free both hands. *"El espectro del Señor Coecke!"* added Niay, even more agitated than before. Williblad was moving the arms of the puppet so that the shadow looked as if it were reaching downward. José's snoring fizzled out. He woke and yelped in fear.

It was time. Bruegel swung open the storeroom door and stepped out, holding Master Coecke's scimitar at the ready. The *wayang kulit* show on the ceiling filled the room with throbbing, eerie light. Slowly, step by step, Bruegel walked forwards. José, Niay, and Carlos were sitting bolt upright, their clothes in a tangle, their faces flushed bright red from the poisons of the nutmeg. José was trembling; Carlos was naked, beleaguered, and at a loss. Bruegel flourished his scimitar, gloating at the vandals' discomfiture. He took another step forward—José broke and ran.

The big, soft soldier scurried across the room and went crashing down the stairs: down past the bedrooms, down past old Mayken's studio, down past the kitchen, down into the basement. Bruegel gave Niay a meaningful glance. If she would flee too, then Carlos would surely follow. But the nutmeg-addled Niay was gazing at him with a complete lack of recognition. Evidently, in her delirium, she truly took Bruegel for a ghost.

"Ayudame, Carlos!" she cried, worming around behind the wiry little soldier. It must have meant "Help me," for Carlos squared his shoulders, snatched up his sword, and sprang at Bruegel. Bruegel froze, holding his scimitar at a defensive angle. He knew nothing, really, about sword-fighting.

The naked Carlos opened his attack with a heavy downward slash of his blade. Bruegel blocked the blow with his scimitar, more by chance than by design. The shock of the impact traveled into the scimitar's hilt and numbed his hand. He stepped backwards towards the storeroom, and Carlos struck again. This time the blow knocked the scimitar from Bruegel's hand. Carlos raised his sword for a death blow. Downstairs, Mayken's cries were coming every instant. What a strange time this would be to die. And to die an utter buffoon.

"Niay!" called Bruegel, not liking for Carlos to hear his voice, but desperately wanting for this hopelessly addled woman to take the emergency action they'd planned. If Carlos grew violent, Niay was to dart forward with her pin to paralyze him.

"Niay!" cried Bruegel again. If she acted now, they could carry the felled Carlos down to the basement, and when he woke he'd never be sure what happened. But Niay sat dazed upon Carlos's pallet, staring with her eyes as big as saucers. Bruegel turned tail and flung himself into the sanctuary of the storeroom, with Carlos and his sword close behind.

Inside the storeroom, Williblad waited pressed against the wall beside the door, and Bengt stood backed into the far corner with the lantern. Carlos saw Bengt, but he didn't see Williblad, and the half-American was upon the soldier before he could resist. There was a thud, a gargling cry, and then Williblad had disarmed Carlos and seized his neck in both hands. Carlos flailed at Williblad, clawing his face. Bruegel got behind the soldier and pinioned his arms. Williblad kept on choking Carlos; the veins stood out in Williblad's forehead from the effort. Slowly Carlos slumped down towards the floor. His tongue slid out of his mouth, dark and thick and bloated. Williblad didn't let up. Two minutes later Williblad had strangled Carlos to death.

The three men looked at each other in silence. Bruegel wondered about what they'd just done. Was the killing of Carlos a justifiable retribution for the beheading of Filips de Hoorne? Self-defense? Or was it a mortal sin? If a sin, to what priest would one dare confess it to? A baby's first, coughing wail sounded through the floorboards.

"My wife!" exclaimed Bruegel, wanting to run down to her. But first he had to conclude the episode up here. "You're a noble friend, Williblad. I'm sorry I teased you before. We were overwrought."

"Go see your baby," said Williblad with a half smile.

"I have an idea," mused Bengt, staring down at the nude corpse. "We'll crate him up. Like a boxed painting. We'll ship him off with the other panels. A fitting revenge for daubing on Master Bruegel's picture, eh? Boxed like a painting himself."

"Good," said Bruegel, edging out of the storeroom towards the stairs. "Do it right away."

"And how's the mad Niay?" said Williblad walking across the studio to where she still sat on the bed, her skirts up around her waist.

"I saw a ghost," said Niay, her eyes unblinking. "It came out of the ceiling."

"You need to sleep," said Williblad in an even tone. "Sit here and watch us work, Niay, and then we'll go down to our shed." He pulled down her skirts and patted her cheek. "My little spider. Caught in her own web."

Bruegel found Mayken propped against a pillow with a tiny red baby in her arms. The baby's eyes fastened on Bruegel, truly seeing him. The eyes of God. Bruegel felt unclean, as if Carlos's death were stuck to him.

"It's a boy," said Mayken. "Let's call him Jan. For your true father."
Upstairs Bengt and Williblad began hammering.

The baby woke them many times in the night, which seemed to last a hundred years. Bruegel was plagued by every manner of strange dream: of Filips's head, of the shuddering in the attic floor, of baby Jan's eyes, of a painting that was a corpse, of a father who denied him, of blood and swords. Every facet of the long strange day was mixed up together, as in the maddest scenes of Master Bosch.

At sunrise Bruegel stopped trying to sleep. His stomach was gnawing with hunger pangs and he felt weak. Yesterday he hadn't eaten lunch or supper. When he used the chamber pot there was an unusually large amount of bright red blood in his stool. He drank some milk, and then he went to the shed in the garden and woke Niay.

She was her old self again, and full of apologies. The gin and nutmeg had gotten the better of her. She confessed she'd never actually sampled the decoction before; it was more potent than expected. At Bruegel's request, she went down to the basement to wake José and find out his state of mind. It was important to know this right away, for if the news was bad, there was no time to lose. Bruegel sat on a stump by the shed waiting for Niay's report.

A patch of the sleeping Williblad was visible through the half-open door, lit by the gray light of dawn. Williblad had saved his life again. A costly friend, but a lethal enemy. And now Bruegel was a father again, with a second son. Peter and Jan. Might both be painters? This business with his stomach—how much time did it leave him? A moot point if Alva learned of Carlos's murder. Bruegel felt a slight pang of remorse. Perhaps they'd get away with the killing. But his stomach could well do him in.

He looked around the yard, feeling lonely for Waf. It would have done him good to have that long furry dog to pet. Poor Waf. Poor Carlos. In his worry and weariness, Bruegel glimpsed something moving at the very edge of his vision, a sly exultant figure seen more with the mind than with the eye. It was lean stinking Death, skeleton Death passing by. Bruegel had seen him before, at that peasant wedding years ago. What was it poor Father Michel had said about the months? February in September.

Niay reappeared from the basement with her report. Everything was fine. José was unclear about what had happened the night before, but above all he knew that he never wanted to sleep in the haunted attic again. On hearing that Carlos was gone, José had expressed neither surprise nor concern. José had said that Carlos was looking for an excuse to desert, and that seeing the ghost had probably decided him. José hadn't liked Carlos all that well anyway, and was just as glad to be rid of him. José was planning to grab some food and to go tell his sergeant that Carlos had disappeared.

Bruegel spent the rest of morning sitting with Mayken, staring at Jan, and discussing the baby with Little Peter. Jan's gaze wasn't so sharp today as it had been yesterday. Big and Little Peter concluded that a baby could see clearly in the hours after he was born, and that then he rested for a day. Little Peter said it was good that Jan had sharp eyes, since they were a family of painters. He was enthralled by the baby's tiny fingers, and he loved it when the baby took hold of his own larger finger.

Meanwhile Mienemeuie and Bengt cleaned up the studio, moved the soldiers' equipment down to the basement, and transferred Bengt's possessions back into the attic. Of the soldier's possessions, they hid the shirt, pants, and boots that Carlos might have worn had he really run away. They could burn them another day.

A little before noon, a horse and wagon arrived to haul the four boxes down to the harbor basin. Shitting out so much blood had left Bruegel feeling rather faint. Bengt, Williblad, and the teamster handled the loading of the wagon. The unmarked box with Carlos was only a little thicker than the others, and seemed not all that much heavier. Oak panels were massive things.

Just to see things through, Bruegel rode along on the wagon to the harbor. Bengt and Williblad followed on foot, with Niay coming along as well. It was in fact almost time for her and Williblad to start their day's work at the Pepper Berry. After all yesterday's turmoil it seemed odd to imagine anyone going to a normal day of work.

The *Luilekkerland* bobbed cheerfully in the black harbor water, her flags and pennants flying. Captain Adam van Haren gave them a warm welcome. It was a simple matter for Bruegel to privately explain to him about the fourth crate.

"I'll see that it falls overboard on a high tide running out to sea when we hit the Scheldt tomorrow," said van Haren. "It'll float out with the rest of the garbage. Don't worry about a thing."

"What if it drifts to shore?"

"The box will bear no witness. And in these times it's common to find a body."

"How soon are you leaving?" fretted Bruegel, still not at rest. "I'm worried the Spaniards might think to come down here and search the ship."

"I'll put a lookout in the rigging, and we'll weigh anchor if we see them coming," said van Haren. "Meanwhile we've still got some lace to load."

"Could you have your lookout send someone into the Pepper Berry and warn me too if there's any sign of the Spaniards?" asked Williblad. "I'm sure there's nothing to worry about, but if they come down here it just might be for me instead of you. I wouldn't care to face the Council of Blood." This last was the name for Alva's tribunal, which was currently handing down scores of death sentences every day.

Van Haren agreed. Niay and Williblad started their day's work at the Pepper
Berry; Bengt and Bruegel returned home. Waiting in the garden were three
armed men: José, a sergeant, and some new Spanish soldier. The sergeant was an
all-too-familiar figure: the Walloon with the heavy mustache, brown leather
jerkin, baggy leather pantaloons, red socks, and smooth blue cap pulled down low
over his round head. Tilting back his head to see out from under his cap, the Walloon gazed nearsightedly at Bruegel. Though this was the fourth time they'd met,
the sergeant still seemed not to recognize him.

"I like to see the room where the soldiers were lodged," he said in his thick
French accent.

The nape of Bruegel's neck tingled as he led the three soldiers up the stairs.
But there was nothing to see in the studio except Bengt's copies of Bruegel's
new pictures, and these were of no interest to the Walloon.

"Where you put Carlos's equipment?" he wanted to know. Bruegel led them
down to the basement, and showed them José and Carlos's things.

"Corporal Miguel will live here now," said the Walloon, indicating the new
soldier, a long-nosed fellow with thick lips and a narrow chin. "He speaks a little Flemish. He going to notice everything that happen and tell me. He going be
in charge of José." The Walloon paused and glared at Bruegel. "Miguel don't
believe in ghosts. If there more trouble in this house we burn it down." Bruegel
said nothing.

And then they were back out in the yard, and it seemed as if everything would
be all right. But still the soldiers lingered.

"Williblad Cheroo," said the Walloon, pointing at the shed in the corner of
the yard. "He live here, no? The image breaker. I see him doing it couple years
ago. Antwerp was wrong to free him. José say Cheroo live here with the woman
named Niay. She a kind of witch, I think, from what José tell me. I hope they not
good friends of yours, because when we finished here, we going to the Pepper
Berry to arrest them."

The soldiers took everything out of the shed and threw it on the ground,
searching for evidence or, more likely, for valuables to steal. But they found little
more than Williblad's fine winter cape and the looted rosary that Niay wore for
a necklace. They took these and clattered down the street towards the harbor.
Bruegel felt sick with worry for his friends. He hoped the lookout would spot
the trouble coming.

He passed the rest of the afternoon trying to draw his vision of the baskets
and the masked beekeepers. Little Peter sat next to him with a charcoal and his
own piece of paper, drawing what he said were tigers. Bruegel was too light-
headed to make much progress. Time had slowed to a crawl. He and Little Peter
played with the baby, chatted with Mayken, looked in on old Mayken in her studio, then tried to draw some more. Near sunset, Bruegel could stand the suspense

no longer. He walked down alone to make inquiries at the Pepper Berry. And, yes, the *Luilekkerland* had sailed, and, yes, the lookout had warned Williblad and Niay in time for them to get aboard.

"Have a beer," said Raos the innkeeper. "Relax." Bruegel took a large foaming mug and seated himself on a bench in front of the Pepper Berry. All day he'd been faintly tasting blood at the back of his throat, and it was good to have the thick, sweet lager wash the sensation away. The sun was low in the sky, gilding the dirty stones of the harbor with warm light. Bruegel ate some bread with his beer, which helped settle the pangs in his stomach. Today, this very day, he'd become the father of a second son. He was well content.

In his mind's eye, Bruegel floated out along the Willebroek Canal, caught up with the *Luilekkerland*, smiled at the escaped Niay and Williblad, peeked into the crates and took one last look at—oh, not at Carlos, may God bless his soul and forgive his killers—took one last look at his *Peasant Dance* and *Peasant Wedding*. Bruegel savored the thought of these two pictures, secret mementos of the doomed celebration he'd attended with Franckert, these eight years gone.

All around him, life was going on. On the bench beside him a red-faced woman was arguing with a toothless man in a cap with flaps down over his ears; on the cobblestones before him two little girls were playing jacks with a leather ball and a handful of pig vertebrae; a new ship was gliding into the harbor with sailors scrambling up into the rigging to strike the sails; a gull and a crow were fighting over a fish head at the wharf's edge; two young men were coming around the corner singing a new Beggar song about yesterday's executions—life was endlessly rich and endlessly various, and it could take a man eight years simply to paint one single moment of one single day.

Bruegel took another sip of his beer. The things he'd painted, he'd painted right. It might be that his stomach was going to kill him before long, and half his life's work might be out of sight in storage, but he knew he'd painted things that mattered. He'd painted what he saw, and more than that, he'd painted what he couldn't see, the God that fills the world, as above, so below.

※ ※ ※ ※ ※ ※ ※ ※ ※ ※ ※ ※

SIXTEEN

THE MAGPIE ON THE GALLOWS
BRUSSELS, JANUARY–SEPTEMBER 1569

It was winter again, the season of black bile, the earth frozen hard, the snow and ice so cold that they seemed made of dry metal rather than water. The sun was orange on the horizon and night was coming fast. Mayken added some wood to the fireplace in her mother's studio. Money was short this winter, and the Coecke house wasn't so well heated as usual; this was the one room other than the kitchen that they always kept warm.

With no particular work to do, Mayken's mother was sitting in a rocker by the fire knitting. She'd taken to wearing spectacles for close work. As an artist, she wasn't content to knit ordinary things; rarely did she knit even a hat with less than three colors.

Little Peter was at the table, daubing with some watercolors. Bengt was at the other end of the table, working on a drawing based on his copy of Peter's *Luilekker-land* painting. They hoped to sell it to Jerome Cock for engraving. Peter lay sprawled upon the couch, staring out the window at the low winter sky, brooding over something, his lips slightly moving. Baby Jan lay asleep on his stomach.

Each morning Mayken was at pains to thoroughly wrap the boys in the colorful wool outfits old Mayken made them, and they were flourishing like greenhouse tulips. Jan was sturdy and lively, with a ready smile, and Little Peter was more fun to talk with all the time. But her poor husband was wasting away. Though Peter didn't like to discuss the matter, it seemed there was considerable blood in his stool every morning. His stomach gnawed at him between meals and in the nights, and of late he was finding it harder and harder to swallow. This week he'd been too weak to do any work on his two new pictures. Always more pictures, though with each one, Mayken wondered if it might be the last. By some slow alchemy, the unthinkable had become a constant background to her thoughts. If nothing changed, Peter must soon die. A sad thought on a gray morning.

There was a light footstep on the stairs; it was their unwelcome lodger, the Corporal Miguel, more spy than soldier, coming up from his lair in the basement. He glided into the room, his long nose pointing this way and that, and paused behind Bengt, studying his work. "It's for fun," Bengt said without looking up. "A fairy tale. Nothing of politics or religion."

Though Miguel understood Flemish, he didn't answer. After another penetrating look around the room he proceeded upstairs to the studio, not that anything had changed there for the last few days. Mayken would have liked to dandle Jan for a distraction, but if you took him off Peter's chest when he was sleeping, he always began to cry. She looked out the window at the bleak monochrome street, then poked the fire again, wishing there could be some good news.

And then, behold, mother's friend Marcus Noot was at the front door, stamping the snow off his feet. Mayken's mother let him in, exclaiming with joy at what he told her. Marcus came up to the second floor to share his good news, sonorously reading it from a scroll of paper that had been slit to ribbons at the bottom so that a big red disk seal could dangle from one of the strips.

"On this same day, by this Communal Council it was decided that Master Peter of Bruegel shall be discharged of the Spanish soldiers quartered in his house, and that the masters of finance of this city shall offer to the same Bruegel a certain gratuity in order that he may pursue his activity and his undertakings in this city."

"What?" exclaimed Peter, his haggard face lit by the first real smile that Mayken had seen for weeks. It was like seeing the sun come out. Peter sat up, cradling little Jan in the crook of his arm. "This is really true?"

"A proper triumph of truth," said Noot, and when Miguel popped out of the staircase with his large dark eyes staring, Noot pointed at him and called, *"Adios!"* Miguel silently padded over to examine the proclamation in Noot's hand.

"The city is paying the cost for you and José to lodge yourselves elsewhere," explained Noot, reaching into his pocket and brandishing a plump little purse. "You and José are to pack up and leave tonight, Corporal. Pick any inn you like."

Miguel peered at Noot's scroll some more and finally murmured a question.

"That's right," said Noot. "I can give you this month's money right now, my man." He extracted two coins from the purse and handed them over. Mayken noticed the purse was still fat. She wondered if perhaps Noot might give them some of that too. Their diet was down to potatoes and mussels. "Mind that you sign a receipt for me," Noot told Miguel. In another moment, he and the Spaniard had finished their business. Miguel sidled down to the basement where he could be heard talking to José.

Little Peter ran over to look at the seal on the city proclamation. "It's a picture in wax, Mama!" Mayken examined it with her son; the seal showed an archangel with a sword. That's the kind of help they needed in this hard time. An archangel.

"You're wonderful, Marcus!" Mayken's mother was saying, her arms around their friend. She kissed him on the cheek, knocking her spectacles askew.

"Perhaps now Peter can do some work on those paintings of the Willebroek Canal," said Noot. Catching Peter's neutral expression, he added, "Or not." Peter had told Mayken he lacked the energy and will to document the building of the canal and that he only wanted to paint a few last things from within his head. One day, in a particularly sardonic humor, he'd gone so far as to say that the best thing about his terminal illness was that, with any luck, he'd die before he had to paint the Willebroek Canal. Mayken always rose to the bait and scolded him mightily when he'd say things like that. It was what he expected her to do and she did it. In the waning of their time together their common rituals had begun to seem like formal dance steps, tiresome but at least familiar, something to fill the hours before the arrival of Death.

"In any case I convinced the City Fathers that you deserve a little peace of mind," concluded Marcus Noot. "A gift from the city." With a flourish, he handed Peter the whole plump purse.

"A miracle," said Peter simply. "Thanks be to God."

Things were a bit better for the rest of the month. The fire in the attic studio was lit again, and Peter and Bengt went back to working up there every day. At the end of January they had another guest: Abraham Ortelius.

"How's Peter?" he asked Mayken at the door. With Williblad fully out of the picture Ortelius had regained his old surface polish and equanimity. Yes, his hair was thinning, but he seemed more energetic and collected than when he'd been running after the other man.

RUDY RUCKER

"Peter does poorly," said Mayken. "He's a handful. Always talking about dying." Though she was intimately familiar with the thought by now, speaking of it still made her voice break. "All he can eat is milk, sometimes with a little bread soaked in it. And always he loses blood. We don't know how long he will last."

Up in the attic, Peter was sitting in his chair staring at his two new pictures, a pair of watercolors on canvas, all in tones of blue, green, and gray. Bengt was to one side, working as usual on some copies. Little Peter was playing by the fire.

"You've done well to get new commissions in these times," said Ortelius, taking a hearty tone. He settled in a chair next to Peter, and Mayken took a seat as well. Jan was safe downstairs with her mother. "Nothing slows the pace of our Bruegel!" continued Ortelius, straining for joviality.

"I don't suppose Mayken had a chance to tell you who these are for?" asked Peter, closely regarding his friend. "No, she was probably talking about my health. I'm a terrible worry to her. Guess, Abraham, for whom might these paintings be?"

"I wonder," said Ortelius, willingly entering into the game Peter proposed. "It's an unusual subject matter. Of your own choosing, I'd wager. Nobody but Bruegel would conceive pictures as odd as these. One panel shows six blind men leading each other into a ditch, most saturnine, and the second one—what is it?"

"I call it *The Misanthrope*," said Peter, with a slight smile. "It's a picture of me about to die."

"Don't say that, Peter," snapped Mayken. Little Peter was lying right nearby playing with some blocks. She didn't like for the boy to hear talk like this every day. Even though Little Peter didn't look up, the stillness of his head told Mayken he was listening. Big Peter glared at her in his most provoking way. His final illness was making him quite unmanageable.

Mayken disliked *The Misanthrope*. Unlike all of Peter's other paintings, it was composed as a circle, a circular scene set against a gray background. The main figure was a bitter-looking, black-caped man walking slowly to the left. His profile, beard, and folded hands did indeed remind Mayken a bit of her husband—turned old and broken and sad. The part of the picture that he was walking into held only a decaying tree and four or five slimy brown mushrooms. He was walking into the Land of Death.

"Quite traditional," said Ortelius in a careful tone. "Like a rondel in a Book of Hours. I see you've even written a caption on it. 'Om dat de Vierelt is soe ongetru / Daer om gha ic in den ru.'" This meant, word by word, "For that the World is so untrue / Therefore go I in sorrow."

"Master Bruegel and I enjoy the *zakkenroller*," put in Bengt, using the Flemish word for pickpocket. "I'm just now copying him. It's a clever bit of work." He was referring to the grotesque little figure crouched behind the Misanthrope to steal his purse. The *zakkenroller* held the heart-shaped red purse in one hand and used a pair of shears to cut the ribbon that attached it to the unaware Misanthrope's waist.

Mayken hated the *zakkenroller*. He looked sly and mean. He was ensconced in a transparent bubble with a cross, his body inside and his arms and legs sticking out. The parts on the inside were drawn a bit darker and fuzzier. Peter had been pleased when he'd achieved this effect; he kept discussing it with Bengt, as if how he laid on the paints was as important as the sad, bitter things that the paints said.

"And look at these," said Peter, letting out a chuckle. Though it was beyond Mayken's comprehension, it pleased Peter to pretend this picture was funny. With a grunt he got to his feet and pointed at some spiky objects painted on the ground before the Misanthrope; these were the "caltrops" that were sometimes strewn on battlefields to lame soldiers and horses. They were four-pointed metal stars shaped a bit like children's jacks, with their points arranged so that one was always pointing upwards. On the floor beside the painting Peter had a real caltrop he'd picked up somewhere for a model. "The Misanthrope is going to step on a caltrop," said Peter. He nudged the sample caltrop on the floor, then wagged his finger at Ortelius. "Beware, Abraham. That's what happens to people who feel sorry for themselves. They get their purses stolen and they step on caltrops."

"I'm glad you're not sorry for yourself," said Ortelius, leaning back in his chair, eager to jolly Peter along. "That's a relief. It makes this visit that much more of a pleasure." But now he caught a glimpse of Mayken's troubled face. "What do you think of *The Misanthrope*, Mayken?"

Mayken simply shook her head. Peter was tired of hearing her nag him about the picture. She already knew what he'd say anyway, he'd say that they could laugh or they could cry, so why not laugh. She herself found it hard to see any point in acting as if dying were funny, especially when you were going to be the one left behind. If Peter thought he could keep his spirits up that way then good for him.

A bit puzzled by her silence, Ortelius turned back to Peter. "What's the glass ball around the pickpocket?" he asked. "The World?" Mayken braced herself for the answer. She'd heard it too many times before.

"With the Spanish overlords gone from our home, I can openly say that it's the symbol of the Habsburgs," said Peter. A hard fanatical glint appeared in his eyes. Despite his assumed airs of mirth, Mayken knew well that his heart was far from peaceful. Thanks to a letter they'd received a few months ago, he'd become more obsessed than ever by the fate of Jonghelinck's confiscated pictures, with sixteen of his finest among them. "The *zakkenroller* is the Archduke of Austria," said Peter, his voice tight. "He's the one who robs us the most. He robs Peter Bruegel. I have evidence of a plot, Abraham. I have it from Cardinal Granvelle."

Ortelius looked askance at Mayken, almost as if he were wondering if Peter had gone mad. "Granvelle is the Viceroy of Naples now, isn't he, Peter? At the far end of Italy. You can't tell me that the Cardinal writes you."

"It is he who commissioned these pictures," exclaimed Bruegel, abruptly lightening his humor. He'd grown quite volatile of late. "The work comes due to the good offices of Granvelle's secretary, this particular man being an old friend of yours and to some extent of mine." Peter allowed himself a little smile now. Even in his weakened state, he had an excellent sense for the dramatic.

"You mean Williblad?" sang Ortelius, the years sliding off him. He beamed like a happy girl. "Williblad is in Naples?"

"The very same," said Peter. "I had a letter from him in October, shortly after the last time you were here."

"I—I don't suppose he mentioned me?" asked Ortelius wistfully. Mayken's heart went out to the frail, balding mapmaker. It would be hard to carry passions the world thought wicked or absurd. Not for the first time, it struck her how odd it was that she and this man had shared the same lover. It wasn't a comfortable thought. But Ortelius's homely, yearning face spoke to her nonetheless.

"He did mention you," said Mayken, gently patting his knee. "Quite warmly." She wished the discussion were over. She didn't want to hear Peter shouting about that letter again.

"Bring the letter," Peter told Mayken, as if reading her thoughts. Again she shook her head. It was no fun arguing with a sick man.

"I'll get it," piped Little Peter, proud of knowing the family hiding place. "Can I?"

"Good boy," said Big Peter, and Little Peter ran across to the corner of the attic where there was a loose floorboard under a bit of carpet. It's where they'd been keeping the papers they didn't want Corporal Miguel to see. Even though the spy was gone from their house, by force of habit they were still being secretive. So Little Peter brought Williblad's letter to Peter, and he read it aloud, sitting in his chair. Mayken braced herself.

"'Williblad Cheroo to Peter Bruegel salutation. Niay and I have made our way to Naples, a climate much to our liking. We have found employment with the Viceroy of the province, who is none other than our old acquaintance Cardinal Granvelle. The Viceroy is in robust health, that is to say fat as a *varken*. He often voices his dismay over the dispersal of the hoard he had amassed in Brussels. He particularly regrets the loss of your painting *The Flight Into Egypt*.'"

"I'm so glad Williblad's safe," exclaimed Ortelius. "Captain van Haren didn't know what happened to him after Amsterdam."

"You hear that about my picture?" put in Peter. "They're becoming more rare and costly all the time. Thanks to the Habsburgs." There was no trace of his earlier good humor. He gave the paper a loud rattle and read on.

"'When I assured the Viceroy that I could arrange for him to purchase some new pictures by you, my position with him was assured. I am again one of Granvelle's secretaries, with the responsibility of advising him on his art purchases, much as I did for Fugger.'"

Peter paused again, glaring as if daring them to interrupt. Stubbornly Mayken held her tongue. "Listen to this next part, Abraham!" said Peter.

He continued reading, his flushed meager face growing smooth and tight. " 'The Cardinal reports that the Habsburg court has a keen taste for your work. Dear Peter, I trust you recall my belief that the confiscation of Jonghelinck's paintings came about so that your works might find their way to the Archduke of Austria. Granvelle confirms this. He himself helped de Bruyne bring about Jonghelinck's financial ruin.' "

"Aha!" shouted Peter, furious all over again, even though he'd read this letter dozens and dozens of times. "Aha! Aha! Aha! The *zakkenroller* in the imperial orb! He cuts away my heart as I slink off to die in the woods!" He burst into a cracked fit of coughing, finally having to fetch up a cloth to his face and spit out some blood.

"That's enough, Peter," said Mayken, more sharply than she meant to. "Calm yourself. You don't have to read the whole letter."

"I can read it myself," said Ortelius, holding out his hand. There was a slight tremor in it that broke Mayken's heart. The poor man was desperate for news of Williblad's feelings for him.

"No, no," said Peter, selfishly clutching the letter to his chest. "I'll read the rest. The rest is easy." He patted off his mouth, took a sip of water, took a breath, and resumed.

" 'The redoubtable Niay is a maid in the Viceroy's household, one among several. She finds it agreeable as there is little work for her to do. There are some Javanese here as well, though Niay has lost her old love for shadow puppetry— for reasons you may well recall.' "

Peter read over that part quickly. Mayken very well knew the reasons why Niay no longer liked shadow puppets, but Ortelius didn't, and in these times there was certainly no reason to tell him. Peter pressed on.

" 'The Viceroy's table is quite to our liking and we are lodged in a room with a window opening out onto an orange tree. The villa is on a hill with a view of the Bay of Naples that looks good enough to paint. Perhaps I shall undertake a second work in my own American style! Since coming to work for the Viceroy, I've brought my wardrobe back into a befitting state. The tailor has made me three costumes of silk and velvet: one yellow, one maroon, and one green. The Neapolitans are very clever with these things. The fasteners on my clothes are Turk's-head knots of silk cord which fit through loops of the same cord, and my boots are of a remarkable softness.' "

"I'd like to see him," said Ortelius with a faraway smile.

" 'The Viceroy instructs me to offer you a commission for two paintings. He places no restriction on the subjects, so long as there are no gross and obvious offences to the Church, the Crown, or the personage of His Worship. As payment for the two works, he offers you four times the commission he paid for your *Flight into Egypt*. Upon receipt and approval of the new works, the Viceroy will send you a letter of exchange for the Medici bank in Antwerp. The Viceroy desires that you paint the new pictures on canvas rather than panel, both for ease of shipping and so that it will be easier for him to take these treasures with him should he again relocate in haste. I implore that you temper any lingering bitterness towards the Viceroy and fulfill this commission. Your acquiescence in this matter will appreciably enhance my standing in his household.' "

Peter paused. He seemed to have recovered from his little fit of fury. "And here's the part about you, Abraham." He read out the end of the letter.

" 'Please give my warmest regards to Mayken and Little Peter. I often think fondly of Abraham Ortelius, remembering the many kindnesses the dear man did for me. Greet him as well. Do know that Niay and I are most content in our new home. With warm affection, Williblad.' "

Peter folded the letter and handed it over to Ortelius, who studied it and then passed it to Little Peter to stick back under the floor. Mayken was glad they were done with the letter once again. It grew tiresome, indulging the whims of a cantankerous invalid.

"Praise God," said Ortelius, still lit up by the joy of having heard Williblad mention his name.

"Except he hasn't sent that letter of exchange," said Mayken, sour with Peter's self-indulgence and angry at his impracticality. "It's a poor price they offered anyway. And Peter's been painting these pictures for free for four months. I don't trust Granvelle."

"The man values my art," said Peter simply. "That makes up for his sins. We'll have our money before Easter, Mayken, long before the city's gift runs out."

"I'm sure you enjoy the freedom to pick the subjects that most speak to you," said Ortelius in a soothing tone. He gave Mayken a sympathetic look. She could see he understood how burdensome it was for her to be with Peter during these last times. "Assuming you don't write a full explication on the back of *The Misanthrope*, I'd say there's no obvious offense to the Crown, Peter. Your modes of thought are too subtle, too oblique. And your panel of the blind leading the blind—how apt an image for these times."

"God knows it's more to my taste than painting some men digging a ditch for the city," said Peter. "Yes, the work's going well, even though I'm terribly weak from shitting out blood. There's little left of me but bile, choler, and phlegm. It's a blessing to have those soldiers gone from the house. In the last two weeks, Bengt and I have all but finished these two paintings. Speaking of money, did you bring something for me, Abraham?" This was a question Mayken wanted the answer to as well.

"Not everything you hoped," said Ortelius, unrolling the bundle he carried. "I sold your little panel of the crippled beggars to Plantin. And Jerome Cock is engraving your drawing of *Summer*, the one with the reaper's scythe sticking out. Fine. But nobody wants to print your *Beekeepers*. I tried others besides Cock; they all feel the same. There's too big a risk of it being deemed heretical. It's your misfortune that there happens to be a new Calvinist tract called *The Beehive of the Holy Romish Church*. The Inquisitors are quite frantic to burn the author of the book, and Cock feels that if he were to publish your drawing he might end up facing the Council of Blood."

Ortelius unpacked Peter's *Beekeepers* drawing and unrolled it on a clean spot of the floor, weighting its corners with some heavy pebbles Peter kept about the studio for just that purpose.

"Spooky, eh?" said Peter, looking down at the sinister masked beekeepers manipulating the hives. "That's the executioners with de Hoorne's and Egmont's heads in their baskets, you understand. And see the man climbing up the tree? That's Williblad escaping to Naples. I drew it to give him good luck and it worked."

"Where are the heads?" cried Little Peter, jumping to his feet. "Is Uncle Filips's head in that basket?"

"Oh, Peter," protested Mayken. "Must you always stir him up with your fantasies?"

"When I saw the execution, it made me think of beekeepers," said Peter stubbornly. "And this is what I drew. Not that anyone has to know that. So remember, Little Peter, it's our secret what's in the basket. Jerome Cock's onto the wrong scent entirely. How can he imagine this has anything to do with Calvinists?"

"Well, we couldn't help but notice that the church in the background has no cross on top," said Ortelius. "One might say it's a Calvinist church. They don't have crosses, you know."

"But the picture is beekeepers," protested Mayken. It was a shame not to sell this well-made drawing. Why did men make everything so complicated? "We've never even seen a Calvinist church," she added. "Are there really such things?"

"There was one in Antwerp," said Ortelius. "Alva's men had its roof torn off. And now the former members of the congregation dangle from the rafters."

"Well, well," said Peter, clearly upset, but trying to keep an even tone. "I suppose we'll perforce add the *Beekeepers* to our studio collection." There were a number of his smaller paintings and drawings on the walls. "Bengt, mount it in a paper mat so we can hang it."

"The Spanish might always come by to inspect your studio again," said Ortelius. "There could be trouble if they saw it." What a fussy old maid he could be, thought Mayken, thoroughly tired of this discussion.

"This will put them off the scent," said Peter, taking out his pen. He was overexcited, not really himself. He knelt down next to the drawing and began slowly inscribing a proverb on the corner. *"Dye den nest weet, dye weeten, dyen roft, dy heeten,"* he intoned.

These days Mayken sometimes wondered if her husband weren't breaking down under the strain of his wasting disease. This was that same motto he'd used about Williblad and Mayken. "Who knows the nest, knows it, who robs the nest, has it."

"Explicate," said Ortelius, humoring his friend. "I do but ill perceive your meaning, Mijnheer." He let out a scholar's dry chuckle.

"The Nest is both God and the Church," said Peter, not looking up from his task. His voice was coming in jagged bursts. "Who knows God, knows God no matter what, and who steals the Church has only the Church. The Tyrant steals our Church and thinks he has our God. Alva makes me ashamed of our Church. Did you hear that he tortured William's steward until he showed them where to find the Bosch triptych sealed up inside in the wall? The *Garden of Earthly Delights*. It's in Madrid by now. Philip *has* the Bosch, but I *know* it. *Dye den nest weet, dye weeten, dyen roft, dy heeten.*"

Again Ortelius gave Mayken that sympathetic look. "The nest of God," he said, sententiously clearing his throat. But then he fell silent. Nobody could make sense of Peter's farrago. Mayken reached over and poked Ortelius, wanting more help. "It's not such a bad thing, you know, to imagine your paintings in the imperial palace," essayed Ortelius. Peter glared up at him, his mouth set in a feral grimace, saying nothing. Mayken poked Ortelius again.

So now the good Ortelius came up with a fresh topic. He began talking about his *Theatrum Orbis Terrarum,* the book of maps he was working on. He'd brought a rough version of it along.

The book took Peter's attention off his obsessions. Ortelius and Peter leafed through it together, taking a little tour of the world, with Little Peter looking on. The two men sat and chatted for the rest of the afternoon, Mayken coming and going. When it was time for Ortelius to leave, he bowed his head and prayed with Peter for his health. And then they embraced for what was to be the very last time.

A few weeks later Granvelle really did send a letter about the money, and Hans Franckert was able to get the cash from the Medicis. There was another tearful parting when Franckert came to bring the money and to say his last words to Peter. Franckert's own health was not so good; his skin was turning yellow and he'd lost the roll of fat from around his neck. But he wouldn't speak of it, he wanted only to talk of Peter, and long after Peter had dropped off to sleep, he sat in the kitchen drinking wine and talking of his old times with Peter.

When Franckert finally left the house it was near midnight, and he was quite overcome with tears. With most of their guests Mayken didn't allow herself the luxury of crying, for once she began, it was too hard to stop, and who would run the affairs of the house if she were blinded with tears all the time?

But seeing Franckert's kind face so pinched and sad broke down Mayken's reserves. She cried on his shoulder for quite some time, though when she was done she felt no better than before. For Mayken it wasn't a matter of enjoying one big emotional farewell. For Mayken in these last months, each moment was a farewell, every day, all day long.

Peter and Bengt finished up the two canvases and sent them off to Naples. With everyone impoverished or at war, Peter had no prospects for a new commission other than the Willebroek Canal panels, which he resolutely refused to paint. He began idly making drawings of Spanish soldiers with the faces of pigs and monkeys engaging in every vile and loathsome act. It made Mayken uneasy to see these sheets. What if, in some fey humor, Peter were to sail one of the papers out of the studio window?

Wearily she remonstrated with him. Why not do another painting, she proposed. A happy painting. Perhaps a cheerful landscape. Just for fun. The idleness was poison for him.

"All right," said Peter. "A happy picture for you. There's an odd little bit of panel that I've always meant to put something on. I'll get right to it."

"Don't overwork yourself."

But of course Peter did overwork himself, as he always did when he became engrossed in something. When he worked, it was always at white heat. He finished the new picture in a month. As for cheerfulness: the centerpiece of the new little landscape was a gallows. But at least it was an empty gallows, nicely lit in the sun, and with a lively magpie perched on top of it.

"That's you," said Peter, pointing to the magpie. "And see her mate, down here on the stump pecking out a worm? That's me."

"The gallows looks twisted," said Mayken, intrigued. "The top and the bottom don't match. Did you mean to do that?"

"Or did your father fail to teach me perspective?" asked Peter with a smile. "No, it's supposed to look wrong. Executions are from another world, a mistaken world, a Crooked World. I saw a gallows like this seventeen years ago, when de Vos and I walked to Italy. What a beautiful day that was. I wanted to put that day into this picture for you. I was young and the whole world was still ahead of me."

"I can see it, Peter. I love the way the leaves of the trees are shimmering." Besides the sweet pair of magpies, there were some merry little dancers, a bagpiper, a village, a castle, a water mill with pigs, a river winding out through cattle pastures to a city by the sea, boats on the river, and a heron in the sky—all these details conjured up by little flicks of Peter's brush. And in the front corner of the picture crouched a bare-assed man taking a shit.

"I shit on death," said Peter. But that night, the last day of February, he vomited up a whole basin of blood.

Peter never got well again. The vitality ran out steadily from the hidden wound inside his belly. As spring turned into summer, Peter grew too weak to go up and down the stairs. He spent most of his time in their bed. Mayken began wondering how many more tears she had left. Not that Peter was one to ask for her pity.

In the afternoons, he would prop himself up on a pillow and draw a little. But by the end of the summer he was too listless to even draw. He grew uneasy about his scabrous drawings of the Spanish soldiers and had Mayken burn them in the fireplace.

In the month of August he did little more than lie in bed, a hollow-eyed stick figure, watching the day's light moving across the wall. Early in September, a priest came to take confession and administer Extreme Unction. It was Father Ghislain, the same man who'd married them and baptized the boys.

"Deep down I never really thought I'd be dead," Peter told Mayken that afternoon. "I wonder what it'll be like."

"You'll be in Heaven," said Mayken softly. They'd long since dropped any pretence that Peter might recover.

"I never painted Heaven," said Peter. "I hope there's crows and trees. And that someday you'll join me. But not soon, no, no, no, not soon."

Mayken stroked his hand, his strong wise fingers. How could he leave her? It was hard to imagine raising her two sons on her own.

"I didn't dare confess about helping Williblad kill Carlos," said Peter after a while. "I don't feel I can trust even Father Ghislain."

"Tell God yourself," said Mayken. "He'll forgive you."

"Yes," said Peter. "I see Him all the time. He shines through everything. I can see my whole life too, Mayken. I can move back and forth through it. You're the best part of it."

"Dear Peter." She leaned over to kiss him, her tears falling on his cheek.

Mayken was wakened before dawn by a shaking of the bed. She sat up, filled with terror. Peter's breath was making a harsh, crackling sound.

"Peter?"

There was an answer, but she couldn't make it out. Mayken lit a candle. Peter was trembling all over and his fingers were plucking at the sheet.

"Peter!"

His eyes fluttered open and he looked at her, seeing her as no other man could see. "I'm ready," he said in a soft voice. And then he died.

That afternoon, Mayken and Little Peter went upstairs to Peter's studio, Mayken carrying baby Jan. Peter's own brushes and palette sat undisturbed where he'd last left them. His spot: a chair, a table with his paints and brushes, and a fresh, unmarked panel on the easel.

The Magpie on the Gallows hung on the wall. How strange it was to see Peter's paintings, thought Mayken, and him no longer here. They were like pools you could dive into, like wells, like Peter's eyes.

After a bit, Little Peter walked across the room and picked up his father's brush.

✳ ✳ ✳ ✳ ✳ ✳ ✳ ✳ ✳ ✳ ✳ ✳ ✳

ACKNOWLEDGMENTS

In writing *As Above, So Below,* I've tried to stick as closely as possible to the known facts of Bruegel's life and times. The historical documentation of Bruegel's life is sketchy. We have Carel van Mander's two-page "Life of Bruegel," written thirty years after his death, and a mere half dozen primary documents. But, of course, we have the artworks as well, and, if *As Above, So Below* is an accurate measure, a picture is worth some ten thousand words.

Among the most useful of the art-historical books on Bruegel that I studied were Bob Claessens and Jeanne Rousseau, *Bruegel* (Alpine Fine Arts, 1981; originally published in 1969) and Roger H. Marijnissen and Max Seidel, *Bruegel* (New York: G. P. Putnam's Sons, 1971).

I'd like to acknowledge my debt to two earlier novels that tell the story of Bruegel's life. These are Felix Timmermans, *Peter Bruegel, or Droll Peter* (Coward-McCann, 1930) and Claude-Henri Rocquet, *Bruegel: The Workshop of Dreams* (Chicago: University of Chicago Press, 1991). Though perhaps more a meditation than a novel, Rocquet's work is a gem.

Two final acknowledgments. Gert Hofmann's *Parable of the Blind* (Fromm International, 1989; originally published in 1985) is a tale in the style of Samuel Beckett, told from the point of view of one of the blind men who posed for Bruegel's painting; the tale served as an inspiration for my description of the St. Luke's group's Landjuweel performance. Michael Frayne's highly entertaining contemporary novel *Headlong* (New York: Henry Holt, 1999) envisions the title *The Merrymakers* for the lost painting in Bruegel's cycle of Seasons paintings.

Further acknowledgments and a complete account of my alchemical novelistic processes can be found in the "Notes for *As Above, So Below*" document posted on the book's Web site, www.rudyrucker.com/bruegel.

My publishers and I wish to thank the following museums and collections for making available copies of the works listed below and for granting permission to reproduce them.

Where a painting bears no date, an estimated date is placed in brackets. The sizes of the pictures are given in centimeters, rounded off to the nearest whole number.

Jacket. *The Fall of the Rebel Angels,* 1562, 117 x 162 cm, oil on oak panel, Brussels, Musées Royaux des Beaux-Arts de Belgique.

Chapter 1. *Mountain Landscape with Cloister*, 1552, 29 x 33 cm, pen and brown ink on paper with washes added by an unknown later hand, Berlin, Staatliche Museen der Stiftung Preussischer Kulturbesitz (bpk), Kupferstichkabinett. "Photograph Copyright © bpk, Berlin 2002."

Chapter 2. *The Tower of Babel*, 1563, 114 x 155 cm, oil on oak panel, Vienna, Kunsthistorisches Museum (KHM, Wien).

Chapter 3. *The Battle of Carnival and Lent*, [1559], 118 x 165 cm, oil on oak panel, Vienna, Kunsthistorisches Museum (KHM, Wien).

Chapter 4. *The Fall of Icarus*, [1556], 74 x 112 cm, distemper on canvas apparently touched up with oil, Brussels, Musées Royaux des Beaux-Arts de Belgique.

Chapter 5. *Luxuria*, 1557, 23 x 30 cm, drawn in pen and brown ink by Bruegel and made an engraving by Jerome Cock, Brussels, Bibliothèque Royale de Belgique, Cabinet des Estampes.

Chapter 6. *The Peasant Wedding*, [1568], 114 x 163 cm, oil on oak panel, Vienna, Kunsthistorisches Museum (KHM, Wien).

Chapter 7. *The Parable of the Blind*, 1568, 86 x 154 cm, distemper on canvas, Naples, Capodimonte Museum.

Chapter 8. *Dulle Griet* (or, *Mad Meg*), 1564, 117 x 162 cm, oil on oak panel, Antwerp, Museum Mayer van den Bergh. "Photograph Copyright © IRPA-KIK, Brussels."

Chapter 9. *The Sermon of John the Baptist*, 1565, 95 x 161 cm, oil on oak panel, Budapest, Szépmüvészetu Múzeum (National Museum of Fine Arts).

Chapter 10. *The Peasant and the Birdsnester*, 1568, 59 x 68 cm, oil on oak panel, Vienna, Kunsthistorisches Museum (KHM, Wien).

Chapter 11. *The Adoration of the Kings*, 1564, 108 x 84 cm, oil on oak panel, London, National Gallery. "Photograph Copyright © The National Gallery, London."

Chapter 12. *The Hunters in the Snow*, 1565, 117 x 162 cm, oil on oak panel, Vienna, Kunsthistorisches Museum (KHM, Wien).

Chapter 13. *The Beggars*, 1568, 18 x 21 cm, oil on panel, Paris, Musée du Louvre. "Photograph Copyright © Réunion des Musées Nationaux / Art Resource, NY."

Chapter 14. *Lazy Lusciousland* (or, *Luilekkerland*, or, *The Land of Cocaigne*), 1567, 52 x 78 cm, oil on panel, Munich, Bayerische Staatsgemäldesammlungen, Alte Pinakothek München.

Chapter 15. *The Beekeepers*, [1568], 20 x 31 cm, pen and brown ink on paper, Berlin, Staatliche Museen der Stiftung Preussischer Kulturbesitz (bpk), Kupferstichkabinett. "Photograph Copyright © bpk, Berlin 2002."

Chapter 16. *The Magpie on the Gallows*, 1568, 116 x 160 cm, oil on panel, Darmstadt, Hessisches Landesmuseum Darmstadt.

CPSIA information can be obtained at www.ICGtesting.com
Printed in the USA
LVOW042155090312

272483LV00001B/100/A